About This Book

The Cataclysm

Nearly a century ago, the world fractured. The new Veil offered easy passage between dimensions...friendly or not.

Alanna McLean bonds with Jekk, a scarred and tortured Fael from the other side—and enters a new world of danger. When Faelinn—large lynx-like cats from beyond the Veil—bond, their human gains supernatural powers.

Now Alanna finds the lost. From lost keys to lost people, she just needs to touch something associated with the missing thing to find it.

Jonathan Burke patrols the border between worlds. When his own Gift requires him to solve a series of child murders, he reluctantly involves Alanna in the case.

Whether Alanna and Jonathan can defeat a creature that makes darkest nightmares come to life depends on their bonds with their Fael... and with each other.

New voice Sarah Husch launches readers into an exciting new world with a romance that will make your heart sing.

Fated Bond

Ebook edition published 2023
by Soul's Road Press

Copyright © Sarah Husch. All rights reserved, including the right of reproduction, in whole or in part in any form, without written permission of the publisher, except in the case of brief quotations embedded in critical articles and reviews.

This is a work of fiction. Names, characters, places, and events are either the product of the author's imagination or are used fictitiously, and any resemblance to actual persons, living or dead, business establishments, events, or locales is entirely coincidental.

Inquiries should be addressed to
Soul's Road Press
info@soulsroadpress.com
http://www.soulsroadpress.com

Cover images © Babak Tafreshi | print.babaktafreshi.com, Viorel Sima | Depositphotos, Christian Roeschert | 500px.com/p/christian_roeschert

Author logo: Funky Book Designs
Soul's Road Press logo: Designs by Trapdoor

For Scott, my one and only. You're my biggest supporter, my soulmate, my partner in crime. I can't imagine my life without you. I love you.

For Fiona, my darling Cryptid. You're my chief research assistant, head of my fan club, winner of the Best Kid Ever award. I love you, sweetpea.

Fated Bond

BOOK 1 OF THE FAELINN CHRONICLES

SARAH HUSCH

Fear glued his shirt to his back. The shadows that crept up the walls reached for him, all sharp edges and taloned fingers. Somewhere nearby, a dog barked. Water dripped. An old piece of plastic scraped down the alleyway. All the sounds but the one he was listening for. He just wanted it all to stop.

He needed to be able to hear the monster stalking him.

There. A footstep. Just one, but too close. He shrank back, trying to hide in the crevice behind the dumpster. Something tickled his ankle, a light touch, maybe a bug. Maybe a finger. He couldn't help the moan that slid out of his lungs. He tried to tuck his foot up tighter but there was no room. The tickle became a grasp, then a clamp.

His leg was dragged out into the open. His fingers gripped the cold dumpster but slid away as the unrelenting hand pulled harder. Harder. On his back like a trapped turtle, he stared up into drowning black eyes.

"Gotcha," Jonathan murmured. His senses reached out, following the tendrils of intent that linked the cold body of the cadaver he was holding to the killer he was hunting.

Jonathan didn't see the morgue he stood in. Instead, he saw the scene of the last murder he'd been hired to solve. It's what he did. Find killers.

We have him, Cateera, his Faelinn bondmate, agreed. Her strength wrapped around his mind, protecting and comforting. They were a team.

Diving forward into the killer's black eyes, Jonathan reached for the tendrils that bound the killer to the victim's body. Murderers always left residue behind. Their intent, their desire, their accidental regret. It was always different, but it was always there. He reached deeper and found what he was looking for. His mind slid along those links, tightening the connection, until he found himself inside the killer.

Looking down, he took pleasure in the terrified man's babbled pleas. The vomit of words soothed him, filling the emptiness inside. Fed him in a way nothing else did. Jonathan slid a little deeper. Cateera was there with him, enhancing his Gift. He needed to see where the killer was now, not where he'd been earlier in the week.

A glimpse of a room. A sense of walls, of doorways. Traffic noise. A generic painting on the wall over an unmade bed. A motel? Maybe. He wanted to look around, search for something to give him an actual location. Jonathan fisted those tendrils of connection, forcing knowledge from the mind he was stalking. A name. A location. Something.

And the eyes turned to look at him. Turned inwards, those nightmare eyes latched onto him with surprise. Something pushed against his mind. He'd never felt anything like it before. None of the killers he'd found had ever felt his presence. Jonathan tried to pull back but he was held fast.

Fingers raked through his mind. Pain and terror settled into the furrows left behind. He became the stalked. Laugher echoed inside his skull as the killer systematically rifled through his awareness, taking his name, his location, his memories. The sensation was horrific. Scenes of torture, crime scenes he'd worked as a detective, bloody and vicious, played out endlessly in his mind. And this time there was no reprieve. He couldn't look away. All of those things were promised him. He would suffer each of them, endlessly.

Jonathan screamed.

Come back, Cateera pleaded. Her panic buffeted him. *Don't leave me!*

Afraid he was losing himself, afraid he'd never get back, Jonathan gave a mighty heave and wrenched his mind away from the killer holding him close. The images dissolved. Pain jarred up into his hips when his knees hit the cold tile floor. Hands gripped him, and he tried to shake them loose until he realized they were the fur-covered fingers of his bondmate.

You're safe, she told him, repeating it until he felt the knowledge begin to settle him.

Safe. He opened his eyes to meet the turquoise gaze of the Faelinn crouched next to him. Her white fur, marked with soft purple swirls, was silky when he threaded the fingers of one hand through her ruff. Gently, he rested his forehead against hers. His throat hurt from screaming; his lungs were on fire from the lack of air.

Failure filled him. The killer was gone. Lost to him now. And there was no way he was going to reach for him again.

"I'm sorry," he told the man standing beside the morgue's cadaver rack. "I can't help you."

For the first time since he'd received his Gift from his bondmate, Jonathan couldn't use it. Regret mingled with the failure because this guy, this killer they'd asked him to catch, was a nightmare. He would kill again. And there was nothing Jonathan could do because the killer's final words before he was able to wrench free still echoed in his head.

I see you, Burke.

Chapter One

Turn left in 50 yards.

Alanna drove forward, scanning for the left turn. Nothing but rock and pine. A mile, two sharp twists in the narrow road, and a frustrated curse later, there was still no left turn. An amazing scenic view of the Shenandoah Valley plunged outside her right window, all dark bare limbs and fallen leaves of red and gold. On the driver's side, sheer rock and trees. No turn in sight.

Frustrated, Alanna poked at the GPS unit on her dash.

Go. Stop. Right right right, the pleasantly British voice instructed her, sounding like a demented cheerleader.

With a snarl, Alanna smacked the machine. The unit emitted a noise that sounded suspiciously like her second-grade teacher tsk-ing her and shut itself off. She stared at it a moment, realized she was wandering too close to the steep drop-off, and returned her attention to the narrow road. Hunter's Forge had to be around here somewhere. She wished she'd paid more attention to the directions she'd received over the phone, but she'd been sure her GPS would get her where she needed to go. It was Fae-spelled and guaranteed to work in close proximity to the Veil.

Obviously, someone had lied.

The road crested, wound around an outcropping of stone and began a gentle descent. A sign informed her that the town of Hunter's Forge was a mere two miles away. Relief filled her. Hunter's Forge was where she was meeting her escort into the Haven. She'd find the shop where they were meeting, take her GPS unit out and run over it a few times. That thought made her smile as she envisioned people stopping to stare at the crazy woman abusing a harmless machine. Alanna was still smiling when she drove into town.

The mountains cradled the buildings between grey arms of rock. A carpet of fallen leaves decorated the slopes of the Blue Ridge in a thousand shades of warm gold and autumnal fire. Green pine rose above them, needled sentinels between the stark bare limbs of their deciduous cousins. Above the trees, playing with the peaks and curling over the outcroppings, the Veil rippled and glowed with iridescent color.

Hunter's Forge was an old town, dated back to the Cataclysm. It had started as a military outpost assigned to watch the Veil. While many of those outposts had shut down after the War, this one had flourished, due in no small part to its proximity to the Haven. Buildings made of local stone lined the narrow road. Store fronts advertised end of season sales. At the height of autumn, tourists flocked to the area to gaze at the fall foliage, to drive the twisting roads over the mountains, and to spend their money in the local shops. A red brick library sporting Federalist-style columns dwarfed a small police station. Beyond that, an elementary school spilled children from its doors and onto the slides and swings of a playground. It reminded her of stories she'd read about small-town main streets. Parades, couples walking hand in hand, and gossips at every corner.

An ornately scrolled sign shaped like a fanciful cupcake advertised the Sweet Indulgence bakery. Alanna pulled into an empty parking spot beneath an iron lamppost. She threw the misbehaving GPS a last withering look and slid out of the car.

Cool air scented with sugar, cinnamon, and the underlying scent of rich coffee wrapped around her, drifting from the store. Alanna closed her eyes, breathing it in, feeling the cobwebs clear. New DC didn't smell like this. She wasn't sure anything else in the world did. She really needed to get out of the city more often.

A bell tinkled when she walked into the bakery. The sweet smells, merely hinted at outside, hit her full blast, and her stomach chose that moment to cheer. She pressed a hand to her stomach. Surely one cinnamon roll wouldn't hurt. And maybe another to indulge in later. Or maybe something with chocolate.

Realizing she was the center of attention as she stood there smiling like an idiot, Alanna focused on the task at hand. She was supposed to be meeting someone. A quick glance around at the iron tables showed that either her contact was even later than she was, or they'd given up and gone home. The only other person in the place was the woman behind the glass counter.

"Hi." The pretty redhead smiled at her.

"Hi," Alanna said, responding to the smile with one of her own. Her stilettos clicked on the black and white tiled floor as she crossed to the counter. "I'm supposed to be meeting someone, but it looks like they're not here yet."

"Oh sure," the woman said. She swiped a towel over the counter next to the cash register and then tucked it back into the loosely tied apron at her waist. "You must be Alanna McLean. Mark Dennison called and told me to be on the lookout for you."

There was open curiosity in the words, and in the big brown eyes. Alanna smiled, but didn't rise to the bait. "I'm a little late. I'm not sure if I've missed my escort."

"I don't think so; no one from the Haven has been in today."

"Is that apple strudel?" Alanna asked, distracted by the slices of apple and pastry in the display case.

"Sure is. It's my grandmother's recipe and there's nothing like it either side of the Veil. Can I get you a piece while you wait?"

"Oh yes please," Alanna said. "And coffee. And a cinnamon roll." And one of everything else, she thought. She would be happy to roll out a cot in the corner and live here, eating nothing but pastry for the rest of her life. "Is your grandmother the baker?"

"Nope, just me. I took over for her when she retired. I'm Gina," she said, glancing up with a smile as she efficiently slid a piece of strudel onto a white plate. "You're a writer, aren't you?"

Small-town gossip, oh my. "That's right. Word gets around a place like this, it seems."

"No, actually, I recognized your name when I was talking to Mark, and when you walked in I recognized you from the photo in your last book." She placed the plate with strudel and a cinnamon roll on the counter and turned to grab a mug. "I have to admit I'm a bit of a fan, but you don't have to worry, I'm not going to go all weird on you."

Alanna couldn't help but laugh at Gina's words and made herself relax. She knew she was stressed about this weekend. She'd all but promised her editor she would get permission to set her next book in the Haven, with the Faelinn and the people who shared lives with them. "I'm flattered," she said.

Gina lifted a steaming mug of richly scented coffee. A small pitcher of fresh cream was in her other hand. "Go ahead and take your plate, I'll carry this to the table for you. I do have to warn you, because I'd feel guilty if I didn't, that if you go into the library, under no circumstances should you tell the librarian who you are. Next thing you know, she'll have called an emergency book club meeting with you as the chief victim."

"Victim?"

"I mean honored guest," Gina said.

"I'll keep that in mind."

Alanna was still laughing as she took the first bite of strudel. It melted on her tongue. That's it, she would move here just for the pastries. The last bite was as good as the first. The strudel and two cups of coffee later and Alanna seriously doubted she would ever move again. The cinnamon bun on the plate mocked her. Ignoring it for now, she tapped the screen of her e-reader. The page in the newest book by her favorite author flipped to the next.

Lost in the book, Alanna didn't glance up right away when the bells over the door tinkled. Only when jean-clad legs stopped at her side did she drag her eyes away from the screen. Her mind hummed in pleasure as her gaze slid up muscled thighs under faded denim, narrow hips, and washboard abs tight enough to play mountain music on. The black T-shirt covering those delectable muscles advertised the use of sarcasm as a weapon. Her lips twitched in a smile that faded as her perusal slid up to his face.

They didn't make men that looked like that in real life. Alanna wrote about them, sure, with the shaggy blond hair curling too long over the collar, the blue eyes that held a slice of summer in their depths, the sculpted mouth with the decadent bottom lip. But those men were fantasies. This one couldn't possibly be human. Too beautiful, too male.

And far too suspicious, given the deep frown on his face.

"You're Alanna McLean?" he asked, standing close enough for her to feel the heat of his body. She narrowed her eyes at him. He loomed over her like an angry bull ready to stomp her into the dust. It was rude. And she didn't like being crowded.

"Yes," she said, meeting his eyes with a cool gaze.

He grunted. "I'm chief of security for the Haven." His voice was low, with just a hint of the South in the smooth tones.

"Don't mind him," Gina said, coming up behind them with a mug of coffee. "Jonathan has antisocial tendencies. Why Mark would send him to get you, I just don't know." She pushed the mug into Jonathan's hand, hooked a chair out from under the table with one foot, and pointed to it. "Sit down and make nice while I pack up the meat rolls for Cateera."

Jonathan blinked at her for a moment, and then obediently dropped into the chair. The frown on his face had gotten deeper. It made him look edgy and dangerous, not the kind of man Alanna generally dealt with. The hands that cradled the mug were long-fingered and scarred, little white lines cutting into the tanned skin over his knuckles, down to his wrists.

"I'm Jonathan Burke," he said. He thrust one of those scarred hands in her direction. There were calluses on his palms.

Alanna liked how he didn't treat her to a limp handshake because she was a woman. She also liked the directness of his gaze, even if there were shadows of suspicion in the blue depths. It was the low curl of heat in her belly that she didn't like. Taking back her hand, she pushed the plate with the cinnamon bun toward him. "Please help me eat this. I overestimated the amount of sugar I could pour into my body at one time."

The quirk of a smile touched his lips and she momentarily forgot how to breathe. If the man ever turned a full smile on her, she was pretty sure she'd melt on the spot. She watched as he snagged her fork and speared a piece of the pastry. He looked tired, she decided. The dark shadows under his eyes made him look like he hadn't slept well in days.

"What do you want at the Haven?"

"I'm a writer," she told him. "I want to set my next novel there."

Jonathan pushed the plate away, the rest of the bun uneaten. "Excuse me?"

"I've spoken with the Dennisons and they're receptive to the idea. I'm staying the weekend to iron out some details and get their final agreement. And hopefully get started on some research."

"You might as well just get back in your car and head home," he told her. "There's no way in hell I'm letting you write a book about the Haven."

"What business of yours is it where I want to set a book?"

"I told you, I'm the chief of security at the Haven. Dennison lets you set a book there and we'll be swamped with even more tourists than we are now. My job is to protect the Faelinn from publicity seekers like you who want to make a profit off us."

Alanna narrowed her eyes, the hot swell of anger in her chest threatening her hold on her manners. "You—"

A rumbling meow to her right stopped her words. The most amazing creature she'd ever seen stood next to the table, eyes focused on Alanna. "Oh," Alanna breathed. "You're beautiful."

The Fael was predominantly white except for the swirls decorating her plush pelt. The markings were soft purple and resembled tribal tattoos. Her long, narrow face was delicately boned, the slanted eyes a shocking turquoise. Her pointed ears were topped by stiff tufts shaded a deeper purple. And she was big, easily weighing several hundred pounds. Even with the narrow face, she resembled a lynx the size of a tiger. Alanna was shocked by the true size of a Fael.

Jonathan grunted. "Cateera says thank you."

Alanna smiled in delight. The Fael sat, tall enough that her head was nearly the same height as Alanna's own. Her tail wrapped around her feet, though the purple tip twitched back and forth. "May I touch you?" Alanna asked.

Cateera inclined her head regally and turned it a little, presenting her neck. Her fur was softer than anything Alanna had ever felt. Her fingers sank into the short, dense strands. She could feel the strength of muscle in the neck, down in the shoulders. Her fingers scratched gently and the Fael began to purr.

Jonathan made a rude noise and pushed back his chair. "You can follow me in your car."

"That's not necessary," she said, her hand falling back to her side. He might be the most gorgeous man she'd ever met, but he was rude and she had no desire to extend her contact with him. "You can just give me directions. My GPS conked out on the way here."

"Don't you know that a GPS won't work this close to the Veil?" he said. "If you want to get to the Haven, you'll follow me. I'll be waiting outside."

Speechless, she watched him grab a white paper bag from the counter and leave the bakery, Cateera at his side. An outstanding ass didn't excuse the attitude, she told herself. Not even in those jeans.

"He can be a jerk sometimes," Gina said. "But he's so hot it's hard to care." She watched him open the rear door of a black SUV parked next to Alanna's sleek sedan. Cateera jumped in and he shut the door before getting behind the wheel.

Alanna found herself laughing as she handed over cash to pay for the baked goods. "He's too pretty to be human. He's a Veiler?"

"You'd think," Gina answered, leaning one hip against the counter. "But no. He's one-hundred-percent human, just with very, very good genes. And I'd sure like to get into them." Gina sighed again and then shook her head.

Alanna had to echo that sentiment. He was a rude jerk, but that didn't keep her hormones from waving madly in his direction. And that was just annoying. "I'll stop by before I head home in a few days, to stock up for the road."

Alanna was still smiling when she left, the door tinkling as it shut behind her. She caught Jonathan's stare through his windshield, held it for a moment, thought about sticking out her tongue, but decided she was too mature for that. Instead, she got into her car and prepared to follow him.

Jonathan drummed his fingers impatiently on the wheel, waiting for the woman to leave the bakery. Damn, he was tired. He hadn't slept in two days.

The last consult had been from hell. For the first time since his Gift Awakened, he'd failed. And now this woman thought she was going to waltz into the Haven and write about them. He just didn't need this right now.

She smells good, Cateera said as she draped her front half over the reclined front seat of the SUV. The rest of her long body took up the back bench. Her tail tapped a tattoo against the back of his seat.

"Gina's cinnamon rolls smell good," Jonathan said. "Alanna McLean smells like trouble." Actually, she smelled like jasmine, but there was no way he was going to share that little nugget with Cateera.

The woman in question left Gina's place. Alanna glanced at him, the animosity clear in her smoky eyes. She looked cool and unruffled in her grey business suit, the short skirt showing off an amazing pair of legs. Dark hair was drawn back into a sleek roll, highlighting the refined bones of her face. She had the body of a forties pin-up girl, soft curves and a narrow, tucked-in waist, the kind of body that would have graced the side of a bomber from the Veil Wars. For all that, she managed to project an air of cool reserve. It made him want to shake her up a bit, see what happened.

Pulling onto the road, he glanced in the rear mirror, checking that she was still there. Curiosity and suspicion warred inside him. Mark hadn't told him anything about her. How was he supposed to keep the Haven protected if he didn't know anything about the strangers who were invited in? Granted, he'd been away for a few days, working on that damned case in Carolina, but he hadn't been gone long enough to be kept out of the security loop. At the very least, his second-in-command, Rivera, should have kept him up to date on expected visitors.

You are getting snarly again, Cateera said. Her narrow head turned to look at him, the purple tufts at the ends of her erect white ears quivering a little from the vibration of the vehicle on the road.

"I'm a snarly kind of person," he said. "You knew that when you bonded with me."

I bonded with you because you are mine. I do not like snarly.

Jonathan took one hand off the wheel to bury his fingers in the thick white fur of his Fael's ruff. The fur was luxuriously soft, the white strands interspersed with bands of the most delicate lavenders. She was one of the most elegant Faelinn he'd ever met, and he was still shocked and awed at the fact that she'd picked him three years ago.

"I'll try to be nicer," he promised.

She coughed, her version of a snort. *And I will try to resist the beef rolls Gina put in the bag for me.*

Jonathan laughed out loud, knowing the chances of that were slim. Gina's beef rolls were one of the finicky creature's favorites. A yawn threatened to swamp him. He wanted to be home, sleeping. He wanted to forget the voice that had reached out and slipped into his brain, whispering of fear and death. His failure to find the killer during the last case was going to eat at him for a long time.

I still think she smells good, Cateera said. She lifted a paw to groom between her wickedly sharp claws. *Your scent changed when you sat next to her.*

It was the nonchalance of the statement that made him look at her. "So?"

She is your mate.

"Like hell," Jonathan responded. "Humans don't have mates."

Humans bonded to Faelinn do, Cateera replied smugly.

"I love you, Cateera, but you're insane. There's no way in hell I have a mate. And certainly not a nosy woman who wants to write about us." He glared at her until she put her head down on her paws and closed her eyes. His Fael was obviously sleep deprived. She was delusional.

The entrance to Old Home Road wasn't easy to find. Trees and shrubs nearly overgrew the turnoff. It was deliberate. This road led to the residential area of the Haven. There was another entrance a few miles farther along that was reserved for deliveries and led to a warehouse where the deliveries were processed. After processing, the deliveries were loaded onto Haven trucks and moved inside the fence. That road was clear and well-marked.

Old Home Road wasn't. The twisting road ran for several miles. Jonathan checked constantly to make sure the writer was still behind him. Periodically the road ran parallel to the Haven's fence line. The ground had been cleared in front of the fence to keep anyone from using the trees to gain access to the private land.

Jonathan pulled to a stop in front of a large wrought iron gate. The fanciful iron curlicues twisted into leaves and trees did little to disguise the sharpened spikes atop each pole. Ceramic conductors were attached in regular intervals to the fencing on either side into the gate. The fence was electrified. For those less knowledgeable, large signs informed them of the fact. Cameras monitored every inch. The Haven was protected from unwelcome guests.

He waited until she pulled up behind him before rolling down his window to enter the security code into the keypad. The wrought iron moved smoothly aside, the paved road continuing forward between arching old-growth trees. Against his better judgment, Jonathan drove forward.

The black SUV moved through the impressive gates. Not entirely sure he wouldn't close the gate on her, Alanna followed quickly. Roads split off on either side, and down one she caught a glimpse of a parking lot. Her escort gave her no time to linger, and she sped up to catch him. The paved road was well maintained. Limbs arched overhead, throwing a splatter of light and shadow onto the road. She thought it was like driving into the heart of a dream. A golden leaf drifted down, dancing a little in the SUV's wake. It touched on her windshield before swirling away.

The road continued farther than she would have expected. The Haven, where most of the Faelinn lived with their bonded human partners, was isolated. The amount of land that the gates encircled must be immense. And it all belonged to the man she was going to interview.

It was an email from Shellie Dennison that originally put the thought in her head. Wife of the reclusive Mark Dennison, Shellie had proclaimed herself a fan of Alanna's writing. Everyone in the world knew who Mark Dennison was. Billionaire and proponent of Veiler rights. One of the first to bond with the elusive Faelinn. The email from Shellie made her wonder what it would be like to build a character around a bonded human. Everyone was curious about Faelinn. The tales about the creatures were contradictory. Viewed as both sweet, overgrown kitties and as monsters to scare children into obedience added to their intrigue and mystery.

Alanna had responded to the email, extending her interest in learning about the race in order to write a romance. Shellie had been receptive to the idea. That was several months ago. After a period of cautious correspondence, Shellie invited her to come to the Haven to meet the Dennison's. To learn firsthand about the Faelinn.

And now Alanna was driving behind a rude jerk who just happened to be the Chief of Haven Security. And he was bonded to a Fael. She couldn't imagine anyone or anything willingly spending any amount of time with him.

Even if that full bottom lip had tempted her to take a bite.

Get over it, she instructed herself firmly. There are enough jerks at home without getting the hots for one out in the middle of nowhere.

Narrow lanes began to veer off the main road. She tried to peer down them as they passed, but trees blocked her sight. Jonathan took a left, the road gradually climbing. Houses began to appear, set back from the road, all large in a variety of styles. Long lawns rolled down to the road, some quite steep. Life in the mountains.

Ahead of her, Jonathan slowed. He honked the horn, an arm waving out of the window. She thought he was signaling to her until she saw an elderly woman raking the scatter of leaves beneath an oak raise a hand back to him. So, he wasn't completely antisocial.

The road curved sharply. The Veil was suddenly right there, filling the sky above the trees with mesmerizing color. It was practically on top of her car. Alanna's foot hit the brake. She couldn't do anything else because the need to stare was overpowering.

The folds of the Veil shimmered in gauzy colors that fluctuated from the deepest jewel tones to the most delicate pastels. It was the closest she'd ever been. No wonder her GPS had malfunctioned. The odd twisting of space and time near the Veil wreaked havoc with electronics all over the world.

Nearly a century ago, ripples had begun to appear in odd places across the planet. Over the next few years, the ripples had changed, strengthened. Sheets of coruscating light had burst from the ground, pushing up first through fault lines and around tectonic plates, and then in other places, with no rhyme or reason. Scientists worldwide studied the phenomenon, investigated the lights.

Cataclysms shook the world. Mountains rose and fell. Islands birthed themselves. Governments fell apart. Millions died in the initial upheavals, more in the wars that followed as each failing nation struggled to gain dominance. The US reshaped itself into territories when earthquakes along the New Madrid fault dropped the Midwest by hundreds of feet. The Gulf rushed in to fill the new basin. It reached the Great Lakes and became the Inland Sea. The new sea divided the nation in half. The federal government tried and failed to maintain control; the cataclysms were too great. The Eastern states remained under the control of the government centered in New DC. The Western states, having lost many of the coastal and mountain cities to tectonic upheaval, centered itself in North Platte, Nebraska, which had the distinct advantage of being both tectonically inactive and far enough from the new Inland Sea that it stayed dry.

The Veil continued to change. In certain areas, the scientists discovered odd twistings, soft spots in reality. They found that those places were passages, dimensional tears that opened onto another earth. Robotic cameras were sent through, but none of them survived the trip. The electronics burned out.

Then the first of the travelers appeared from the other side. Children recognized them first. They were the closest to the old fairy tales, their imaginations still pliable enough to put together the newcomers with the creatures of legend. Only it wasn't just the sweet fairies of those children's stories that came. It was the darkest of nightmares as well, and all manner of creature in between.

What was left of the world panicked. The Veilers, as they were dubbed, had no intention of staying on their side of the dimensional tear. Trying to contain them was impossible; the Veil had opened in too many places. A child's closet did indeed lead to a wonderland. The Marianas Trench glowed with magic down in its formerly black depths. Reality had changed.

The Veil changed the world even more than the geographical upheavals. Humans discovered the passages went both ways, and the brave and the curious travelled to the other side. Not every place could sustain human life. A meadow on one side might lead to the deepest ocean depths on the other. A town in upper New York was abandoned because the Veil opened onto a vast volcano. The heat and lava had a disturbing habit of making its way through to change the landscape for miles around.

Like the Earth, the world on the other side was home to different groups of people, different creatures, not all of which were happy that humans were their new neighbors. The face of war changed as humans found enemies that brought them together. Over the years it became obvious which portions of the Veil were dangerous, which areas led to places it was best to leave alone. For the worst of those, military bases kept watch, ensuring that nothing passed through that had harm in its heart. Even then, the clashing of cultures and technology exploded into a war that pitted human weaponry against magickal. It was brutal, with massive casualties on each side. It became apparent early on that there would be no clear winner. The two sides would just whittle away at each until there was no one left.

A shaky peace formed. A few skirmishes popped up periodically, but a hard-won treaty was fashioned and upheld. And a new Earth was born.

People of Alanna's generation grew up with the Veil. They'd never known the world without it. But knowing about the Veil was far different from living with it in the backyard. The Veil's beauty left her breathless. And she swore she could feel it against her skin, a warm tingling like the barest of static shocks

An impatient series of honks yanked her out of her reverie. Alanna waved a hand to let her escort know she was still with him, and put the car into drive. Another five minutes and Jonathan turned again. The road climbed steeply and suddenly the trees gave way to a rolling lawn. An immense house dominated the landscape. It was a fairy tale fantasy of a house with fancifully carved gingerbread decorating the eaves. Turrets like white castle towers stood guard at each corner, and she spared a moment to dream of a study in one of those rooms, being able to look out of curved windows while writing. A wing swept backwards through land-scaped grounds, and she could see several separate buildings a short distance away. A deep porch stretched across the front, fall flowers spilling from flower boxes on the railing. The SUV pulled to a stop at the bottom of the steps.

Alanna parked and climbed out quickly to stare up at the three levels of stone and brickwork. The main roof was a dream of crenellations and gables. She blinked a moment, realizing that what she had first taken for a bird was in actuality a gargoyle captaining the rainspout. Before she'd looked her fill, the front door opened and a petite blond ran down the steps.

"You made it," Shellie Dennison said. Her flowing gauze skirt floated like a turquoise cloud around her trim ankles as she came to a stop next to Alanna. Dangly silver earrings tangled in the blond curls that framed a narrow, pretty face dominated by amber eyes. Those eyes sparked with excitement.

"Hello, Mrs. Dennison," Alanna said. The woman's smile was infectious and brought an answering one to Alanna's mouth.

"Oh no, it's Shellie," she said. "We've emailed so much I feel like we're already friends." She linked an arm through Alanna's and began drawing her toward the house. "How was the drive?"

"It was fine," Alanna said. She felt like an Amazon next to Shellie, and found herself wishing she'd worn flats. Even then, she would have been several inches taller than the petite woman.

"Until she got lost," Jonathan said. He leaned against the side of the SUV, arms crossed over his chest.

"In that case, thanks for rescuing her," Shellie said. She tugged his face down to give him a resounding kiss on the mouth. "You'll stay for dinner, won't you?"

Quick warmth brightened his eyes, but he still shook his head. The beginning of a smile flirted with his lips. "Not tonight, but I do want to talk to Mark."

"He's going to yell at me," the man who'd joined them said. He extended a lean hand to Alanna, a welcoming smile curving his thin mouth. "I'm Mark Dennison."

He wasn't what she'd expected. For one thing, he was young. Short dark hair swept back from a smooth-skinned face. For a man who'd reportedly bonded with a Fael more than seventy years ago, he showed no sign of that age in his face or bearing. The lines that fanned from his grey eyes, carved into his cheeks, seemed to be more from smiling than the press of years. Dressed in grey slacks and a white shirt rolled up over muscled forearms, he seemed no older than she did.

"Thanks for inviting me to your home," Alanna said, meeting his palm with her own. His grip was dry, firm.

"Your books have given my wife many hours of pleasure," he said, inclining his dark head toward her. "And she can be very persuasive when she wants something."

"She wants to write about the Haven," Jonathan said. Those summer-blue eyes pinned her. He angled himself so that his body moved smoothly between her and the Dennison's. It was a deliberate move, meant as both insult and warning.

"I know, isn't it exciting? She's the best," Shellie said. "Her romances have all been on the bestseller lists." She gave him a sly smile. "You should read one, Jonathan. You might learn something."

Alanna had to bite the inside of her lip to keep from laughing. The look on the man's face was worth putting up with every minute of his rudeness. She had a feeling she was going to like Shellie Dennison. A shiver touched her spine, the feeling of being watched. Something touched her side, moved along her hip.

She gave a startled yelp and spun around. Briefly, her fingertips touched something silky-soft. A hard hand steadied her, fingers wrapped around her elbow.

"Careful," Jonathan advised. His breath whispered over the soft hair around her ear.

Jonathan's hand at her elbow and the warmth of his breath on her cheek sent unexpected arousal zinging through her veins. Her breath stuttered and it took an act of sheer willpower not to sway into him. It pissed her off. She yanked her arm away and concentrated on the fur she'd felt beneath her fingertips. She knew it had been a Fael; the feel of the fur had been a dream beneath her fingertips. It wasn't Cateera because she was too far away, but there were no other Faelinn nearby.

"They'll show themselves when they're ready," Mark said. "If they come to trust you."

Alanna took a deep breath, pushing down the excitement. Rumors abounded about the chameleon-like abilities of the Faelinn. To see—so to speak—actual confirmation of those abilities excited her. "Of course, the choice is theirs. I can only hope I'll earn that trust."

"Come inside," Shellie said. "We'll talk."

The inside of the Dennison home was another surprise. If she'd been asked to predict what it would look like, it would have echoed the crazy mix of styles that made up the outside. Instead, it welcomed her with warm wooden walls, polished so that the rich red tones gleamed. Marble tiles on the floor were inlaid with gleaming jeweled stones that swirled into a complicated mosaic she couldn't quite make out. A massive silver chandelier hung from the tall ceiling, throwing warmth and light around the room.

Shellie didn't give her time to linger. She led her down a corridor carpeted with a beautiful antique Persian rug, the colors complementing the paintings on the walls. "The parlor is through here," she said, indicating a set of folding doors. "You can freshen up across the hall and then join us."

"Thank you," Alanna said. She definitely needed a moment to herself. The closeness of the Veil, her first glance of its iridescent majesty up close, and the thrill of meeting her first Fael had all combined to fluster her. She needed to settle before she could begin learning everything she could about the Faelinn.

And she needed to get a grip on her unexpected physical reaction to the Haven's arrogant chief of security.

Chapter Two

Jonathan watched a hawk above the nearby trees. It glided in lazy circles, angling to catch the updrafts. It screeched and took a sharp dive, disappearing into the pines. Closer to the house, he heard the solo croak of the bullfrog that lived in the fountain. He was surprised it hadn't found a place to settle in for the coming winter. The fountain had been turned off weeks ago. Of course, that was Dennison's problem; his was the writer.

"What is she doing here?" Jonathan demanded once the women had gone inside.

Mark tucked his hands into his pockets, rocking back on his heels. "She's here to interview us about the Faelinn."

"Why? She'll write about them and then we'll have twice as much trouble as we normally do with people coming around here."

Mark was silent. Jonathan met those cool eyes with a stubbornness of his own. "How am I supposed to do my job if you don't even warn me that you've invited a writer here? When you asked me to pick her up, I thought she was just a friend of Shellie's, or a business contact."

"You're right, of course," Mark said. "I should have told you. But the decision to allow her here wouldn't have changed." He stroked a slow hand over Cateera's head when she appeared beside him, smiling down at the bewhiskered face. She nudged his side and then took off across the lawn, racing to disappear into the afternoon dimness of the wood.

"I would never do anything to harm the Faelinn, you know that," Mark said.

Jonathan pushed his hands through his hair. The tension at the base of his neck had crawled upwards and threatened to sink claws into his brain. "I know, so explain to me why you allowed her here."

"Shellie," Mark said. He smiled a little at Jonathan's grimace. "One day you'll fall hard for someone, and you won't be rolling your eyes at me that way anymore.

"It just so happens that I agree with her, this time," he continued. "We've kept ourselves cloistered here, allowed a mystique to grow up around us. We say it's because it's safer, but is it really? You've heard the stories people have concocted about the Faelinn. They're vampiric, they suck the blood from children, and their bones can be ground into a paste to heal the most traumatic of wounds. Half the stories are meant to terrify, the other half to entice."

"The terrifying ones have the benefit of keeping people away," Jonathan said.

"No," Mark contradicted. "They make the Faelinn, and us, targets. People want to kill what they fear, Jonathan. I would rather have children dreaming of a magical Fael of their own than have bounties put on our heads because someone wants us dead. Or worse, captured for experimentation."

"Won't the truth encourage that anyway?" Jonathan asked bitterly.

"If the truth is known, then we can lobby for protection, for laws to penalize those who would hurt us. As it stands, we have no protection. Only a few of us can use our Gifts to help where it's needed. We can offer so much, once we're understood and protected."

"You've already made up your mind," Jonathan said.

"Yes. If that means we talk to a writer who wants to make a character centered around a Fael/human bonding, then that's a start. I've read her work. The books are well written, and more importantly, well researched. They may be fiction, but it's a place to start."

Gazing into the trees where Cateera had disappeared, Jonathan reflected on what his friend, his employer, had told him. As head of Haven security, he knew the risks that they'd run into over the past few years. Intruders, trappers, hunters. Human Righters. He thought that publicizing who and what they were would only bring more of the same down upon them.

"I'm against this," he said.

"I'm sorry, Jonathan," Mark said. "I know it worries you. I know it makes your job harder, but I think it'll be okay."

"Did Shellie tell you that?"

"She foresees a change," Mark said. "She believes it trends to the positive, and she knows that the next few days will determine how it plays out. That's all I have to work on."

"All right then," Jonathan said. He looked up at the house, at the whimsical design that he thought was so ridiculous, but somehow captured his friends' personalities so well. "I'll trust you both. But I'm keeping an eye on the writer."

A quick grin twisted Mark's thin mouth. "I'll just bet you will. Try not to scare her off, okay?"

"No promises," Jonathan said as he swung into the SUV. No, he wasn't going to make any promises where that woman was concerned. There was something about her that got to him. He didn't trust all that big-city polish. He'd left that all behind when he moved to the Haven. His life here was simpler. When he needed a rush, needed to use the Gift that Cateera had Awakened in him, he did some consulting work. He didn't want any of that disturbed.

Especially not by a woman whose sleek glamour made him want to ruffle a few feathers. Made him wonder what was beneath that designer suit.

The parlor was a haven of creams and greens, with wide, deep sofas of loden green. A massive fireplace held logs prepared for flame. Photos lined the beautifully carved mantel, and above it a still life seemed to glow. More than just a masterwork, Alanna suspected it might be a Veiler's work, magic captured in each petal and leaf.

One wall of the room was made entirely of windows with French doors in the center. Outside, a tiled patio held a profusion of stone pots filled with plants that thrived in the late fall air. A long, lush lawn ran down for at least an acre before opening onto an incredible view of the Blue Ridge. Above it, the Veil shimmered.

"I've never been this close to the Veil," Alanna said. She couldn't look away from it, drawn to the windows as soon as she'd entered the room.

"It moves, you know," Shellie said. "It's not constant. Not everyone realizes that."

"Is it dangerous living so close?"

"Only when the Veil cuts through the kitchen," Shellie answered.

Startled, Alanna looked at the woman, saw the laughter in those shining eyes, and grinned. "You're pulling my leg."

"Well, no, but it only happened once, and it was only for a few hours."

Nervous now, Alanna eyed the Veil with suspicion. She absolutely didn't want to wake up in the morning with it glowing at the foot of her bed. Or worse, wake up on the wrong side of the dimensional curtain.

"You're making our guest nervous," Mark said. She hadn't heard him enter and turned at the sound of his voice. "It hasn't moved that much in more than thirty years, so I think we're safe."

Somehow, Alanna didn't find that terribly reassuring. She cast one last look out the window and then let Shellie lead her to a sofa. A tray of sweet tea and pastries had appeared on the low table between two of the sofas. She could have sworn it hadn't been there when she'd entered the room, but then again, her attention had been directed outside.

"You had a good trip then?" Mark asked, taking the glass his wife handed him. He perched on the edge of the sofa next to Shellie, one hand drifting along the tips of her golden curls.

"I did, yes," Alanna said. The tea was cool and sweet, perfect. She wanted to take her shoes off and curl her legs up underneath her. There was something about the room, about the couple, that made her feel at home. "Although I made the mistake of trusting the GPS specifications that said it would work near the Veil."

Mark laughed, and the lines beside his grey eyes crinkled. "That happens, I'm afraid. If you spend any time here, we'll take care of that. You'll find your cell phone won't work particularly well, either. You're as likely to dial a number and get someone in the Western States as you are the number you wanted. You're welcome to use the house lines while you're here. There's a laptop in your room that will allow you onto the Internet. I'm afraid yours won't access it."

"Thank you," Alanna said. "I'll want to take notes when we start to talk."

"Shouldn't be a problem," Mark said. "Your laptop will work fine, just not the Internet."

Shellie nudged him with her shoulder. "Enough electronic talk. I want to hear about the ideas for your next novel."

Now that was a topic Alanna was comfortable with. As a writer she was used to discussing her work. Between signings, readings, and conferences, Alanna was pretty sure there weren't many questions she hadn't been asked.

"I want the main character to be bonded to a Fael," she began. "I'm thinking the heroine, but it will depend on how the story develops after I've talked with you both. I've done a lot of research in the past month, but I have to tell you there's not a lot of fact out there."

"That's on purpose," Shellie said. "The Faelinn themselves are private creatures, and there aren't many of them to begin with." She lifted her shoulders in a light shrug, sending the silver earrings dancing. "We're nervous about putting too much information out there."

Leaning forward, Alanna met the woman's gaze. "No matter what you tell me, you have my word I'll treat it carefully. If you agree to the book, you'll have the chance to look over everything before I send it to my agent. I may not take it out, but I'll certainly listen to your concerns."

"We appreciate that," Mark said. "It's important to protect the Faelinn, and the Haven."

"I'm curious why you agreed to speak with me at all."

"Because it's time," Mark said softly. "The Veilers, as we call them, are a part of our world. There's no indication that things are going to go back to the way it used to be. The war has been over for decades, but we're still learning to live together. That means making laws to protect both dimensions. The Faelinn are a sentient race and they deserve the same considerations other sentient races do."

"They need to be protected," Shellie said. "Two weeks ago, we caught a trapper at the edge of the Haven setting bear traps. Before that, it was hunters with tranquilizers. When they were questioned, they admitted to being hired by a pharmaceutical company to capture a Fael for a bounty."

"In the past ten years, we've lost six Faelinn. Their bonded partners have reported that the Faelinn were either killed or captured," Mark said. "They told us that before they died. The ones with captured Faelinn lasted longer, but once the Faelinn were dead, their partners died too."

Alanna stared at the pair in shock. "You die when your Fael dies?"

"And vice versa," Shellie said.

"Which equates the killing of Faelinn with human murder," Mark said. "But there are no laws to protect us."

"Does anyone outside the Haven know that?" Alanna asked. "You can't expect the killers to be brought up on charges of murder if no one knows that people have died."

"Why?" Mark demanded. He got up to pace, his movements agitated. When he looked at her again, his expression was cold. "As I've said, the Faelinn are sentient. Should we differentiate between their murder and ours just because they aren't human?"

Alanna shook her head slowly, her mind racing. Bonded at the most basic level, lives entwined so tightly that when one died the other died, too. It would be murder then, should be considered murder. Two counts. The part of her that was the writer began to plot, to rewrite her basic premise. The part of her that lived and breathed wanted to track down the people responsible for those deaths and bring them to justice.

"Do you realize how dangerous it will be to let this knowledge out? The Faelinn are hard to catch, but for the most part humans are easy targets," Mark said. "An unscrupulous party can capture a bonded human, and the Fael will fight to reach them. Kill the human, and the Fael will die, leaving it in the hands of whoever engineered the kidnapping."

"That's why you live here in the Haven," Alanna said.

"Not all of us live here, but the Faelinn are social creatures so we prefer to live together for that reason as well as for safety," Mark said.

"The bounty offered to the hunters I mentioned was in the millions," Shellie said.

"Then I don't understand why you want any more information out there about the Faelinn," Alanna said.

"Consider the book you'd like to write the first step in a public relations campaign to change how people think of the Faelinn. Hiding the truth hasn't worked," Mark said. He tucked his hands in his pockets, his clever eyes fixed on hers. "So we're going to let it out. Getting public opinion on our side is the first step toward lobbying for change, for laws."

Alanna felt the sudden heavy weight of responsibility on her shoulders. A romance novel, an erotic escape into fantasy for a reader, had suddenly taken on more important undertones. What she wrote would be the beginning of change. If she screwed it up, she would carry that with her always.

"Why me?" she asked softly. "There's any number of authors you could have asked. People who write nonfiction would have been a better choice. Write about the history of the Faelinn, the truth."

"And relegate it to nonfiction hell? A few people will read it out of curiosity. A few scholars may peruse it. But the masses will read fiction," Mark said.

"I picked you because I love your writing," Shellie said. She smoothed the folds of her turquoise skirt over her knees, looking faintly embarrassed. "Everyone reads you."

"Thank you," Alanna said with a laugh, "but I think that falls into the realm of fantasy, too."

"You spent six months on the *New DC Dispatch* bestseller list with your last hardcover," Mark said. "Five weeks of that were spent in the number one slot. If you sold stock in your writing, I'd have bought a big chunk. The people we need to reach read your work. The people we need to reach will be sympathetic."

"It will work," Shellie said. "I have a good feeling about it."

Looking from one to the other, Alanna considered what they were asking. Her storyline already had the elements of mystery in it. She could rebuild the plot, structure it around the concepts that needed to be addressed. She could have a hand in guiding minds into the acceptance of the Faelinn and their plight. What writer would pass that up? And how arrogant was she to assume such lofty dreams?

"I can write a story. I can build it around the truth; make the readers see how much needs to be changed. But I can't do more than that," Alanna said. "I can't put an end to the myths that have grown up around you. I can't make anyone lobby for new laws."

"You leave that to us," Mark said. "We have lawyers and politicians who can do that. We just need public opinion behind us. We need to change the fear of the unknown."

"And I want to read a really juicy romance," Shellie said with a wide smile. "With a gorgeous hero," she continued, looking over at her husband.

"Did I hear talk about heroes?" A woman bounced into the room, a tote thrown over one shoulder. A short cap of red hair framed a pixie face, and the jeans and T-shirt showed off a curvy body. When she saw Alanna, a broad smile broke over her face. It changed her from merely pretty to beautiful.

"You're here," she proclaimed when she saw Alanna. "Oh my gosh, I am such a fan. I brought all your books with me so you can autograph them. Say you will!"

Mark cleared his throat. "Alanna, I'd like you to meet our granddaughter, Daphne."

Alanna blinked slowly, staring from the young face of the college-aged woman to the man who even now was putting an affectionate arm around her. Granddaughter? No way. There was just no way. There couldn't be more than ten years between the two.

Before she could voice the obvious question, two paws landed on her knees. Slanted aquamarine eyes stared into hers out of a broad face covered in dark fur that shaded more towards midnight blue than black. She stared into those eyes and felt her mind go blank.

The Fael resembled a lynx with his whiskered feline face and long tufted ears. The cupped ears were erect and ended in stiff bristles of royal blue fur. The broad paws that rested on her knees were large and heavy. Surprisingly, the Fael had long fingers and a thumb, almost hidden beneath the dense fur of his paws. The size of a golden retriever, but broader through the chest, he was utterly adorable with his eyes looking into hers so seriously. The Fael gave her a long sniff, whiskers tickling against her cheek, and then with what could only be a sound of disappointment, he dropped back to the ground.

Looking stricken, Daphne knelt to run a hand through the thick ruff of fur around the Fael's neck. There was a collective release of breath when the creature ran to the French doors, used a paw to unlatch them, and disappeared outside.

"I'm sorry," Daphne said, looking toward her grandfather. "Riordan wanted to come with me. He wanted to see if she was his."

"We should have discussed it," Mark said. His eyes were hard, his lips thinned with disappointment.

"I'm sorry," Daphne said again. Looking at Alanna now, she repeated the apology. "I should have spoken to you first before bringing him here."

"What just happened?" Alanna asked. Her heart was gradually slowing, the surprise and shock she'd felt easing off. As it did, she became aware of the edge of tension in the room. She could almost see the lines of it between her host and his granddaughter.

"Riordan was hoping that you were his bondmate," Daphne explained.

For a second time, shock left Alanna speechless. She looked over at the doors and through the windows to the rolling edge of lawn. But there was no Fael in sight.

"He's only a kit, you see," Daphne said. "He wants to find his bondmate, and I thought maybe you could be it. I'm sorry, I should have asked."

"It's okay," Alanna said faintly, looking back into the worried eyes of the woman looking at her so earnestly.

"It's not all right," Mark said. "That's not how we do things, and my granddaughter knows that full well."

Shellie stepped forward, placing one arm around Daphne's shoulders. "She just wants him to be happy and settled, Mark," she said to her husband.

Recognizing when someone was on her side, Daphne kissed her grandmother's cheek. "Thanks, Nana."

Alanna's lips twitched as the smile threatened. The look on Mark's face when he realized that he was going to lose the argument made her long for a camera. Irritation, exasperation, and a deep love warred in his eyes before he threw his hands into the air. "Fine. But you keep control of him, Daphne, and tell his mam that she needs to give him another lecture about manners."

The smile that blossomed over Daphne's face lit the room. "I will,

Granddad, I promise." She dropped her tote onto the floor and began pulling books out of it. "Now will you sign these for me?"

The laugh escaped before she could control it. Alanna covered her mouth, but the giggles continued, and she was afraid they were going to think she was a lunatic. At her feet, the pile of her books teetered and spilled over, the bright, romantic covers staring up at her.

When the others joined her, she relaxed. The laughter removed the last of the tension, brightened the corners and spilled out the doors. It called to those that were listening, those who had waited, tense and worried. It teased calls from their throats, a joyful release of sound. It echoed through the Haven, from one to another, until finally circling back to drift inside and mingle with the human joy.

The strange yowling coming from outside filtered in through Alanna's amusement. With a last hiccupping gasp, she stopped laughing to listen. "What is that?"

Shellie came to sit next to her. "Those are the Faelinn," she explained. "And I do believe they're welcoming you."

"Oh," Alanna said softly. The noise wasn't pretty; it was rough like the sound of an old tomcat giving a midnight serenade, only magnified a hundred-fold.

"You see," Shellie said to her husband. "I told you things would be okay."

Jonathan heard the calls, and they stilled his fingers on the keyboard. From her position sprawled on the sun-warmed planks of his deck, Cateera lifted her head. She gave one long stretch, her front legs crouched low while her back arched in a move that would have likely broken Jonathan's spine. She opened her mouth, long canines glinting, and joined her voice to the others.

Through their link, Jonathan felt her happiness. He was clueless to understand it, but she was ignoring the query he directed toward her. She continued to call, to sing with her brethren until finally giving herself a great shake and sitting back down to begin the slow process of grooming her whiskers.

"What was that about?" Jonathan asked. He reached for his coffee and found the mug empty. He didn't even remember drinking it. Exhaustion pushed down on him but he needed to finish the report on his last consultation. It helped to get the information down on paper, even if it was just for his own files. And this one had been bad. He hoped that by writing it all down, he'd be able to push the details out of his head.

We are happy, she answered. A big pink tongue bathed her paw. Using the now damp fur, she swiped it delicately over her jowls, slicking each whisker into place.

Leaning back in his chair, Jonathan stretched long legs toward his friend and nudged her lightly. She swiped at him with one paw, claws carefully retracted, before returning to the long task of keeping her vanity in check. "Why are you happy?"

Because she is going to write about us. Berren says that is a good thing, Cateera answered. *I told you I like how she smells.*

Scowling, Jonathan drew his legs back, tension tightening another notch at the nape of his neck. "Help you how?"

She will make people want to protect us. Then we will become accepted, and not hunted, Cateera answered. She turned her head a little. *We do not like being hunted.*

Silence settled over the deck, broken only by the sound of tongue on fur. The house was his, far too big for him with its sprawling first floor and enough bedrooms to hold a large family, but the rustic wooden exterior with the wraparound porch had suited him somehow, and he'd bought it from Mark, wanting to make part of the Haven his own.

No matter what the Faelinn thought, this woman had the ability to wreck that serenity. Safety would become a dream and not the near reality it was. Oh sure, he knew just how fragile things were here, but it was still far safer than anywhere else on either side of the Veil for the Faelinn. He didn't like the threat Alanna represented. He didn't like the polish, the sleek city feel of her.

She was trouble.

A few taps of his fingers brought her information onto the screen of his laptop. He'd called in a favor when he'd gotten home and had a friend run her info. Now Alanna McLean's life spread in front of him. Date and place of birth, education, current address. She owned a townhouse in a swanky neighborhood in New DC. Her financials showed it paid for free and clear, with a good bit of cushion in the bank and in a variety of safe investments.

Apparently, her writing was successful enough that it paid well.

She'd published nine books, the last seven of which had made it to the bestseller lists, both in hard copy and e-format. She was a bona fide rock star of the romance world.

She had no business making money off the Faelinn.

You are being grumpy again, Cateera complained.

"I'm always grumpy, according to you," he responded, still reading Alanna McLean's stats.

That is because you are. You need your mate. And kits.

"I don't have a mate," he answered, irritated by this new twist on an old mantra. Cateera had been nagging at him to get a woman since he'd bought the house. Apparently, she wouldn't consider him settled until there was a family inhabiting his space, careening from wall to wall and making far too much noise. He could find female companionship when he wanted it without making one of them a permanent fixture. And there was no way in hell it would be Ms. Swanky Address McLean.

"I need a beer," he told her, staring at her over the top of his screen.

And I need another meat roll, she replied. Haughty eyes held his. *Do we have a deal?*

"You've already had two," Jonathan pointed out.

Cateera continued to stare at him, and her silence held a wealth of meaning.

"Fine," he said with a laugh.

The kitchen was large, divided by a long butcher's block. The cooking area was on one side with state-of-the-art appliances, gleaming counters, and a battered coffee maker. A scarred farmer's table currently covered with books and sketches took up the alcove by the big bay window. It was a bright, sunny room and one of the things that had sold him on the house. The refrigerator let out a cold blast when he retrieved a bottle of lager. He popped a meat roll into the microwave for a few seconds to take the chill off, because Cateera was nothing if not spoiled, and then leaned one hip against the counter while she ate. The beer was cold and felt good going down.

"You knew about Mark's plans? You've been talking to him?" It was unusual for any Faelinn to talk to a human other than their bondmate. In many cases, they were unable to; in some, they just couldn't be bothered.

We all talk to Mark, Cateera replied. Tiny flecks of pastry clung to the white whiskers around her mouth. There was going to be more grooming in her future. *He is Berren's bondmate.*

That was true, Jonathan thought. Had been true from the very first, from what he understood. Mark Dennison had bonded with the Fael who had once been king on the other side of the Veil. Builder of the Haven, protecting and nurturing not just the Faelinn, but their human companions. In many ways, he was a father to them all.

That didn't mean Jonathan had to fall into line with this current plan. He might be retired, but his cop instincts still told him this could be a bad idea. And his role now as head of Haven security meant that it fell to him to make sure any repercussions stayed far away.

"I need you to be careful," he said.

Cateera sat, tucked her long, purple-tipped tail around her legs. She regarded him coolly, her head reaching higher than his waist. *I am always careful,* she told him. *I do not leave the Haven unnecessarily. The hunting is good here, and I am safe.*

The kitchen tile was cool beneath his knees as Jonathan knelt in front of her. He threaded his fingers through her ruff, the deep lavender strands of fur thick and soft. "You're my best friend. I worry that the publicity from a book will put you in danger."

I believe it takes a certain amount of time to write a book, Cateera said. She butted him with her head, and then swiped her tongue over his face. *Plenty of time for you to figure out how to stop her.*

"Am I that obvious?"

I know you better than anyone. Your instincts to protect are very strong. You will make a very good father.

Jonathan growled with irritation and rose to his feet. "I'll be uncle to your kits."

Wistfulness touched her thoughts. *Perhaps one day.* She gave herself a vigorous shake, from her head to the tip of her tail. *We should talk about what happened in Carolina. It is very worrisome that our prey escaped.*

It didn't take a lot of empathy to know she was changing the subject.

There were slightly fewer than 300 Faelinn in the world, most living in the Haven, and none of the males had met Cateera's exacting standards. Work would take both of their minds off things, and she was right when she'd said that it took time to write a book. Alanna McLean, even though she was an annoyance, was not an immediate threat.

The immediate threat to his peace of mind was what had happened two days ago in their last consult. The Gift that Cateera had Awakened in him closely echoed his prior career as a police detective. The Gift, though, cut to the heart of the chase. It allowed him to mentally track a killer. Over the past several years they'd honed the skill with success after success. Until this last job in Carolina.

He should not have gotten away from us, Cateera said. *We had a firm grip on his location.*

"He shouldn't have been able to crawl into my mind like that, either," Jonathan added. Restless, he rifled through the sketches scattered on the table. He picked up one covered with fine lines and colored notations and then dropped it again. "You felt him there, Cateera. He knew who we were."

He took that straight from your mind, she said. *I honestly think he is a Veiler. There was something inhuman about his thought patterns. And he scared you.*

Only with her could Jonathan admit that he had been scared. Something about the way that bastard raked through his thoughts had been terrifying. He scrubbed at his face with his hands. He was tired. Pouring the rest of the lager down the sink, he tossed the bottle into the recycling bin.

"I'm heading to bed," he told her. "We'll dissect the consult tomorrow."

I am going to run. I do not want to sleep yet. She let herself out the back door, throwing a last glance at him over her shoulder. *Dream of your mate,* she told him.

Cateera's words chased him up the stairs.

Chapter Three

Throwing open the balcony door, Alanna stepped out into the night air. It was cold, and she wrapped her arms around her ribcage. The season was closer to winter here than it was at home. She briefly considered going back inside to find her robe but discarded the idea. Instead, she settled into the soft cushion of one of the chairs and drew up her legs. Rippling lights danced in the sky above the tree line. Seen against the star-strewn dark, the colors of the Veil took on an intensity that defied understanding.

She had travelled to Europe once, a harrowing flight that had hopped from zone to zone over some of the shorter dimensional curtains. Not all of them reached high into the atmosphere. After the Veil Wars, new sea travel routes had been plotted, helped along by the knowledge of the Merpeople. As air travel continued to progress, both magickally and technologically, routes were drawn up over and around the Veil's manifestations. Now there were routes mapped around the globe. Air travel was possible if you had the patience to endure the endless winding safe zones. The trip had afforded her the opportunity to view the aurora borealis. It was nothing compared to this. The sweeping sheets of color that the northern lights threw across the sky were beautiful but limited. Human eyes could see only some of the colors that spilled through the atmosphere. Originating from deep within the earth, the Veil was something more. She felt its pull, felt the magnetism that tugged at the soul. It was no surprise that from the moment it appeared, dotted and striped across the Earth, people were drawn to it.

Layers of color moved, hidden and then revealed in teasing glimpses. It was endless and depthless. The palest of ice blues would suddenly turn almost black with a deep richness that hinted at other colors invisible to the human spectrum. Greens to make a man weep. Purples that alternately soothed and raged in the heart. Golds wept into reds with a swiftness that stole breath. It was compelling and beguiling.

And the most frightening thing she'd ever seen.

Alanna knew she should be working. Earlier, she'd expanded the list of questions she'd compiled before leaving home. There was so much more going on here that she hadn't expected. Hadn't had any cause to suspect. They wanted her to help save them. No, not save, that was wrong, she knew. Help them to be understood and protected. Shellie saw her book as a mix of romance, adventure, and public relations.

Which all led to another slew of questions. Were other less humanoid races also hunted for the secrets they held? She knew there were few laws in place to offer rights or protection for the Veilers. And even those differed from nation to nation. Most of the laws centered around the Fae and the other human-like Veilers. Those races with something to offer, a skill to trade or treasure to barter, held far more rights than the others. What kind of protections were there for the Veilers who were more alien to a human viewpoint? She realized her knowledge was woefully inadequate.

The only things she really knew about Veiler rights came from the hateful Human Righters campaign. They advocated violence, hatred, and above all, humans first in everything. No matter where you were on social media, there they were. Just recently she'd seen an article about a farm that had held lesser earth Fae as slaves. What would they do if they got their hands on the Faelinn? It was a frightening thought. No wonder Shellie and Mark wanted to change people's thoughts about the race. If they were seen as animals instead of sentient beings, then there was no telling what could be done to them.

What was happening to her romance novel? Alanna had envisioned a heroine bonded with a Fael. She'd wanted the mystery of their connection.

Now she was faced with the choice of keeping that or writing something that could have real repercussions. And wasn't that a good bit of hubris rearing up in her head?

Laughing at herself, Alanna stood up and stretched. Tomorrow she'd deal with the questions, and maybe figure out a way to work both concepts into her writing. Her editor would be thrilled.

The Veil rippled, spat colors into the night, as she shut the door. It would still be there in the morning.

~

Brambles twisted around her feet, thick thorns piercing the bare flesh. Running. Escaping. The sound of pursuit close. A pause for breath, drawn harshly into her lungs. Which way? Which way? Panic drove her on, over the rocks now. A leap for safety across a small chasm silhouetted her against the sky. A voice cried out in triumph. Hated. Feared.

Running again. No time to breathe, no safety here. Down, hide in the rocks. In the scrub. Icy water stinging in the cuts and tears, surging around her feet. Cover her scent. Lose the pursuit. Escape.

A splash behind her. No time to look. Just run. Faster.

Pain. A fiery slash across her flank. Tripping, tumbling, the sharp rocks tearing and bruising. Blood hot as it poured from the wound. Steamed as it hit the snow.

There was nowhere to go. No way to go. Turning now, facing her pursuer. He wielded a sword, the winter moonlight glinting on its blade. Her blood discolored the edge. He smiled, sharpened teeth wicked in the tattooed face.

She bared her own, growling. Preparing. There would be only one chance. Focused. Waiting. Ignoring the taunts, the weaving tip of iron. One chance. Just like in the Pit.

He moved in. The sword flashed moonfire from the sky, scattering it across the icy stream, the snow-dusted rocks. Dodging, the blade whipped by, and it was now! Now! Teeth skating across boiled leather and into reeking flesh. Blood, hated blood, bitter and rancid in her mouth.

Punches, nails tearing at the wound in her side, screaming. Was it hers? No, her mouth was full of flesh. A shake of her head. Another. Arms fell away and her pursuer, her captor and tormenter, stumbled, dropping to his knees. Flesh and blood were bitter in her mouth.

Escape now. No time to see if he could follow. Hurting, crawling away. Moving to the light that called her.

I'm coming.

The day was hot, the sky bleached of color. It seemed that autumn had stepped back and summer had moved in for one last hurrah. The air was thick with humidity. Even the trees at the edge of the lawn seemed listless, the oranges and reds dull, the greens dusty and tired. The Veil seemed to glimmer like a mirage through a haze of heat. The flower beds trimmed back for the coming winter drooped in the warmth, the last late-blooming flowers nowhere near as vibrant as the colors painted in the sky.

The crisp grey linen slacks and the sleeveless silk tank Alanna had donned that morning clung to her, but she was too restless to be inside. The braided coil of hair at her nape seemed to pull her head down, and a headache lurked behind her eyes. The sickening taste of blood had coated her mouth when she woke up that morning. Her stomach had rebelled and she'd barely made it to the bathroom in time to retch. Even now, her stomach was queasy.

But there was work to be done. The laptop was open in front of her, a glass of cold sweet tea beside her. Shellie had graciously agreed to have the interview on the patio where the scent of pine and fall grasses drifted through the humid air. Shellie somehow managed to look cool despite the glow of perspiration on her skin.

"Are you sure you're okay?" Shellie asked. The charms on her bracelet jangled as she reached for her tea.

Alanna forced a smile. Her head really was pounding now, but there was no way she was going to give up any of this opportunity for a silly thing like a headache. "Yes, I'm fine. I just didn't sleep well. I think it's being so close to the Veil. It's almost like I can feel it on my skin."

A small frown touched the smooth skin between Shellie's eyes. It was obvious she didn't believe Alanna. Finally, one shoulder lifted in a small shrug. "All right, then. What do you want to ask?"

Alanna was grateful when the other woman chose to let it go. "I have a list of questions, but honestly, I'm not sure what to ask first," Alanna admitted. Impulsively, she closed her laptop. "How about we start at the beginning. How did you meet your Fael?"

The smile that curved Shellie's mouth now was soft with remembrance. "That's tied up with how I met Mark. We met at a USO dance in Luray. I remember how handsome he was in his uniform. He was enough to make my heart tremble.

"He still is," she confided, making Alanna smile.

"He was stationed at the base outside of Luray." She paused to take a drink of tea, looking out over the lawn. "It was bad in those early days. The tribe of Gargoyle that had come through the Veil and taken up residence in the caverns were vicious. Not all of them agreed with the peace that had been brokered between us."

"I remember reading about the Luray Massacre," Alanna said.

A shudder shook Shellie's slight frame. "It was worse than anything you could imagine."

"At least they're peaceful now," Alanna said. She remembered the Gargoyle she'd seen perched on the roof when she arrived. She was positive he was real and not a statue.

"Yes," Shellie agreed. "But it was bloody while it lasted. Every so often we still hear about a youngling earning his manhood by stalking the locals. It hasn't led to any killings in a few years, but there's still an army outpost there, just in case.

"And I'm wandering off topic, aren't I?" She shook her head, today's earrings casting colorful patterns on her cheeks when the sunlight caught the crystals. "We moved here to Mark's family home after we were married. Setasha came through the Veil not long after. She became my bondmate. We've been bonded for sixty-eight years." The blond smiled slightly. "My, that was a long time ago."

"You don't look a day over twenty-five," Alanna said. She startled as a bird flew down from a nest, a squawking red streak of feathers.

There were no lines on Shellie's face. Her skin was smooth, taut with the resiliency of youth. The Dennisons certainly had the wealth to invest in the finest health care and cosmetic work, the priciest of magickal glamours. Alanna sat back in her chair, considering. One finger tapped a restless beat against the glass table.

"It's something to do with the Faelinn, isn't it?"

The door to the patio opened, and Shellie turned her head to smile at her husband. The casual khakis and white shirt open at the throat gave him a relaxed look. Lifting one hand, she caught his fingers, holding them briefly to her cheek as he sat in one of the empty chairs. "I was just telling Alanna how old I am."

Mark laughed. "And did you tell her that I'm an old codger of ninety-seven?"

"We hadn't gotten that far," Shellie said.

"The Faelinn keep you young," Alanna said. A tumble of puzzle pieces fell into place in her head. "That's why so many people are hunting them."

"One of several reasons," Mark admitted. "It's a symbiotic relationship."

The scrape of chair on stone forced Alanna's attention to Shellie. The woman was on her feet, staring intently at the barrier of trees beyond the lawn. There was tension in the line of her shoulders, in the rigid length of her spine.

"Setasha says there's a new Fael coming," she said. "She and Berren are following his scent." She looked at her husband. "He's hurt."

"What's wrong?" Alanna asked. Her skin prickled with the knowledge that there were Faelinn out in the woods. She still hadn't met any except the surprisingly large kit that Daphne had brought the day before, and Jonathan's Fael, Cateera.

"A Fael came through the Veil," Mark explained. The line carved between his brows deepened as he listened to Berren through their mental connection. "A newcomer." He took out his cell phone, speed dialing.

"We have a situation," he said, never taking his eyes off the trees. He snapped the phone shut, glanced down at Alanna. "It might be best if you went inside."

"Whatever it is that's going to happen, I want to see it," she said stubbornly. "If you want me to help, then I need to see as much as I can."

A curt nod and he strode down the stone steps to the lawn. Alanna stood, too edgy to stay still. A sudden bout of dizziness shot blackness around the edges of her vision. Shellie caught her arm, held her when she would have fallen. The headache pushed against the inside of Alanna's skull, travelled down her spine in painful spasms. She was desperately thirsty. Unable to look away from a spot at the tree line, Alanna reached for her glass of tea, drank until the ice cubes clinked against her teeth. She was still thirsty.

A flock of dark birds took flight from the woods. Bushes shivered. Alanna didn't realize she'd walked forward until her fingers bit into the stonework of the decorative fencing around the patio.

Three Faelinn stepped from the tree line, a pair flanking a third who staggered between them. The center Fael was huge, larger even than the two escorting him. Dun colored fur covered his body rather than stripes. He, and it was a he, she knew it instinctively, paused, raised his head as if scenting the air. He came closer, one limping step at a time. Even from this distance, she could see the gold of his eyes.

"He's hurt," Alanna murmured when she drew up next to Mark. He glanced over at her but she barely acknowledged his presence. The headache was nearly intolerable now, pulsing behind her eyes, the base of her skull. She clutched Mark's arm, nails digging in. "He's hurt," she repeated, forcefully this time. A lancing pain stabbed into her side and she moaned.

Mark looked at her. His grey eyes were cool and assessing. "I see," he said softly. "Is this what you want? You need to be sure, Alanna. Bonding is forever."

The words barely penetrated the nearly overwhelming need to embrace the creature that had stopped halfway across the lawn. He stood between the two other Faelinn, his sides heaving. His legs trembled but he didn't fall. He just stood and waited. She couldn't look away from his golden gaze. When Mark stepped in front of her and framed her face with his hands to force her to meet his eyes, she hissed at him.

"Is this what you want, Alanna?" he asked again. "You can deny the bonding. You have a choice. I will not have this forced on you by a wild Fael."

There was no choice. How could he even suggest that? The Fael staring at her with his soul in his eyes was meant to be her partner and friend. Alanna knew this was why she was here. Not the promise of a story. Not the chance to see what so few saw. This tenuous, shining link that stretched gossamer fine between the two of them. "Yes," she whispered. "This is what I want."

The spider-web strand of belonging thickened with every step she took. It tugged her, spinning through her psyche to anchor deep within her. The grass was silky and cool beneath her feet. She'd run out of her flats. There was no hesitation when she dropped to her knees in front of the Fael who looked at her as if she was his everything.

"I'm here," she said. When he finally collapsed at her feet, she lifted the great head into her lap. Golden, sun-drenched eyes looked up at her. His pelt was rough under her hands, full of dirt and briar. Twisted scars showed through the patchy fur. Blood marred the dust-colored fur of his muzzle. It was dried, clotted around his whiskers. The great wound along his flank wept red. Through the blood and dirt, she thought she could see white bone. His sides shuddered with each shallow, panting breath.

I came, he said. The words pierced the pain in her skull, sending it scattering away.

"Yes, you did," she murmured. Her fingers found the silky tufts of his ears, and he purred as she stroked. The left ear was tattered, long healed. It looked like a bite had been taken out of the side.

Mine, he told her. His tongue curled over her wrist.

And teeth sank into her flesh.

The pain was immense. It radiated from her wrist up her arm, every nerve screaming with shock. Fire raced through her. Something inside of her twisted, warping out of shape. Her brain exploded with sensation. Too many colors. Too many scents. She tried to tear her arm away from him, from those sharp piercing teeth, but a paw slapped down on her arm, surprisingly strong despite his injuries. Each draw of blood from her body sent a fresh spasm of pain.

Through it all, those great golden eyes held hers. Full of love. Full of trust. And she couldn't look away. And then she didn't want to.

Mine, he told her again, the words whispering into her mind. The pain ebbed, soothed by the balm of his voice. *I am Jekk, and you are my bondmate.*

The sensation of him in her mind was overwhelming. There didn't seem to be enough room for both of them. Memories of a past she'd never experienced nestled against her own. Hopes, fears, dreams that were foreign to her settled into her heart. It was too much. The last sensation she felt before the world skittered away was the rough silk of Jekk's neck ruff against her cheek.

∾

A situation, Mark had said. Jonathan paused at the top of the patio steps, Cateera at his side.

A situation, my ass. Cateera chuffed lightly in agreement. He was going to have words with Mark about his use of understatement.

Ebon-furred Berren, the alpha of the Haven Faelinn, stood guard over the prone body of a Fael Jonathan had never seen. Berren's copper-tipped ears were slicked back with mistrust. Setasha, his pretty mate, stalked back and forth, her tail slashing the air. Cateera ran to join them. Mark rose from his crouched position next to the writer when Jonathan approached. Alanna McLean lay sprawled over the body of the unknown Fael.

They have bonded, Cateera told him. She stalked back and forth, examining the newcomer with narrowed eyes.

"Oh fuck," he muttered when he saw the blood drying on Alanna's wrist. Claimed and bonded. Assessing the wound in the Fael's side, Jonathan wondered just how long either of them would last.

"You got here quickly," Mark greeted.

"Too bad it wasn't quicker," he answered. He knelt, hands hanging loosely between his thighs, and stared at the newly bonded pair. Even out cold, Alanna maintained an air of cool elegance. The grass stains on the knees of her grey linen slacks, the slender bare feet, neither did a thing to change it. His heart gave a hitch because she was just so still, so pale. The pulse in her wrist beat reassuringly steady beneath his fingers. Bewildered, he snatched his hand back. When had he reached for her?

Cateera nosed the Fael at her feet, giving a long slow lick to his muzzle. *He is wearing a collar.*

Reaching out, Jonathan carefully smoothed back the dirty fur of the Fael's ruff, revealing the black iron encircling his neck. It was tight, buried in the skin, and was going to be a bitch to get off.

"That complicates things," he said.

"Let's get them in the house," Mark said.

43

Jonathan slipped his hands beneath Alanna's thighs and shoulders, easily lifting the unconscious woman into his arms. Her head turned, nuzzling into the softness of his T-shirt. Strands of her sable hair lay loosely across one cheek, night-dark across her pale skin. It crossed his mind that she did smell good, and heard Cateera's laughter in his head. Ruthlessly, he shut his bondmate out. Turning toward the house, he left Mark to deal with the several hundred pounds of wounded Fael.

"I've called Bethany," Shellie said as she fell into step beside him. "We'll need her to heal his wounds."

Jonathan nodded. The bite marks at Alanna's wrist had stopped bleeding, were even now healing over, but her bondmate would need care if he was to live. "There'll be more when the collar is removed."

Shellie nodded and held open the patio door. "Take her to the infirmary. We'll ask Ichirius to bring her mate. I didn't foresee this possibility, you know."

Sparing her a glance, Jonathan noted the worry in the woman's eyes. He wasn't feeling generous though. "But if you had, you'd have still invited her."

"Yes," Shellie answered serenely. "What comes of this will be good for all of us."

He grunted and followed the woman into a fully equipped examining room. He laid Alanna gently on one of the two gurneys. She moved restlessly. Her fine-boned hand was cold and clammy when he picked it up. Turning her wrist over, he examined the damage the Fael had done.

"It's already healing," Shellie said, peering down. "It's a true bonding."

Jonathan bit back his answer. Cateera was always cautioning him against speaking his mind. At the sink, he scrubbed his hands and dried them before snapping on latex gloves. Shellie was ready with sterile pads. Gently, he began cleaning away the blood to reveal two neat holes already pinking over with new skin. It was a true bonding, and that only increased his irritation. If it hadn't been, the flesh would have been torn, still bleeding. He shook his head, even as he tossed the dirty gauze into a bowl.

"This shouldn't have happened."

"But it did," Mark said, pushing through the wide swinging doors. "And now we have to deal with it." Behind him, a tall Gargoyle followed, glossy black wings tucked neatly at his back. He cradled the newly bonded Fael in his muscled arms. Ichirius's tourmaline eyes were bright in a face that was grey and craggy like the rock he resembled. His needle-sharp teeth could inflict a venomous bite on his enemies. He was terrifying, and had a heart that prized loyalty to his friends above all.

"Lay him on the gurney, please," Mark instructed.

With a deft tenderness, Ichirius settled the Fael on white sheets. The black pinfeathers of his immense wings quivered, a clear sign he was upset. Shellie linked her arm through his, patting the hardened skin. "We'll see that he's taken care of," she promised.

"The Kellian will be angry," Ichirius said. His basso rumble of a voice caused the water in the bowl to shiver just a little. He pushed Alanna's gurney over so that it butted up against her bondmate's. Even unconscious, she reached out a hand to clutch at his fur.

Mark shared a glance with Jonathan after the Gargoyle left. It would be time to hunt, Jonathan knew. The fact that the Fael still wore a collar told him that the Kellian who owned him was still alive.

Hunting is better than working, Cateera said.

He hid a smile. His prissy Fael who so hated to get her fur dirty turned into a bloodthirsty fighter when they went on a Hunt.

I am not prissy, she denied hotly. *You just do not appreciate the beauty in grooming.*

You're such a girl, he told her on their mental pathway. She gave him a swat across the thigh, her claws only partially sheathed. He did smile when she leaned into him, the warmth of her muscular body pressing into his side as she stared at the unconscious pair.

He is a warrior, she observed. *I may consider him.*

The Fael stalked out of the room, the lavender end of her white tail swishing. Staring after her, Jonathan shook his head. That she could find anything mate-worthy in the tattered, emaciated Fael on the gurney surprised him. And worried him if he were being totally honest.

This was shaping up to be a hell of a day.

Drawing Mark away from the bed, Jonathan spoke in a low voice. "I'll gear up and then cross through the Veil."

"You have the standard offerings?"

"Yeah, I've got everything I need in the SUV. Cateera will backtrack his crossing point, and we'll go from there."

Gripping his arm, Mark nodded. "Don't take any chances."

"It's not the first time I've had to do this," Jonathan reminded him.

"And it won't be the last, I know," Mark said. "But Shellie would kill me if anything happened to you. She's rather fond of you."

The grin that curved Jonathan's mouth was there just to piss his friend off. "Maybe I'll think about stealing her away from you when I get back."

"You're far too young for her," Mark said. "But just in case, I can still kick your ass."

"You could try, old man," Jonathan laughed. He sobered up as he glanced back at the unconscious pair. He ignored the fact that his eyes lingered primarily on the writer's graceful curves. "I'll be back as soon as I can. I hope you figure out a way to keep this from becoming a total disaster while I'm gone."

Mark shoved his hands into his pockets, watching his wife bustle around, setting out the necessary supplies for Bethany's arrival. "It's only a disaster if she dies."

Cateera waited for him at the bottom of the stairs. *Will he live?*

"I hope so," Jonathan answered, striding across the marble floor, the heels of his boots tapping out a quick rhythm. "If he dies, so does she, and I don't know how Mark will spin that one."

The Fael should have asked her, Cateera said. She slid out the door before him, bounding down the stone steps to where he'd left the truck. *I shall speak to him about it when he wakes. It was very bad manners.*

The precisely spoken words, the haughty tone, had him laughing. "I'm sure he'll be thrilled to listen."

Opening the rear hatch, Jonathan released the hidden catch that popped open the storage area beneath the SUV's bed. Beneath lay an arsenal and his survival gear. He stripped off his T-shirt, replaced its bright blue with a faded grey silk to wick away moisture. He layered his clothes, switched his boots for another all-terrain pair, and ended with a winter camouflage jacket. He was already sweltering, but he'd need the warmth on the other side. He ignored the guns, their notoriety for misfires across the Veil making them more of a hazard than a tool. Knives at his waist, thrust into his boot. Field provisions and fresh water were in a small pack along with a first aid kit and rock-climbing gear. Finally, he drew a scabbard from the specially cut foam that cradled it. The sword inside was wickedly sharp, the steel oiled and tended.

You just didn't know what you'd need when you crossed the Veil. The Kellian tribes that lived on the other side were fierce, war-like. They didn't like to lose what belonged to them. And they considered the Faelinn their property.

Securing the scabbard so that the sword jutted up over his shoulder, Jonathan was reassured by its weight. He hated crossing the Veil, hated even more the brutal creatures that occupied the little corner of it that abutted Mark's property. But like all things, with the bad came the good. The Faelinn lived there as well, and one of them was worth more than every one of the tribesmen put together.

The muscled weight of his bonded Fael pressed against his thigh. He felt the deep love that came through their link and knew that in a million years he would never be truly worthy of it.

"Are you ready?" he asked her, knowing she hated crossing the Veil as much as he did. She'd strapped on a pack with extra provisions, survival gear if it took longer than anticipated to follow the Fael's back trail. A lethal crossbow was secured tightly to her back. With her teeth and claws she rarely needed it, but she believed in being prepared for anything.

We will find the slaver and kill him, Cateera said. *And then I will have the last meat roll.*

Laughing, he followed her into the woods as she backtracked the new Fael's trail.

Chapter Four

Dr. Bethany Ingraham straightened from her examination of the unconscious Fael. She pushed one hand through the short dark curls falling over her forehead, the other into the soft chestnut fur of Flexa, her bondmate.

"I won't lie to you—it's bad," she told Mark. "The collar is embedded in the neck. I'd say he's worn it since he was a kit. It's at its largest expansion, but it's still far too small." She spread the dust-colored fur apart, revealing hideous black metal. The collar was obviously too small and the Fael's skin had pushed out at the sides, growing over the edges of the collar so that any attempt to remove it would require a knife to slice away the excess flesh.

"That poor thing," Shellie murmured. Her hand tightened on Mark's arm. Tears glittered on her lashes.

"That's on top of the injuries he's sustained," Bethany continued. "The slash over his hip is deep; I really don't know how he continued to walk. His ribs are broken, and he has some internal bleeding. His left front leg is deformed from a badly healed fracture. He's seriously malnourished. He's little more than skin and bone."

"Pit fighter?" Mark asked. The Fael's muzzle was scarred, one long slice stretching over the bridge of his nose.

"That would be my guess."

"Can you help him?" Mark asked. His fingers twined with Shellie's as he drew her even closer to his side.

Flexa turned her head, a snort of air showing her disdain. A quick smile tilted Bethany's lips. "You doubt us? Of course, we can help him."

"What do you need?" he asked.

"Go and boil some water and bring me some towels."

He turned on his heel, heading for the door.

"Mark, I'm kidding," she said with a laugh. "I'm not birthing a baby. Just let us work."

Glancing from the unconscious Fael to Alanna, Mark frowned. The writer was so pale, her hair a stark black against her skin. Compared to the Fael's slow breathing, Alanna's was too quick. Her body struggled with the bond, trying to assimilate the psyche of a desperately injured Fael.

His own Fael, Berren, head butted him hard. *You can't help until they're well,* the black-furred Fael told him. The dusting of bronze tipping the ends of his ears and tail glittered in the stark light from the medical lamp.

"I know," Mark said. Standing next to Alanna's gurney put him directly opposite Bethany. He would be able to monitor everything that she did. There was a waiting room, but he knew he wouldn't be able to stay there. He never could. Every time a Fael joined them, he felt the responsibility to oversee the newly bonded pair. And in this instance, with the bonding being so unexpected with a woman who wasn't informed of the consequences, he needed to stay. To watch. To minimize the problems. He wrapped his arms around Shellie and waited.

Bethany's hands hovered over the gaping slash in the Fael's flank. It still leaked a slow dribble of blood. Flexa stood on her hind legs, her furry fingers agile as she began to sponge away both the dried blood and the new. All too quickly there was a pile of stained gauze in a basin. The healer placed her fingers over the wound. A pale gold glow enveloped her hands, shining in the overhead light. It stretched filmy tendrils towards the wound and then slowly sank inside.

The wound began to shimmer. The seeping blood slowed and then stopped. The stark glimpse of bone disappeared as muscle fibers reconnected. Flexa's paw covered her bondmate's, aiding Bethany as they worked together to heal the Fael. Bethany's hands moved slowly over the

Fael's body. Golden light flickered through the fur, dancing in and out of tortured flesh. Internal injuries were healed with the aid of the healer's Gift.

Setasha, Shellie's ivory furred Fael, paced at the foot of the bed. Her long tail twitched impatiently. She peered over Alanna's prone body, watching the healing pair closely. It was in her nature to supervise.

The Haven was fortunate that the doctor had been willing to move her practice to the area. Of course, the Faelinn preferred to stay close to the Veil, and to others of their kind, but that didn't always work out with their human partners' careers. Bethany and her family lived in the Haven, but she ran a general practice in town. Her abilities to heal, however, were a closely guarded secret.

Slowly, the doctor worked her hands along the wounded Fael's legs. Mark winced when he heard an audible crack as she broke one of the front legs to reset the bone. Flexa pulled hard to straighten the limb, holding it in place while Bethany healed it. The skin rippled as the muscles shaped themselves back into their normal patterns and then stilled. His cracked ribs received her attention. Minor cuts scabbed over, healed from within. Finally, with a shaky sigh, Bethany stepped back. Flexa nuzzled her cheek, and then dropped her paws to the floor and lay down.

"I've taken care of his major injuries. What do you want to do about the collar?" she asked. She accepted the bottle of cold water that Setasha gave to her. Half of it disappeared before she stopped drinking.

"Is it spelled or welded shut?" Mark asked.

"Spelled," Bethany said, smoothing away the patchy dun colored fur to point out the sigil carved into the black iron. "But it might as well be welded it's embedded so far into his skin."

"Can we afford to give Jonathan a little time?"

"The Fael's had it this long," Bethany said with a shrug.

"It would be kinder to keep them asleep," Shellie said. She smoothed back Alanna's hair where it had come loose from its braided coil.

"Leave them for twenty-four hours," Mark said decisively. "If the collar's lock doesn't release by then, we'll have to take it off manually."

Bethany nodded and touched each of the sleeping pair's foreheads with a gentle finger. They'd sleep awhile longer.

And God help them all when they woke. Mark had no idea how Alanna was going to react to her new situation.

~

The Veil buzzed against his skin. Jonathan gritted his teeth as he studied it from his crouched position at Cateera's side. It flickered and sparked, the occasional tendril reaching out to graze him. He jerked away every time. He hated the way it felt. A low static charge that could change in a heartbeat from a tickle to a burn. The colors looked solid, nothing visible through them even though walking into the Veil showed how insubstantial it really was.

He came through here, she said.

"I see the blood on the grass," he agreed. He stared a little longer at the flowing colors a foot away, and then straightened. "Let's go."

Together, she said.

The anxiety behind the words panged in his heart. "Always," he promised, and then stepped into the Veil.

Color burst over his skin, each hue a different tactile sensation. The reds slashed like knives; blues, so cold they burned. Jonathan gritted his teeth. A low whine came from Cateera's throat, but she kept pace with him as they walked farther into the inter-dimensional tear. Static electricity ran along his skin and ruffled his hair like wind. They'd learned early on that electrical devices never survived the journey.

I will rip him limb from limb for making me go through this, Cateera swore. Her fur stood on end, making her look like a lavender and white puffball. She caught the image from Jonathan's mind and turned her head to nip at his fingers.

There was no up, there was no down. There was only forward. Cells stretched to the limits of their elasticity. Neurons fired randomly, shimmers of pleasure followed by stabs of pain. The ground rolled under their feet. If he thought too hard about breathing, he was convinced they would suffocate. And then abruptly, they were through.

The only resemblance to Earth's side of the Veil were the mountains. Everything else was different. No shades of green to please the eye covered the bare slopes. Rocks tumbled with knife-edged danger down the steep grade, each in varying shades of grey and icy white. It was a harsh, unforgiving landscape and every time he saw it, Jonathan understood the Faelinn desire to wear joyous colors in their pelt.

Cateera sneezed. *Once I have removed his limbs, I will drag them to the nearest cliff and drop them.*

Jonathan grinned. The Kellian stood no chance against his fierce bondmate. He watched as she gave a great shake and then crouched low. Her sleek fur darkened, color fading into the mottled winter greys of the world around them. She became virtually invisible to the eye. It was some form of light-bending chameleon magic, no one knew for sure. Of course, since they refused to allow scientists to examine the Faelinn, there was no way to determine exactly how it worked.

And Jonathan was okay with that.

The sun was high, but its light was cold. It lanced off icy drifts of wind-driven snow to stab at his eyes. Jonathan tugged his goggles into place and the glare was cut off. With the Veil at his back, the energy it threw off still prickling his skin, Jonathan centered himself. He loosened the sword in its scabbard, and with a last threading of his fingers through Cateera's fur, began an easy loping stride that carried him down the trail.

Blood droplets dried to a brown crust speckled the rocks. The faintest of claw scratches showed up as minute whiter stripes on the darker grey stone. He felt a wave of admiration from Cateera as they wended their way through a dry gully, icy pellets of snow shifting like sand beneath their feet.

He tried to hide his tracks even though he was injured, she observed. She stopped to nose at a patch of dead scrub grass. *He rested here.*

The brush was shaded by overhanging rock, but it was narrow and provided little relief from the frigid wind. Jonathan knelt, looking for tracks, but there was little to see. The Faelinn had obscured his presence, hiding the signs of his occupation. Only his scent trail remained, and Jonathan's senses weren't acute enough to pick it up.

Cateera led the way along the gully before scrambling up and out. She raced through a narrow canyon, tempering her pace so that he could keep up. Gradually they worked their way downhill, the stunted scrub giving way to the occasional copse of pine and bare elm. The snow weighted down the branches and lay in thick drifts around their bases. The trail led them around the trees. Even wounded, the Fael had taken the long way around rather than leave his footprints in the snow.

Looking back up the slope they had descended, Jonathan realized how far they'd come from the Veil. He could see its glow in the sky, but not the Veil itself. The sun was beginning to slide lower, hovering over the bare shoulders of rock. It was the long rays of the sunlight that reflected from the Veil and threw its colors up into the sky. Turning away, he resumed the steady pace that Cateera set.

The run loosened his muscles, loosened his thoughts. This wasn't the first hunt they'd had. The very first had been revenge for what had been done to Cateera. Their bonding had been hard, both of them wounded. His body had been recovering from the gunshot that had forced him into extended leave from the police department. He'd been driving the Shenandoah Parkway, no destination in mind, trying to make decisions, searching his soul for reasons to go back.

There'd been no one to go back to; his last relationship had ended months before the day he'd taken the bullet that had nicked his lung. His world had consisted of work, sleep, and more work. The future spread out in front of him with endless vistas of more of the same. It propelled him to drive, to aim the car in a direction and keep on until something changed.

The scenic pullover beckoned him from the road. The need to stretch his legs and suck some of the mountain air into his recovering chest drove him from the vehicle. Climbing over the guardrail, he ignored the drop down into the valley at his feet. He didn't much care if he fell or not.

The low mewl of pain coming from the side of the road made him reach for a gun that wasn't there. Cursing, Jonathan moved cautiously around the car, his eyes scanning the underbrush beside the road. At first, he saw nothing beyond the edge of the parking lot. But that low pained cry pulled him forward until he was close enough to see the great beast collapsed under the bushes.

She'd been grey then, the color of the mountains she'd fled. The iron collar around her neck inhibited her natural camouflaging talent. So thin, he could count every rib. Even then, before they'd bonded, he'd felt her thirst and had returned to the car for a bottle of water. She lapped at it from his hand, and when she raised those turquoise eyes to his, he knew that the change in his life he'd been looking for had come.

You were meant for me, Cateera told him now, dropping back to pace at his side for a time. The fall of her paws on loose rock was silent. She leaped down a short drop and he followed, landing lightly beside her. His lung had recovered quickly after they'd bonded. The scars from the original wound and the subsequent surgery were almost gone. The bonding had many advantages.

"He came a long way," he said softly. They'd descended from the steep slopes of the mountaintop to nearly valley level. The ground rose and fell in gentler waves, but even here the environment was inhospitable. The trees were still stunted, twisted into unnatural shapes. The ground was hard beneath the layer of snow. The snow drifted in unexpected holes and made each step an effort. This was nothing like the verdant Blue Ridge of home.

Birds burst from the trees, their harsh calls echoing in the otherwise still landscape. Jonathan stopped, melting back into the shadows of a stand of pine. He crouched and felt the pressure of Cateera's body against his. They waited, and a wafting of icy breeze brought them both the scent they'd been expecting.

The sour smell of dirt and sweat. The unmistakable tang of the oil the Kellian used in their beards. The scent of blood.

"Is he alone or has he brought Faelinn to hunt with him?" Jonathan asked silently through their link.

Drawing a deep breath, whiskers quivering, Cateera considered. *He is alone. The blood smells fresh.*

A feral smile spread across Jonathan's face. If the hunter was already wounded, it would make the coming fight that much easier. Perhaps the Kellian would bargain for the life of Alanna's Fael rather than risk another wound. The race was notoriously hard to kill. He would take whatever advantage he could get.

I will circle around, Cateera told him. Indiscernible from the surrounding trees she slipped away. Her fur reacted instinctively to changes and it was only because he was tuned to her that he knew she ghosted between the trees. He stalked forward, trying to minimize the crunch of snow beneath his boots. To one side, a tumble of boulders blocked Jonathan's view. He was betting the Kellian was on the other side.

A harsh curse in a language Jonathan recognized told him he was right. He reached for his sword, and then hesitated. The faint sound it would make leaving the scabbard might give his presence away. Instead, he waited.

I see him, Cateera said. *His back is against the rock. There is a lot of blood on his chest.*

"Stay back, dear one," Jonathan replied. "I want to see if he'll negotiate."

The Kellian grunted. He appeared from behind the rock, his head thrown back to scent the air. The movement revealed the savage bite in his throat. Dark blood stained the skin, thick clots around the wound. It coated the iron rings sewn into his boiled-leather chest plate. It lingered on the long length of blade that was suddenly in a hand that would easily match the size of Jonathan's head.

"I can smell you, little human," he said, his tongue twisting the English into guttural syllables. Eyes as black as a Fael's collar scanned the trees. "Come out, come out."

The steel sliding from Jonathan's scabbard was nearly silent, but those deadly eyes honed in nonetheless. The smile that split the rugged features revealed sharpened teeth. The Kellian warriors painstakingly sharpened their teeth upon achieving manhood. And they braided their beards, one braid for every enemy kill. This one had a lot of braids.

Leaving his pack behind, Jonathan stepped from his hiding place. The Kellian looked down at him from a height of more than eight feet. The race as a whole was bigger than humans, but this one was huge.

"You're the one the Faelinn call their Champion, aren't you?" the Kellian said. The words were rough, spoken with a heavy accent and made worse by the wound to his throat. "Where's your pet?"

Jonathan smiled. He didn't know he'd been given a nickname. He found that he liked it.

Do not let him stroke your ego, Cateera warned.

The words centered him, and he settled into a waiting stance. The sword was a familiar extension of his arm. The leather-wrapped hilt fit his palm perfectly. The balanced steel was so well made he could hold it for hours. He studied the giant. It wasn't just the height; it was the width of shoulder, the long stretch of arm that made him formidable. It should have made him slower, but a slow Kellian was a dead Kellian, and they were a warlike race. None that he had faced were hampered by their size.

"My name is Jonathan Burke. I've come to bargain for the life of a Fael." He might be hoping to bargain, but his rule was to never approach a Kellian without a weapon in his hand. He'd learned that the hard way.

The Kellian spit into the snow. "There's no bargain good enough to pay me for the cost of that Fael. He's mine and I want him back."

"I'm sorry to say he's out of your reach," Jonathan said. "He's passed through the Veil and he's with us now. I'm ready to compensate you for his worth." He reached for the bag nestled in an inside pocket. The laces loosened as he tossed it. Shining gold coins scattered across the white snow. A few jewels glowed red and green amongst them.

"I will have him back," the giant said. He lunged forward, his boot crushing a ruby into the snow. The tip of his blackened sword darted close.

Jonathan stepped aside smoothly and the initial lunge missed him. The Kellian was no novice and made a sideways slice that would have separated Jonathan's shoulders from his chest if he hadn't parried. Jonathan felt the blow ring up his arm even as he twisted gracefully aside. He rolled his shoulder as his muscles absorbed the energy of the blow.

"My name is Oktar," the Kellian said. "I'll be known as the one who killed the Champion." He struck again, hammering down onto Jonathan's weapon.

This Kellian was too big and too fast. If Jonathan didn't end it quickly, the sheer mass of the giant would wear him down. The wound in Oktar's throat didn't seem to be hampering him, likewise the long-scabbed scratches trailing down his massive arm and thigh. Still, the best Kellian negotiations were done at the end of a sword.

"You can walk away from this a very rich man," Jonathan said. "You can be the wealthiest man in your Tribe, enough to overthrow your chief and rule in his place."

"I'm already wealthy. That Fael is a Pit champion, and he belongs to me. Why should I bargain with you?" He grunted as Jonathan's weapon darted inside his guard, slicing into his biceps.

"You can't touch him once he reaches the other side of the Veil. I just want to compensate you for the loss of your fighter," Jonathan said. He was quicker, smaller, and his feet left graceful patterns in the snow as he moved around the brutal giant. He made an effort not to show how the depth of the snow slowed his down. What came up to his lower knee was barely ankle high on the Kellian.

Oktar laughed. "There is nothing you have that I want."

Jonathan fell back from the driving rain of blows. Each one temporarily numbed his arm. He slid away from a vicious thrust, ducked under the sideways slash that followed. "Jewels and spices to tempt your women," he said. "To make them appreciate you all the more."

"My women already appreciate me. They fight to be in my bed." Oktar snapped. "They obey my every command."

Another quick dip of his hand to his boot and Jonathan flung a long steel knife. It buried itself in the snow in the place the Kellian had been only a moment before. It was meant as a bargaining chip, the steel highly prized on this side of the Veil. It would have been nice if it had wounded the Kellian as well, but his reflexes were too quick.

"Steel that will never rust, that will run red with your enemy's blood. You will be a god on the battlefield."

Barking laughter filled the clearing. Oktar barged forward inside Jonathan's defenses. "I am a god now. You want me to release his collar. I tell you I won't. I'll come for him and none of your weakling brethren will stop me." One fist connected with the side of Jonathan's head.

Blackness was sudden. One minute Jonathan was standing, the next he was flat on his back in the snow. He struggled to stay conscious because it would be his death if he didn't, but the black void in his head sucked him down. It was Cateera's scream that wrenched him out. He rolled instinctively and pain thrust him into blinding awareness. The pain was exquisite, fire consuming him, each nerve ending blazing with it. There was a black knife protruding from his shoulder, and he had no memory of how it got there.

Another scream assaulted his ears, followed by Cateera's voice in his head. His roll carried him to his feet, his body's training taking over when his brain couldn't. Unbelievably, the sword was still in his hand. Too many screams, deep bellows of pain and the growling hiss of an enraged Fael.

The pain nibbled at his vision, trying to cast him down into the black again. He shook it away and focused. His first thought was to wonder why Oktar was wearing a cloak. A moment later he realized it was Cateera clinging to the Kellian's back. Wicked claws were buried in his flesh and the leather of his chest plate. Her long, sharp teeth gnawed at his exposed neck. Blood covered her muzzle and poured down his side.

The Kellian fell backwards in an attempt to crush her. His sword was forgotten in the snow. Cateera leaped free, twisting in midair to land on his chest. Her teeth clamped into the soft flesh of throat. Hatred poured through the link between Cateera and Jonathan, woven strongly with satisfaction at the taste of her enemy's blood. Utter rage filled his heart. Jonathan opened himself to her, throwing wide their connection. He felt the triumph, the joy in the destruction of the hated Kellian. This one tribesman stood for all the others throughout the centuries who had enslaved her race. And she allowed Jonathan to share this victory with her. He felt flesh shred beneath scything claws, tasted the bitterness of foul blood in his mouth. It gave him strength. With a roar, Jonathan stepped forward, his mind broadcasting his intent. In perfect unison, Cateera released Oktar as Jonathan's sword cleaved through flesh and bone to sever the Kellian's head from his shoulders.

Jonathan collapsed to his knees. Blood soaked Cateera's muzzle, the fur hidden beneath the wet, red gleam. Streaks of it stained her paws. She met his eyes a moment and then threw back her head and shrieked her triumph. The call echoed through the mountains, and Jonathan felt it all the way through to his soul. When she came to him, he threw his good arm around her shoulder and buried his face in the fur of her side. He didn't feel it. His sole focus was the pain that had expanded to burn out his mind. Stupid, stupid, stupid. Only a sliver of the blade showed beneath the black leather hilt of the knife protruding from his jacket. Damn it, it was the same side that had been injured three years ago. He felt hot blood dripping down his chest, his left arm. Every movement twisted the knife deeper.

"Are you hurt?" he asked Cateera.

No, but you are, she said. *We must take care of you.*

He pulled back from her, grunting. Jonathan found a relatively clean bit of cloth on the Kellian's pants to clean the blood from his sword. It was an effort to seat it in the scabbard, the movement causing the knife to twist in its bed of muscle and flesh.

"We need to get moving back toward the Veil," he said. His teeth were clenched against the pain. "Scavengers will be here soon. I'd rather not be around when it gets really dark."

Agreed, but they will follow your blood trail, she pointed out.

She opened the traveling pack she wore, the long fingers hidden by her thick fur making short work of the zipper. A bottle of water tumbled out. She opened it and offered it to him. He took a long swig. The icy water soothed his throat. He poured a stream over her bloody muzzle, washing the worst of the clots away. Cateera shook her head, spraying water droplets before taking a long drink of her own.

His vision doubled and his heart pounded in his chest. The agonizing fire in his arm faded, but it left a void behind. He couldn't feel his fingers, couldn't move his arm. The knife hadn't exited his back because he could feel the tip digging into the inside of his shoulder blade. Even that pain was beginning to fade.

Poison, Cateera whispered. *We need to get you home.* Claws retracted from her fingertips, Cateera examined where the blade entered through his coat. *This must come out. The source of the poison must be removed or it will spread even more quickly.*

"Shouldn't remove it," Jonathan said. He chanced a glance at the wound. The knife doubled, wavered, and then merged back into a single weapon. "Might bleed out."

You will certainly die if we do nothing, she said. The pack yielded up a first aid kit, and she quickly spread out what she'd need. *I will not lose you.*

The knife yielded to her strong grip. The hooks fashioned into the iron shredded skin and muscle on the way out. The pain broke through the numbness. His own scream was the last thing Jonathan heard.

Chapter Five

The click was faint. Despite his light doze, Mark heard it anyway and was at the side of the bed before his brain caught up with his feet. Bethany gently pushed past, careful fingers smoothing back the matted fur surrounding the iron collar. The Fael slept on, completely limp in the healer's induced slumber. The collar was dull black beneath the bright lights. Only one thing had changed. The locking mechanism was open. The separation of the halves had ripped part of the collar away from the tender flesh beneath, and blood already matted the fur.

"You need to give Jonathan a raise," Bethany said.

"I'll make a note of it," Mark said with a quick smile. "How can I help?"

"I need to take the collar off," she answered. Leaning close, she peered intently at the scarred flesh of the Fael's neck. "All right. Give me a few minutes to set up, and we'll get started. See if you can get him turned onto his back."

Gently untangling Alanna's fingers from her bondmate's pelt, Mark pushed the gurney far enough away to allow him to stand between the two. Berren took the spot across the gurney and added his strength. Between the two of them, they managed to move the pad beneath the Fael so that he flopped over onto his back. Berren growled when he saw the bare patches on his kin's stomach. Thick ropes of scar tissue distorted the skin between clumps of filthy fur.

He's been tortured, Berren said. The alpha's eyes narrowed, the fur along his back raised. *Some of these are barely healed.*

"Pit fighter," Mark agreed. He winced as his head filled with Berren's cursing. It had been long decades since he and Berren had bonded, but the Fael had never lost the deep need to care for his pride. He'd been a king before he'd crossed the Veil. He was still a king. Mark took Bethany's place at the sink, lathering his hands with antibacterial soap before snapping on a pair of sterile gloves.

"Oh, that's good," Bethany said when she saw the Fael again. Her hands weren't gloved. Her healing touch worked best skin to skin. "I'll be able to get to the cannula from here." She frowned down at the unconscious Fael. "Poor thing," she whispered to him. "We're going to help you."

Flexa took a position beside her bondmate. Her ears were erect, her gaze intent. Long chestnut whiskers quivered. She had just as much of a role in the healing as the doctor. Between the two of them, the magic that generated from their bonding enabled them to heal. Mark was damned glad that such a Gift had developed in a bonded pair.

"I'm going to loosen the collar from back to front. I'll try to control the blood flow as I go. Flexa, if you'll turn his head so I can reach the collar's clasp, we'll get started." Her partner mewed her agreement. Balanced back on her haunches, she gently turned the Fael's head so that the healer could see where the collar opened.

With a delicate touch, Bethany used a scalpel to cut away the ridges of scar tissue trapping the collar against the skin. Rich red blood swelled from the raw flesh even though she healed it as she went. Beneath her fingers, smooth pink skin emerged. The Fael would heal with few scars.

A low moan drew Mark's gaze from the painstaking operation to the woman asleep on the other examining table. Alanna was still unconscious, but she'd turned to face her bondmate, one hand reaching blindly to touch him. Her arm didn't stretch across the distance.

"Watch her, Berren," Mark said. His Fael chuffed in response and moved to stand next to the bed. By far the largest Fael in the Haven, he could look down at Alanna's face without even trying. The tip of his tail twitched back and forth.

The operation to remove the collar continued. As Bethany loosened the iron, it opened on hinges set on either side of the cannula. Blood stained her hands, dyed the Fael's dun fur. The skin grown over the iron resisted the removal of the collar, clinging to the iron, forcing her to use the scalpel more and more frequently.

With a scream Alanna sat up, nearly falling off of the table in the effort to reach her bondmate. Berren caught her easily.

"Hold her," Bethany said calmly.

Choking. The pain in her throat was fierce. Her skin was being ripped off. She tried to drag in a breath but couldn't get it past the tearing pain. She wanted it to stop, needed it to stop. Dragging herself up, Alanna flailed with her hands, hitting something, but it didn't help. Something tight was pressing against her thighs, holding them down, and she fought to be free.

"Alanna, calm down!"

The words slashed into her consciousness, but they meant nothing. She fought, kicking out, using her claws. Teeth bared, she tried to bite but couldn't reach a target.

Something rough and wet scraped over her face. The heat of it was shocking and she sucked in a breath. Before she could scream, it repeated. It made her focus on something other than the pain. Opening her eyes, she realized she was face to face with whiskers, fur, and slanted bronze eyes. Alanna stared, blinking rapidly, still trying to draw air into her lungs past the obstruction in her throat. The great head, bigger than her own, moved forward and gently nuzzled her cheek.

It's all right, Alanna, we're taking care of him. The voice tickled inside of her head.

"What's happening?" she asked, and through the confusion she heard how weak her voice sounded. She clung to the Fael who was trying to comfort and calm her. "I can't breathe."

"Yes, you can," Mark said. He appeared at her side and took her cold hands in his own. "Slow and easy."

She tried, but it hurt. Her throat hurt so badly the panic began to swell again. She scratched at her throat, but there was nothing there.

"Berren, let her stand."

The heavy weight disappeared from her legs. Seeing Jekk, she moaned in fear. Without realizing she'd moved, Alanna stood at the side of the wide gurney, her horrified eyes taking in the collar and the red blood. Jekk's four legs were splayed ungracefully. Her Fael was as still as death.

Fingers caught hers. Mark pulled her hand away from her throat and gently guided it. She felt fur under her fingers, warm skin beneath that, and the sudden sense of relief had her drawing in a long breath. A second breath, easier still and her head began to clear. More importantly, most importantly, was the Fael sprawled bonelessly in front of her. Her fingers had clenched in his fur. She felt the hard muscle and bone of his shoulder beneath the dingy, dirt-filled pelt. A woman worked over him, wielding a sharp knife at his throat. At the head of the gurney, a Fael with silky chestnut fur held his head gently. Terror ripped through Alanna. Berren must have sensed it because he nuzzled up against her, allowing her to lean into him.

Bethany isn't hurting him, Berren said. *Be still now or you'll get him agitated.*

"She's hurting him, I can feel it," Alanna whispered, her voice rough with sudden tears.

"His collar has to be removed," Bethany explained, pausing long enough to look at her. "Don't worry, I'm a doctor and I've done this before. He's unconscious and isn't feeling any pain. You're feeling it for him."

"How?" Alanna asked. She realized she was stroking the rough fur where his shoulder met his front leg over and over.

"Do you remember what happened?" Mark asked softly.

Her fingers stroked the length of Jekk's arm while tears tracked down her cheeks.

"I remember you saying a Fael had come through the Veil," she answered. She couldn't tear her gaze from the hideous black collar dug into the scarred flesh of Jekk's neck.

"Can I help?" Alanna asked. She didn't know why she'd asked; she just felt that she had to do something. Her anxiety level was climbing again and the only thing that seemed to help was touching the Fael and feeling the warmth of life beneath her hand.

Bethany spared her a surprised glance out of light brown eyes and then turned back to the operation. "I'm nearly done with this side," she said, indicating the part of the collar across from Alanna. "Come around here and hold the collar out of the way while I remove the other side."

"I'm not sterile," Alanna said.

"Wash up at the sink and put on gloves." A jerk of her head indicated the large sink in the corner. "I'm a healer; I'll deal with any chance of infection."

The water was hot, the soap sweet-smelling. The suds in the sink were pink as the blood on her hands sluiced away. The gloves were a quick struggle and then she was back at Jekk's side. Taking the collar into her hand, Alanna felt the weight of it, slick with blood. She'd never gotten queasy, even watching every doctor show on the Discovery Science channel. She'd even been allowed to observe a knee replacement as research for a novel. But this, this was different. The collar was barbaric, the depth of the skin grown up over the edges evidence that he'd worn it for many years. She felt an overwhelming sympathy, and a fury that swamped her.

"His name is Jekk. He's mine, isn't he?" she asked softly. With her free hand, she stroked the edge of his ear, feeling the stiff, bristled tuft at the end. He resembled a lynx to some extent, only much bigger, with a narrower face, and a long tail.

"Yes," Mark said. "You weren't given time to make an informed choice, and I'm sorry for that, but, yes, he's your bondmate."

Holding up her half of the collar, Alanna saw where it hinged. Saw, too, the odd plug between the hinges, centered over the carotid. She leaned in for a closer look, and the Fael assisting the doctor gently nudged her aside.

"It's a cannula," Mark explained. "The Faelinn are kept prisoner, and their blood is used to prolong life."

"That's horrible," she said. She couldn't quite get her head around the knowledge that she was now half of a bondmate pair. Nothing seemed real.

"All right, I'm going to remove the cannula now," Bethany said. "There'll be a lot of blood at first, are you ready for that?"

"Yes," Alanna said. She thought she was. And it wasn't the blood that made her panic. It was the hot slicing pain in the skin of her neck. She gagged, slapping at her throat with one hand, expecting to feel blood.

"I'm almost done," Bethany promised.

The scalpel sliced swiftly, opening the skin above and below the cannula. Alanna breathed as deeply as she could, one trembling hand holding the collar, the other buried in the thick fur at the side of Jekk's head. The pain was tremendous and she swallowed it back, struggling to remain calm.

Alanna focused on the Fael whose senses were tied into her own. His fur was a dusty, dun color, a vague suggestion of stripes shadowing the fur between tall, erect ears. The bristled tuft at the end of his right ear was dark, giving him the look of an Earthan lynx. The tip of his left flopped a little; there was a chunk missing from the base of the ear. He was big; stretched out on his back on the oversized gurney, he looked easily over seven feet. Dirt and bramble clung to his pelt, matted into the soft cream fur of his belly. Twisted scar tissue across his ribs and stomach made her heart ache. Blood, both dried and fresh, smeared his neck and right flank. He was emaciated, ribs outlined clearly along his sides. Despite that, she thought he was the most beautiful creature she'd ever seen.

"Here comes the hard part," Bethany warned. With gentle fingers, she pulled the cannula free. Vibrant carotid blood splattered Alanna's hand, and she swallowed rapidly against the pain in her neck. The sides of the cannula were barbed. Had anyone tried to remove it without precautions, it would have ripped the Fael's throat out.

Flexa quickly clamped off both ends of the exposed carotid, long fur-covered fingers skilled with the surgical tools. Bethany tossed the collar with its barbed cannula into a metal pan. Her fingers reached into the incision and grasped both ends of the artery. Flexa deftly released the clamps. Blood welled around Bethany's fingers, pulsing with each beat of Jekk's heart. Alanna felt her pulse skitter. She closed her eyes, dizzy and sick. The taste of blood was meaty and thick in the back of her throat. Light played across the inside of her eyelids, coalescing into a scene of terror and violence.

She was a kit, small and helpless. Huge hands held her down, rough with calluses and cruelty. Trying to bite earned her a blow to the side of the head. It made her dizzy and she couldn't resist when her neck was stretched. Something wickedly sharp pierced her throat, driving into her with unbearable force. Her blood began to pour down her small chest and she whimpered. Hard hands tightened a collar around her neck and then her blood was spilling into a cup. No one came to help. No warm soothing tongue lapped her pain away. She was alone.

"No," Alanna shouted, and pulled herself from the memories. She leaned down so that her lips brushed the soft fur at the base of Jekk's ear. "Not alone, never alone again. I promise." She threw one arm over his chest, not caring that his blood was staining her clothes and skin. Holding her bondmate tightly, she let the warmth of Bethany's healing magic engulf her.

~

Your mate needs you.

The words pierced her sleep and jerked her upright. Alanna blinked into the dark, confused by the voice. A dark shadow loomed at her side and she fought back a scream. The purring snore and sense of utter contentment calmed her, made her aware of the identity of the shadow. Jekk grumbled a little and she soothed him with a stroke of her hand down his back. It was utterly strange to be so connected like that, to feel so intimately the emotions of another being. It frightened and exhilarated.

The low light that had been left on in the corner showed a room far different from the one she'd been in. The curtains at the window, the chairs grouped around a small table, the regular beds all gave the illusion of a normal bedroom. It was only the medical equipment pushed into the corner that told her they were still in the medical section of the house.

The blanket draped over her was too hot. Pushing it off revealed her bloody clothes. Jekk's blood. Frantically, she rolled to her knees, leaning over her bondmate to push aside the fur at his throat. The collar was gone, the bloody wounds carved into his throat healed into faint lines. The only remnant of his scars was the blood staining his fur.

"What am I going to do with a bondmate?" she whispered into the dark. A mix of apprehension and anger fought for dominance. Why hadn't anyone told her that gaining a bondmate was a possibility? She was answered with a rumbling purr, but no change in Jekk's sleep pattern.

Too disgusted with the state of her clothes to go back to sleep, Alanna got up, taking a chance that one of the doors in the room led to a bathroom. The first was a closet, but the second yielded a large bathroom equipped with a luxury shower and soft towels. Leaving her filthy clothes in a pile, she stepped under the hot pulsing water and let it sluice away the dried blood and all the questions that circled in her mind.

Your mate needs you.

The words shot into her head in a female voice, harsh with urgency and fear. It was the same voice that had disturbed her sleep. She straightened from smoothing lotion onto her legs. She was still wrapping the robe around her shoulders when she ran into the bedroom. Jekk continued to sleep. There was no one else there. Confused and wondering why she was hearing things, she went back into the bathroom. A pile of clothes that hadn't been there before sat in a neat pile on the counter. Too spooked to question them, she dressed quickly.

The bedroom door slammed open. The shadow of a Fael filled the doorway. It wasn't until Cateera's teeth clamped around her wrist and the same panicked voice shouted in her had that she recognized her.

Your mate needs you! Come!

Alanna's eyes sought out Jekk's recumbent form. Not even the slamming door had infiltrated his sleep.

Not Jekk. Jonathan. Cateera tugged her to the door, her teeth tightening just enough that Alanna had no choice but to move or risk her skin being torn. *Come!*

Cateera's panic was infectious and by the time the Fael had pulled her into the hallway, it had taken root in Alanna's chest. Her heart pounded in dread when Cateera pushed through a set of swinging doors, revealing a room that resembled the one where Jekk's collar had been removed. For all she knew, it was the same one.

But Jekk wasn't the one on the table now. Her gaze fell on a prone figure she recognized, should have anticipated given Cateera's mental state. She barely noticed when Mark and Bethany looked up. The panic was her own now, not to be explained or examined, but there nonetheless. Cateera released her wrist so that her hand fell onto Jonathan's. Instinctively,

Alanna curled her fingers. His hand was cold but she felt the faintest squeeze in return.

"What happened?" she demanded. Her eyes did their own examination, seeing too much blood, the dark bruise spread across his jaw and up to his temple. His blond hair was disheveled and sweat-soaked, falling into closed eyes sunk in violet shadow. Long lashes flickered and Alanna realized he was conscious.

Mark tried to draw her away, but she resisted. Cateera bared her teeth in an unfriendly hiss and he quickly let her go. "He was hurt seeing that Jekk's collar came off."

A quick, confused glance at Mark and then back down at Jonathan's strained face. "What?"

"I'll explain later," Mark promised.

Cateera issued a short meowing demand.

"I'll do what I can," Bethany reassured her. Sharp scissors flashed and his coat fell away, the shirts beneath following.

Alanna sucked in a sharp breath when she saw the bandages on his shoulder. Dark red lines spread out across ashen skin.

"The blade was poisoned," the healer said while removing the bloody bandages. "You did well removing it, Cateera."

Ripped muscle and skin hung from a puncture wound. Dark blood oozed out and rolled down to soak into the ruined shirt trapped beneath him. Blood covered the side of Jonathan's body, darkening the jeans at his waist. It stood out in stark relief against his pale skin. Blood loss had turned him almost ghostly beneath the bright surgical lamp. Flexa slipped an IV into his arm and attached a bag of blood.

"Ah hell, Jonathan, you should have dodged faster," Mark said when he saw the wound.

"Yeah, thanks for the advice," Jonathan growled, his voice hoarse. "Now stitch me up."

Cateera stood on her back legs, front paws pressing into the sheet next to Jonathan's leg. Her distress was evident in the sounds she made. She placed one paw on top of Alanna's hand, connecting with her bondmate through Alanna.

Jonathan's fingers twitched and Alanna tightened her own. With her free hand, she pushed his hair back from his forehead. Even damp the strands felt like silk. "You're all right," she whispered, leaning close. She saw a flash of blue when his eyes opened a sliver.

"I need to remove the poison from his system before I heal the physical wound," Bethany said. Left unsaid was the reality that if the poison wasn't removed, there would be no need to heal the knife wound. "You've outdone yourself this time, Jonathan," she said to him.

He grunted in response but didn't look at her. His gaze remained locked on Alanna.

"What can I do?" Alanna asked. Not for a second did she look away from the man whose intense gaze seemed to draw her ever closer.

"Kiss me."

The faint words drifted up, wrapped around her, and settled awareness into her skin. There shouldn't be that sudden fluttering in her stomach. Of course, she shouldn't be this upset about his wounds either. The man was arrogantly annoying. Her gaze drifted over the bare chest, hard stomach. She was honest enough to admit that he was also deliciously lickable. He was long and lean, muscles defined from his biceps to his abs. It didn't matter that blood painted a Rorschach inkblot on his side. A woman would have to be dead not to appreciate the view.

"Kiss me," he whispered again.

"We haven't even had a first date," she replied. Her fingers were still in his hair and she stroked slowly. Smooth, like the skin of his good shoulder, the sharp angle of his collar bone.

"So go out with me."

"No," she answered. Hard muscle under sexy, smooth skin. She splayed the fingers of her hand over his stomach, feeling the ridges of those muscles. "You're an arrogant ass."

One side of his mouth twitched into a smile, revealing a dimple. He winced when it pulled at the bruise covering nearly half his face. "Does that mean you're not going to kiss me?"

"If you're going to kiss the man, do it now," Bethany said drily. "I need to knock him out to repair this damage."

One dark blond eyebrow twitched upwards in a dare.

She wouldn't give him the satisfaction of letting him win a dare. Alanna let her hand continue to stroke over his skin, enjoying the feel of the muscles twitching beneath her light caress. She ignored the girly fluttering in her abdomen and bent to brush her mouth across his. Just a little kiss, that was the plan. Before her lips felt the soft welcome of his. Her eyes drifted shut even as the knowledge that this man was dangerous to her sanity rolled through her. His lips shaped her name. It was the most erotic thing she'd ever experienced. Touching her tongue to his bottom lip, she absorbed his flavor, a combination of sinful male and melted toffee. She felt it the instant Bethany sent him to sleep, his lips relaxing away from hers. Alanna was trembling when she lifted her head, and if she could have throttled the healer at that moment, she would have.

Yes, Cateera said with distinct satisfaction.

A haunting cry echoed through the house. Alanna felt it down to her bones as it reverberated both inside and outside of her head. The fear and emptiness were too much and she staggered back a step. Cateera pressed up against her side, anchoring her.

"It's your Fael," Mark said. "Reassure him that you're safe. He woke alone, and he's panicking."

"How?" She could feel Jekk's panic, his terrible fear that she was gone.

"In your head—he'll hear you," Mark said.

Struggling through the panic, aware that her heart was racing with it, Alanna concentrated on sending all the reassurance she could through the new bond between herself and Jekk. She felt the tenuous line between them steady and strengthen. Heard the whisper of her name in her mind in that strange, gruff voice.

"He'll come to you," Mark reassured her.

Alanna could see it in her mind, the crazy kaleidoscope of images as Jekk ran along the hallway, following her scent or merely tracking along the invisible line that ran between them. And then the doors pushed open and he was there. Alanna had braced herself, unsure of what to expect, but the great beast stopped just short of her and looked at her with cat-like golden eyes.

I thought you were gone.

In the face of all that need, the love she could feel pouring into her, Alanna knew that whatever happened next, it would happen with the two of them together. The anger she'd felt at having her choices taken away evaporated. Falling to her knees, she wrapped her arms around Jekk's newly healed neck. Blood had dried in his fur, but she didn't care. He was the most wonderful, amazing thing that had ever happened to her. When he started to purr, his happiness and relief filling her, Alanna began to cry.

Knuckling the tears from her eyes, Alanna kept her grip on Jekk, but turned to look at up at Jonathan.

Jekk stirred, leaning forward to sniff Jonathan's hand. The Fael's lips peeled back, revealing sharp fangs. He growled, ears flattening, the hair of his ruff rising. Cateera hissed a warning and smacked him in the head with one white paw, the claws only partially sheathed. He reeled back, golden eyes huge with surprise. A second later he snarled back. The fur along his back spiked and his ears flattened. Cateera stood her ground, protecting her bondmate.

Alanna hugged him tight, feeling the muscles beneath his fur bunched and ready to spring. "Jonathan won't hurt you, Jekk."

He smells of Oktar, Jekk said.

"Who's Oktar?" she asked.

"I would say that he's the Kellian who enslaved Jekk," Mark said. "Since the collar released, Jonathan must have killed him."

Is this true? Jekk demanded of Alanna. His eyes were fixed on Jonathan. His tail whipped back and forth with consternation. He was still poised to fight.

He is dead by our hands, Jekk. The collar is gone, and you are free. Cateera spoke the words to both Jekk and Alanna.

Jekk swiveled his head, stretching his neck. One long-fingered paw probed at his throat. Alanna dug her fingers into his fur, scratching the now-smooth skin where the collar had been, showing him that it was gone. His fur smoothed, lean muscles relaxing. His purr deepened while his eyes closed for a moment in sheer ecstasy. He shook his head abruptly and let out a roar of triumph that stopped everything in the room.

When the sound died away, Jekk stepped forward, keeping a careful eye on Cateera. He bowed his head to her, lowering it onto outstretched paws. It wasn't an act of submission but one of thanks. Cateera's iridescent white fur glimmered in the light, the lavender-tinged scrolls making lovely contrasting patterns. She gave him a long sniff. Her whiskers twitched, but she condescended to lick the fur between his ears. He lifted his head and stared at her, whiskers twitching a little.

She says I smell bad, he complained, looking at Alanna.

She choked back a laugh, trying not to hurt his feelings. But she had to agree. He did smell bad.

Shellie came in, dressed in bright pink silk pajamas. Matching slippers adorned her feet. Except for the sleep-tussled hair, she didn't look like she'd been pulled from her bed. She took in the scene with a practiced eye and clapped her hands sharply. Instantly, house Brownies came from their hidden places and looked at her expectantly. Only a foot tall, their broad, wizened faces were sharp-chinned and big-eyed. Dressed in sturdy, utilitarian clothes and leather shoes, the half-dozen Brownies jostled each other, poking and pushing, unable to be still. Clearing her throat, Shellie tapped her foot until she had their complete attention.

"The Faelinn need food and water. Nothing too rich for Jekk, please. Jonathan's room needs to be prepared. We'll need coffee and food so you might as well start breakfast; it's nearly dawn. We'll be there shortly. Thank you."

Alanna watched in fascination as they scattered to their tasks. Jekk tracked them intently, the tip of his tail twitching violently. Startled, she saw into his memories where creatures very similar to the ones who had just disappeared into hidden openings in the walls had been used to train him to attack. His instincts vibrated with the need to catch and kill. It was only his fierce will that held him still. Wordlessly, she hugged him again. There were no words to share that would make up for what he'd gone through.

A gentle hand stroked her hair and Alanna looked up. Shellie smiled down at her. "Come downstairs with me. There's nothing we can do here and Jekk could use a good meal. Mark and Bethany will follow when Jonathan is healed."

Realizing that the pang in her stomach wasn't just from worry and fragile emotions, Alanna stood. Jonathan's breathing had strengthened. That unexpected worry eased a little only to be replaced by Jekk's hollow hunger. The Fael stayed pressed to her side as they followed Shellie. He hesitated at each closed door, holding her back with his body as if an attacker was going to jump out of each room. His ears were erect and tipped forward, his whiskers bristled. He was unused to the freedom to wander, the safety that surrounded him.

Alanna soothed him at each intersection of hallway and door. His physical wounds might be healed, but the mental ones would take time and gentle care. He reminded her of the inhabitants of the abused women's safe house she'd researched and used as a setting in a book. Hypervigilant, waiting for the attack that was sure to come. Not yet willing to hope that they might be safe at last.

Don't be sorry for me, Jekk said.

"How can I help it?" she asked him. She stroked the coarse fur between his ears. His head reached nearly to her shoulders. "I see what they did to you. I remember it."

There was a long silence, and she could feel the distress in his mind. *It was the only life I knew. Now I have you to show me how to live a better one.*

Tears stung her eyes and Alanna blinked rapidly. She might have his memories, be able to feel what he felt if she chose, but she didn't know the heart of him. The essence of him. That would take time. It both terrified and thrilled her.

"Here we are," Shellie said. "We can see the sun come up from here."

The room was lovely, painted in crisp white with one wall an intense green. Violet cushions padded the chairs of a table set beneath a wide expanse of window. The sky outside was edging towards the light, the starlit black merging into indigo and navy at the horizon. The mountains were a ridge of blackness beneath the lighter tones. The air was redolent with the scent of the fall flowers that decorated the table and the rich smell of coffee.

Alanna immediately poured herself a cup. It was as good as it smelled.

"Which do you prefer, Jekk, to join us at the table, or to eat on the floor?" Shellie asked.

Jekk looked to Alanna for guidance. Guilty because she'd seen to her own needs and not his, Alanna silently asked what he preferred. At his silent request, she made herself comfortable on the plush carpet, her back against one wall. "I think Jekk and I will eat here," she said to Shellie.

The blond smiled and settled down next to her. "Perfect. We'll have a picnic."

Jekk sat next to Alanna. She hugged him close, one arm draped over his neck. She didn't want to be parted from him. She needed to keep touching him. He was exhausted, and it was a dragging ache inside of her. Feeling the flow of his thoughts tumbling like a river just beneath hers was an odd sensation. She knew if she concentrated, she could hear what he was thinking, but she didn't want to invade his privacy. She sensed that that would be the key to maintaining a sane relationship with someone who could communicate mind-to-mind with her.

A small door in the wall opened and Jekk was immediately alert. He crouched, body tense and ready to spring. The low growl that came from his throat made the hair on her arms stand up. The Brownie that popped out of that door took one look at him, squeaked in terror, and fled.

Alanna petted her bondmate soothingly. "He won't hurt you, will you, Jekk?"

Hungry, he answered, but the muscles in his shoulders relaxed.

Wary Brownies peeked from the doorway. The first one peered suspiciously at Jekk and then stumbled out, obviously pushed from behind. Amazingly enough, the plate he carried never spilled. Jekk watched closely as the Brownies climbed a staircase attached to one end of the sideboard to place dishes of steaming food on the table. One male, bigger than the others by an inch, edged closer to the Fael, his arms cradling a large bowl of water.

He slid it in front of Jekk and raced off again. Before Jekk could do so much as lower his head to drink, another brought a bowl of food. This one was braver, poking Jekk's nose with a long finger and laughing as he dodged the quick snap of teeth and was gone. Chunks of raw meat, cooked vegetables, and brown rice filled the bowl. Jekk's head wavered between the two bowls before he finally settled on the water, drinking deeply.

He was so thin. His bones pressed against his skin, stomach concave between ribs and bony hips. The lackluster fur was coarse, without the shiny health of Cateera's. It was also filthy, matted with dirt. Blood had dried to a reddish-brown crust down his throat and neck and along one lean flank. Bare patches revealed old scars and Alanna wondered if the fur would ever grow back. He was easily seven feet long, and weighed several hundred pounds, but she had a good suspicion he was seriously underweight. She'd "seen" the conditions he'd lived in and felt a huge wave of anger at whoever this Oktar had been. Once things calmed down, she was going to have a long talk with everyone. There were a great many questions that needed answering. To hell with her book. The questions had taken on a whole new, personal edge.

A Brownie female approached with a tray, keeping one eye on Jekk. The Fael kept his own eyes on the little creature even while he drank noisily. Alanna murmured her thanks and balanced the tray on her lap, sure she would never be able to finish the tower of scrambled eggs, potatoes, sausages, pancakes, and bacon. The cold glass of orange juice, though, tempted her beyond words. When Shellie stood and helped herself to the food on the buffet, Alanna realized that she'd been given a tray so she wouldn't have to leave Jekk's side.

When Alanna finished, she couldn't believe that most of the food was gone. Beside her, Jekk rested his head on his paws. The bowl of water was nearly empty. The food was gone. She felt his contentment roll over her.

Mark strolled in, followed by Bethany and Flexa. He grinned at the three of them on the floor and joined them once he'd filled a plate of his own. He kissed his wife's cheek before downing most of a cup of coffee. "Jonathan is fine. She's given him a second transfusion because he lost so much blood, but the poison is gone and the wound is healed."

The relief Alanna felt was inexplicable. She barely knew the man. He was rude and arrogant. He'd irritated her beyond belief in the few minutes she'd spent with him in the bakery. But his mouth was addictive and even thinking about it made her want to taste him again. Maybe she was just hormonal. The bonding with Jekk had rattled her head and made her more emotional than normal. That had to be it.

Flexa, Bethany's chestnut-furred Fael, nudged Jekk with interest. Alanna had the distinct impression that they were talking. Flexa nudged him again with her head, and then licked between his ears. His eyes closed and he settled down, chin resting on his front paws. His long sigh of contentment made them all smile.

"What did you mean when you said Jonathan killed Oktar to release Jekk?" Alanna questioned.

Mark put down his plate and cradled the coffee mug in his hand. "There are two branches of Faelinn on the other side of the Veil here. One group lives wild and free in their own society in the mountains across the Veil. The other has been enslaved to the Kellian for millennia. The Kellian hunt the wild ones, catching them and enslaving them when they can.

"Jekk was enslaved. The Kellian use the blood of the Faelinn to prolong their own lives. They pierce the carotid with a cannula and use it to tap the blood when they need it. It's held in place by an iron collar that is spelled shut and keyed to the owner. The only way the collar can be released without endangering the Fael is for the owner to willingly open it, or through death. Sometimes the Kellian will barter with us for the cost of the Fael. Other times, like now, they will choose to fight to the death. Jonathan takes care of both of those things for us. The collar popped open when the Kellian's heart stopped."

"But that's awful!" Alanna said.

"It's a horrible life," Shellie agreed. "Short of going to war with the Kellian again and wiping them out, we can't stop it."

"That's not what I meant," Alanna said. "Why do you make Jonathan fight? Having to kill someone like that must be terrible. How many times have you made him do it? How often has he been hurt?"

Mark's eyebrows arched in surprise. He shared a quick look with Shellie before answering. "Jonathan is head of security here at the Haven. When he joined us a few years ago, he crossed the Veil to free Cateera. Before that, we would break the collar and tear it off. Sometimes that didn't work and the Fael died. We've never asked Jonathan to be our hunter. He just does it."

"It's not right," Alanna said stubbornly. Her thoughts tumbled over themselves. She knew her reaction was overblown, but anger fizzed in her blood and she couldn't help it. "He shouldn't have to do it. Someone else should take care of it."

Jekk's wet tongue licked around her wrist in an effort to soothe her, but she wasn't having any of it. "He's been hurt. You need to make him stop."

"I believe you'll find that you can't make Jonathan stop anything he's intent on doing," Shellie remarked.

I'll help him in the future, Jekk promised. *I'm a very good hunter. I'll see that he's safe.*

"You will not," Alanna replied. "I don't want you hurt either. Am I surrounded by macho males with no sense?"

Bethany laughed. "Wait until you get to know my husband, Aron. He thinks he's in charge, too."

Mark cleared his throat. "Ladies, I believe I'll leave you while my manhood is still in place. Alanna, anything you need is yours. You'll probably sleep most of today while the bond between you and Jekk strengthens. We'll talk again later. In the meantime, welcome to the family."

Alanna smiled back. Family was nice.

But she still wasn't happy that Jonathan had been hurt.

The suite was huge. Put Jekk into the equation, though, and it seemed so much smaller. Alanna stood in the middle of the bedroom. Jekk seemed to take up the rest. He really was huge. What on earth was she going to do with him in New DC?

Is this where you live? he asked. He sniffed at the bed, the dresser, the door leading into the bathroom. He glanced over his shoulder at her, the golden eyes questioning.

"No, I'm just visiting here." She sat down on the bed and tucked her feet up under her, watching while he explored. She felt his exhaustion, but his curiosity in his surroundings was temporarily winning out.

That explains why I never felt you before, he said. He opened a drawer in the dresser. It was empty, but he gave it a thorough sniff anyway.

"What do you mean, you felt me?"

He came to sit in front of her, his head on a level with hers, even though he was on the floor. Multitasking, he began to lick a paw, swiping it over his whiskers. *Two days ago I woke up and felt you in my head. I didn't know who you were; I just knew you were here and I had to get free.*

"I dreamed about you," Alanna said. He was so cute, the delicate swipes of paw over whisker and ear. Unfortunately, it wasn't making much of a dent in the crust of blood and dirt on his face. "At least I think I did. You were running through rocks and someone was chasing you. He caught you and cut open your side."

Yes. That was Oktar.

"I thought you had killed him," she said.

I slowed him down, that was all. Kellian are very hard to kill. I owe your friend Jonathan a boon.

Apparently, so did she. The thought didn't sit well with her. Above and beyond the fact that he'd risked his life for Jekk, she never liked owing anyone anything. And the concept of owing Jonathan made her grit her teeth. Maybe she could just make him cookies or something and call it even.

"Can I ask you how you got free of Oktar? Why didn't you escape sooner?"

You can ask me anything, Jekk told her. *I never had anywhere to go before.* Seemingly satisfied that his face was as clean as he could make it in one session, he laid his chin on her knee. Her fingers automatically began stroking, scratching under his chin lightly. His eyes closed in pleasure.

Images began to fill her mind. Horrific, blood-soaked images of a massive earthen pit, a roaring of sound that rang through her mind, and the snarling of other Faelinn. The flash of fangs, long deadly claws striking out. Opponents falling at his feet, their blood mingling with his. Alanna shuddered, more terrified with his acceptance of the events than the reality of them.

That is the Pit. I fought to stay alive. I am the champion.

"Why would Oktar put you there to fight? I thought that Oktar would drink from you. Wouldn't he be afraid you would be killed?" she said.

I made a lot of money for him, but at the heart of it, I was replaceable. There was no bond between us. We don't bond with the Kellian. If I died, he would replace me.

The matter-of-fact tone in his voice broke her heart. He lifted a paw bigger than both of her fists put together and gently touched her cheek. *I'm here now, and that's what matters.*

The images continued in her head. He let her glimpse the day he escaped, the feeling that his bondmate was out there, waiting for him. The desperate need for freedom that compelled him to attack, to kill, and flee the Kellian town. He left a bloodbath in his wake.

The horror she felt slipped through their link, and he drew his head away from her caress. *You hate that I'm a killer.*

"No," Alanna said, grasping the thick fur at the side of his head and making him look at her. Those golden eyes with their vertical pupil, bright with an intelligence that rivaled any human's, held misery. "I hate that you were forced to kill to protect yourself. I could never hate you."

Unblinking, he studied her for a long moment. She felt him slide through her mind, looking for the lie in that statement. He didn't find one. Jekk gave a long sigh that turned into a jaw-cracking yawn.

Alanna laughed. "Get some sleep, Jekk. Later, we'll get you clean."

That would be good, he agreed. He paced the room, choosing a spot where he could easily see her. He coiled his big body into a tight circle, covering his nose with his tail. His eyes regarded her solemnly. *Will you be here when I wake up?*

"I will always be here," she promised him. She settled herself into the covers and smiled as his eyes slipped closed. Watching him, the steady rise and fall of his chest, Alanna felt a great weariness claim her. The big breakfast she'd eaten coupled with the feeling of his exhaustion made her crave sleep. Even with early morning sunlight slipping through the lace curtains, she found that she couldn't keep her eyes open any longer. Her head touched the pillow, and she slipped into dreamless sleep.

Chapter Six

The sun warmed his fur. Despite the layer of clouds, the rays that made it through felt wonderful. Closing his eyes, Jekk raised his head, angling it so that he caught the best of the light on his face. He'd never spent much time outside. It was a little overwhelming. There was no press of walls or bars at his flanks, just the wide-open space that smelled of possibility.

The bondmate who was so new to him still slept. She was a wonder. He'd felt the beat of her heart through the Veil, all the way into his fetid cage. It had fluttered in his chest at first like a captured animal before settling into sync with his own. The need to be with that heart spurred him on to do what he'd never attempted before. The element of surprise had allowed him to tear past Oktar when he'd opened the cage. It had given him speed to flee through the gated town, climb the wall and jump for his freedom. The beat inside was a homing beacon that set his feet in the right direction.

Freedom was the golden light warming him, the wind ruffling his fur, and the human who now shared his heart.

A new scent surged rich in his nostrils. His muscles lost their relaxed languor and tensed into knotted readiness. The scent was one of the two Faelinn markers that permeated the house behind him. This one was the dominant, the male. Jekk was expecting this.

The black male stalked across the lawn. He approached in full view, making no effort to hide. Years of Pit fighting led to an automatic assessment. The male was big, taller in the shoulders, but narrower in the chest than Jekk. Lean muscle flowed beneath night-dark fur. He was well fed and healthy. A formidable opponent. But Jekk could beat him. He knew it in his sinews and bones, in his blood. The big male was softer than he could be. Jekk was sleek and fast, his claws honed to razors, as capable of fighting on two legs as four. He would win in a fight with this male, but the question was, did he want to?

Sunlight flashed on the metallic copper of ears and tail when the black male stopped a respectable distance away. Eyes of the same color studied Jekk carefully.

Aware that he was facing the Alpha of this place, Jekk made a conscious decision to allow a portion of the aggression to seep out of his muscles. It was one of the hardest things he'd ever done. He nodded his head slowly. *I'm Jekk. I ask your permission to stay in your territory.*

I'm Berren. You and your bondmate are welcome here but if you have any intention of challenging me, tell me now and we'll get it over with.

A surprised laugh coughed from Jekk's throat. He could count on his fingers how many times he'd laughed in his life. With fingers left over.

I'm done with fighting, Jekk said. *I think I want to learn how to live.*

Berren chuffed his agreement. *Your bondmate will help with that,* he said. *Bondmates are to be treasured.* He walked forward but stopped a foot away.

Knowing what was expected, Jekk lowered his head, chin resting on the ground for a long moment while Berren gave him a good sniff. It stretched his self control to the limit to hold still while the male walked around him. He never allowed enemies at his back. To do so would be suicide in the Pit.

It was that thought that kept him still. He wasn't in the Pit any longer. He would never be there again. It was time to put aside his savage half and embrace peace. Doing so would be hard but he was a rational being first, a savage fighter second. So he held still and when Berren faced him again, he allowed his muzzle to be gently held between a massive jaw.

Welcome, Jekk. The Haven is your home now, Berren said softly.

Jekk nodded.

When you've gotten used to the Haven, I'll expect you to join our patrols. Every Faelinn here patrols the fence line. You'll be trained and assigned a partner.

There's danger here? Jekk asked. His whiskers bristled. Nothing would be allowed to hurt his bondmate.

Walk with me, Berren said.

Jekk fell into step next to the dark male. They paced around the huge house. Each step past a window, beneath a balcony, sent Jekk's nerves into overdrive. It just didn't feel safe not to pause and verify the safety of each potential trap. Berren pretended not to notice. Jekk was grateful for the other male's reticence. The constant vigilance was going to be a very hard thing to overcome.

As they rounded the edge of the house, another building appeared a short distance away. Trees that still retained their golden leaves gave it shelter. A sturdy branch disappeared into the building through a gateway cut into the upper level.

There's danger on two fronts, Berren said. *From outsiders who covet us, and from the Veil. There hasn't been trouble from the Veil in years. No Kellian have crossed over in decades but we keep alert. It would only take one to break our Truce. Humans have tried to gain entrance through the fence more recently. So we guard both.*

I will train him.

The words slipped into Jekk's mind. He turned to see a white and lavender female slip from the trees and walk towards them. He lifted his muzzle, sniffing the air. Her scent was solo, hers alone, not overshadowed by a male's. Interest pricked his ears forward. She was unmated.

I will train him, and I will partner him, Cateera said. *He is bonded to Jonathan's mate.*

She was beautiful, Jekk thought. Her lines were long and sleek, her fur shining like silk in the sunlight. He liked the arch of her neck, the delicacy of her muzzle. Partnering with her could prove to be interesting.

Jonathan's mate? Berren asked. *Does he know that?*

I have informed him, Cateera said. *He is still in denial.*

Humans have mates like we do? Jekk asked. A warm female scent tickled his nose and he breathed it in deeply.

They do if they are bonded to Faelinn, Cateera said. She gave him a haughty look, and a sniff. Her nose wrinkled.

The sniff made Jekk aware of just how much he needed to bathe. Dried blood pulled against his fur. The stench of the Pit was bone deep. He was used to it, but it was obvious she found it offensive.

The three of them reached the building. Two stories tall, it was made of local stone. There were no windows on the lower level so he couldn't catch a glimpse inside. From the front, he couldn't see the tree branch. Berren reached the door first and threw it open. Heat and moisture poured out. Jekk approached with interest, following Cateera's swishing tail inside.

Heated bathing pools of various depths were staggered around the room, interconnected by narrow sluiceways. Water ran through the channels, proof of constant circulation. Lounging benches and human chairs were grouped in a corner. The upper story was reached by a series of ramps and ledges and he caught a glimpse of more padded benches. Through one wall, the thick pine branch provided a perfect upper story exit.

There's another water play area in the Haven's community hall. It's larger, but while you're staying at the house, you're welcome to use this one, Berren said. *Get cleaned up, and if you like, we'll go hunting later.*

❧

"You look better," Alanna remarked. She leaned back in the lounger, her hands cradled around a steaming mug of coffee. Jekk rinsed the last of the shampoo from his fur. After many repetitions, the water finally ran clear.

I don't smell bad anymore, Jekk answered.

She laughed and took a drink of the coffee. She'd panicked a little when she'd woken up and he was gone, but a query along their personal link had reassured her. A Brownie showed her the way to the bathhouse and then fussed long enough to provide her with coffee and cinnamon rolls from the small kitchen.

Cateera raced to the highest point of the building and threw herself onto a water slide. Jekk watched carefully. When she tumbled off the bottom safely, he walked to the top and stood peering down the slide.

"Might as well do it, Jekk," Jonathan called. "She'll give you hell if you don't."

The lounger creaked as he settled next to Alanna. "I don't suppose you know if there's a beer in the fridge?"

"Tea, coffee, and juice, I think," Alanna answered. "Should you even think about beer with all the blood you lost?" She glanced over at him and tried not to drool. Long legs clad in faded denim, a tight shirt stretched over sleek muscles, he was the poster boy for hot sex.

"Probably not," he answered. He stared at her, lazy blue eyes slowly moving over her arms, curvy hips, and long legs. His perusal was making her breathless. Her nipples hardened, and she refused to look to see if they were visible through her top. Judging by his lingering look, they were. She should be irritated, but she was too busy telling herself that the liquid heat pooling between her thighs had nothing to do with furious want.

Jekk flung himself down the slide. Panic, hers and his, filled her, but his plunge off the edge of the slide was fairly controlled and his panic faded. The faintest hint of surprised enjoyment colored his thoughts instead.

"How's he doing?" Jonathan asked.

"He's going to be fine," she said, her first instinct to protect her new bondmate.

"He's strong," Jonathan agreed. "It will help him over the hurdles. He may suffer periods of disorientation or panic, though. He was a Pit fighter?"

"I think so, yes," Alanna said. "I've seen things in his memories." Her hand trembled as she brought her coffee to her mouth.

"He's likely been confined for most of his life. Being out in the open might bother him at first. He may react aggressively to perceived threats. You'll have to watch him," Jonathan said. It was the gentleness of his voice that made her listen. Anything else and she would have bristled at the perceived criticism to her bondmate.

Nodding slowly, Alanna watched her bondmate cautiously paddle the length of one of the deeper pools. Cateera matched his pace, nudging him occasionally with her head.

"They told me you freed him."

Jonathan shrugged, the muscles of his shoulders bunching and relaxing. "Part of the job."

"Everyone seems so damn casual about it," Alanna said. She turned on the lounger a little, angled her body towards his. "You could have died. There was poison on that blade, wasn't there?"

"My fault—I miscalculated the Kellian. Cateera got me home safely and Bethany fixed me up. I'll move a little faster next time."

She leaned over the arm of the lounger. "You could have been killed," she repeated slowly, emphasizing the last world.

Intense blue eyes watched her carefully. The dimple in his cheek threatened to peek out. "You were worried about me."

"I don't want your death on my head," she said. "Knowing my luck, you'd come back and haunt me."

The dimple flashed full-blown. He shook his shaggy blond head. He leaned over the arm of his lounger until his breath brushed the hair near her ear. "That's not it. You were worried. Admit it."

The warmth of his breath on her skin led to the desire to climb into his lap and nuzzle. Oh hell no. Alanna scrambled to her feet but as quick as she was, he was quicker. Strong fingers wrapped around her wrist. Her pulse fluttered under his grip, speeding up when his thumb began to swirl slow pleasure into her palm. Jonathan tugged and she ended up in his lap anyway. "You kissed me."

"You begged me to," she protested. She could feel the heat of his body. It melted into her skin. She wanted to sink her free hand into his hair and drag his mouth to hers. She wanted to experience the dark toffee taste of his kiss again. "I took pity on you because you were wounded."

He outright laughed at that. His mouth was a breath from hers when Cateera shrieked and tore out of the door, Jekk close on her heels. "What the hell?" Jonathan said. He tossed her to her feet and headed after them.

Alanna reached for Jekk's mind but found herself shut out. Fearful of what he was doing—afraid he'd hurt Cateera—she ran after Jonathan. He caught her with one strong arm, pulling her to a stop against his side.

"Wait," he murmured.

"He might hurt her," Alanna protested.

"I don't think so," Jonathan said. "Watch."

Cateera stood facing Jekk. He waited, every hair on his body quivering. She purred something at him. He responded with a harsh bark. Her tail swished and she turned her back. Waited a beat. Then gave him a coy look over her shoulder and raced away. With a low growl, Jekk took off after her. They raced across the lawn, the tawny male just a few paces behind the white female. Even from here, Jonathan could hear her taunts.

"What just happened there?" Alanna asked.

Jonathan shrugged. He was damned if he was going to tell her that his bondmate was interested in hers.

The cell phone in his pocket buzzed. He pulled it out and read the message from Ed Rivera. The Jensen boy was acting up. He'd been caught spray painting the community center wall. Again. Normally, Ed, his second-in-command, would have written it up and left it on Jonathan's desk, but the kid was getting to be a problem. He texted a quick message and put the phone down.

He really liked the fact that, for the most part, being head of Haven security involved only the occasional teenaged prank or a curious tourist at one of the two gates into the Haven. Beat the hell out of what he'd left behind when he'd quit the force. Of course, when things went really wrong here, they tended to do so in a big way.

"Your phone works!" Alanna said, interrupting his musing.

"My GPS works, too," he said, fighting the urge to grin. He had no intention of telling her that they had a way of fixing the electronics problem. He stole a quick glance at her, and the look in those stormy eyes had the grin winning out.

"You know, I really don't like you," she said. Crossing her arms over her chest, which had the nice side effect of pushing her breasts even higher in the low-cut top, she glared at the two Faelinn who were still chasing each other around. Jonathan let his eyes linger on her for a moment. Her dark braid fell over her shoulder, nearly as thick around as his wrist. When he started to wonder what her hair would look like loose and spilling over those enticing breasts, he made himself look away.

Trouble. Oh yeah.

Cateera was teasing the male by slowing down just enough to let him get close, and then speeding away again. *He's going to catch you,* he thought at her.

No, he will not, she replied. *He is far too slow.* She proved it by increasing her speed to leave Jekk several yards behind, reversing her direction and swatting him with her tail on the way past. Jekk shook his head and reared back on his hind legs a moment before chasing after her again. He seemed very determined.

Jonathan continued to watch, knowing that Jekk could end the game at any time. Even exhausted the male was dangerous. Jonathan was amused with Cateera's actions. She turned her nose up at the attentions of every unmated male in the Haven. Several had repeatedly tried to win her affections, to no avail. He knew she wanted a family, a mate and kits. He knew, too, that it had to be completely on her own terms. Her slaver in the Veil had tried to use her for breeding. She'd seen her first litter taken away and enslaved. That was when she had escaped. The loss of her young was still an unbearable ache in her heart.

And here she was now, teasing a male who had barely evaded death. Underweight and downright scrawny, with a tattered ear and a dull coat, she somehow found the male very interesting. Jonathan just didn't understand females, no matter what species they happened to be.

Jekk stopped, his head hung low with exhaustion. Jonathan knew how he felt. They'd both lost a fair amount of blood the day before. He knew he wasn't up to racing around the lawn. Realizing she was no longer being chased, Cateera stopped, watching the male. Cautiously, she approached, the lavender tips of her ears quivering. Jekk crouched, exhaustion and disappointment in every line of his body. Cateera edged closer. The male sprang, his jaw closing around her throat, teeth sinking into the fur at the back of her neck. He mounted her, holding her in place just long enough to let her know he was the dominant, and then released her.

And slowly sauntered back toward the house.

Jonathan felt Cateera's indignation. She'd been outsmarted and she didn't like it. And yet, somehow, her fascination for the tawny male had just increased. She followed him, and when he collapsed into a sprawl in a particularly nice spot of grass, the sun spilling warmth onto his fur, she placed one paw on the back of his neck to hold him down and began to clean his ears.

Jonathan could swear he heard the male's purr from here. He certainly heard the laughter from the woman beside him. Damn it.

Shellie waved at them from the patio. Alanna waved back and began walking across the lawn. Her hips swayed enticingly. He thought that maybe Cateera had a good idea. He would really love to hold Alanna down and lick her until she purred.

"That man is going to be the death of me," Shellie declared when they reached her. A cascade of interlocking golden hoops dangled from each ear.

"What's he done this time?" Jonathan asked. The petite blond radiated irritation. Even her curls seemed to vibrate with it.

Narrowed amber eyes glared at him. "Are you getting smart with me, young man?"

"No ma'am," he replied promptly. She might look like a younger sister, and he thought of her as one, but Shellie Dennison took every opportunity to remind him that she was old enough to be his grandmother.

She sniffed. One foot tapped restlessly on the flagstone. "All I did was casually mention that I felt the market was going to take a drastic upswing this morning, and now I can't tear him away from the phone and the computer. We have a guest."

"Don't let me interfere with his work, please," Alanna said.

"You casually mentioned a drastic upswing?" Jonathan asked with a laugh. "That's like a red cape to a bull. His Gift probably roared to life and won't subside until he's made another billion."

"So now it's my fault?" Shellie asked, glaring at him.

Jonathan held his hands up. He dared a glance at Alanna and saw no help there. If anything, those stormy eyes held a dancing amusement that irritated him to the core. "Of course it's not your fault, Shellie. He's just doing what his Gift needs to do."

Peach-tipped nails tapped the arm of the chair, and then mercifully, Shellie let him off the hook. He relaxed back in the chair, rotating his shoulder against the stiffness that lingered. He'd have died from blood loss and poison if he'd been any longer getting back, or if Bethany hadn't come so quickly. It was a sobering thought.

"I see he's settling in," Shellie said, watching Jekk and Cateera.

Setasha approached the pair, and Cateera hissed a warning at the new female, one paw still resting possessively on Jekk's back. Jonathan focused on Cateera's thoughts but backed away when he felt a shaft of anger at his intrusion. Faelinn hierarchy was both plainly simple, with Berren as the alpha of the Haven's Faelinn and Setasha his mate, and drastically complicated as the other Faelinn jostled for position. And it seemed to him that his Fael was staking a claim on the new male. Even though Setasha was already mated, Cateera wanted it known.

Trouble trouble trouble.

"What's this Gift you keep referring to?" Alanna asked.

"That's something we don't talk about with outsiders," Shellie said. "If you hadn't bonded with Jekk, I might not answer that question. Not even for a book we hope will help the Faelinn."

Alanna curled her legs beneath her. "I have to be honest, I don't know what's going to happen to the book I planned. So much has changed. I feel things taking a new direction in my head. I think the story I leave here with won't have much in common with what I planned."

"Life is fluid," Shellie said. "And it's so very hard to anticipate what each new ripple will bring." She toyed with an earring. "The way Jekk came to you is not normally how it's done. We can't anticipate when a new Fael will escape to us, but we try to make sure that a potential bondmate is aware of the changes that will take place."

"I would have said yes," Alanna said.

"You might wish you'd been given a choice once you learn everything," Jonathan said. "But short of death, there's no changing what's happened."

"Are you always this cheerful?" she asked him.

"You seem to bring out the best in me," he answered with a wide smile, just to see the flash of annoyance in those haunting eyes.

"Children," Shellie snapped, the quick bite in her voice silencing them. "Despite his charming way of telling you, Jonathan's right. There is no going back from the bond. You and Jekk will be together until one of you dies."

"That must be so lonely for the one left behind," Alanna said softly.

"You don't understand, dear," Shellie said softly. She reached out and caught one of Alanna's hands, squeezing gently. "When one bondmate dies, so does the other. We talked about it briefly the other day. Bondmates can't survive alone."

Alanna paled, her skin stark against her dark hair. "You know this for sure?"

"For every Faelinn death we've had, the bonded human has died as well," Jonathan answered her. "Usually within hours. No human has died before a Faelinn, so we have no way of knowing if the reverse is true."

"But it would be logical," Alanna murmured, her eyes going to where Jekk slept in the sun.

"There is a silver lining," Shellie said. "You already know how old I am. Time seems to stand still for us. In fact, I think I'm healthier now than before I bonded with Setasha. We heal faster, and so far, none of us have contracted any major diseases."

"I'm not sure I want to live forever," Alanna said. Her voice was pensive, her gaze fixed on something only she could see. Tugging her braid forward, she curled the loose end around a finger over and over.

"We don't think it's forever," Shellie said. "The Faelinn seem to have vastly extended life spans, but they are mortal."

"But I'll outlive my friends and family," Alanna said.

"Yes," Shellie said. "You will."

"Not much of a silver lining, to outlive everyone you care about," Alanna said.

"It's why most of us live in the Haven," Shellie told her. "We've become each other's friends and family. And of course, it's safer here."

"But I don't live here," she pointed out. "I live in New DC. In the city."

"We'll help you move," Shellie said. "There are several houses you can look at. I'm sure one of them will suit the two of you."

Jonathan had been waiting. He'd known she wasn't going to take all of this easily. He saw the minute her eyes clouded, a narrow line appearing between her brows. Across the expanse of lawn, he saw Jekk's head come up.

"I'm not moving here," Alanna said. "What makes you think I would?"

Shellie's mouth opened, then snapped shut again. She looked over at Jonathan, and he shrugged. She was on her own with this one. After all, bringing this woman to the Haven had been her idea. He'd known from the moment he looked at the elegant pin-up curves of her that she was trouble.

"Most Faelinn and their bondmates live here. It's safer for us. We're a complete community here with everything we need. I'm sure you'll love it once you give it a chance."

Alanna shook her head the moment Shellie started to speak. "No. I live in the city. My life is there, I'm happy there. I have no intention of moving here or anywhere else."

"There are certain things that Jekk will need that won't be easy to find in the city. He'll need to hunt, for instance."

"We'll work things out," Alanna said. Her mouth was set in a tight line. "You said that not all of you live in the Haven. I'll be one of those."

"I see," Shellie said, sitting back. She folded her hands neatly in her lap. The slightly flighty woman metamorphosed into someone Jonathan rarely saw, a cool, level-headed woman who'd helped her husband guide the Haven for many years. A woman who could convey disapproval with a look, while her words outwardly agreed with you.

"Well, that's your decision, of course, dear. You know what's best for Jekk and yourself. I'm sure you'll find plenty of places there for him to run free and hunt."

"My life is there," Alanna repeated. The mutinous line remained between her brows, but the stubborn look in her eyes was wavering. "My friends, my house. Everything."

Shellie poured two glasses of tea from the pitcher on the table, the amber liquid catching the sunlight. She handed one to Alanna. "I know. You'll have to stay here a few more days, though. In all good conscience we can't let you go until after your Awakening."

Jekk padded over to them, sitting at Alanna's side, and leaning in so that he rested against her. She slid an arm around his neck, anchoring herself to his solidity. They were already a pair, Jonathan acknowledged. As much as he wished it wasn't true, it was obvious that they belonged together. He picked up his glass of tea and drained it.

"There are compensations for being bonded to a Faelinn," Shellie said. She tucked a stray blond curl behind one ear. "Shortly after the bonding, we undergo what we've chosen to call the Awakening. The Faelinn seem to tap a latent talent in us and bring it to the fore."

"What kind of talent?" Alanna asked. Jekk watched Shellie as intently as she did. His ears were erect, the dark tuft at the end of the whole ear vibrating slightly.

"It differs from person to person, but it seems to be psychical in nature. There's no way to predict what Gift you'll have, or its strength. But it will come, and we prefer that you be here when it does."

"Is this Awakening dangerous?"

"It can be," Jonathan answered. "Although usually only to the newly bonded pair. We did have a problem when Jack Berenger Awakened. He's a pyrocant and burned his house down. Of course, now he's the Haven's fire chief, so it worked out in the end."

"My Gift is a small one," Shellie said. "I see glimpses of the future and I can predict trends, feel whether the outcome of a situation will trend positively or negatively. Mark finds it useful when I see the stock market going up and down."

Alanna was quiet for a moment, obviously thinking this over. "Mark's Gift has to do with money," she guessed. She waited until Shellie nodded. "And Bethany is a healer?"

"Yes," Shellie answered. "She's a trained doctor and has a general practice in town, but she serves as the Haven's healer when we need it. She keeps her Gift hidden and uses it in town only when it can be done without jeopardizing us."

"If the people who hunt the Faelinn found out about our Gifts, they'd try even harder to capture them," Jonathan said. He leaned forward and propped his elbows on his knees. "I won't let that happen."

Alanna nodded slowly. "Oddly enough, I find that reassuring." A small smile tilted one corner of her mouth, and he found himself suddenly fixated by it. Her top lip was just a little fuller than her bottom. It added a softness to the cool elegance of her cheekbones, the arching sweep of her dark brows. And it made him recall her honey and citrus taste. His body tightened.

His cell phone rang again and with a curse, he glanced at the screen. Rivera again, but a phone call rather than a text told him it was something more important than teenaged pranks. Rising from his chair with a quick apology, he strode to the far end of the patio where he had privacy but could still watch the women.

"Burke," he answered.

"We've got alarms going off along the northeast wall, section eight. I'm on my way out there now, but thought you'd want to know."

"I'll meet you there." Jonathan glanced over at Cateera. She was napping in a sunspot, the light glistening on her the fur.

I am sleeping, she told him without opening her eyes.

"Right," he thought with a laugh.

"I have to go," he said, walking back to the chairs. He leaned over to kiss Shellie's cheek. "Tell Mark I'll talk to him later."

"Is everything all right?" Shellie asked.

"Rivera called. There's an alarm going off. Probably another deer, but I thought I'd head out there to be sure."

"All right, dear," she said. "Be careful. I don't want to have to call Bethany again."

Chapter Seven

"Don't let him get to you," Shellie told her.

Alanna grimaced. "Too late."

Shellie laughed, the clear sound making Jekk's ears perk up from where he dozed on his feet at Alanna's side. "Second to Mark, he's the one who keeps things running around here. As security chief, he keeps us safe. You already know what he does when an enslaved Fael comes to us."

Her crazy reaction yesterday had faded a little, but the quick spike of anger still bothered her. She let out a slow breath before she spoke again. "Is that his Gift?"

"Not quite." Shellie switched seats so that she was on the lounger Jonathan had vacated. With a sigh, she toed off her shoes and stretched out her legs. "He hunts killers. He does consulting work for several police departments." She gave Alanna a bland look. "He's also our most eligible bachelor."

"And likely to stay that way with his attitude," Alanna said sourly. She would not be happy about that. Oh no she would not.

Shellie laughed again.

Alanna took a long drink of tea, feeling the sweet liquid cool her throat. "So is there any rhyme or reason to the Gift I'll get?"

"It usually runs along the lines of a latent talent, but not always. It will come in the next few days. Oh, don't look so horrified. We won't let anything happen to you."

"What if I burn the house down?" Her voice sounded anxious even to her own ears. She didn't like feeling that way. Liked even less the unknown Gift she was going to develop. She really didn't care for surprises. "Or cause an earthquake? A bolt of lightning through the living room?"

Shellie covered her mouth but the giggles escaped. After a moment, Alanna laughed along with her, realizing just how silly she sounded. Still a little on the hysterical side, but she figured that was okay. After all, she was being told she was suddenly going to have some kind of superhero power.

"Or you could suddenly develop a talent for making the perfect cake."

"It would have to be chocolate," Alanna said, still laughing. "Double fudge cake with lots of frosting."

I'm hungry, Jekk informed her. *But I don't want your cake.*

That sent Alanna into another bout of laughter. She felt Jekk's bewilderment. Swinging her legs off the chaise, she wrapped her arms around him, still laughing as she buried her face in the fur at his neck. He smelled of sunshine and shampoo, his fur silky now that he was clean.

Cateera is going to take me hunting, he told her. He did the mental equivalent of rolling his eyes. *She thinks I can't hunt for myself.*

Alanna gave him a last hug and drew back to look at the lovely white and lavender Fael who'd come to stand at Jekk's side. Turquoise eyes met hers. She listened in her head for Cateera to say something, but the Fael remained silent.

"Have fun," she told them both. With an excited yip, Jekk took off after the female, heading for the woods.

"Hm," Shellie said, watching the pair closely.

"What?"

"I believe Cateera is interested in your Jekk. I've never seen her like this." She slanted a knowing glance at Alanna. "If the pair end up mated, you'll have more contact with Jonathan than you might like. They mate for life, you know."

"Now I really need chocolate cake," Alanna said.

"Up for a drive into town, then? We can get lunch and finish off with cake at Sweet Indulgence."

"That sounds perfect. Give me fifteen minutes to change, and I'll be ready to go."

~

Jonathan pulled up behind Rivera's truck. A road ran the perimeter of the Haven, making it easy to reach every inch of security fencing. Before Jonathan could get out of the SUV, a Fael landed on the hood, appearing out of thin air. One of the smaller Faelinn, Rivera's bondmate, pushed his nose against the front window, showing a lot of teeth in what passed for a smile.

"Jesus, Kallek, are you trying to give me a heart attack?" Jonathan asked as he shut the door.

The Fael jumped to the ground. The tires of the SUV sighed in relief. Even small, the Fael weighed several hundred pounds, and reached Jonathan's hip. Green and brown striped fur ruffled as a breeze passed through it.

"Hey, Burke, how's the shoulder?" Rivera asked, stepping away from his truck. He wore the standard Haven security uniform of black jeans and T-shirt. They didn't bother with a badge or insignia. Everyone in the Haven knew who was who. No one outside the Haven needed to know.

"The doc fixed me up," Jonathan said.

"Good. Where's Cateera?"

Touching his Fael's mind quickly, he focused in on her whereabouts. "Showing the new addition the best hunting grounds." Quickly, he filled Rivera in on the new Fael and his bondmate, most of which seemed to come as no surprise to the man. One thing about a small community, Jonathan mused, was that there were few secrets. The gossip grapevine was more efficient than a room full of grandmothers.

"I hear she's hot," Rivera said.

"You're married, and I don't think Rick would put up with you looking at a woman," Jonathan reminded him. Oh yeah, Alanna was hot, Jonathan thought, remembering her in those tight jeans and low-cut shirt. But there was no way he was going to tell Rivera that.

"Yeah, but I can still appreciate the curves," Rivera answered with a laugh.

Jonathan grunted. "Tell me about these alarms," he said, scanning the length of the fence. Nothing appeared out of place. The twelve-foot-high chain-link wasn't compromised in any way he could see. The barbed wire coils along the top showed no sign of tampering.

One tanned hand rubbed the back of his neck as Rivera scanned the same areas. His gold wire-framed glasses did nothing to hide the serious brown eyes. "Walk with me."

Jonathan fell into step beside him, walking slowly along the blacktop. No trees grew close enough to reach the fence. They maintained an empty twenty-yard swath of land on both sides, trimming and culling any new growth that threatened to provide a way over the fence.

"It wasn't the physical alarms that were set off," Rivera said. He consulted his data pad before stopping in front of a section of chain-link. "The magickal safeguards lit up across the board on this section, then nothing."

"What do you see?" Jonathan asked. To his eyes, it looked like a boring fence.

"I was waiting for you to get here," Rivera said. Kallek joined him, sitting on the blacktop at his side. He uttered a short chuffing sound and Rivera nodded, and then extended one hand toward the fence. His fingers flared, and Jonathan watched as the force field his second-in-command had placed around the Haven lit up.

To Jonathan's eyes, nothing appeared out of place. The pale shimmering gold held no blemishes, no burn marks where something had tried to force its way through. Strands clung to the chain-link, twisted around the barbed wire. The electrical conduits appeared as shining orbs. Not only that, but the warding extended out a few feet beyond the fence and a few feet above and below.

Rivera saw something different. He stepped into the warding and pointed out several places. "There are marks here and here, like something brushed up against the field." He indicated the bottom of the field where it twined around a fence pole. "There's a small fracture pattern here."

"Someone tried to get in?" Jonathan asked. He stood as close as he could without getting caught in the delicately woven power strands. He squinted at the places Rivera pointed out but couldn't see a thing.

"I can't say for sure. It could just be a large animal that strayed too close. We've had some false alarms from animals since we recalibrated last week. Maybe there's a faulty tie-in with the security link to the main unit at the station. I'll give it a thorough check today."

"You don't think that's what it is," Jonathan said.

"No," Rivera said. "I think something with some power came along here. The non-magickal sensors didn't pick up anything. Whatever caused this had some juice."

"Recommendations?"

"I'm going to reinforce and reset the shield, and I think I'm going to have to tweak the sensitivity of the system. I don't like all the false reports."

"Call Agneta in, if you need her," Jonathan said.

"Will do."

Jonathan turned to go and then stopped. Something disturbed him. Deep down in his animal brain where instinct dwelled. That prickly feeling of being watched crawled across his shoulders. He studied the tree line beyond the fence, searching for something, anything, to account for the feeling. "Kallek, your eyes are better than mine. Do you see anything out there in the trees?" Jonathan said.

The Fael turned to look. He stalked along the fence line, staying just far enough back to keep away from the electrical current. He looked quizzically over his shoulder at Jonathan and lifted one shoulder in a shrug.

"What is it?" Rivera asked.

"I don't know," Jonathan replied. He was silent for a long moment, listening for something he couldn't hear. "Increase the drive-bys for the perimeter. I want eyes on these fences. Let me know if you find anything with the diagnostics."

"Will do," Rivera said.

Jonathan leveled a finger at Kallek. "You jump on my SUV like that again, I'll have your hide for a rug."

They were both laughing as he walked away.

~

"Tell me about the Haven," Alanna said, sliding into a chair. The glass-topped table held a small bouquet of wildflowers, two mugs of coffee, and two pieces of amazingly rich-looking chocolate cake.

Shellie took a sip of coffee. "Mark set it up after he bonded with Berren. He owned the land the house is on, which included a section of the Veil. He negotiated an agreement with the government to maintain and police the Veil here and bought up as much land around it as he could. He's added to it over the years."

Shellie took a bite of her cake and closed her eyes. "I could live here."

Alanna sampled her own cake and had to agree. The dark, sinful taste dissolved on her tongue. This one piece easily wiped out her chocolate allowance for the entire month. Possibly longer than that. It was completely worth it. She felt Jekk nudge her mind and shared the taste with him. His approval was obvious. She promised to bring him a piece. Apparently, he wanted her chocolate cake after all.

"You know the Haven encloses the entire segment of this part of the Veil."

"Really?" Alanna asked.

Shellie nodded. "It starts about a mile from the house and disappears back into the ground just shy of the southern wall. Mark bought up the land at the southern tip of the Veil not long after Cateera came through. Now, any Faelinn that make it through come directly into the Haven where they'll be safe."

"They only come through the Veil here?" Alanna asked in surprise.

"Here and one other place in Europe. I don't know much about the Faelinn there. I've met only one unbonded male from that area. He seemed to be more advanced technologically. Of course, the Faelinn there aren't in danger of being wiped out, either. With the depredations of the Kellian here, there just aren't many. The Faelinn don't breed often, although the female will take a mate when she finds a compatible male. They struggle to maintain a working population level."

"How many free Faelinn are there?"

"Here? The numbers vary. The unbonded will cross back and forth. There's always the danger that they'll be captured on the other side. Most of the bonded pairs here were made with the free Faelinn. It's not often that we see an enslaved Fael escape."

"Like Jekk?"

Shellie nodded. "Like Jekk, and Cateera, too. A few others."

Alanna was silent, warming her hands with her mug. Outside the window, trees rustled in the breeze, shedding fall leaves. Across the street, the antique store seemed to be doing a brisk business. So normal, which made the things that Jekk had shared of his life so much worse. One scene after another of cages and blood and pain flickered through her mind. It was heartbreaking.

"Do they have to stay?" Alanna asked. "The Faelinn here in the Haven. Does the security fence force them to stay inside?"

The anger that darkened Shellie's eyes was unexpected. "Do you honestly think we hold them prisoner like the Kellian do? They're free to come and go whenever they want. They all know the passwords to the gates. And they're more than capable of leaping over the fence. The magickal safeguards we have are keyed to let them through."

"I'm sorry," Alanna said. There was still so much she needed to learn, both for herself and for the book she was going to write. She should be taking notes, but she'd jot everything down later. "I didn't mean it like that. You were telling me that most of the bonded pairs stay in the Haven. Other than for protection, I wondered why."

Cradling her coffee, Shellie sighed. "I'm sorry. I didn't mean to jump down your throat. Most Faelinn prefer to be with others of their kind. They also like to remain close to the Veil. It's something to do with the energy it gives off."

"So you weren't kidding when you thought I was going to stay."

"No, I wasn't. But New DC isn't far away; you'll be able to visit whenever you want."

"I'm sure we'll be fine," Alanna said. They'd make things work. They'd figure out a place for him to run and hunt. There were plenty of rabbits in the parks. Although she wasn't sure how many rabbits it would take to fill Jekk up. Earlier, he'd tried to share a taste of the rabbit he'd caught, and she had politely declined. She'd hurt his feelings and had to explain she didn't eat raw meat. Apparently, Kellian did, and that was all that Jekk had ever known.

A family clattered through the door, setting off the bell. Two children crowded the counter, hands pressed to the glass as they surveyed the goodies. They looked like twins with their matching jeans and green shirts, though the girl had shining blond pigtails. They both pointed at what they wanted and raised hopeful eyes to their mother. Gina appeared out of the back, rubbing at the streak of flour on her cheek, and smiled at her customers.

"There are almost two hundred bonded pairs living in the Haven, plus their families. There are easily five hundred of us. There's a small elementary school for the kids, although the older ones go to a local high school. We have a library, a community center."

"A fire station," Alanna said, remembering the conversation.

Laughing, Shellie nodded. "Yes. We even have a general store that carries staples and a few other things."

"So it's mostly self-contained," Alanna noted.

"It is, but we shop the local stores too. This town is an extension of the Haven and we want it to thrive. Most of our residents work outside the Haven."

"Do any live away from the Haven?"

A teenaged girl came in, greeting Gina by name. She ordered a skinny soy vanilla latte, no whip, and a napoleon approximately five inches high. Alanna hid a smile at the disparity of the two. The girl took her order to a nearby table and promptly began texting.

"I never quite got the hang of that texting business," Shellie confided. "Daphne tells me I live in the dark ages."

Alanna laughed. She had to keep reminding herself that the youthful blond woman sitting across from her was in her nineties. She wondered how she would look when she was that age. Did humans bonded to Faelinn age at all, or just slowly? She had so many questions to ask, but the bakery was filling up, and there was no privacy.

The conflicts in her head raged, and no amount of double fudge chocolate cake was going to fix that. Instead, she asked the question that was nagging at her. "How is she texting? I thought the Veil interrupted the cell signals."

"We have a method to fix that. We'll get that done for you on the way home."

Laughter drew her attention. The family had settled at one of the larger wrought iron tables. Steam curled from large colorful coffee cups while glasses of milk sat in front of the children. Frosting smeared their faces and while Alanna watched, the mother pulled a wet wipe from her purse and attacked her son's face.

"I miss that age," Shellie said. "I'm waiting for Daphne to settle down and give me great-grandchildren."

"Is she bonded?"

"Yes, to Riordan's mam. You remember the kit she brought with her?"

"He was cute."

"He's a handful. One of only of a dozen kits born this side of the Veil. That's why he has an Earthan name. He desperately wants a bondmate."

"How do they find them?" Alanna took a long drink of coffee, still watching the family. The face washing had finished. As far as Alanna could tell, it had been a waste of time. The frosting had reappeared. "Jekk said he could feel me when I got close to the Veil here."

"We don't know," Shellie admitted. "There seems to be some kind of psychic connection that kicks in, but since we refuse to let anyone examine the Faelinn, we just don't know for sure."

"There's a lot that you don't know about them," Alanna observed.

"And we're fine with that," Shellie said. "Setasha is as intelligent as any human, more so than some I've met. The thought of her being caged and studied like a lab rat terrifies me."

The scenes Jekk had shared with her were still fresh in her mind. A small cage with barely enough room to turn around. A larger cage where he trained to fight. And then there was the Pit. There would be no more cages in his future. He would have a whole room to himself. She had a spare room. There would be no bars, no prison. Just freedom.

"I understand," Alanna said softly.

Tucking a blond curl behind one ear, Shellie observed her. Alanna waited patiently, not at all offended by the scrutiny. The family clattered out the door, all smiles and laughter.

"Yes, I think you do understand," Shellie said finally. She finished the last forkful of cake and sat back. "If you're finished, we'll head back to the Haven. I want to get your cell phone sorted out."

"Sorted out?" Alanna asked, gathering her purse.

Shellie smiled. Her earrings tinkled as she stood. "You'll see."

A bag with a piece of chocolate cake for Jekk in one hand, Alanna walked out of the bakery. The sidewalk was striped with shadow, the sun playing peek-a-boo through the trees planted along the road. Across the street, a man loaded a set of tapestry chairs into a pickup truck bed. The large dining room table was already there. The antique shop's proprietor observed from her doorway.

Alanna liked the town. It was the type of place you'd find in a book about small towns and multigenerational families. The kind of place where everyone knew each other, and newcomers to the area would be newcomers for decades. Down the street, a sidewalk board sign advertised a sale at a small bookstore. She made a note to stop in before she left. Independent bookstores were hard to find in this age of big box stores and ebooks.

But it wasn't the city.

Something flashed on the sidewalk. Bending, Alanna picked it up. A child's barrette sparkled in her hand. Iridescent crystals were set into the wings of a small butterfly. She remembered seeing it in the little girl's hair. Looking up and down the sidewalk, she realized the family was gone. Absently, she slipped the hair clip into her pocket before joining Shellie in the car.

The drive back to the Haven took no time at all. Shellie pulled into the driveway of one of the three houses Alanna remembered seeing when she'd followed Jonathan to the Dennisons'. She recognized his SUV in front of the house on the right. The house was a modern log cabin, though "cabin" was hardly the word she'd use. Large windows and skylights would let in lots of light. Perched on a small rise, it looked as if it had pushed up whole from the earth. It appealed to her.

"You'll love Agneta," Shellie said as she walked up to the house on the far left. Fall blooms spilled from pots on the wraparound porch, gold and white, blues and blush pinks. Wind chimes played, long thick tubes providing bass notes amongst the lilting piccolo sounds of the smaller chimes. Stained glass set into the oak door portrayed an enchanting scene of Veiler denizens, their faces peeking from behind trees and leaves. It was a work of art, and Alanna wondered who the artist was.

Bells tinkled inside the house when Shellie pressed the doorbell. Alanna walked along the length of the porch, examining the sun catchers hanging amidst the plants and chimes. Each was different, each depicting a flower or herb. The colors glowed with the light falling through them.

"Yoo-hoo, Shellie," a voice called from the garden. A silver-haired woman hurried across the yard. She held an empty coffee carafe in one hand. Her hair was long and thick, held back by a black band. When she got closer, Alanna saw that her eyes were the blue of a late fall day edging to twilight. And they were examining her very closely.

"I was over at Jonathan's," she explained, hugging Shellie with one arm while smiling widely at them both. "That boy works too hard. He was injured again, but I'm sure you know all about that. Anyway, I took him some coffee and zucchini bars. I have to sneak the healthy food in when he's not looking. You must be Alanna; I've heard about you. Read a few of your books, too." She thrust a hand in Alanna's direction. "I'm Agneta Ingridsdottir."

Nearly breathless with the effort to keep up with all of that, Alanna smiled and shook hands. Agneta's hand was warm and strong, completely unexpected. Looking more closely, Alanna realized that despite her first impression, the woman was younger than she seemed. Wrinkles edged her eyes, but her skin lacked the papery dryness of age.

"Come in, come in. I'll put on another pot of coffee and we'll have a nice chat. Are you going to be moving here? The house next door is empty. It's a lovely place. Where's your Fael? Jekk's his name, isn't it? The two of you can look over the place together."

Alanna was going to get dizzy; she just knew it. Trying to keep up with Agneta's conversation had her thinking that more coffee was probably a really good idea. She followed Shellie into the cool interior of the house. Sunshine fell through the stained glass, splashing in multicolored hues on the floor and wall. A lovely hand-knotted rug covered part of the floor. Rooms opened up to either side, and a staircase climbed to the second floor, the banister the same honey-colored wood as the floor.

"The stained glass is lovely," Alanna said. It seemed easier to change the subject than to try to explain why she wasn't moving to the Haven.

"Oh, thank you, dear. Jonathan is very talented." She led them down a hallway and into a bright kitchen. The counters were covered with computers, phones, CD players, and all the wires and gizmos that belonged inside of them. More were piled on a table with no discernable organization. Cords and cables snaked over the floor, hung off the counters, and dangled from the top of the refrigerator.

Alanna tripped over an extension cord, still trying to process the information that Jonathan was the artist responsible for the stained glass. The delicacy of the work didn't jibe with the sarcastic, irritating man she'd met.

"Be careful, dear, it's a minefield in here. Of course, it's nothing compared to my workroom. That place needs a good cleaning, but when I'm in there I get distracted. It's better that I acknowledge that side of my personality, though, otherwise I might annoy myself." Agneta stuck the carafe she'd been carrying under the faucet, filling it with water and beginning a new pot of coffee. The coffeepot seemed to be the only thing in the kitchen free of technological clutter.

The sound of snoring drew Alanna's attention to the other side of the table. Peeking over, she saw a Fael lying on his back, paws sticking up. A sunbeam hit him square in the stomach and turned the grey of his fur into glittering silver. His whiskers quivered as he snored, and Alanna had to fight off a giggle.

"We have company, you big lump, wake up and say hello," Agneta said. "Meet Felix."

The Fael opened one glittering cobalt eye. The meow sounded so much like "hello" that Alanna found herself saying hello back. Rolling to his feet, Felix stretched, rear high in the air, before padding over to a sleek aluminum box. Its front was half computer screen, half dispensing unit. Alanna watched in fascination as he used a delicate finger to operate the touch screen. A stream of clear liquid that looked like water but smelled of something sweeter poured out into a bowl, which he then settled down to drink from.

Bemused, Alanna took the mug from Agneta. Ducks wearing tutus and sunglasses danced across it. "His name is Felix? He was born this side of the Veil, then."

Shellie nodded. "He's Flexa's kit." She shoved aside a pile of motherboards and settled herself at the table.

"And he's a big lump of love," Agneta said. Felix looked up at her, droplets hanging from the tips of his whisker, and smiled. It was a little Cheshire cat-ish. "And very smart," she added. "He said to tell you that."

"I can see that," Alanna said.

"He'd have to be to teach a seventy-five-year-old woman how to deal with technological gadgets. So other than bringing you by for us to meet, what can I do for you?"

Alanna carefully removed a pile of tech manuals from a chair and sat. Felix came over, put a paw on her leg, and let out a long string of meows, punctuated by flicks of his long silvery tail.

"He wants to know where Jekk is," Agneta said.

Reaching for her Fael's thoughts, she discovered that he was already on his way. His tummy was full, and he felt content. Cateera was leading him, and Alanna caught a glimpse of her as she ran ahead. Happiness poured through the link from Jekk, and she found herself smiling.

"He's on his way," she told Felix. He gave a short trill of acknowledgement.

"Can you fix her cell phone?" Shellie asked Agneta.

"Of course, give it here," she said, wiggling her fingers in Alanna's direction.

Digging it out of her purse, Alanna passed it across the table. Agneta cracked it open, pulling out the sim card. She slipped the phone into a small vise, tightening it gently until the phone was secure. Felix padded over to peer into the phone. One long claw dipped into the open back. There was a crackle, followed by a spark.

"Is that normal?" Alanna asked Shellie.

"Don't worry," Shellie said. "It's what they do."

Agneta pressed the sim card between her palms. A glow leaked from between her fingers, throwing sharp shadows across the table. Felix's eyes glittered in the cast-off light. There was a spark from the sim card, although it didn't seem to bother Agneta. The smell of burning wire overpowered the scent of coffee.

"Okay, that should do it," Agneta said. She removed the phone from the vise, popped the card back into it, and closed it back up. "You'll be able to make calls no matter how close to the Veil you are. Bring me your laptop sometime and I'll fix the Wi-Fi on that too." A smile quirked her lips, a mischievous glint in her eyes. "And I understand you had problems with your GPS."

"Everyone's going to know about that, aren't they?" Alanna asked.

She took the cell phone and examined it curiously. A full signal showed in the upper corner. Whatever they'd done, it was receiving again.

Shellie laughed. "Of course. Newcomers are an endless source of gossip around here. For instance, we all know you find Jonathan Burke incredibly annoying."

"You're kidding," Alanna said.

"Not at all," Agneta told her. Retrieving the coffeepot, she refilled the mugs. "There's a pool going for how soon the two of you are going to hook up. Sorry dear, but I have to back him on this. I think his charm will have you in his bed within a week."

Alanna choked. Shellie gave her a friendly pat on the back. "That's not going to happen. I'm not staying here. And he's not charming."

Felix padded to the back door and opened it. Cateera nosed her way in. Felix waited patiently. Jekk stopped in the doorway and eyed the other male carefully. Alanna felt a low buzz in her mind that she was learning meant that the Faelinn were communicating. Jekk allowed the other to sniff at him, holding himself rigidly. The emotions spilling across their bond spoke of barely contained control. He wasn't used to viewing another male as a possible friend and ally. His experience with males had always been in the Pit. Blood had always been spilled. Slowly the fur on Jekk's neck smoothed out, the tension leaving him. Felix stepped away from the door and Jekk stepped in.

The three Faelinn took up so much space in the kitchen that it suddenly felt extremely crowded. Jekk crossed to her, keeping an eye on Felix as he did so. He sniffed the mug she held in her hand. He shook his head and sneezed.

That doesn't smell good, he informed her. *Cateera said the next house is empty. Are we going to live there?*

Alanna closed her eyes. Even her Fael was ganging up on her today. "No," she told him through their link. "I live in a city a few hours away." The sudden wariness that filled her told her exactly how he felt about that. She wrapped an arm around his neck, leaning her head against his. The feel of his fur against her cheek comforted her. "It will be fine."

Felix filled another water bowl and handed it to Jekk. Just as carefully, Jekk bent his head to drink. Having offered hospitality and had it accepted, Felix bounced a little and it came to Alanna that for all his size, he was still fairly young. There was another buzz in her head, and then the three Faelinn left the room.

Agneta grinned. "I'm sorry to tell you this, but Felix is about to corrupt your Fael with the joys of television."

"They watch television?" Alanna asked in surprise.

"They do almost everything we do," Shellie said. "They absorb language directly from our minds, and reading as well. This world is so different from Jekk's, though, that it will be confusing for him for a while."

"Felix told him that he can see what a city is like on the television," Agneta said.

That didn't sound like such a good idea to Alanna, but Jekk seemed content so she let it slide. She realized, having watched Felix fix her cell phone, that they were not children nor should be treated as such. "I have so much to learn," she said.

"Then let's get started," Shellie said. "And we can discuss men while we're at it."

A cold breeze blew through the window, sending the curtains into a frenzy. It flipped the pages of a small notebook Alanna used for notes. Slapping one hand down on a page, Alanna shivered. The room had grown cold while she was working. The desk sat near the window and she reached out to slide the pane shut. There were goose bumps on her arms. A glance at the laptop's clock surprised her. She'd been working for several hours transcribing notes. It was nearly three a.m.

Saving the work, Alanna closed the laptop. She'd spent time cataloging everything she'd learned about Faelinn in the last few days. They were far more complicated than she'd realized. Far more intelligent. And the story that was taking shape in her head was going to be so much more than she'd planned. Excitement swept through her. She couldn't wait to get home and plunge into the writing.

A long stretch popped the vertebrae in her spine. Dropping her arms to her sides, Alanna wandered into the bedroom. Jekk stirred in his sleep, raising his head from his paws to look at her. He'd wedged himself into a corner after dragging the comforter from the bed. From his position, he could see both the door to the sitting room and the one to the balcony. Alanna walked over to him, her bare feet sinking into the lush pile of the carpet. He purred as she sat down, leaning back against his side.

There aren't any bars, he told her. *I'm not used to that.*

"You're free now, and safe," she assured him. Her fingers found the sensitive place at the base of his ear and scratched gently. His purr ratcheted up a notch. "You never have to sleep in a cage again."

It's very strange to go where I want, Jekk said.

Sadness filled Alanna for what he'd been through. Sadness and absolute, pure fury. Responding to her emotions, Jekk turned his head and rasped his tongue over her bare knee. The rough wetness made her laugh. She leaned into his warmth and closed her eyes. She'd had a cat when she was a kid. He would curl up in front of her at bedtime, and she'd fall asleep with her fingers buried in his fur, his purr rumbling against her chest. The fury leached away, replaced by a drowsy peace.

Are you going to fall asleep?

Alanna laughed. "Maybe." She opened her eyes and found him smiling, or as close to one as he could get.

Something glittered on the carpet, catching the light from the bedside lamp. Curious, she reached for it. It was the barrette she'd found outside the bakery. The crystals sparkled as she held it up to the light. Her fingertips tingled. Shaking her hand at the sudden pins and needles, she watched the light scatter across the rug.

The tingle turned to a burn. The sparkles solidified into pictures. As the burn spread up her arm, down her torso, the scenes wrapped around her. She saw two adults eating cake. She saw herself across the bakery, talking to Shellie. Flash forward and she was riding in a car, pulling into a motel parking lot. The mountains pushed up behind the rooms, trees marching along the slope. A playground sat at the end of the parking lot.

Flash. The ground arching away beneath her feet, and then back as she urged the swing higher and higher. Something moved in the trees, visible only when she was at the apex of her flight. Her mother sat on a bench, reading a guidebook. Her bratty brother was digging a hole in the sandbox. Letting go, she flew forward, her sneakers hitting the ground a fraction of a second before her knees. It hurt a bit, but the peek-a-boo movement through the trees was far too interesting to care.

Flash. Thick tree trunks around her now. Downslope, the playground was out of sight. Ahead, the silky flowing shape moving from tree to tree. Close, the whip of tail, the flop of an ear.

Flash. Thick brush, her sneaker caught by a root. She couldn't see the animal anymore. She couldn't see the motel. The trees blocked most of the light and she began to be afraid.

Flash. A man, smiling, releasing her foot. A dog panted at his side, no longer hiding in the trees.

Flash. A hand over her mouth.

Flash. Screaming.

Alanna was on her feet. She had to go. The burning drove her forward. Jekk was in her mind, wrapped in her thoughts. She felt the need to hunt, the harsh imperative driving her out into the night. And she ran.

Chapter Eight

His cell phone rang, the guitar riff jarringly loud. With a grunt, Jonathan reached for it. By the time he had it in his hand, he was awake. A holdover from his cop days.

"Sorry to wake you, sir. Patrol just called in. Alanna McLean was spotted running down the street near your place. She wasn't dressed for the weather."

It took him a minute to place the voice. Brown, the security officer handling the night shift. Jonathan's head was still trapped in the spider claws of a nightmare. Remembering his manners at the last minute, he bit back the curse. "Thanks, Brown. I'll take care of it."

They are Awakening, Cateera observed.

"Looks like," Jonathan said. He grabbed jeans, pulled them on. Sweatshirt, jacket, shoes. He pushed his cell phone into his pocket and ran out the door.

It was cold. Fall weather in the mountains meant warm days and icy nights. His breath frosted as he began a brisk jog down the street, his loping strides matched by his Fael. Rounding a corner, he saw Alanna and Jekk ahead. Now he cursed. She was dressed in silky shorts and a white tank. They were meant for sleeping, not running down the street in the middle of the night. Barefoot.

Jekk snarled as they drew up. He bared his teeth. Alanna ignored them completely. Her bare feet slapped at the pavement.

"Keep him off me long enough for me to get this jacket on her," Jonathan said to Cateera.

I will do my best.

Jonathan slipped off his jacket. Increasing his pace, he caught up to Alanna. Jekk lunged and Cateera muscled him aside, cuffing him as she drove her way between them. Wrapping his arms around Alanna, Jonathan jerked her to a stop, nearly lifting her off her feet with the effort.

Her hair was long and loose; it whipped into his face. Any other time, he might have enjoyed the cool silk against his skin but trying to hold her still long enough to get her arms through the sleeves of his jacket didn't leave him a lot of room for enjoyment. Her angry cries at his throat puffed warm air against his skin. He felt the nip of her teeth before he jerked his head back. At his side, Cateera fought to hold off Jekk. She used the mass of her body, her paws and teeth to keep him back. The larger Fael could easily overpower her, but he was still cognizant enough to hold back. The Awakening trapped him, forced him to protect his bondmate, but he understood no one was hurting her.

Jonathan realized there was no hope of getting the zipper up, so he let Alanna go. She sprinted away. He trailed her, Cateera at his side. He had no idea where she was headed or what awaited at the end.

Veering off the road, Alanna leaped the narrow ditch between the pavement and the rough grass. In a heartbeat, she'd disappeared into the trees. Cateera took the lead. Jonathan was nearly blind beneath the branches. The starlight didn't come close to lighting the way and the Veil was behind him.

She is making enough noise that you could follow just from the sound, Cateera said dryly.

The smile that tugged at his lips did so despite his worry. "She's a city girl," he commented back.

Her snort was as unladylike as anything he'd heard from Cateera. His bondmate didn't like cities and tolerated them only when they had to work in one. A few steps ahead, he heard a soft cry and almost tripped over his feet as he came to an abrupt stop. Alanna had tumbled into a deadfall. He reached to help her and narrowly avoided Jekk's teeth taking off his hand. By the time Cateera pushed Jekk away, Alanna was already up and running, her mind focused on something only she and her bondmate could see.

He didn't want to think about what the ground and underbrush were doing to her bare feet and legs.

The slope took a downhill slant. The Awakening pair began a headlong rush down the slope. Jonathan increased his speed, circled them, and placed himself and Cateera in front so that if Alanna fell, he could catch her. A moment later, he realized where they were heading and began to curse even as he pulled out his cell.

"It's Burke," he snapped into the phone when the security center answered. "Kill the power to the southwest sector now!"

"What? Why?"

"Just do it! The whole sector, Brown, do it now!"

The trees ended abruptly, spitting them out by the road surrounding the Haven. A shimmer of moonlight caught the coils of razor wire atop the fence. Alanna headed straight for the chain-link. Catching her arm, Jonathan dragged her to a stop. He shook her hard, trying to get those faraway eyes to focus on him. Teeth clamped onto his hip, and he grunted with the pain. Jekk growled, trying to shake him loose from his bondmate. Cateera pushed between them, biting Jekk's muzzle to get his attention, to call him off.

"Alanna, you can't go over the fence!" He yelled into her face, desperate to make her understand. "The gate is a mile away; we can go that way. I'll show you!"

Sharp incisors bit through his jeans. A paw the size of a dinner plate slapped him in the ribs. Claws opened long slices along his flesh, and Jonathan gritted his teeth. Hot blood soaked into his sweatshirt.

"Alanna, listen to me!" He shook her again. Her arms felt impossibly fragile through his jacket.

For a moment, the briefest sliver of time, her eyes focused on his. "Can't think," she whispered hoarsely.

"I know," he said. He rubbed his hands soothingly up and down her arms. The wind blew her loose hair around them both. "But you can't go over the fence."

"Have to," she said. Tears streaked her cheeks as she struggled to free herself from his grip. "She's screaming."

"Who?" Jonathan demanded. "Who's screaming?"

An animal groan ripped from Alanna's throat, and she wrenched herself free. Jekk released him at the same time, cuffing Cateera aside as he followed his bondmate.

"Fuck!" Jonathan yelled and ran to catch up. He caught her arm again. "At least let me go first."

He made a leap for the chain-link and caught the metal halfway up. He had a moment to be grateful that his orders to turn off the electricity had been obeyed, and then she was clambering up behind him. Jonathan climbed rapidly to where the razor wire began. The Leatherman was in its customary spot in his back pocket. Clinging to the cold metal fence, he used the wire cutter attachment to snap the wickedly sharp coils. The ends whipped out. A quick jerk of his head was all that saved him from a nasty slice.

Jekk sprang over the fence, his powerful hindquarters easily clearing the twelve- foot height. Turning at the bottom, he peered up. The moonlight made lanterns of his eyes. He crooned to his bondmate. Jonathan made a lateral move and Alanna climbed higher. Her toes clung to the open links. Holding the wire out of the way, he steadied her as she swung a leg over the top. For a moment, icy fingers clung to his, and then she slipped down, quick and agile.

Jonathan followed and cursed as the sharp wire sliced his sweatshirt. He let himself hang loose for a second and then dropped lightly onto his feet. Cateera leaped the fence. She nosed against his hip, licked his fingers, and got a quick scratch under the chin before they resumed the chase.

Alanna and Jekk disappeared into the trees. A flashlight would have been useful, Jonathan thought as he caught up to them. The moonlight disappeared, not a silver glimmer visible through the fall leaves. Each pounding step brought a stitch of pain where Jekk's claws had torn through his skin. He could feel blood oozing from the bite on his hip. At least the Fael hadn't eviscerated him.

He was holding back, Cateera said. *He did not want to hurt you.*

"I know," Jonathan answered. He quickened his pace, realizing the pair were leaving him behind.

What was driving her? The phrase "she's screaming" played over and over. He could still hear the tormented determination in Alanna's voice. Whatever Gift was Awakening wasn't going to be an easy one. He thought of his own. The ability to hunt a killer meshed well with his criminal science background and his time on the force, but it wasn't one he'd have willingly chosen.

It is a good Gift, Cateera said. *We are very good at it.*

He acknowledged that she was right. They made a good living, helped bring closure to people, and had seen some brutal sons-of-bitches put away. But it was a hard Gift to carry inside.

I hear traffic.

Even concentrating, Jonathan couldn't hear anything over the slap of Alanna's feet in the underbrush, the harsh panting of her breath. But sure enough, they burst through the trees onto a narrow state road. A pickup sped by, horn blaring as it missed Alanna by inches. Not seeing it in whatever interior landscape she inhabited, she ran across the road. Jonathan could see dark footprints on the asphalt. Her feet were bleeding.

He wondered how much farther they had to go.

The world had narrowed to pain. Sharp, slicing pain lanced up from her feet with each pounding step. Her skin was so cold it burned where it was exposed to the night. Her chest was a tight constriction of muscle, each breath forced in and out of straining lungs.

And her head held the screams of a young girl, each agonized howl pounding against her skull.

Fear dragged her forward. Fear of being too late. Fear that the girl's screams would end in the worst possible way. Fear that she would fail.

A fishhook of pain pierced Alanna's chest. Whoever—whatever—was on the other end was reeling her in. She had no choice but to follow.

Reaching for Jekk's mind, she found the same imperative. He crooned encouragement, his thoughts wrapped around hers. He brushed against her thigh, but even his soft fur hurt her icy skin. They'd covered miles, how far she had no way of knowing, but the safety of her room was far behind.

The fishhook yanked her off the road. The hard asphalt changed to the softer carpet of pine straw and frozen leaves. Underneath, though, lurked the sharp points of fallen branches and rocks. Agony lanced her right foot and she stumbled, an involuntary cry breaking from her lips. A steady hand wrapped around her elbow, gave her just enough stability to keep from falling. When Jekk turned to nip, she forced him back. Jonathan was helping, not interfering.

She wanted to say thank you, but the words were trapped inside. She knew he was there, had known from the moment he'd caught up to her and trapped her in his arms to yank his coat around her. Without his help, she would never have made it over the fence. The imperative driving her wouldn't allow a detour.

A flash of white raced past. Cateera paced them, sometimes running ahead, sometimes falling behind. It was only the occasional flicker of moonlight forcing its way through the thick pine branches that allowed her to be seen. She moved like a spirit, soundless in her stride.

A fresh scream crashed through Alanna's skull. Ignoring the bush that snarled twiggy fingers in her hair, yanking some loose, she increased her pace. The screams were louder. Blond pigtails shuddered behind her eyes. They were getting close.

Through the underbrush came the glimmer of lights. They should have been warm and welcoming. Should have been. Instead, they launched shards of terror into her heart. The screams lay behind those lights.

Hard hands caught her a moment before she broke from cover. Her momentum carried them down. The breath crashed from her lungs, leaving her momentarily immobile. She had a brief awareness of sprawling atop lean, hard muscles before she was flipped and pressed beneath him. Jonathan's breath warmed her face.

"Stop! Think it through, Alanna," he whispered. His legs trapped hers, his hands cuffed her wrists as she instinctively tried to push free. He grunted when Jekk's powerful forelegs smashed into him. The Fael's teeth closed over his shoulder. Cateera snapped at Jekk, protecting her bond-mate. The male snapped back, his teeth missing her by inches.

"Let me go," she begged. Pain gathered inside of her. Her heart beat so fast she thought it might erupt from her rib cage. His body warmed the length of hers. She wanted to snuggle into him and feel all that hard muscle keeping her safe. She wanted to be wrapped up tight in his arms and have his heartbeat steady her own. But the hook jerked hard, threatened to rip her heart from her chest. The screams trapped inside her mind were forcing her skull apart.

"You can't go running up to that house. You have no idea what might happen." Jonathan grunted as once again several hundred pounds of Fael hit him in the side. The force of the blow pushed him off balance, and Alanna used it to roll him over. He sat up, trapping her arms, her wrists still cuffed in his hands.

Shudders ripped through her slender frame. She was freezing, but heat raged down her spine. "Please," she whispered. Something sharp dug into her left knee, the pain swallowed by the overwhelming influx of sensation. She buried her face in the crux of his shoulder. He smelled good and he felt wonderful—what woman wouldn't enjoy his muscled thighs beneath hers, the hard chest against her breasts. Any other time, she might take advantage of the situation—even if he was a jerk—because the man was too hot to be believed. But now, right now, she just wanted the pain to stop and it wouldn't as long as he held onto her.

The barking of a dog interrupted the snarling of the two Faelinn. Cateera shivered into invisibility. Alanna felt the shock of surprise from Jekk and then a curious twisting before he disappeared. Jonathan's arms tightened around her when the door to the house opened. A rectangle of light slanted across the long yard before a man blocked it.

"There's nothing out here, you stupid mutt," he said. The words carried in the still night air. A dog wormed around his legs, wiggled free, and streaked across the yard toward them. Jonathan cursed, his hands momentarily going slack. Using that to her advantage, Alanna twisted free. The sharp hook yanked. The tug eased with each step she took toward the house.

The dog yelped and tumbled end over end. Alanna felt the brush of fur against her hand and knew that Jekk was with her. Behind her, a snarl and a whimper told her that Cateera was taking care of the dog. A driveway curved across her path and sharp rocks from the crush and run lacerated her already tortured feet.

The porch light flicked on. A thin-shouldered, bearded man stepped forward, his brows drawn together in a brutal scowl. Plaid flannel pants and a white undershirt covered a narrow frame. "Who the hell are you?" he demanded as Alanna approached the porch.

Jekk hit him full on, knocking him flat. His head hit the wooden floor with a thud. His startled scream became a groan. The Fael flickered back into view. Jekk's lips were curled back from sharp predator's teeth, paws as big as the man's head planted firmly on his chest. Limping steps took Alanna up the stairs. The man bucked, gasped for breath, tried to throw Jekk off. He flailed out with a hand and caught Alanna's ankle. A sharp tug brought her to her knees, pitched her forward so that splinters gouged her palms.

The screaming was still inside her head. The child's high-pitched wails of pain and terror pulsed in her brain. Alanna crawled forward, numb to everything but the need to stop the noise. She tugged against the hand but couldn't get free. Jekk solved the problem by biting down on the man's arm. His scream was hoarse from lack of breath, but his fingers released their lock on her ankle.

"Enough, Jekk," Jonathan commanded. "Tend to your bondmate."

Jekk obeyed, releasing the man into Jonathan's care. He immediately nudged Alanna with his nose, crooning down low in his throat. She sank her fingers into his fur, taking strength and comfort from the contact. She staggered to her feet and stepped into the house.

The sharp, hooking pain was unbearable. Hot tears spilled down her cheeks, warmed frigid skin. The cabin wasn't large. To the right, the front room held an old beige couch and a recliner in green plaid. Flames in the fireplace spit heat into the room. Rifles hung in a rack over the mantle. To the left, a small dining area held a table covered with papers, a laptop, and DVD cases. A couple of barstools stood unoccupied on the near side of a half wall separating a kitchen. The room smelled of fried onions and burning pine. All of that blurred as Alanna's knees gave out.

Down the hall, a girl screamed for her mommy.

"Who the hell are you people?" The angry voice was behind her. "Get out of my house! You have no right to be here!"

"Shut up and sit down," Jonathan said. The man tried to twist away from Jonathan's hand on his shoulder. With an easy shifting of muscle, Jonathan flipped the man onto his stomach and wedged a knee in the small of his back. The bearded man shrieked when Jonathan twisted one arm up behind him. Blood from Jekk's bite stained the carpet.

"Get off me! You have no right!"

Jekk loped forward to push his face close to the man's. Sharp incisors below dangerous eyes and the rumbling growl from his chest was all it took to still the man.

"Oh God, get it away from me!"

Cateera came inside. Turquoise eyes assessed the situation. She padded over to Jonathan and leaned down to take a long sniff of his captive. A delicate sneeze made her whiskers shake. She gently nudged Jekk away, sending him to his bondmate's side.

Jonathan leaned down, his voice pitched low and dangerous. "I don't know why there's a little girl crying for her mother, but I'm going to find out. Now, Cateera here is going to watch you, and she doesn't like you. If you don't move, she won't bite you. If you do, she'll rip your head off your neck. Do you understand?" A jerk of the twisted arm and the sight of Cateera's teeth reduced the man to babbling agreement.

Jonathan helped Alanna to her feet and stepped into the hallway. There were four doors. Only one mattered. The wood-paneled door was warped at the bottom, the veneer peeling from moisture damage. The doorknob was dull brass. There were scratches around the keyhole. Above it was a second lock, a deadbolt.

Both were locked.

Frustrated, Alanna yanked on the knob, twisting it over and over, trying to get in. The pain in her head erupted from her mouth in a tortured keening. Jekk shoved against the door with his shoulder. The wood groaned, splintering around the knob. The deadbolt held firm.

From the other side of the door came heart-wrenching sobs.

Jekk exploded against the door, leaping so that his shoulder took the brunt of the hit. The deadbolt held, but the wood around it shattered. The door swung inwards.

The room was dark. The light from the living room only illuminated a small portion of the rug. Blocking the doorway so Alanna couldn't get inside, Jonathan flicked the light switch and chased away the shadows.

The room was a little girl's fantasy. Pale pink paint colored the walls, with a scrolling border of roses around the top. A bed fit for a princess dominated the room. Its white canopy arched high, streaming panels of lace tied to each post. The curtains matched, though the windows themselves were shuttered. A delicate vanity with tiny roses painted on the drawers sat beneath a window. There was a scatter of hair bows across the top.

Hundreds of stuffed animals lined shelves on the walls, brown bears, purple dragons with iridescent wings, white tigers. Every one of them looked soft and cuddly. Their eyes watched, alert for the tea party that was sure to happen. Another tumble of stuffed toys hid amongst the pile of pillows on the bed. In the middle of that mound of fanciful animals was a little girl sucking in breaths in shuddering sobs.

Blond hair hung down one side of her face, the other still caught up in a pigtail. Her eyes were bruised violets swollen and hopeless with fear. Alanna recognized her beneath the tears. Beneath the bruise swelling one side of her face. Beneath the blood from the split lip painted across her chin. It was the child from Sweet Indulgence who had laughed her way through a piece of cake mere hours ago.

The hook in Alanna's chest ripped free as she staggered forward to the edge of the bed. The little girl shrank back in fear. "You're safe now," Alanna said softly. "I found you, and you're safe."

"I want my mommy," the girl said.

"We'll get you to your mommy," Alanna promised. Jekk crooned his agreement. He leaned closer, and gently licked the small fingers clutched tightly into a bear's fluff.

"Kitty," the girl said. Surprising them both, she launched herself forward to wrap thin arms around his neck, burying her face in his fur. He began to purr as he jumped onto the bed. The mattress groaned under his weight. With gentle paws, he shifted her so that he could circle his body around hers. No one would be able to reach her without his permission.

Shivers of reaction shook Alanna. Her feet throbbed uncontrollably, and she looked down to see a puddle of scarlet spreading around her feet as her blood soaked into the carpet's cream pile. It was the sight of the blood that made her realize how much pain she was in. Her knees buckled and she caught one of the bedposts. The adrenaline that had kept her going through miles of woody mountainside was flushing from her system, leaving her with the reality of what she'd done.

An arm caught her around the waist, hauling her up against a muscled chest. The implied comfort almost did her in. There was that little girl, angelic face bruised and swollen. The pile of stuffed animals hid most of what Jekk hadn't covered with his legs, but it was obvious that she was naked. As she sobbed, Alanna caught a glimpse of blood on skinny white thighs. Realization kicked in. How could she have been so stupid? A bubble of innocence she hadn't even known she had burst.

Turning into Jonathan's embrace, she saw what was in the corner. A black tripod sported a professional-looking video recorder aimed at the bed. Rage drove away the pain in her feet. It drove everything from her except the need to hurt. She yanked free of Jonathan's grip quickly enough that she caught him by surprise.

The living room seemed to magically appear before her. Cateera looked up from where she crouched eye-to-eye with the man on the floor. He never saw Alanna coming. The first kick drove his breath from his body in a long wheeze. The pain she felt in her toes was nothing compared to what was in her heart. The second kick to his ribs broke something. The snap was audible, but whether it was a rib or a toe she didn't know or care.

He rolled into a ball on his side. Jonathan caught her just as her third kick nailed the monster hard in his groin. Then her feet were lifted off the ground, her legs still kicking out. Someone was yelling. She struggled to get free, but Jonathan wasn't letting go. She went limp, lifted her arms, and slid right out of his grip, leaving his coat behind as she slipped free. She grunted as her foot connected with the man's stomach.

Through it all, Cateera sat and watched, her lips peeled back from her teeth in a Fael version of a feral smile.

"Enough!" Jonathan shouted. When he lifted her off her feet again, he bodily moved her away. He dropped her onto the couch, and when Alanna went to clamber off, Cateera draped her upper body across Alanna's lap, effectively pinning her in place.

Be calm, Jekk told her. *The child is scared enough. She needs help.*

The words shamed her. Alanna stopped trying to push Cateera away and forced herself to relax. The feeling of warm fur against her cold legs set off a series of painful shudders.

Jonathan watched her, a fierce expression in those summer-blue eyes. She gave him a small nod and he nodded back.

"Quit whining," he told the man curled on the floor.

"She broke my balls," he wheezed. His hands cupped his crotch, tears of pain soaking into the grey-flecked beard.

"You won't need them anymore, trust me," Jonathan said, pulling out his cell phone. He walked to the pine dining table and flipped through papers until he found an envelope. It must have had an address, because she heard him giving it to the person on the other end of the call. And the man's name—Peter Samuelson.

Closing her eyes, Alanna leaned back into the smoky-smelling couch. Jekk let her look through his eyes down at the little girl cradled against him. She'd fallen asleep, one hand clutching the teddy bear, the other clutching Jekk.

We found her, Jekk said. Satisfaction curled through the words.

How? Alanna asked through their bond. Violent shivers wracked her body as her core temperature slowly began to normalize.

It's our Gift. It's what we'll do together.

Alanna remembered Shellie talking to her about an Awakening. The bonding between her and her Fael would solidify until something inside of them Awakened a power. She'd had no idea what it would be like. Shellie had tried to explain. She'd talked about a sudden understanding, a need to do something that you'd never been able to do before. The reality of it was far different. The visions that had driven Alanna to run through the cold autumn night had been terrifying, but the result was amazing. Somehow, she'd come here, to this place, in response to a child's screams only she and Jekk had heard. She wouldn't change that. If this was what had manifested, this need to find a lost child, then Alanna could live with that.

But next time she was going to stop for shoes.

Chapter Nine

"The police and EMTs are on their way," Jonathan told her. He crouched in front of her. "There was a girl reported missing from a local motel earlier today."

"I saw her," Alanna said. "I was in town with Shellie, and I saw her in Sweet Indulgence with her family. How could he do that to her, Jonathan?" She wanted Jekk to comfort her, to feel his warm sturdy body leaning against her, but he was protecting the girl. Her mind flooded with reassurance though, a depthless kind of love that she returned with her whole heart.

"Fuck you, bitch," the man said. He tried to straighten up and Cateera immediately dropped from Alanna's legs to move in front of him. He froze.

"Don't talk to her," Jonathan warned him. "Don't even look at her, or I'll let her kick the rest of your ribs in." Reaching for the jacket on the floor, Jonathan draped it over Alanna's bare legs. Her bloody feet stuck out from underneath.

Alanna fought back a smile, but not before Jonathan saw it and smiled in response. Oh, not fair, she thought. Here she was, frozen and in pain from her lacerated feet, a pedophile curled up on the rug, and an abused child in a princess's nightmare of a room, and the most beautiful man she'd ever seen was smiling at her. She wished he'd just scowl and stare at her in that way he had that annoyed her so much. It would be so much easier to remember he was a jerk, then.

Jonathan's cell phone rang, and he pulled it out of his pocket as he rose to his feet. He kept his eyes on their prisoner while he talked. Alanna listened to his side of the conversation, realized he was talking to Mark, and closed her eyes again. She didn't want to be sitting on this couch. She didn't want to be touching anything that belonged to the man on the floor.

Her childhood had been middle-class idyllic. Both her parents had worked, but somehow dinner had always appeared on the table at night. There had always been help with her homework, a ride to a friend's house. Clubs and sports were always supported. Her dad had even coached her softball team. Nothing in that life had prepared her for what she'd seen in the bedroom down the hall.

Stranger danger was something she'd learned about in school, heard about over and over again from the friendly policeman who'd come to talk to them once a year. Don't talk to strangers. Don't get in a strange car. Remember the safety word. Hers had been *pizza*. She'd never needed it. Strangers were something that hovered at the edges of bad dreams. They were the shadowy figures that she and her friends scared each other with at sleepovers. None of them knew what strangers did once they caught you, but they'd known it wasn't good.

Not once had she ever thought she'd meet one of those frightening strangers face-to-face. She never thought she'd have to look into the eyes of a victim and know what had been done. The need to hurt the man on the floor, to make him feel every measure of the pain he'd inflicted, was so strong she was afraid if she looked at him, she'd lose control of herself again.

If you let him free, I'll track him into the woods and hunt him down, Jekk said. *It will make both of us feel better.*

"We can't," she answered. "That's not how we handle justice here." She sent him mental pictures of a court trial, and a penitentiary she'd visited once for research.

You weren't thinking of those things when you were kicking him, Jekk pointed out.

A confusing mix of shame and satisfaction swept through her. The satisfaction made her feel worse, but only a little. "We still have to follow the law."

The growl that reverberated through her mind told her exactly how Jekk felt. *Then your justice doesn't match the crime. He preyed on this child,* Jekk argued. *He deserves to know fear and pain. Our young are precious. No one should be allowed to hurt them.*

"If I could, dear one, I would help you hunt him down and make him pay," she said. "We can't. We just can't."

The sense of helplessness that flooded into her brought tears to her eyes. His own captivity was only days behind, and Jekk identified with the little girl. They'd both suffered atrocities beyond their control. His need for visceral justice was as much for himself as for her. It hurt Alanna that she couldn't allow it, because it was what she wanted as well.

Alanna forced open her eyes to look at the man responsible for what had happened tonight. Samuelson was still curled into a protective ball. His short dark hair was flecked with. Everything about him looked harmless and unassuming. He might have been a plumber or a teacher, a mailman or a CEO. His eyes were wild, though, darting around the room, but never leaving Cateera's bared teeth for more than a few seconds. Blood stained the patchy beard growing over his chin and neck. He looked less like a monster and more like a shrunken, helpless scarecrow. And she absolutely hated him.

Lights splashed blue and red across the wall, racing from one end to the other. The sound of car tires on gravel came in through the open door. It brought Samuelson's head up sharply. "Hey, man, we can sort this out. I have money, I can pay you. I won't press charges for the assault. Let's just be reasonable. I wouldn't have done it if he hadn't made me. Come on, man, it's not my fault!"

Alanna saw the utter disgust etched on Jonathan's face. She wasn't at all surprised when Cateera snarled and almost delicately closed her jaws on the back of Samuelson's neck. Blood drained from his face so quickly it was as if he'd instantly become a corpse.

Why does she get all the fun? Jekk demanded. Alanna covered her mouth, trying to muffle her laugh.

"You good?" Jonathan asked, watching her from the door.

Alanna nodded. She pulled Jonathan's jacket around her shoulders, slipping her arms into the sleeves. The fire was warming her legs, but her torso still felt like solid ice. The jacket was too big for her and she overlapped the front for extra warmth. A trace of his aftershave clung to the collar. It smelled delicious.

A dog started barking. It caught her by surprise. She thought that the dog had been killed. Car doors slammed and a deep male voice ordered the dog to shut up. It gave a last unrepentant bark and then subsided. Jonathan glanced at her, down at their captive, and then stepped outside. She shoved her hands into the pockets of his jacket and sat back to see what would happen next.

~

The night had gotten colder. Jonathan thought they might see snow early this year. Red and blue cop lights spun a kaleidoscope of color on the surrounding trees. The artist in him was intrigued. He wondered if he could catch that effect in glass. The sheriff and two deputies clumped up the three steps to the porch. He knew all three. He'd worked with them before.

Nodding at the deputies, Michaels and Voight, he held his hand out to the sheriff. "Sheriff Jacobs," he said, clasping the work-roughened hand warmly. Jacobs had a couple of decades on him, but that had never slowed the man down. He'd been sheriff for the past eighteen years, and there was no reason to think that the next local election wouldn't see him serving another term. Sharp, pale eyes took in the blood on Jonathan's shirt and pants, the grim look on his face.

"Burke," the sheriff answered. "EMTs are about a mile behind us. What the hell's going on?"

"There's a little girl in there, in the back bedroom." Jonathan pushed a hand back through his hair, remembering the look in the girl's eyes. "The room's set up with a professional video system."

"Ah shit," the sheriff said. "You and your Fael found her?"

"Not quite. We had a new Awakening. It led the bondmates here."

Jacobs grunted. "That would be the writer woman who came up here."

No surprise he knew about Alanna. Jonathan was aware that Jacobs made it his business to know everything that went on in his community. He considered the Haven part of that community, and Jonathan was glad for it. "That's right. She's in the living room. Her Fael is guarding the girl in the bedroom. She's got some injuries of her own. She'll need the EMTs to look at her."

The sheriff grunted. He took off his hat, scratched at the close-cut rim of hair that was all that remained of the dark springy curls he'd had when he'd first been elected sheriff, and returned the hat to its accustomed place. "Will the Fael give us trouble?"

"No," Jonathan said. "But the pedo Cateera is watching might."

The ambulance came up the drive, pulling to a stop behind the cruisers. Two EMTs jumped out and moved quickly to retrieve equipment. Their navy uniforms blended into the night. Turning to the two deputies who'd been listening in, Jacobs instructed them to secure the homeowner. They disappeared into the house. The sheriff turned to the ambulance crew when they came up the walk and asked them to wait outside until he gave the word. Jonathan followed the sheriff into the house. Cateera was sitting in front of Alanna. She'd remained visible, and her lavender-tipped white ears were stiffly alert while she watched the deputies handcuff Samuelson.

"He looks a little ill," the sheriff noted. "Got some blood on him."

"Tripped over his dog and fell down the stairs when we got here," Jonathan said blandly.

"Damn shame," the sheriff answered.

"That's a lie!" Samuelson yelled. "That bitch kicked me. I want her arrested."

"Got a witness said you fell down the stairs," one of the deputies said. His eyes were hot and hard as they met Jonathan's and then slipped away. He hauled Samuelson to his feet, and then held him steady while the man bent over at the waist, groaning about his balls.

Alanna must have really done some damage, Jonathan thought. Funny, he couldn't find it in himself to feel sorry for the guy. Cateera watched with interest. It was obvious she was just waiting for an excuse to bring him down again.

"Did you read him his rights?" Jacobs asked Deputy Michaels.

"Sure did," the crew-cut deputy answered. Tall and lanky, his uniform hung a little on his frame, but there was a shine to his shoes and a precision crease in his pants. He was the kind of man that took pride in his work and made sure all the details were perfect. "He even said he understood the part about anything he says can and will be used against him in a court of law."

"Good enough," the sheriff said. "Haul him out."

Cateera stalked them to the door, growling low in her throat. Samuelson squealed and moved a little faster when she playfully nudged the back of his knees with her head.

"You have style, Cateera," Jacobs told her. She turned to him, cocking her head, looking very pleased with herself.

The sheriff turned his attention to Alanna. "Ma'am, I understand there's a little girl back there?" the sheriff asked, a nod of his head indicating the hallway.

"Yes, in the back bedroom."

"Can you ask your Fael to let us get to her?"

A smile touched Alanna's lips. "Jekk won't hurt you."

"Thank you. Let's go," he said to Deputy Voight. Cateera paced around the room before settling in front of the fire.

Outside, Jonathan could hear Samuelson threatening Michaels with a lawsuit for illegal entry and police brutality. That would be in addition to the assault charges against Alanna, of course. Jonathan shook his head and crossed to the couch. The nap on the arm had been worn off, and the cushion he settled on had a permanent dip in the center. He ignored both as he focused on Alanna.

She was too calm, he thought. Since she'd exploded into rage, she'd been too quiet. She seemed to be almost tranquil. It worried him a little. He'd seen victims with similar reactions in his time as a cop. So traumatized by what they'd seen or experienced that they shut it all off. Sometimes it took days or weeks before it all came out. But it always did. He could only hope that it was soon.

Her hair was a wind- and wood-tangled mess and much longer than he'd thought it would be. He reached out and gently plucked a leaf from the thick strands. There was a scratch on her cheek where a branch must have caught her. Her bare legs were covered with dirt and dried blood; one particularly nasty gash on her left calf was still bleeding sluggishly. Her feet were a tortured mess and it surprised him that even with the strength of the Awakening upon her, she'd been able to keep going.

"Mark is on his way to pick us up," he told her. "He'll bring a truck so the Faelinn can ride in the back."

"That's good, because I don't think I can stand up right now," she confessed.

Before he could answer, a child's screams drove him to his feet. He took a step toward the hall and then made himself stop. He wasn't a cop anymore. The sheriff knew what he was doing. Still, it was damn hard to keep from rushing to help. He met Cateera's steady gaze and shoved his hands into his pockets.

"She just woke up," Alanna said softly.

Turning, he saw that there was no worry in her eyes. That stormy grey held many things, but worry wasn't one of them. Jonathan felt his shoulder muscles loosen a bit, and he put a hand to his nape to rub at the tension there. Hell of a night.

"Jekk says they startled her when she woke up. They're being very careful with her."

"That's good," Jonathan said. A clatter on the steps alerted him to the arrival of the EMTs. They pushed the stretcher ahead of them, a medical supply bag sitting on top. He knew one of them. The younger of the two, Darrin Rogers, had a sister in the Haven, married to a bondmate. They shared a nod on the way past. At least he would know how to deal with a protective Fael.

This bothers you, Cateera said. She was curled in front of the fire, grooming her paws.

Of course, it bothers me, he thought back. *This isn't the first time I've been in a situation with an abused child.*

Yes, but Alanna found this one, and that bothers you.

He snapped a glance at Alanna. She was still quiet on the couch, wrapped up in his jacket. She was so pale she looked like a ghost with all that dark hair snarled around her face. Those feet were going to need some attention. He'd make sure Darrin looked at them before the ambulance left. And he was beginning to worry about shock. He'd expected tears and hadn't seen them.

"She doesn't seem like the type of person who's seen this before. So, yes, it bothers me. What did you do with the dog, by the way?"

Cateera indicated her disdain with a flick of her tail. Standing up, she performed one of the spine-distorting stretches that always made him wince, and padded over to sit by Alanna. *He was hardly worth bothering with. I caught him and put him in his kennel. His bark was very annoying.*

Jonathan couldn't help the smile. Crossing to the small kitchen, he opened the refrigerator. The contents disgusted him. Bottles of cheap beer stood beside cheery containers of chocolate milk. A stained container of Chinese food had leaked down onto the shelf below, leaving a dark sticky-looking puddle. Plastic tubs contained odd-looking leftovers. There was no telling how long some of them had been there. Digging around, he managed to locate a couple of bottles of water.

A quick search in a cabinet revealed a large bowl. He filled it with water from the sink and took all of it over to the couch. He put the bowl in front of Cateera, caressing her ears for a second before returning to Alanna. Opening a bottle of water, he handed it to her.

"Drink. You're probably dehydrated from the run," he said.

She drank obediently, a small sip. Her eyes closed in pleasure, and then she was taking long gulps from the bottle, almost draining it dry. He opened the second and took a long pull of his own.

"Those had better not be from the refrigerator," the sheriff said. "I don't need you tainting my crime scene."

"I'll add it to my statement," Jonathan said easily.

"How is she?" Alanna asked.

The sheriff pushed back his hat. "Bruised, she must have fought some. I think you know she's been violated."

Alanna nodded. A tinge of something dark and painful crossed her expression before it smoothed out again.

Jekk pushed past the sheriff, crossing to his bondmate. She leaned forward to hug him, put pressure on her feet, and cried out. Jekk immediately lay down and began to lick the bloody streaks on her legs. She hissed in a breath and pulled her legs out of reach.

"Let him," Jonathan said. "He can help speed up the healing."

Gritting her teeth, Alanna nodded. She clenched her fingers in Jonathan's jacket when Jekk resumed licking.

"The girl is Amber Leigh Jones," the sheriff told them. "She went missing this afternoon from the motel playground. Her parents have been notified and they're meeting us at the hospital. Before I head over there, I have a few questions."

"All right," Alanna said. She hissed when Jekk began cleaning a particularly deep gash on the sole of her left foot. Jonathan sympathized. He knew how rough a Fael's tongue could feel.

Unzipping his jacket, Jacobs settled on the couch. Jonathan moved to where he could see both down the hallway and out the front door. The EMTs were loading the little girl on the stretcher. Outside, the deputy in charge of Samuelson was by the cruiser, talking on his radio. They needed to get the suspect out of here before they wheeled the girl out. There was no reason she needed to even catch a glimpse of him again.

"We can start with your name," the sheriff said. He took off his hat and laid it on the arm of the sofa. He gave Alanna a smile guaranteed to charm. The man might be in his fifties but that only meant he'd had more time to hone his skill.

"Alanna McLean," she answered. "I live in New DC. I can give you my information if you need it."

"All right, Ms. McLean. I'm going to ask you a few questions."

Jonathan crossed his arms over his chest. She was handling herself well, but he was still worried about delayed shock. He kept expecting her to break down. The fact that she hadn't yet concerned him. Maybe she wasn't that kind of person. Or maybe she was holding it in. If it was the latter, the sooner she let it out, the better.

"Is that all right?" Jacobs asked.

Alanna gave a quick nod, following it up with a quiet yes.

"Good. Now, we'll get your official statement down later. Right now, I just want you to take me through what happened when you got here."

"The dog started barking," she said softly. "We were in the woods and the dog must have heard us. He started barking and the man opened the door to look outside."

"Peter Samuelson," Jonathan inserted.

She gave him a grateful smile. "The dog got out. Cateera raced after it." Restlessly, she reached for Jekk. He stopped licking her left foot to lay his chin on her knee so she could scratch the soft fur between his ears.

"What happened then?" the sheriff prompted.

"I...I could hear her screaming. I'd been hearing it and I had to find her to get it to stop. I had to get into the house. Jekk knocked him over so I could get in. The door to the room was locked but Jekk broke down the door." She looked squarely at the sheriff. "Did you see the video camera and the way the room is set up?"

"I did," he said softly. "I'm sorry that you did, Ms. McLean."

"I want everything done right. I know I broke in and I damaged his property. I'll accept any charges you have to make against me. I'm aware of what I should and shouldn't be telling you. But he's a monster," she told him. Her voice was fierce. "I don't want anyone making mistakes, mislabeling evidence, or otherwise screwing things up. I want this man to be put away for a long time."

The sheriff took her words in stride. "So do I, ma'am."

"I don't want a plea deal made."

"I can't control that," the sheriff said. "That's up to the District Attorney."

The hand restlessly petting Jekk stopped. "No plea deal. If it even looks like there's a plea deal in the works, you call me. I know some people that will put an end to that."

I like her, Cateera said. *She will make you a good mate.*

"Whoa, back up a second," Jonathan thought tightly along their connection. Cateera's laughter filled his head. "I'm glad you can find humor here."

She continued to laugh, the oddly accented roughness of it making him smile. His Fael had a way of defusing his tension. He would never have thought it possible that anything could make a situation like this better, but she did it consistently. When they were working on a case, searching for a killer, she could draw him back, ground him in reality. Sometimes he thought it was the only thing that kept him from going insane.

"And I am considering her Fael for my mate," Cateera continued. *"It is possible that I find him acceptable."*

The urge to sit down was sudden and sharp. He was saved an answer by the rattle of the stretcher coming down the hallway. Amber Leigh was curled up, her arms around the stuffed bear she'd been holding when they found her. The blood on the swelling curve of her bottom lip was the most colorful thing about her. It hurt his heart to see innocence broken like that.

There was a commotion outside. Jonathan followed the EMTs out the door to see a caravan of vehicles pulling up. Two more local cruisers, and a couple of state vehicles. Another ambulance. And behind them, a local news truck. Cateera had followed him out, and he felt that peculiar twisting in his head that marked her shift to invisibility. The lone deputy immediately started for the news truck, one hand held up.

"Sheriff," Jonathan said, poking his head back in the door. "The circus is here."

Jacobs hurried down the steps. His voice bellowed, cutting through the commotion. Order began to prevail over chaos as his deputies moved to contain the news crew, to maintain a perimeter around the house so no enterprising reporter could sneak in the back. Obviously alerted by the sheriff, the second ambulance crew began to move toward the house. He knew they needed to get Alanna out of the house to protect the crime scene. Even as he thought it, a forensics truck drove around the news people to pull up behind a cruiser.

"Is there another victim in there?" an EMT asked him, pausing on the steps as the second deputy stepped out of the house. Jonathan realized he'd forgotten Voight was still in the house.

"She's not a victim," Jonathan said, "But she needs her feet looked at."

"Will do," the EMT said good-naturedly. Carrying the medical bag, he and his partner hurried inside.

Following them in, Jonathan saw Jekk bristle, his lips peeling back from sharp incisors. The EMTs froze so fast, he almost bumped into them. Before anyone could say anything, though, Alanna gently nudged Jekk to the side. The low whine in his chest was distressed, but he took a step back. The dark-tipped ears twitched with irritation and his ruff remained full, but the teeth disappeared.

"Jekk won't hurt you," Alanna said. She looked at Jonathan. "I feel like I keep having to say that."

"Uh, can you ask him to go outside?" the dark-haired one asked.

"No, I can't," Alanna snapped. Leaning heavily on the arm of the couch, she forced herself to her feet. The look of pain on her face had Jonathan pushing past the medics. When her knees crumpled, he caught her, lifting her into his arms.

"Put me down," she yelled, shoving at his shoulder with one hand. "I don't need you to be carting me around."

There it was, he thought. The temper, the reaction. Something other than the unruffled cool he'd been seeing so far. "No chance, sweetheart," he told her with a smile. He looked at the EMTs still lingering at the door, still watching Jekk cautiously. "I'll carry her out to the ambulance. You can look at her feet there."

"I'm not your sweetheart," she told him. She shoved his shoulder again, trying to wriggle free.

"Nope," he agreed, following the two relieved EMTs. "But Cateera thinks you should be."

Enjoying the shock on her face, he dropped his mouth to hers. He knew the second he did it that it was a very bad idea. He also knew that he'd tasted her before. The dream of her kiss hadn't been a dream. Her small squeak of surprise turned into a sigh of pleasure and the sound nearly undid him. She tasted like every forbidden night time yearning he'd ever had, seductive and dangerous. The hand that had been pushing at him relaxed and slid into his hair. He forgot how to walk and just stood there and kissed her.

There was a very sharp tap on his shoulder. Breaking the kiss, he threw what he knew was a thoroughly pissed-off look over his shoulder. The petite woman standing there was dressed in a white Tyvek suit, booties, and gloves. She carried a metal case that probably weighed about as much as she did, and she was glaring at him.

"You're in my crime scene. Get out," she told him.

"Yes, ma'am," he answered. Because really, what else was there to say? As he slipped past her, still easily carrying Alanna, he saw that her eyes had already moved past them. She was studying the room now, intense concentration on her face.

"Why did you kiss me?" Alanna asked as he carried her down the steps. Her breath left a tracing of ice crystals in the air.

"It seemed like a good idea," he answered.

"Don't do it again," she told him.

He angled them away from the news crew that was shooting footage even as the police forced them back into the van. That was all they needed—their faces plastered across the early morning news. "Why not?"

"Because I don't like you," she said.

Jonathan tried very hard not to smile. She might not like him, but she'd kissed him back with the same intensity he'd felt. And her fingers were still stroking the fine hair at the nape of his neck. It was making him insane with want. He intended to kiss her again, the sooner the better. Her soft curves snuggled against him. The silky skin of her legs draped over his arms had him imagining what it would be like to press her lush body into the mattress and have those legs wrap around him. Had him aching to hear that soft, needy whimper again. He was going to get her into his bed. Even if it was a very bad idea.

Depositing her on the edge of the ambulance's open back, Jonathan was pleased to see that some color had returned to her cheeks. But it was still too cold out, and she began to shiver again with her legs exposed to the air. One of the medics produced a space blanket and wrapped it around her. She smiled at him gratefully.

"Let's take a look at your feet," he said, crouching down to peer at the lacerated soles.

When the second EMT aimed a light, Jonathan saw just how bad it was. Jekk had cleaned away much of the dirt and dried blood, but that just made it easier to see the jagged cuts and tears, places where the skin had been torn away in raw open wounds. The dark tip of a twig protruded from one instep. There was no telling how long it was, or what it had torn on the way in.

"We're going to have to take you to the hospital," the EMT said.

"No," Alanna said, shaking her head fiercely. Jekk responded to her distress by edging closer, brushing up against the medic. The man jerked away in surprise, and then when Jekk didn't threaten him, cautiously extended a hand. Realizing it was gloved, he peeled the latex off and lightly touched the fur along Jekk's flank.

"He's soft," he said wonderingly.

Jekk's head whipped around so quickly that the medic fell back onto his butt.

"He likes to be scratched under his ears, like this," Alanna said, demonstrating. The medic reached out and cautiously sank his fingers into the thick fur. Jekk responded with a rumbling purr that brought a wide smile to the man's face.

"He says thank you, but a little to the left," Alanna told him. When he obliged, Jekk's purr deepened.

"You still need to get to the hospital. Your feet need more attention than we can give you here. What did you do, go running through the woods?"

"Yes," Alanna said. "Jekk and I heard Amber Leigh crying, and we came looking for her."

Disapproval drove Jonathan a step forward. It was bad enough that Jekk had remained visible, even though that could be put down to his inexperience at dealing with humans. Hopefully, the camera crew hadn't gotten any decent shots of him. For Alanna to be openly discussing her flight through the woods to find the lost girl was dangerous. Word would get around and the efforts to capture Faelinn would ramp up again.

No, Cateera said. *Do not stop her. We want humans to know. We are tired of being protected. If they know what we can do, they will value us, and protect us.*

"If they know what you can do, they'll capture you and study you like lab rats."

Perhaps, because some humans can be as cruel and evil as a Kellian. But we believe that the majority will value our abilities and see that we are given the rights of sentient beings. We do not wish to hide any longer.

Everything in him rebelled at the idea of making the Faelinn so vulnerable. Partly because he'd seen evil and knew what men could do. Mostly, it was personal. The thought of losing Cateera terrified him. She was so tightly bound up in his heart and soul that he knew he wouldn't be able to go on if something happened to her. He completely understood why one bondmate couldn't survive without the other.

I do not wish to lose you, either, she said. *But we take those risks every time we work. Alanna saved a child. Those are the sorts of things that humanity needs to see as valuable in us. If they value us, they will protect us.*

He thought she was being wildly naïve. There was no guarantee they would be protected. Stolen and used, yes. Protected, not necessarily.

Sharing the knowledge of what Alanna and Jekk could do just wasn't smart. Short of slapping a hand over Alanna's mouth, though, he couldn't do a damn thing about it.

"I'm not going to the hospital. Dr. Ingraham can stitch me up," Alanna said.

Jonathan felt a stab of relief that she hadn't revealed Bethany's Gift. At least the woman had some sense.

"Then at least let us clean your feet up, do what we can."

Jonathan watched the expressions flitting across her face. That top-heavy mouth tightened, and he was sure she was going to refuse. She surprised him when she nodded.

"Good. Let's get you into the ambulance. It will be warmer for you in there."

Before the EMT could do anything, Jonathan hopped up into the ambulance, scooped Alanna up, and deposited her on the stretcher inside.

"Would you stop carting me around?" she said.

He ignored the question. "I'm going to check with the sheriff. I'll be back for you in a little while."

"I want to have a look at your injuries, too," the EMT said, nodding at the blood on Jonathan's shirt.

Jonathan waved him off. "I'll be fine." He glanced at Alanna. "Don't go anywhere."

He heard her mutter a very unflattering name under her breath as he jumped to the ground. Since he took a perverse sort of pleasure out of annoying her, he smiled. He'd been right when he met her; she was trouble. It didn't look like that was going to change in the future. But what she'd done tonight might just make up for it.

Hot cocoa steamed up into her face. Alanna breathed in the rich scent before lifting the Styrofoam cup to her lips. It was still too hot to drink, so she blew on it for a moment before taking a cautious sip. It burned her tongue but felt wonderful going down. She didn't know where it had come from. One of the deputies had shown up at the ambulance with it.

She was grateful enough that she was considering naming her firstborn after him.

Drowsing at her feet, his back making a nice footstool, Jekk snored lightly. He had the right idea. She was so tired she felt like she could fall asleep sitting up.

Beneath gauze wrappings, her feet throbbed painfully. The EMTs had been as gentle as they could, but they'd hurt her. They'd cleaned rocks and grit from the bloody mess of her feet. Apparently, there was a sliver of wood that was going to have to be removed. There was going to be Novocain involved. She would insist on it. She and Bethany were going to be best friends before this was all over.

The ambulance with Amber Leigh had left a little while ago. Mark had arrived, had nodded at her from across the lawn, and then gone to find the sheriff and Jonathan. So, she sat, feeling tired, annoyed, and a little emotional. Too much. The whole night had been too much. Dragged through the woods by a compulsion she couldn't control, finding a little girl too late to save her from a monster, kicking the crap out of the same monster. And yes, she had broken a toe and wasn't going to be able to wear heels for a while. And then Jonathan had kissed her. And that was a whole other issue.

"Where'd you get the coffee?"

The bestower of the kiss sat down next to her on the edge of the ambulance. His shoulder brushed hers, and if she'd had room, she would have scooted away. "It's not coffee, it's cocoa. A very nice deputy gave it to me."

"Care to share?"

"No," she said, and took a deep swallow. And tried very hard not to show that it was still too hot.

"You did a good thing tonight, Alanna."

His voice, that velvety deep voice that would be perfectly suited for reading romance novels for audiobook sales, was actually complimenting her. And for some reason, some stupid reason, it broke her down.

"I was too late," she said through a choking wave of grief.

"What do you mean you were too late?"

"I should have gotten there sooner, before he—before. I was too late." The tears were hot, a rush of them down cheeks still cold in the night air.

Gentle hands caught her legs, still wrapped in the space blanket, and swung them over his so that he could draw her into his lap. The arms that circled her provided warmth and comfort, and a haven where she could give in to the emotion she'd tried so hard to lock away. Great shaking sobs were muffled against the soft material of his sweatshirt, her face pressed into the curve where his shoulder met his neck. A distressed crooning and the press of a cold nose against her cheek had her blindly reaching out to wrap one arm around Jekk's neck. Her distress had woken him. His broad paws rested behind her, his bulk warm against her back.

"You weren't too late," Jonathan told her, stroking the tangled mess of her hair. "You found her when no one else could."

"But he hurt her," she managed to get out between teary gasps.

"But she's alive," he countered. "She was taken this afternoon, Alanna. Chances are she was molested before you began to track her. You can't blame yourself for that."

The words bounced off her misery. All she could see was the smear of blood on those pale thighs. She should have run faster, gotten there sooner. Jekk whimpered in distress, echoing her emotions. He licked the tears from her cheeks.

"Listen to me," Jonathan said. "Has anyone told you what my Gift is?"

She stirred enough to turn her head and answer him. "You find killers."

He nodded and tipped her head up so that she had to look at him. His fingers were gentle on her skin. "I have no chance to find the victims. My Gift won't work until they're already dead. No matter how fast I find the killer, the victims are always dead."

"But—"

"No," he said. His eyes were shaded with fatigue, dark with memory. "I can only hope that by finding the killer fast enough, there won't be any more victims. So finding your little girl alive is a Gift I can only wish for, no matter what happened before you got there."

A hot, scratchy tongue moved to lick the tears from her other cheek. Jekk's whiskers tickled her skin.

"Hey, big guy, get your fur out of my face," Jonathan said, shoving at the Fael, whose head was blocking his.

An unexpected giggle turned into a hiccup. The tears began to slacken, the sobs easing in her chest. Jekk dropped back to the ground but stayed close enough so that she could keep contact. Closing her eyes, she laid her head on Jonathan's shoulder. A stray thought skittered through her brain as she drifted to sleep.

He made her feel safe.

Chapter Ten

S omething tickled her face. Grunting, Alanna buried her face in her pillow. The tickling moved to her ear. Smacking blindly, her hand collided with something solid. She groped at it, outlining a nose, the line of a jaw. Bristly whiskers. Sleep fell away in ragged streamers, and she opened one cautious eye to stare into a pair of amber ones.

Wake up, Jekk said. *The sheriff will be here soon.*

She contemplated pulling the covers over her head. And then sat right up and stared at him in shock.

"You're blue," she said aloud. Not just blue, but a lovely turquoise color that echoed Cateera's eyes.

He caught the thought and nodded. *Her eyes are beautiful.*

Alanna wiggled around until she was comfortable. The pillows cushioned her back against the headboard, the blankets a cozy haven of warmth. She scooped her hair out of her face and found a twig.

"I didn't know you could change color. I thought you could just be invisible."

I was never allowed to do it when I was a slave to the Kellian. The collar kept me from changing. Do you like the way I look now?

Understanding that the answer was of great importance, she studied him carefully. The tips of his ears, tail and whiskers were still black. Everywhere else, turquoise fur glistened in the light. Darker hints of stripes ran along his back and sides, and the fur of his chin and throat was a paler shade. He was a fanciful dream.

"I think you look amazing," she told him truthfully. "I thought you were beautiful before, too."

Choose, then, he told her.

Alanna shook her head. "No. You choose what you like. You're free now. You can change every five minutes if that's what you want, and I'll love you no matter what."

Her bondmate paced to the floor-length mirror in the corner, peering at himself carefully in the glass. A shimmer flowed over him. She felt it as a tickle in the back of her mind. He stood now as he had when she'd first seen him. But no, that wasn't quite right. He'd been a dusty tan before. Now Jekk's fur held the richness of sunlight through honey. There was still the hint of stripes, still the paler fur beneath his chin, still the dark tips of ears and tail, but the fur glistened with light and health.

This then, he said. *This is me.*

"You're perfect," she said with a smile. She swung her legs out of bed, her feet hitting the floor before she could think about how much it might hurt. Instead of pain, the plush carpet tickled her soles.

The doctor healed you while you slept.

"I don't remember," Alanna said. She peered at her feet and gave her toes an experimental wiggle. Even her broken toe was fixed.

Mark and Jonathan brought you home. I rode in the back with Cateera. He came and sat in front of her. *Are you well now?*

"Yes," she said. Alanna caught a glimpse of herself in the mirror and stared in horror. Her hair was full of dirt and pieces of tree. It felt matted and greasy, and she wore the same tank and shorts she'd worn for her race through the forest. They were filthy and they were going straight into the garbage. "I need a shower."

The sheriff is here, Jekk said. He paused a moment and then continued. *He's going to talk to Jonathan and Cateera first.*

"All right, but I still need a shower," she said, heading to the bathroom.

Alanna?

She stopped and looked at him curiously. He rarely used her name. "Yes?"

We have a good Gift, don't we?

It was a plea for reassurance. She dropped to her knees and circled his furry neck with her arms. He smelled of sunshine and forest. "We have an amazing Gift."

One furry arm held her tightly. *That's good then.*

Alanna was still smiling as hot water pounded the last of the aches and pains from her body. It took forever to get the twigs and leaves from her hair. She must have looked like a wild forest witch. It was mind-boggling that Jonathan had kissed her. She stopped in mid-lather. Filthy, bruised, bleeding, looking like hell, and he'd still kissed her. She supposed since he'd been filthy, bruised, and bleeding when she'd kissed him, it didn't matter.

Still, it irritated the hell out of her that not only had she liked it, but that she really wanted to do it again. And again. His dark toffee taste was addictive.

"Stupid, stupid, stupid," she said out loud. She finished her hair and attacked herself with a scrubby sponge soaked in jasmine-scented bath gel. Her skin tingled and she wondered how it would feel if it were Jonathan's hands smoothing the lather over her breasts and stomach.

"Stop it," she told herself fiercely. "He's a jerk. He's arrogant and obnoxious. You don't even like him."

Like has nothing to do with want, a tiny voice in her head chimed in. The same voice went on to point out that a jerk wouldn't have run alongside her, wouldn't have helped her over an electrified fence.

Wouldn't have shown the compassion she'd seen when they found Amber Leigh.

Squashing that little voice, Alanna raced through the rest of her shower. She toweled off with a brutal efficiency that left her skin glowing. There was no way she was going to allow that man to get under her skin even more than he was. Besides, she was leaving for home soon, and he wouldn't be bossing her around.

End of mental discussion.

Dressed in black slacks and a silky blouse patterned with swirls of purple, her hair braided into a coil at her nape, she felt like herself again. Jekk led her to Mark's office on the third floor and then abandoned her. He couldn't seem to get enough of the freedom to run. Stepping into the office, she expected to see the sheriff, but Mark was alone. A desk roughly the size of the *Titanic* occupied a small section of the massive room. Seated behind it, looking like the captain of industry that he was, Mark smiled. Phone to his ear, he waved her to a seat in the casual grouping of sofa and chairs before a massive fieldstone fireplace. Instead, Alanna browsed the shelves the length of one wall, impressed with the wide variety of books. Most of them showed wear in the spines. They were obviously not there for decoration. Interspersed amongst the novels and books on nearly every subject under the sun were quirky pieces of art, and even quirkier pieces of clutter. A malformed bowl graced a shelf, little lumps of clay twisted into odd designs stuck to its sides.

"Daphne made that for me," Mark said from behind her. "I think she was in second grade at the time."

"It reminds me of something I did for my mother when I was about the same age," Alanna said with a laugh. "She keeps it on a shelf too."

Mark laughed. "I'm sure she loves it, too."

Alanna smiled and noticed the coffee service on the low table in front of the sofa. She would swear it hadn't been there when she came in. The house Brownies were not only efficient but magickally silent. Perhaps she could investigate employing one when she got home.

"The sheriff was delayed," Mark told her. "He's still with Jonathan. That will give us time to talk."

The leather sofa was soft, and Alanna sank into it with a sigh. When Mark handed her the mug of coffee, she finally began to feel human. Sipping at the black liquid, she decided it was quite possibly the best coffee she'd ever had.

"I don't suppose one of your Brownies would like to move to New DC," she said.

Mark laughed. "You can ask, but they're a clan. Usually they prefer to stick together unless there's marriage involved. The men will move to another clan once they're married, but rarely until then."

"And the women don't leave?" Alanna asked.

"Only if there's a conflict," Mark said. "Or occasionally a headstrong young woman will want to make her own way, start her own clan. They're highly matriarchal."

Alanna filed all that away. She'd add it to her notes later. She never knew when information like that would come in handy.

"You've had quite an eventful stay," Mark said.

"Well, that's an understatement," Alanna answered drily. "Thanks for bringing me back last night."

"My pleasure," he said. He looked at her keenly over the top of his mug. The faint lines beside his eyes deepened a little. "How do you feel?"

"Still a little confused. What happened to me?"

"The blood bond between you and Jekk deepened enough that your Awakening was triggered. There was probably a catalyst that started it all."

"The barrette," Alanna said. "She lost her barrette on the sidewalk yesterday and I found it. It fell out of my pocket in the bedroom and when I picked it up, I started having flashes of her. All I knew was that I had to find her."

"It shouldn't be as powerful next time," Mark said. "The Awakening is beyond our control. We must follow it to its conclusion, like you did. You'll learn to control your Gift and use it when you want."

"I don't ever want to experience that again," Alanna said. "I don't like not being able to control what's happening to me."

"I understand," Mark said. "My Awakening involved the stock market. It was still in its infancy when the Veil came and destroyed functioning society. After I bonded with Berren, I was driven to reform it, to buy and sell until I made my first million."

Alanna choked on her coffee. She accepted the napkin Mark handed her, glad that the coffee stain blended with the purple swirls on her blouse. "That's a handy Gift to have."

"It is," he agreed. "I've used it over the years to expand the Haven, to make sure we all have what we need. Shellie helps. Her Gift is precognition, not only the visions of the future, but whether the outcomes of some acts will be positive or negative. She can tell me if there's going to be a good day on the market or not. I use that to enhance my own Gift."

"And here I am running through the woods in the middle of the night," Alanna said drily.

"Here you are, finding lost children," he said gently. "I know you didn't choose to be bonded, Alanna. As I've said before, it's not the way we do things. Still, I'd be hypocritical if I said that I'm upset about it. Shellie felt so strongly that your visit would be a positive one, and I think this is part of it." He leaned forwards, elbows resting on his knees, hands dangling loosely between. "If you choose to use your Gift, you can be a very visible advocate for the good the Faelinn can do. I'm hopeful that will lead to positive changes for us all. The Faelinn—all of us—need to be protected."

"That's a very big burden," she said. Crossing one elegant leg, Alanna strove to appear cool and unshaken. "You asked me to use my novel as a platform for your cause. Now you're asking me to stick my own neck out, to be public with this new talent."

"But not alone," he said.

"Yes, alone," she answered hotly. "You told me Bethany hides her Gift. I understand that revealing it would bring an endless pilgrimage of people wanting to be healed to her door. Don't you think that will happen to me? How many people can I expect to see every morning, begging me to find their lost child? How could I look into their eyes and turn them down?"

"You're right, of course," he said. "It's well past time for us to take a more active role in the world, but it's unfair of me to ask you to be the first. It was a lot clearer when you were just a writer we wanted to use. Now you're one of us and stand to win or lose the same things we do."

"Shellie is against revealing our Gifts to the world."

He scrubbed his face with his hands, dragging them back through his dark hair. "I know. It's the one thing we differ on. It's in her nature to want to protect us as much as she can. I want to use our Gifts to provide a reason for laws to protect us. It's a topic we both approach cautiously."

Restless, Alanna stood. The window drew her. His office faced away from the Veil, looking out over plush lawn. The tops of trees disappeared down the slope to provide a dizzying view of the valley. Houses were dotted here and there, what looked to be a small town peeking in and out of the swells and hollows of land. It was peaceful, bucolic. From here she could pretend that the big bad world was far away.

It wasn't, though. It was around the corner and through the woods, to a pedophile's house we go.

"I need time to adjust," she said.

"Of course," he said. He came to stand next to her. "All that you see here is the Haven. That town is ours."

"It's not Hunter's Forge?"

"No, that's in the other direction. Although we own a good portion of that, too. We have almost everything we need here and some of us might never want to go anywhere else. But we're part of a larger community. Perhaps it's time we took another step and became part of the world. We all need time to adjust."

"Shellie told you that I'm not staying here, didn't she?"

"Yes," he said. "It won't be easy for you or Jekk. Faelinn aren't pack animals, but they do like to be with their own kind. I'll do what I can to help you."

"Thank you." She turned to look at him. He wore what she'd come to see as his normal outfit, a pair of slacks and a button-down shirt with the sleeves rolled up. He had a casual air about him that was disarming. You would never think he was one of the most influential men in the world until you looked into his eyes. They were intense, focused, and burned with an inner drive. He carried a heavy load of responsibility, but only those eyes gave it away.

"It will be baby steps, Mark," she told him. "And I'll count on you to support me in every one of them. I won't throw myself out there alone."

"You have my word."

"The novel comes first," she told him. "My agent has already sold it, so I have contractual obligations. After that, we'll see what happens."

"That's all I can ask," he said. Then he smiled, and she realized how easily he'd manipulated her. Oddly, she couldn't feel anything but admiration.

The sheriff is ready, Jekk told her.

"Thanks," she thought at him. "Are you enjoying the sun?"

I was, but I think he wants to see us both, Jekk said. *We're a team.*

Alanna was still smiling at that when Sheriff Jacobs knocked and entered.

Jekk followed him in, then pushed the door closed with a paw. He greeted Mark with a meow, nodding to him before moving to Alanna's side. The Fael poured a bowl of milk from a jug on the table. The specially designed handle on the bowl allowed him to hold it and drink. A Fael's muzzle made it nearly impossible for him to drink easily from a human cup.

"Thanks for seeing me, Ms. McLean," Jacobs said as he settled himself.

"I imagine you need an official statement," she said.

"Yes, I do." He accepted the mug of coffee Mark handed him with a grateful smile. "And you probably have questions for me."

"I do," Alanna said, taking her spot on the couch. Her hand sought Jekk's back, the contact settling her nerves.

The sheriff took out a digital recorder, turned it on, and placed it on the table next to the silver coffee service. "I hope it won't bother you that I'm recording this," he said.

"Not at all," Alanna said. She waited while he recorded the official data, who was present, time and date of interview. "Do I need a lawyer present, Sheriff Jacobs?"

"You're not under suspicion for anything, Ms. McLean, but if it makes you feel more comfortable, I believe Mark is capable of acting as your council."

"What Jacobs is trying to tell you is that among other things, I have a law degree," Mark said. At her look of disbelief, he grinned. "Living a long life gives you a lot of time to explore your interests, Alanna. I passed the bar exam in the Seventies, and if you want, I'll watch out for your interests."

"Well then, I think I'm ready for your questions, Sheriff," she said with a smile.

"Good," he said. He flipped open a notebook, licked the tip of a pencil, and jotted a few notes. "Never lost the habit of taking notes," he explained. "I'm just old-fashioned. Now, I understand that you're bonded to Jekk, here, and that it happened recently. Take me through what happened yesterday."

Beginning with seeing the family in the bakery, and finding Amber Leigh's barrette on the sidewalk, Alanna recounted everything that she remembered. Jekk helped, providing details she'd either forgotten, or hadn't noticed. The sheriff let her go through it once, and then asked her to repeat it. This time, he asked questions along the way, had her explain a point here and there. She'd been interviewed many times, and he was among the best. He drew more from her admittedly dim memory of the events than she thought she'd remembered. So much was bound up in the hazy compulsion to "find" that it had many aspects of a dream. He questioned her over and over about how they'd gained entrance to the house, how Samuelson had come to be injured. She understood that a decent defense attorney could turn her invasion of the house into unlawful entry. It was only her word that she'd known the girl was there, screaming. Hers and Jekk's.

Finally, the sheriff snapped the notebook closed. "Thank you, Ms. McLean. I appreciate your help. I'll have this interview transcribed. Be warned that you'll probably be called upon to testify when this goes to trial, but I think that's all I need for now."

"Testifying will be no problem, believe me," she said. "Now please tell me how she is?"

Jacobs rubbed a hand over his head. "About as good as you can expect, considering. The physical damage she can recover from, but psychologically she'll have a hard road. With any luck, she'll tuck it all away in the back of her mind and forget it ever happened."

"I hope not," Alanna said. "I would think it's best to deal with it now rather than wait for it to explode like a time bomb sometime in the future."

"Maybe you're right." He considered. "There are other things that I'm going to trust you to keep to yourself. The Crime Scene Unit found dozens of homemade DVDs, and at least at first glance, it looks like they were shot in the same room you found Amber Leigh. I recognized one of the girls. I'll be going to speak to her parents when I leave here. I'm not looking forward to it."

"How?" Alanna demanded. "How did he get access to girls without someone coming forward?"

"Intimidation, most likely," Jacobs said. "Fear. Samuelson hasn't lived here long, less than a year, but he's been a busy boy. He teaches language arts out at the high school. In his evenings, it seems he volunteers as a reading tutor for the elementary kids needing help. Weekends he volunteers at the library, in the children's section. He also teaches children's Sunday School at United Baptist."

Alanna didn't know what to say. Jekk, however, had plenty, and proceeded to snarl his desire to chase the man down and slowly torture him.

Jacobs looked at him in surprise. "I don't understand a word you just said, Jekk, but I have a feeling if I did, I'd agree with every one of them."

"The man is a monster," Alanna said.

"What else?" Mark prompted. "There's more, isn't there?"

"Yes, I'm afraid so," the sheriff said. He poured himself another cup of coffee and then sat there, staring at it. "At first glance, it looks like he may have been uploading the videos to the Internet. We found two computers in his house, both password protected, but it was easy enough to get past that. There were files and files of downloaded kiddie porn, and the e-unit is looking at his Internet records now. We're all hoping to use what they find to track down more of his group of pervert friends."

Alanna felt sick. "Did he film Amber Leigh?"

"Yes," Jacobs said gently. "But we haven't found any evidence he got that out online."

"Yet," Mark said.

Jacobs nodded in agreement. "You and Jekk have helped us a great deal, Ms. McLean. There's no telling how many other girls he would have hurt if we hadn't caught him now."

That helped a little. The wish that she'd found Amber Leigh sooner, that she could have gotten to her before her innocence was stolen away, was still a heavy weight in her heart. But his words did help. She just wished she could get the image of blood on that skinny white thigh out of her head.

"Well," Jacobs said, standing up. "I'd better get on to my next stop, as awful as that's going to be. Someone from the station will call when the written statement is ready. If you could come down and sign that, I'd appreciate it."

The sheriff's cell phone beeped. Unclipping it from his belt, he took the call. The skin around his eyes tightened. Lips thinned down to a tight line and his voice held barely contained fury. He snapped the phone closed. "Samuelson is dead," he told them. "I don't know how yet. Mark, I'll talk to you soon."

"Let me know how we can help," Mark said.

Jacobs nodded sharply and extended a hand to Alanna. "Take care of yourself, Ms. McLean. I'm sorry you had to see what you did, but I'm really glad that you found her."

"Me, too," she said.

The sheriff extended a hand to Jekk, and she felt a quick ripple of surprise pass through her mind. The Fael placed a big paw in his hand. "Take care of yourself, Jekk."

The Fael coughed agreement, nodding once to be sure the sheriff understood.

The phone was pressed to Jacobs's ear again before he left the room.

"I don't know whether to be happy he's dead, or mad because he won't be punished," Alanna said.

Mark looked troubled. "Jacobs will find out what happened. You must have a terrible opinion of this area now," Mark said.

Alanna picked up her mug, took a drink of the almost cold coffee, and put it back down on the table. "Bad things can happen anywhere."

I'm glad he's dead, Jekk said. He paused. *What's a game of tag?*

"Why?"

The Faelinn are playing tag in the woods and want me to play. I don't know how.

Opening her memories to him, Alanna showed him images of her childhood, and the endless games of tag she'd played in the schoolyard and in the great field behind her house. She showed him the laughter, the triumph of avoiding becoming "It," and how much fun it was to chase down someone to tag them.

Jekk purred approval. *I think I'll tag Cateera and make her "It".* With a bound, he was gone down the hall.

Alanna was still laughing when she headed back to her room and the laptop that waited.

～

The body was on the bunk. Samuelson had died there, his arms shielding his face. His legs were tucked tight to his chest. The smell of evacuated bowel was stomach-turning. No matter how often he smelled death, Jonathan had never gotten used to it. When Jacobs called, Jonathan headed straight for the jail. He'd pulled into the lot just behind the sheriff.

"Who was back here?" Jacobs said. He squatted at the side of the bunk, hands dangling between his knees.

151

Deputy Voight answered. "No one until I came back here with his lunch. Cell was still locked. I had to unlock it to get in to see if he was still alive. Couldn't find a pulse, so I called you right away. Called for an ambulance too. Funny thing, they moved him to give him CPR, shocked the hell out of him. Soon as they stopped trying, his body curled right back up again. Creepiest damn thing I ever saw."

Jacobs grunted. "Forensic squad? ME?"

"They'll be about an hour," Voight said. "Domestic call with a fatality. Once they finish, they'll head here."

Hands on his knees, the sheriff pushed himself to his feet. "Get the pictures going, Voight. I want digital for every inch of this cell. Make sure you get plenty on the lock as well. If there's anything to be found, I want to see it. The security footage will be secured for review." He scratched his scalp with blunt fingers. "Shit. The paperwork on this is going to be a nightmare."

"No sympathy for the victim?" Jonathan asked from where he leaned against the wall outside the cell.

"Shit no, not after what he did to those kids." Jacobs stared back into the cell. "If it had been me, he'd have suffered a long time before dying. Still, I don't see any obvious marks. Maybe he had a stroke or a heart attack."

Fear, Cateera said. Her whiskers bristled as she sniffed the air. *He reeks of it. I would say that he died of fright.*

Something cold trailed down Jonathan's spine. There was a low chuckle deep down inside his mind. It echoed before slowly fading away. He shuddered at the feeling. He passed on Cateera's observations to Jacobs. The sheriff cocked his head. He stared through the cell bars at the body folded tightly on the bunk.

"Fear, huh? The only thing he'd have to fear here is if I let in the parents of the children he abused. We'll have to wait and see what the ME says about cause of death."

"You'll let me know?"

"You bet," Jacobs said. "Fucking nightmare."

It was cold enough to see his breath condense as Jonathan walked across the parking lot. Cateera had the keys, deftly unlocked the door of the SUV, and had it started before he'd even reached it. The heat was ruffling her fur when he slid behind the wheel. Even with all that fur, she loved the warmth.

"Did you feel that back there?" he asked as he pulled out of the parking lot.

Only through you, she answered. *Whatever it is, it does not seem to touch me. But you have felt it before.*

"Yes." His knuckles were white on the steering wheel and he forced them to unclench. "I felt it on our last consult, and I felt it when we first got home."

An elegant head rubbed briefly against his shoulder.

"I don't know what it is, but it worries me, Cateera. It's almost a voice, almost laughter, but not quite either. And it scares the shit out of me."

You think it is involved with what happened in Carolina. It followed us?

He shrugged, stopped to let a delivery truck finish backing into the alley beside Hunter's Forge's biggest grocery store, and headed on toward the hospital. "Maybe, I don't know. Keep your eyes open, will you? The last thing we need is some spook taking a liking to us."

The sharp smell of antiseptic cleanser permeated the very walls of the local hospital. It was a smell Jonathan always associated with his recovery from the gunshot wound to his shoulder. It made him want to turn around and walk right back out. He dodged a laundry cart, stepped to the side to allow an orderly pushing a gurney to pass. Cateera moved silently, invisible to everyone. The alert excitement trembling in his mind was hers. New things to see, a child to visit. Not even the alien smells and the frightening pieces of medical equipment could deter her.

The nurse at the station glanced his way. She was cute, her dark hair tied back in a swinging tail. Cartoon mice decorated her scrubs and a stethoscope looped around her neck. Any other time he might have stopped, flirted a little. But he was here to see Amber Leigh, not to pick up a date for Friday night.

Besides, she is not your mate, Cateera said. *It will be good when it is the four of us. I have decided that Jekk will be my mate.*

Momentarily, Jonathan's brain stopped working. He wasn't sure which image he found the most disconcerting. Playing house with Alanna and the two Faelinn, or his Fael mated and no longer putting him first in her life. Reason kicked back in after a second. The first would never happen. The second he would deal with. It wasn't fair to keep Cateera from having a life and family of her own.

You are my family, she assured him. She pushed against his hand, rough tongue licking his fingers. *We will all be a family.*

"No, we won't," he told her silently. "Alanna is not my mate. You just need to get that into your head."

You just need to accept that she is, Cateera countered.

He wasn't in the mood to argue. Besides, there was a deputy stationed outside one of the rooms up ahead. Jacobs had told him that there'd been a problem with reporters so he'd put one of his men on guard duty while Amber Leigh was there. The deputy looked young enough to be in high school, a dusting of acne fresh on his cheeks, but his eyes were sharp when Jonathan stopped.

"Can I help you?"

"Jonathan Burke. Sheriff Jacobs said it would be okay for me to visit."

"Yeah, he called. Can I see your ID first?"

Jonathan handed him his driver's license, appreciating the caution. The name stitched above the pocket of the brown uniform shirt said Soames. The boy was cautious. He liked that.

"All right, Mr. Burke," Soames said, passing back the ID. "Her family is all in there."

"Thanks," Jonathan said. He knocked lightly, and then pushed the heavy door open. He'd always wondered why hospital room doors were so heavy. With the amount of traffic in and out of one he would have thought they'd be lighter.

Four pairs of eyes looked his way. Amber Leigh was sitting up in bed, golden hair down around her narrow shoulders. Her lip was swollen and puffy, but the violet bruises under her eyes had faded. She froze when she saw him. Her parents moved protectively. Her mother tightened her fingers around her daughter's while her father rose to his feet, moving forward to intercept him.

"Who are you?" Mr. Jones demanded.

"I'm Jonathan Burke, Chief of Security for the Haven," he said. "Sheriff Jacobs was supposed to let you know I'd be by."

"Oh, of course," he said. The man moved forward, hand extended. His grip was firm, the eyes that met Jonathan's a direct brown under a shock of pale hair. The logo of an expensive designer was stitched onto the navy sweater he wore, brown loafers peeked out beneath pressed khakis. The watch that winked on his wrist was one Jonathan recognized. There was wealth here.

"I'm Carl Jones, this is my wife, Becky."

"Hello, ma'am," Jonathan said, moving forward to shake the narrow hand that was offered. The woman was pretty in a petite, bird-like way, and her grip was pure Southern belle, a brief pressing of her fingers in his palm.

"Becky, please," she said. The soft blue eyes held a wealth of exhaustion and fear. "You were there last night. You helped find my daughter."

"I was there, yes," he agreed. He smiled at Amber Leigh. She regarded him gravely. He saw that her grip on her mother's hand was tight.

There was a sharp tug on his hand, and Jonathan looked down to see a tow-headed boy a year or so younger than his sister holding up a truck. "I'm Bobby, and this is my truck."

Jonathan knelt to inspect the toy. "Hi Bobby. That's a very fine truck. Do you think it might go with this one?" He pulled the dump truck out of the bag he held. He'd stopped by the gift shop before heading up to the room. Jacobs had filled him in, told him about the younger boy.

The boy's eyes grew wide and he grabbed the truck. "It's cool!"

"Say thank you, Bobby," his father said.

"Thank you," he said obediently, already working at the plastic holding it to the cardboard package. Carl took it from him and pulled it free. Bobby immediately took it over to the corner and began to play.

"That was nice of you," Becky said.

"I didn't want him to feel left out, since I got something for Amber Leigh," Jonathan said, and handed her the large pink bag he still held.

There was caution in the girl's eyes, and it hurt his heart to see it. Still, she took the bag, pulling out the tissue paper to look inside. Her breath hitched in. Carefully, she pulled out the stuffed toy. The Fael was hand-made by one of the Haven's bondmates. She had her own small business making the stuffed animals. This one was sky blue and silky soft.

"Look, Mommy, it's a Fael," Amber Leigh said reverently. She cuddled the toy close, her eyes closed.

"I thought you might like it," Jonathan said. "I was hoping you'd like this more." He gestured to where Cateera waited by the door. She shimmered into view. The fluorescent lights glowed on her fur, highlighted the lavender tips of her ears. There was a collectively indrawn breath in the room. He felt Cateera's satisfaction with the reaction and was amused when she moved with regal grace to the bed.

The little girl took one look at her and launched herself forward. Cateera purred as the little arms circled her neck. Blond hair mixed with soft fur, and he found himself wondering if he could capture the mixture in stained glass. He thought he might like to try. Bobby squealed, running forward, but his dad caught him and swung him up in his arms.

"Not right now, son," he said softly. "Wait a few minutes."

"It won't hurt her, will it?" Becky asked cautiously.

Jonathan forgave the woman her ignorance and thought that Mark might be right. It might be time to bring the Faelinn into the world, if only so that people wouldn't be afraid of them. Wouldn't ask if the gentle race would hurt an innocent.

"No, she won't hurt her. Children are very important to Faelinn. Cateera wanted to come to make sure that Amber Leigh is all right."

Bobby chose that moment to wiggle free. He dropped to the ground and wrapped his arms around Cateera's side. The Fael nuzzled him, tickling his face with her whiskers, and making him laugh. She needed a family of her own, kits of her own. He was glad she'd chosen her mate. Hopefully, a kit would come from it. There were so few of them born.

"Thank you," Carl said quietly. "We came to Hunter's Forge with the hopes of seeing some Faelinn. We didn't realize the Haven was so reclusive."

"We don't want to be a tourist attraction," Jonathan said, meeting the other man's eyes. "We don't want to put the Faelinn in danger."

"I've heard stories," Carl said. "I've heard of some instances of kidnapping. I understand why you'd want to keep them away from people."

Jonathan pushed a hand through his hair. Becky was sitting on the bed, stroking Cateera over and over. The rumbling purr was loud. Cateera was being adored and she loved every moment of it. "Not everyone," Jonathan said. "We don't want to keep them away from everyone."

"Listen, can I buy you a cup of coffee?"

"Sure," Jonathan answered. He had the feeling that Carl Jones had things to say, things he needed to say.

"You'll be okay here for a while?" he asked Cateera.

Of course, she said. She was holding Amber Leigh with one leg and grooming her hair with slow rasps of her tongue, much to the girl's delight. She was utterly content. He left her, feeling confident she was safe.

The hospital coffee was rumored to be terrible. That probably accounted for the long line at the Starbucks concession in the lobby. Finally, they settled into a corner of the cafeteria. The room held a mix of medical staff in a rainbow of scrubs, and patients' family members. The unifying expression on the faces of the latter was a mixture of irritation, exhaustion, and fear. Not even the calming blue paint and the tranquil mountain scenes framed on the walls helped. Jonathan tried to adjust his long frame to the uncomfortable plastic chair and finally gave up. The potted Ficus next to the table wilted over them as if eager to listen in.

"Thank you for finding my daughter," Carl said. His hands cradled the paper cup. His short nails were neatly manicured, a wide golden wedding band on his left hand.

"I was there, but I wasn't the one who actually found her," Jonathan said. He debated how much to tell the man. His own instincts told him to walk away, to protect the Faelinn and the Haven by keeping silent. Still, he remembered the happiness he'd felt from Cateera when the children had embraced her. She enjoyed contact with people. Perhaps Mark had it right. Maybe it was time to carefully make their way into the wider world.

"I'd love the opportunity to thank him, then," Carl said. "My children —" He closed his eyes a moment, letting out a slow breath. "My family is my world. I can't imagine what I would have done if Amber Leigh hadn't been found."

"Don't dwell on it," Jonathan advised. He didn't correct Jones about the gender of the person who'd found Amber Leigh. "You can't get caught up in the what ifs."

Carl leaned over the table, his voice dropping to a harsh whisper. "He touched my little girl. I want to rip into him with my bare hands, see him suffer every imaginable atrocity. How am I supposed to not get caught up in that?"

"I don't know," Jonathan admitted. "But maybe it will help to know that he's dead. He was found in his cell a few hours ago."

Carl sucked in a breath and then let it out sharply. "Who killed him? Did he suffer? I hope it hurt like hell."

"We don't know how he died," Jonathan said. "You can talk to the sheriff about that. I thought it might soothe your mind to know that he can't hurt your family again."

Carl nodded. "It does, thank you."

The coffee in his cup was getting cold, but Jonathan took a long drink just the same. "Is Amber Leigh going to be all right?"

"The doctors say she will be. Bodies heal, don't they?" The question held a desperate need for reassurance.

"Bodies do, yeah," Jonathan said.

"Yeah," Carl echoed. He didn't sound convinced at all. "We'll look into therapy when we get home. Jesus, what are we going to do?"

Jonathan rescued the man's coffee. It was in danger of being squeezed into an explosion of caffeine. "Where's home, Carl?"

"Atlanta. I'm city editor for the *Atlanta Sun E-times*."

"Good paper; I read it sometimes."

"Thanks." The man took a deep breath and reached for his coffee again. "You still haven't told me who found Amber Leigh. I assumed it was a man, but was it the woman the TV reporters caught you carrying out of the house?"

Jonathan had seen that footage. He'd been recognizable, but Alanna's face had been hidden by the dark tangle of her hair. No doubt she'd be mortified to have been seen like that. He wondered if she'd caught the local morning news. "That was her," he said.

"Was she injured? How did she find my baby girl?"

"Are you interviewing me, Carl?"

"Would you let me?"

Jonathan laughed. The sound cut through the clatter of silverware, the drone of conversation. Heads turned his way. "I don't think so," he said. "But Mark Dennison might."

The man's eyes widened a touch. "Really?"

"He wants to further the cause of the Faelinn. He wants them protected by law, granted the rights of other sentient beings."

"Are they sentient?" Carl asked.

"Generally, they're smarter than some people I know," Jonathan said. "Alanna and her Fael, Jekk, found your daughter last night. Remember that if you write about us."

"Believe me, I'll remember it until the day I die."

Jonathan took a business card from his wallet and pushed it across the table. "I'll talk to Mark. Call me and I'll let you know if he wants to be interviewed."

Carl took the card, studying it before slipping it into his own wallet. "Since it's obvious you're not going to let me thank the woman who actually found Amber Leigh, will you at least pass on our gratitude?"

"I will," Jonathan said. He finished the cup of coffee and pushed his chair back with a scrape of metal on tile. "I'll go up to collect Cateera, and we'll leave you to your family."

Carl thrust out his hand. "I have no real words for what I owe you all, but thank you."

～

The words echoed in his head as Jonathan drove away from the hospital. It wasn't often he enjoyed the thanks of a civilian. Usually his work kept him away from living victims. The thanks he received came from the police departments who'd called him in to find the killers haunting their districts. It wasn't the same.

I would like to visit other children at the hospital, Cateera said. Her eyes were closed. He'd thought she was dozing. *It is a sad place. I would like to make them happier.*

"Like a therapy dog," Jonathan said.

Now her eyes opened. Her gaze was scathing. *I am not a dog.*

"No, dear one, you're not. But therapy dogs are trained to help the patients. That's all I meant."

Well, that is all right, then. I will be a therapy Fael. We will go there again.

And that, Jonathan realized, was as close to asking his permission as she was likely to get. He reached out to stroke the silky fur of her head, enjoying the purr that filled the SUV. "If it makes you happy, I'll look into setting it up."

It makes me happy, she said. *Thank you.*

Chapter Eleven

Why don't we have our own house? Jekk asked. He was sprawled out on the sofa, his head resting on the arm so he could watch her while she wrote. His tail twitched lazily back and forth. Every time it hit the sofa, it made an audible thump.

"We do," Alanna said. Her fingers flew over the keys, translating the flowing images in her head into words.

Then why are we here in Berren's house?

"I came here to interview Shellie and Mark for a book I'm writing. The woman in it is bonded to a Fael."

He rolled off the couch and padded over to her. Resting his chin on her shoulder, he peered at the screen with interest. *Am I in it?*

Alanna laughed, resting her head against his. "No, Jekk."

He snorted. She felt a presence moving in her mind and had to force herself not to push him out. It still disturbed her sometimes to feel him there. "What are you doing?"

I'm learning to read, he told her.

She hit Save and swung her full attention to him. "Really?"

Yes. It's how I learned English. Now that we're bonded, you can learn my language, too, but Cateera said you won't be able to speak it. Human throats are inferior.

"Cateera is a bit of a snob," Alanna said with a laugh.

But she will be a good mother for my kits, he said. *Is the house next to hers ours?*

She was still trying to process what he'd said about kits. "No, we don't live here. I've told you before we live in the city. Kits, Jekk?"

She felt that shuffling in her head again and knew he was sorting through her memories. She concentrated and was able to see that he was viewing her memories of her home, of New DC. And because she was concentrating, she felt his growing dismay.

I don't want to live there. I want to be here with the other Faelinn. I want to be here with my mate. His ears were back, his eyes narrowed, the cat-like pupils expanded so that his eyes appeared black. She felt his rebellion growing. It was a new bud. Rebellion had been beaten out of him as a kit.

"Jekk, I don't live here. I have a life in New DC. That's where my home is, where my friends are. That's where we're going tomorrow."

No, he snarled into her head.

"Yes," she answered. "We leave in the morning."

The snarl was out loud this time, echoing through the room. There was anger and frustration in the sound, and Alanna extended an imploring hand to stroke the fur of his neck. He yanked away, whirled, and ran to the balcony door. A push of his paw on the handle and the door banged open. A gust of cold air blew in. The muscles of Jekk's legs bunched and then he was over the railing and gone. Alanna rushed for the balcony, caught sight of him as he fled across the wide lawn toward the trees. He'd cleared the two stories easily. And he'd shut her out of his mind.

New DC was home. She loved Jekk, she truly did. Even after only a few days, he was wound so deeply into her soul that she'd never get him loose. Nor did she want to. But she'd already changed her life so much; she wasn't going to change it any more. Her home was in New DC. Her friends were there, and she adored the city life. Moving here was just more than she was willing to do.

You must talk to her!

The command cut right through his brain like a sharp knife into jelly. Jonathan froze, the ax poised at the beginning of a downswing. Slowly, he lowered it, grateful that Cateera's words hadn't come half a second later, or he might have missed the block of wood and chopped off his own leg.

The lavender and white blur that was his Fael streaked across the deep lawn behind his house. He sank the ax blade into the chopping block as a precaution and waited until she came to a stop in front of him. Her thoughts were a muddle of emotion, fury, worry, and despair. Lavender-tipped ears were fiercely erect, the sensitive hairs at the ends quivering.

"What's wrong, dear one?"

She is going to take my mate. You must tell her she cannot do this. He is mine, and he has to stay with me.

Jonathan reached out to soothe her, and she nipped his fingers. He snatched his hand back.

Do not try to placate me, she said sharply. *You must tell your mate that she has to stay.* Jekk appeared beside her, his fur golden in the last stray fingers of sunshine that lingered over the mountains. He'd shivered into visibility so that Jonathan knew he was there. The big male with the tattered ear rubbed his cheek gently against Cateera's.

Things clicked into place, and Jonathan finally knew what she was talking about. There was no use arguing with her that Alanna wasn't his mate. Cateera had decided it was so and in her current state of agitation, trying to deny it would only make it worse. When she'd informed him earlier that she'd accepted Jekk as her mate, he should have paid more attention. He should have realized the consequences.

"You know that Alanna doesn't live here," he told her.

Neither did you when we bonded. Tell her to move. She cannot take Jekk away from me. The words were tinged with the beginning of panic, and through the muddle of her thoughts he caught glimpses of memory. The devastation of her kits being taken away, leaving her alone. Even though the pregnancy hadn't been her choice—had in fact been forced upon her by a Kellian breeding farm—it hadn't made any difference at all in how she felt about her babies. And now, her chosen mate was being taken.

"Cateera, I have no control over what she does. I'm sorry."

You can talk to her. You can convince her. Jekk is her partner, he should have a say in where he lives, but she will not listen to him. Please, Jonathan!

How could he possibly do anything but attempt to change the world for her? "I'll try," he said. "I doubt she'll listen to me, but I'll try." Two paws landed on his shoulders, a raspy tongue dragging over his face. He staggered back under the assault, missed his balance, and ended up on his ass. "Get off me, you crazy female."

Hands full of fur and muscle, Jonathan attempted to shove his Fael off. Her joyful washing of his face felt like it was slowly peeling the skin from his bones. Designed to clean thick fur and alternately to strip flesh from the bones of prey, a Fael's tongue was rough with barbs. Laughing, Jonathan finally gave up the fight, submitting while she groomed his hair, her purr a wild sound in his ears.

This was not going to be fun.

Sitting in the kitchen, hair still damp from a quick shower, Jonathan stared at his phone. Cateera and Jekk stared at him expectantly. The weight of two pairs of slanted eyes made him twitchy. Finally, he pulled out his phone and sent Alanna a text. It was a good thing that Agneta had tweaked Alanna's cell and had made a note of the number. Grabbing his jacket, he headed for the SUV. He hadn't given her a choice about meeting with him. He just hoped she showed up at the front door.

Torn between irritation over being summoned and an annoying kind of anticipation that she was going to share a meal with Jonathan, Alanna paced the foyer. She'd deliberately put on the oldest pair of jeans she'd packed. She absolutely refused to dress up for the man. She still couldn't reach out to Jekk and that added another layer to her already roiling emotions.

"You know, if you jump when he calls you, he's going to expect it every time," Shellie pointed out from where she sat on the stairs. A full, rainbow-hued skirt puddled around her feet.

"There's not going to be an 'every time,' since I'm going home tomorrow," Alanna replied. Still, she forced herself to stop pacing and plopped down on the riser next to Shellie. "Jekk won't talk to me."

Light from the crystal and silver chandelier overhead gleamed in Shellie's curls, sparkled off her diamond wedding band. "Faelinn are people, too," she said. "It can be easy to forget because they're big and fluffy, but they have the same feelings we do."

"He and Cateera are mated."

"Setasha told me," Shellie said. "I have to say I'm surprised. Cateera is very picky. For her to have claimed him in just a few days must mean he's extraordinary."

Alanna managed a quick smile that disappeared immediately. "He is, and now he's furious with me because we're going home tomorrow."

"If you were married and someone forced you to leave your loved one, how would you feel?"

Alanna picked at a nonexistent fluff on her jeans. Shellie's words stabbed to the heart of the matter. They hurt, made her feel petty, but damn it, she had a life in New DC. Was she expected to give it all up? The front door opened and her thoughts dried up and floated away. Oh my, what that man could do for a pair of jeans and an old jacket.

"Hey, Shellie," Jonathan said with a smile that showed off the quick dimple in his left cheek.

Alanna remained seated for the simple reason that her knees were knocking just a little and she wasn't sure if they would hold her up. She didn't mind that he hadn't greeted her yet, that he was asking about Mark. It gave her time to study him. The wheat-blond hair waving over his ears made her want to stroke it back. She wanted to trace the line of his lips with a fingertip and then with her tongue. Just those images alone started heat throbbing between her legs. He made her hot, and it had been a long time since a man had affected her like that. But why did such a gorgeous man have to come in such an annoying package?

"Are you ready?" he asked.

Change that to annoying and rude. "No hello, how are you?"

His mouth twitched up at one corner. "Hello, Alanna, you look beautiful. Are you ready?"

Shellie apparently couldn't contain her snort of laughter, although she did cover her mouth to try to muffle it.

Alanna's cheeks were hot and she knew she was blushing. She really hated to blush. She gave him a look designed to reduce him to a pile of smoldering ash and stood up. His eyes began a lazy perusal of her body, lingering a long moment on her breasts where her nipples had tightened beneath her T-shirt. Instead of being insulted, she felt heat wash through her. That made her cheeks color for a whole other reason, twisted her into knots, and made her want to launch herself at him. Instead, she stalked to the door. He somehow managed to beat her there, and held it open.

"Have a nice time, children," Shellie called out. "I won't wait up."

There was no time to reply to that because Jonathan was already closing the door.

"This isn't a date," she snapped.

"I never said it was," he answered.

Which of course made her feel like an idiot.

Everything else was forgotten when she saw Jekk watching from beside Jonathan's SUV. His golden eyes gleamed in the darkness, catching the ambient light and reflecting it. Cateera sat next to him. They were leaning against each other. Running to the vehicle, Alanna reached out to stroke Jekk's neck, but he jerked away. Turning his back on her, the two ran with easy grace and disappeared into the dark.

Hurt struck hard, straight through her, and Alanna took a step back and collided with Jonathan. His hands steadied her waist for a moment before dropping away. Determined not to let any of them see how she felt, Alanna walked to the passenger side and slid onto the seat. It was warm in the SUV, and she caught the lingering scent of Jonathan's aftershave. Alanna closed her eyes and tried to get the emotional whirlwind she was experiencing under control.

A blast of cold air chilled the SUV when Jonathan got in, cut off when he shut the door. She hazarded a glance in his direction. He was watching her, and in the dark she couldn't see his eyes. His fingers trailed across her cheek, thumb lightly brushing her lips. It was exactly what she'd wanted to do with him inside. The contact was unexpectedly sweet, drained the tension from her shoulders, and made her sigh softly.

Made her aware of how close they sat.

"Are you okay?" he asked.

"I'm having a bad day," she told him truthfully.

He laughed softly. "So I've heard. I'm supposed to change your mind about leaving."

"Jonathan—"

"Don't worry, I'm admitting defeat up front. But I'm still hungry and I know where we can get the best chili cheese fries."

Alanna's stomach chose that moment to rumble. She clapped a hand over it, embarrassed.

"And bacon cheeseburgers, did I mention bacon cheeseburgers?"

~

The building was backlit by the Veil. Climbing five stories into the night, it seemed to take up at least a city block. Arched windows on every floor spilled light onto the surrounding lawn. A huge tree loomed above, taller than the surrounding tree line, and Alanna squinted up at it as Jonathan pulled into the crowded parking lot.

Alanna hopped out of the SUV. The van next to her had a set of family stickers in the back window, Dad, Mom, son, and baby. The son was holding a skateboard. Next to the baby were two larger Faelinn stickers.

"I hate those things," Jonathan said. "Nothing like advertising how many kids you have and what kind."

"That's the cop in you talking," she said, falling into step at his side.

"Yeah, can't seem to help it."

"Thanks for what you did for me last night," Alanna said. "I didn't want to forget to say that."

"No problem," he answered. He held the door open for her. When she passed through, he bent his head to whisper, "Besides, I got to see you running around in skimpy clothes."

Startled, Alanna stumbled. The wicked glint in his eyes rendered her breathless. A vision of being in a corset and stockings, his hands and mouth on her, sparked heat between her thighs. Then his lips twitched, and she realized he knew exactly what he was doing to her. She gave him what she hoped was a scathing look and marched through the door.

And stopped. The lobby held a variety of couches, chairs, and tables. A bulletin board stretched the length of one wall, covered with everything from ads and notices for community events to children's drawings. A large counter, currently deserted, occupied another side of the room. None of which had stopped her.

The carpeting ended, replaced by a lush green meadow. A tree grew in that meadow, a tree that stretched immense branches both upwards and down. The trunk was gargantuan. Houses were smaller than its girth. Stairs had grown up its side, circling around, disappearing and reappearing through arches cut into the bole. The branches were flat walkways, broad platforms dotting larger intersections. Vines snaked down, twisted into ladders, or hanging free. Everywhere on the tree ran Faelinn and their human friends.

"What is this place?" she asked. It couldn't be another World Tree. There was only one, and that one was an ocean away.

"We call it the Playground," he told her. Catching her hand, Jonathan pulled her towards a staircase in an alcove along one wall.

Balconies ringed the atrium, each floor devoted to a different use. Amazing smells drifted through the air. Part of the second floor had been turned into a restaurant. Burgundy leather booths lined the far wall, tables scattered across the open floor. About a third were occupied, and every pair of eyes turned their way. Jonathan called out a few greetings and then led her to a table along the railing. Farther along, the railing opened, permitting a flat branch to grow within stepping distance.

Shrugging out of her jacket and tossing it onto a chair, Alanna leaned over the rail to get a better look. Golden leaves glowed here and there amongst the branches. The sheen of the warm metal reflected amongst the myriad shades of green leaves. This was a World Tree, hidden here in the Haven. How had they kept it secret?

The other Tree had sprung up out of nowhere in the center of what had once been Salisbury Plain. The plain had become a lake, the Tree an island. Mythology abounded with stories of a World Tree and how its roots bound the worlds together. The one in England was immense, even bigger than this one. It was sentient and held the history of ages in its wood. Human scholars vied to speak with it and only a very few succeeded. Alanna had visited the Tree in Salisbury Lake, had gaped in awe from the far shore. It was beautiful and frightening, and she'd never forgotten how one golden leaf had drifted like a coracle in the waves. And here was another World Tree, protected by the Haven. There was no doubt in her mind that no outsiders knew of it.

"How?" she asked softly, glancing at the man standing next to her.

Jonathan's shoulder brushed hers as he shrugged. "That's not my story to tell. All I know is that the Seed was a gift. It's grown here for the past fifty years, changing its shape as our needs have changed."

"It's amazing," she said. Craning her head back, she saw that the uppermost branches reached higher than the building's roof. A shimmering haze marked the spot where the brick and mortar stopped and magic began. No doubt it kept out the elements while allowing the Tree to grow as high as it wanted.

A shriek of laughter startled her. A tow-headed boy no older than six raced along a flattened branch, running full tilt while a purple Fael chased him. He leaped across a space, grabbed a vine, and swung to another branch. The Fael followed in one leap, what passed for a grin on its furry face.

"He's going to fall," Alanna said, clutching Jonathan's arm in alarm.

"It's okay," Jonathan said. "No one gets hurt here, especially not him. Keep watching."

The boy dodged through an archway of leaves, appeared out the other side and into the lounging spot of another Fael. He tried to stop but momentum tumbled him across the branch. He laughed again and flung himself into empty space. The Tree moved. A thin branch whipped forward, wrapped around the boy's narrow waist, and gently lowered him to a safe spot. His pursuer flopped down next to the other Fael and rested her chin on her paws.

"That's Bethany and Aron's son, Stevie. He thinks he's Spider-Man. The Tree never lets anyone fall."

"Well that's great here, but what happens when he thinks he can fly at home and jumps off the roof?"

Jonathan snorted back a laugh. "Oh, he tried that. Broke both arms and a leg. After Bethany finished fixing him up, she tore off a strip of his hide with her tongue. He's never done it again."

Alanna shook her head. She wasn't sure she wouldn't have killed the boy herself. It would have scared her half to death. "Is that her husband's Fael?" she asked, indicating the purple Fael who had already jumped to where Stevie waited.

"No, that's Fiona. She's an unbonded Wild Fael. There's a lot of speculation that when he comes of age they'll bond."

Alanna continued to watch the two, not at all surprised when Stevie mounted the Fael like a horse and clung to her fur when she took off at top speed. The myriad walkways, both narrow and broad, the ladders, and the climbing vines all looked like fun.

"Can we play?" she asked.

Jonathan's blue eyes narrowed, and a predatory gleam lit their depths. A shiver of pure awareness ran up her spine. Instinctively, she backed up a step. A chair bumped her hip. Quickly, she toed off her heels and pushed them under the table.

"If you run, I will catch you," Jonathan promised.

"Do I get a head start?" she asked, edging toward the open rail. She could never resist a challenge.

The wicked smile that curved his mouth was pure promise. "Two minutes. It starts now."

The challenge issued, Alanna hopped through the open rail and onto the Tree. Bare feet hit the branch. It was shockingly warm, smooth as the finest marble. Taking a moment of her two minutes, she knelt and placed her hand flat on the wood.

"Thank you for the gift of your branches," she murmured. An unexpected pain stabbed her palm. A droplet of blood dripped from her skin onto the limb. It shivered a moment, and then sank into the pale golden wood. A deep intelligence brushed her mind, vastly different from the feel of Jekk's thoughts. There was a touch of curiosity coupled with a deep joy. Almost words throbbed inside her, too deep and slow to be comprehended, but Alanna had the sense that she'd been claimed and welcomed.

A glance over her shoulder showed Jonathan watching her intently. He tapped his watch with one finger. She stuck her tongue out at him. Laughter chased her as she took a few running steps along the broad path and then leaped for the narrow branch she'd spotted from the table.

The limb gave a little as her hands gripped it. It was as smooth as she'd hoped, and even though her hands weren't chalked, they moved easily on the wood. Using her momentum and the energy of the branch's pliancy to swing her legs out and back, she drew herself up, her hips hitting the bar. She swung again, flowed through the move to leap to the next limb. Toes gripped and she tucked herself and somersaulted down to another branch. She turned her momentum into a handstand, held it for a few seconds while scanning her route and then used the downswing's energy to fly to a narrow walkway. A twinge in her back chastised her that she hadn't warmed up first.

All those years in gymnastics had paid off. Puberty had changed her body enough that she couldn't pursue her competitive dreams, and she'd discovered both boys and writing shortly after. But she'd never given up the sport entirely. She still practiced, and volunteered at a local gym, training the young tumblers.

Tonight the skills had put her a distance away from the second-floor restaurant. Jonathan would have to take a longer route to reach her position. Alanna ran along the wood toward the trunk, keeping an eye out for useful branches. A broad ladder took her up another level, and she shared a smile with a woman climbing down. Faelinn eyes watched her from within a bower of leaves. A glance behind her was useless; she couldn't see the restaurant from her position, but she was sure her two minutes were up.

If she could circle the girth of the Tree and make it back to their table before he caught her, she would consider herself the winner.

Are you playing tag?

Jekk's voice tickled her mind. Joy flooded her and she looked around but couldn't see him. If he was talking to her, maybe he wasn't mad anymore.

Maybe, she said.

Your mate will win. He's a hunter.

Mate? What?

Jonathan isn't my mate, she said. *I'm not even sure he's a friend.* She leaped from one branch to another, ran along it, and reached the trunk. Steps wrapped around and she headed up. Hopefully, she'd be able to go around completely and begin moving back to the second-floor railing.

Cateera is my mate, Jonathan is yours. You'll miss him when you go home.

"I don't think it works like that. Just because you've mated with his Fael doesn't automatically make him mine." And just why did the thought of belonging to him make her breathless? Maybe she was more out of shape than she realized. The breathlessness was no doubt from her fast pace through the Tree branches.

No, Jekk answered. *He's your mate because he is.*

There was a twisted logic in that. Of course, it led to an incorrect conclusion, but at least she understood what he meant. "Help me get back to the table without him catching me."

If I do, will we stay here in the Haven?

"I can't do that, Jekk. I'm sorry."

Silence again. Bitter, stunningly empty silence. Then, grudgingly, Jekk spoke.

Follow the stairs a little further, then step onto the first large branch, then jump down two branches. Go back to the stairs. Twenty feet beyond is an alcove to hide in. He's very close.

"Thank you, Jekk."

Alanna followed the instructions. She paused for two teenagers to pass and then ran out onto the branch he'd indicated. The first leap down was longer than she thought, and her feet stung as she landed. The second was much shorter. The stairs cut into the rough bark of the trunk were narrow, and she realized that not all the stairways connected. These led her down. The alcove Jekk had told her about was just up ahead. She smiled and ducked inside. Down a short twist of hall she hadn't realized was there and then into an unexpected room carved from the living wood. She'd be hidden here. Fingers curled over her wrist. Alanna had time for a quick, breathy cry of alarm before she was pushed up against the wall.

Chapter Twelve

The wood at Alanna's back was warm. Soft light came from jewels embedded in the wall and illuminated the room enough that she could see benches curving along the alcove's inner walls. In that half-light, Jonathan's eyes gleamed and his smile was triumphant. Jekk had led her straight to him.

"Traitor!" she thought at her bondmate. Laughter poured into her. She made dire threats about withholding chocolate, but the laughter snickered on.

"That wasn't much of a chase," Jonathan remarked. He shoved his hands into his back pockets and mocked her with his presence. "I was impressed by your start, but then you seemed to run right into me."

"I was betrayed by my Fael," she said. Alanna ground her teeth. She had to. If she didn't, there was a good possibility she'd drool on the polished mosaic floor. The man was pure sex standing there. Long and lean with jeans that molded to his thighs and a T-shirt that showed off the breadth of his shoulders. She wanted to tear that shirt off so she could see for herself that he was healed from his knife wound. It had nothing to do with the fact that she wanted to lick all the smooth skin underneath.

Jonathan took a step forward, crowding into her space. One finger traced her jaw so lightly that she leaned into the caress to feel more. His thumb stroked her bottom lip. The teasing contact made her pulse skitter, her breathing quicken. And everything south of her waist melt.

His head bent. His mouth was a shadow away from her jaw. She could feel the fan of his breath against her skin. "I would have caught you anyway."

Lips touched the sensitive skin beneath her ear. She'd expected demand and dominance. This was something different. His hair tickled her jaw and she shivered. Eyes closed, Alanna arched her neck. His teeth scraped against the sensitive tendon. The tip of his tongue tasted her there. It was the merest shiver of contact. A whimper of pleasure broke from her lips.

Body heat flared between them, leaping across the slight distance to send flames licking at her nipples. His hands flattened against the wood beside her head. He murmured softly against her throat, the words indistinct in her haze of arousal. Just that slight contact of lips skating over sensitive skin, of teasing flicks from a damp tongue, was driving her insane. Pleasure corkscrewed tighter between her thighs with each nip of his teeth. When his teeth bit her collarbone, Alanna moaned. Her hips arched and brushed against his. He was rigid in his jeans, and the contact set off a lightning storm in her veins. The desire to press herself tightly to that enticing ridge made her whimper. If he hadn't smiled at the sound of it, if she hadn't felt the curve of his mouth against her skin, she might have wrapped her legs around his waist and seen where it would take them. But he did smile, and she felt it.

Her hands tightened on his waist, and then slid between their bodies, invading that narrow empty space. She felt the trembling of his stomach muscles as she splayed her hands and slowly stroked up. With the last brain cells left to her, Alanna pushed him away and ducked beneath his arms.

"Last one back to the table buys dinner."

His laughter once again drove her along the tree limbs. Damn it, why did the Tree have to be so big? And why did her brain have to be so scrambled? Just because he was cute—gorgeous, her brain corrected. Drop dead, die-if-you-don't-have-him gorgeous—didn't mean she had to fall at his feet and beg for his kiss. Really, it was just too much.

The table was empty. Feeling triumphant, Alanna stepped from the

Tree branch to the floor and claimed her chair. And realized he was right behind her. Irritated beyond belief that he'd let her win, she glared at him. Jonathan ignored it, smiled at her as he sat, and pushed a menu across the table. As if he hadn't just had her on the cusp of orgasm with the simple contact of his lips on her throat.

"Everything is good here. The chef's Gift is food."

A teenage girl approached the table. A black apron circled her hips. A smile showed off her braces. "Hi, Jonathan."

The barely contained adoration in her eyes both relieved Alanna and made her want to snarl. At least she wasn't the only woman he affected. Opening the menu, she scanned the drink offerings. Deciding to order plain water, she found herself ordering a grapefruit-infused IPA instead. Jonathan ordered a lager for himself, and a plate of chili cheese fries.

"Okay," their waitress said. She focused on Alanna and her smile became shy. "I'm a really big fan, Ms. McLean. I'm not supposed to ask, but can you autograph a book for me? I have it in my backpack. I was going to bring it by Mark's but my mom told me not to bother you. So I'm really glad you're here tonight, because I really love your writing. Oh, and I'm Anne."

The gush of words stopped and Alanna found herself grinning. The girl hadn't breathed once while she'd been talking. "I'm happy to."

She gave a little hop of excitement, her brown hair swinging. "I'll bring it right out with your drinks." She danced away and through the swinging door to the kitchen.

"Quite a fan club you have," Jonathan remarked.

Oh good, neutral ground. Do not mention those few moments of weakness in the Tree. Good plan. "If I didn't have fans, no one would buy my books. Then I'd be stuck doing a job I didn't love. And I'd still be writing, but only for myself. I like sharing my worlds with other people."

"Is that why you're in New DC? More stores for book signings, fan access?"

"No, I'm in New DC because I love it there. My friends are there." She smiled at Anne when she brought the beers. She signed the title page of her latest hardcover, dedicating it to Anne, and was still smiling as the girl walked away.

"I thought you weren't going to try to change my mind about going back," she said. The beer was cold, sliding down her throat. It tasted wonderful.

"I'm not," Jonathan answered. He held up his own beer, taking a swig from the frosted bottle, his throat moving as he swallowed. She wondered what he'd taste like there, found herself thinking that it wasn't fair he'd gotten a taste of her and she was left wondering. Reminded herself she was the one who'd pulled away.

"I'm just trying to understand what pulls you back so strongly," he continued.

"It's my home," she said simply. The words printed on the menu didn't seem to make any sense and she closed it with a snap. He'd mentioned bacon cheeseburgers earlier, and that sounded wonderful. She'd burned too many calories last night. Her body craved fuel.

Bethany stepped from the Tree to the restaurant floor. She smiled as she stopped by their table. "Hi, you two. I heard you were here."

A tall slender man joined her. Deep green hair streaked with gold was tied back in a tail that shimmered down his back to his waist. It drew attention to the exotic angles of his face, the slant of deep green eyes. He was impossibly beautiful, moving with a foreign grace that no human could match.

"This is Aron, my husband," Bethany said. Long fingers curled around Alanna's for a moment in greeting. His smile was heartbreaking. And it didn't affect her at all. He was gorgeous in his own way, but his beauty left her cold. Not like Jonathan, whose smile seemed guaranteed to make her think sinful thoughts.

"Thank you for your gift," Aron said. His voice was surprisingly deep, the words spoken in a breathy accent. "The Tree will always know you now."

"It was my honor," Alanna replied. Her hand had healed completely. There wasn't even a scar to show where the blood had flowed.

"He's the Tree's Warden," Jonathan explained when the pair had moved on in search of their son.

"Does he have a Fael?"

Jonathan shook his head. "Only those with human blood can bond with the Fael. The other races beyond the Veil can't do it."

Alanna filed that away for use in her book. It partially explained how the Kellian could enslave the Faelinn. If they bonded, there was no way they could possibly subject their bondmates to such cruelty. At least she hoped so.

Anne brought the chili cheese fries, took their orders for burgers, gazed adoringly at Jonathan a moment, and moved on to another table. The steaming plate of fries were slathered with a thick layer of dark red chili and melted cheese. Alanna could smell the spiciness of the sauce, and her mouth watered. The first taste had her moaning as the flavors celebrated along her tongue.

Jonathan coughed a little at the sound and leaned toward her. "What do I have to do to make you moan like that?"

The words made her thighs clench together. She forced her voice to steadiness, made herself look in his eyes. "It doesn't matter, since you won't get the chance."

His smile widened to show his dimple. "Oh, I will. I'm just going to have to try different things until I figure it out."

Any one of the visions that poured into her mind would have had her moaning if they'd been trying them. "Won't happen," she said, striving for an unaffected tone. She glanced around, looking for something, anything, that could change the subject. Across the atrium, more balconies showed off the other floors of the building. Pointing, Alanna asked, "So what's the rest of this place used for?"

His smile held a touch of laughter that she chose to ignore. "Right across from us is the fitness center that connects back to the first floor where there's an indoor pool. There's a water park similar to the one at Mark's, too. Third floor holds the community library, a video lounge, and arcade. A movie theater takes up parts of both the third and fourth floors."

Trailing a French fry through the chili and cheese, she managed to get it to her mouth without spilling any of the beans back to the plate. It was a minor victory. "What's above us?"

"Directly above us is a mini bowling alley. Parts of the fourth floor and all the fifth floor is office space. The Haven's security center is there, at the other end of the building. It has a separate entrance around back."

"That's where you work?"

He nodded. Leaning across, he swiped a bit of cheese off her lower lip with a finger, and then sucked it into his mouth. His eyes challenged her to say something. The arrival of two huge bacon cheeseburgers gave her a reprieve.

Alanna looked at the thick burger layered with cheese, lettuce and tomato, and what had to be at least six strips of bacon, and groaned. There was no way she could eat all that. Where was Jekk when she needed him?

"We monitor every inch of the fence line," Jonathan said. "We also monitor the Veil, especially the parts that are easily accessible from the other side. Occasionally we have an internal matter to take care of, but that's usually just kids getting into trouble. This isn't a utopia, but there's very little crime in the Haven."

A yowl drew her attention to the Tree in time to see half a dozen Faelinn racing through the branches. They leaped from limb to limb, jostling for the best route, the quickest path. She saw Setasha and Berren, the immense black male well in the lead of the pack. Humans watched them go by, moving aside to let them pass. A flash of golden fur through the branches drew her eye in time to see Jekk jump from an upper branch down into the restaurant.

Amber eyes looked pointedly at the burger, and then at her. Slicing it in two, Alanna gave the larger portion to Jekk. He put the bread back on her plate, took a strip of bacon, and made it disappear. The rest of the burger didn't last much longer, including the vegetables and finally the bread. He was still too thin. It was hard to believe he'd only been with her a few days because he'd changed so much. But the ravages of starvation and abuse were still evident in the sharp lines of his ribs.

Anne appeared with a huge platter of raw meat and placed it on the table in front of him. He was purring as he began to eat. Cateera appeared, the lavender swirls of her fur delicate against the white undercoat. With a big paw, Jekk slid the platter in front of her so that she could eat. She took a small piece and then pushed the tray back.

The sweetness of it was a pang in Alanna's heart. She looked down at her plate, afraid someone would see the quick shine of tears. Anne delivered a second tray to Cateera, giving the Fael's ears a good scratch. It gave Alanna enough time to blink away the moisture. Was she seriously going to split the two of them up?

Propping her chin in her hand, she gazed out over the vast atrium.

People laughed, ran along the Tree branches, lounged in seating areas that had been created at broad intersections. The Faelinn played in the branches with each other and their bondmates. They were a community, an extended family with ties that bound them together. Part of her wanted that, wanted it with a fierceness that surprised her. Another part shied away. She was settled in her life. She had her townhouse, her routine. If she wanted company, there were people she could call to share lunch or a show.

There are people here, Jekk pointed out.

She laughed; she couldn't help it. His logic couldn't be denied. "You are a very sneaky man, Burke," she said, pointing at him with her fork.

One dark blond brow quirked upwards. "How so?"

"You brought me here so that I'd see what a community this is. The Faelinn are a family. You're all family."

"I brought you here for the chili cheese fries," he said, illustrating his point by popping one into his mouth.

"No," she denied. She grabbed one of the few remaining fries and munched on it. "You brought me here so that I'd see how much Jekk needed to be with the others."

"You give me too much credit," he said. "Maybe I just didn't want to eat alone."

"I very much doubt you lack dinner partners when you want them," she said drily.

He rested his elbows on the table, leaning forward. The look in his eyes matched the wicked smile that curved his mouth. "Maybe I wanted to eat with you."

Alanna placed her fork down on the plate so that he wouldn't see it tremble. When Jonathan looked at her like that, it was as if they were completely alone. She felt a little like prey singled out of the herd by a very hungry tiger. The instinctive desire to run and the completely feminine desire to drag him across the table and kiss him warred within her. "Don't change the subject."

A flash of white teeth before he controlled the grin. He leaned back again, fingers tracing the condensation on his beer bottle. "We are a family, Alanna. But we don't live in each other's pockets. You can be as involved as you want or keep yourself separate. There's room for all of that here."

An earsplitting whistle made Alanna jump in her chair. Jekk's entire body tensed, his whiskers quivering. His ruff bristled, making him appear even larger. He made a low growl, his lips peeled back from his teeth. He crouched, ready to protect his bondmate and Cateera. Sliding forward, he reached the rail and peered out.

"It's all right, Jekk," Jonathan said softly. "There's no danger here."

The big male's tail whipped back and forth in agitation. The growl changed to a low whine, but he didn't relax. Alanna leaned to peer through the rail, and he used his shoulders to push her back. She placed a gentle hand on his back. His thoughts were confused; foremost was the need to protect her against a perceived threat. She caught a glimpse of a sandy pit, heard the phantom sound of another whistle.

"Never again," she promised him. "We're safe and with friends. Relax, brave one." She felt a slow easing of the knotted muscles.

A sandy-haired man cupped his hands to his mouth and yelled. A voice nearly as loud as the whistle reached them from the atrium floor. "Hey all, has anyone seen my keys? I can't find them and the wife wants to get home."

"Hey, Dan, up here," Jonathan yelled down.

"You have his keys?" Alanna asked, leaning over to see the man taking the stairs two at a time. He was cute in a bookish way, with short, sandy-brown hair and glasses.

"Nope," Jonathan said. He took a slow pull of beer. "Dan, meet Alanna," he said when the man reached the table. "Alanna, Dan. She's going to find the keys for you."

"What?" she asked Jonathan, even as she met Dan's palm with her own.

At the contact she saw a flash of keys on a tile floor. Tiny little tiles, in shades of grey and blue. White grout. Silver key ring swollen with keys.

"Where are they, Alanna?" Jonathan asked softly.

Her fingers tightened around Dan's. The picture expanded. Keys on a tile floor telescoped out to include the porcelain base of a toilet.

"Bathroom," she told him. She met the soft hazel eyes behind the tortoiseshell frames. "I think they're on the bathroom floor."

The smile took him from cute to hunky. "Thanks, you've saved me from the wrath of Miranda. Nice meeting you."

We're a good team, Jekk said with satisfaction. He nosed at his plate, relaxed now. He swiped his tongue over the plate, licking up the last of the blood. He sat back and began to groom his whiskers with one large paw.

"Nice work," Jonathan said. "Good to know you can find objects as well as people."

"Great," Alanna said. "I have a career to fall back on." She stared at the empty, chili-smeared plate and the pickle spear that was all that remained of her dinner. "If you can find me a hot fudge sundae I might upgrade my opinion of you from annoying to tolerable."

"Be still my heart," Jonathan said with a laugh. "What do I have to do to get you to like me?"

"It's not possible," Alanna said. Want him, yes. Have the hots for him, most certainly. Like him? No thank you.

The taste of fudge lingered on her tongue when Jonathan pulled the truck to a stop in front of Mark's mansion. There'd been no problem finding a sundae; turned out the chef made his own ice cream. She'd had to share it with Jekk, but that was okay. His pleasure at the taste of the chocolate had been worth it. He was gone now, off with Cateera. They'd disappeared into the night and the lightest touch of her mind to his showed him running through the woods, chasing his mate. With a smile, she shrunk the contact down, leaving him his privacy.

"Thanks for dinner," Alanna said as Jonathan came around the truck to join her.

"You're welcome." He stroked back a strand of her hair that curled across her cheek. His fingertips were cool. The contact shivered through her. "So you're really leaving tomorrow?"

"Sometime in the morning, yes," she answered. "I'll try to come back as often as I can, so Jekk can be with Cateera."

"That's good," Jonathan said. He shoved his hands into his jacket pockets. "We'll come up, too, if that's okay. I have business in New DC sometimes."

"That would be fine," she said. They sounded so stiff, like the worst dialogue. If she'd written it, she would have instantly deleted it and started again. But somehow, she just didn't know what to say to him. She made her living with words, but this man, this moment with starshine competing with the Veil in the sky, left her tongue-tied.

Jonathan's mouth twitched in amusement. Her eyes narrowed in response. It was okay for her to feel awkward. It was not okay for him to find it funny. Curling her fingers into the leather of his jacket, she hauled him close and kissed him. His lips were cool. His mouth was hot. And every nerve ending in her body flared with pleasure.

A growl rumbled from Jonathan's throat and one broad-palmed hand came up to curve around her nape. Alanna's back arched when his other hand slid down her spine, lingered at her hip, and then curved possessively over her butt. He tasted of fudge and sin and she sucked his tongue lightly. Her reward was the flex of his fingers drawing her tight against his hips, the hard ridge of his erection pressing just *there*, exactly where she needed it to be.

A gentle nudge pushed her back against the side of the truck. The metal was briefly cold at her back before the heat of him melted her bones. Blond hair was cool and silky as Alanna threaded her fingers through it. Liquid pooled low in her abdomen with each throb of her body.

She was swiftly losing any desire to say good night.

Scratching her nails lightly down his neck, Alanna reveled in the sound he made. The low male groan vibrated through her. Stroking her tongue along the inside of his bottom lip, she nipped him suddenly. Jonathan yelped and drew back. She immediately regretted it, missed his warmth and the pleasure of his mouth.

"Wicked woman," he murmured. He shook his head a little and took a step back. "You're leaving in the morning."

"Yes," she agreed. Lightheaded and breathless, she straightened up from the truck. A long empty night stretched from now until tomorrow. The desire to spend it in his bed was very appealing. Appealing enough that she might not want to leave it in the morning, and that wasn't going to happen.

"Thanks again for dinner, Burke. I'll see you around."

Walking quickly but trying not to look like she was running away, Alanna still heard him mutter something about trouble. She smiled and thought again that it was a good thing she was leaving. He was just far too tempting.

Chapter Thirteen

Jonathan pummeled his pillow, trying to beat it into a comfortable shape. He'd been lying there for hours and sleep was no closer than it had been when he'd first crawled under the comforter. He couldn't get the feel of her out of his mind. More to the point, his body wouldn't let him forget. The addictive flavor of her mouth, the jasmine scent of her skin. The way her body had felt under his hands, soft and firm all at once. She was making him insane.

It was a good thing she was leaving in the morning.

Trying and failing to find a good spot on the pillow, he flung it across the room. It thumped into the wall and dropped onto his shoes. It was no use. His cell phone blared on the table beside him and with intense relief, Jonathan grabbed it.

"It's Brown," the voice said with no preamble. "The fence has been compromised. A pickup crashed right through it."

Jonathan was already reaching for the jeans thrown over the back of the chair by the window. He listened to the concise report, verified that men were already heading for the breach, and hung up. He was out of the house in less than three minutes.

Cateera answered his mental call immediately. The Faelinn had their own alert system and were already spreading through the woods, silent, deadly hunters. They would find anyone who had entered the Haven.

He took the mountain curves too fast, but he knew the roads and could drive them in his sleep. Lights were visible through the bare-branched trees before he reached the breach. He pulled up behind two security vans, angling the SUV so that his headlights joined theirs to illuminate the scene. A black pickup had crashed through the fence. The chain-link had snagged on the undercarriage and been dragged across the road and then into the drainage ditch before the truck had stopped, nose pointing down. The Haven's emergency system had cut off the fence's electricity, but not before sparks had blackened patches of the ground.

"Where's the driver?" he demanded, ground-eating strides carrying him to the truck. Brown grass thick with frost crunched under his feet.

"Take a look," Brown answered. He pointed to the open driver's side door, his flashlight picking out the dark interior. Jonathan peered in. He took the flashlight from Brown, aiming it around the empty interior. The key was still in the ignition. One key, no ring.

"The door was already open but I did turn off the engine," Brown said. "Used gloves." He waggled his latex-covered fingers. "Nothing else has been touched."

"Good man," Jonathan said.

Meticulously, he directed the light around the cab. It was clean, no dust lingering on the dash, no smudges to be seen on the windows. Pulling on his own pair of gloves, he eased open the ashtray. Empty, not even a lingering trace of ash. The glove compartment was spotless and empty. There were still vacuum marks on the floor's worn carpet. Jonathan stepped back to survey the entire truck. Long scratches clawed down the sides where it had torn through the fence. The front end had taken a lot of damage and he was frankly surprised the truck had gotten as far into the Haven as it had. The truck wasn't new, but it wasn't a clunker either.

"Whoever did this had a plan, and money to put into it," he told Brown. "No one throws away a vehicle like this just for the hell of it." He nodded tightly at Rivera as he joined them. The man's glasses caught the light, obscuring his eyes. "I want every road in the Haven patrolled tonight. Call up whoever you have to and make sure it's covered. Cateera is already working to account for every Fael. Berren and Setasha are helping her. Berren is also doubling fence patrol. Between the Faelinn and human security, if anyone made it inside the Haven, we'll know about it.

"Have the truck taken in. We'll be going over every inch of it for any clue to who did this. In the meantime, run the plates and the VIN."

"No plates, and I'll lay odds that the vehicle ID number was lasered off," Rivera said.

Jonathan circled the truck. The plates had indeed been removed. "Shit," he said. He gazed out at the fallow pasture beyond the fence. He couldn't see far past the pool of light but there was evidence of tire tracks in the winter field. He had a good feeling he knew where they'd end. The mountain was crisscrossed with old logging roads and older military roads from the battles that had been fought here when the Veil first sprang up. Local farmers used them to access their remote fields. He'd check with old man Barnes but he doubted the farmer would have any clue who'd used the old road past his place that led to the field he leased from Mark.

"Check the field, follow the tracks back to the road. Look for footprints along the way. That cinder block didn't get stuck on the pedal by itself. I want everything photographed, impressions made of the tracks and any prints you find.

"Send the crew out to repair the fence. I don't want it left unsecured, so Berren is posting Faelinn here until the work is done."

Jonathan scraped his hair back in frustration. "I want to see the video."

Brown looked up from where he'd been keying Jonathan's instructions into his tablet. "You want to see them now, or back at the office?"

"Quick impression now, a longer review later."

Brown nodded, typed something into the tablet, and offered it to Jonathan.

Darkness filled the screen. When two spears of light slowly brightened, he realized he was seeing the approaching headlights. The automatic perimeter lighting kicked on as it registered the large, rapidly approaching object. The truck's speed never decreased. When it crashed into the fence, sparks flew up. They twinkled like fireflies before the safety precautions clicked on and cut the power.

"Infrared?" he asked with a quick glance up at Brown.

The man took the tablet back and accessed another file. He handed over the tablet again. "There's not a lot of detail here. It'll be clearer back at the office."

Jonathan hit play and watched as the warmth of the truck's engine registered in shades of orange and red. He played it through twice and didn't see anything that stood out. But whoever had placed the cinder block had to have driven the truck to a certain point. There should be some record of a heat signature. His mouth tightened, irritation and worry fighting for precedence. This wasn't just a random occurrence. He had the gut feeling that the earlier electronics problems were all related to this break-in. What he didn't get was why no intruders had been found. Why break down the fence if not to get inside? The Faelinn reported that they'd found no one, and he trusted them. They were the best hunters he knew and no stranger in the Haven would remain hidden from them. The security patrols were for his own peace of mind.

"Did your shields detect anything?" Jonathan asked Rivera, referring to the man's magickal wards along the fence line.

"The shields went down when the truck crashed through. They're meant to alert us and to deter smaller animals, not stop anything. Once they're down, I can't scan to see if anything set them off." Rivera frowned thoughtfully. "That's a glitch I need to work on, I think."

Jonathan silently agreed. He felt a brush of fur in his mind, a polite "knock" from Berren. The Alpha informed him that all the Faelinn were accounted for and unharmed. "Thanks, Berren," he replied. "Will you have some of the Faelinn accompany my men across the field? I want those tire tracks traced back to the road. I'd like to know what they sense out there. Someone had to be driving that truck."

Of course, Chief, Berren replied. *I'll take care of it myself, and I'll bring Jekk. I'd like to see what skills he has.*

"Thanks. Mark's up?"

The minute I told him about the truck.

"Okay, I'm heading back to the office. I want to review the video footage. Let Mark know he can join me there if he wants."

Berren said he would, and the contact with the Fael ended.

"All right, I'll head back to the office and look over the video and infrared again. Where the hell is that tow truck? I want to go over the pickup first thing in the morning."

Brown turned away, his cell phone already at his ear.

Jonathan motioned Rivera aside. "This is bad," he said softly.

"I know," Rivera answered. "I'll get things moving and then I'm going to ride and scan every inch of the fence."

"Good," Jonathan said. "We've either missed something, or someone lost their nerve and didn't follow when the truck came through. I'll talk to Sheriff Jacobs as well, see if he's heard anything around town that I need to know about."

"All right," Rivera said. "I'll keep on top of Brown and make sure things are handled."

That helped, Jonathan thought. Rivera wasn't his second-in-command because he had a pretty face. The man had a dogged tenacity to go along with his eye for detail and Gift for magickal wards. He'd make sure things got done while Jonathan handled the details and the politics. And carried the worry like a pile of cement blocks on his back.

Coffee steamed beside him, completely forgotten, as Jonathan leaned forward to peer more closely at the large screen. The control room was dark to prevent glare on the monitors. "Play that back slowly, please, Julie," he told the woman sitting next to him.

Her deft fingers manipulated the video feed to where the truck first became visible. The angle of the camera was such that he saw the approaching lights, and then the passenger side of the truck. No view at all of the driver's side. The footage ended with a blaze of light as the truck collided with the fence and the camera was destroyed.

"I don't see anything, sir," she said. Julie Murphy knew how to pull the finest detail out of the imaging programs. He was extremely grateful for the fact that she was working the night shift.

"Neither do I," he said. He picked up the coffee and took a gulp. He was tired and needed to stay focused.

Julie's fingers began flying over the keyboard. "We haven't tried the other cameras, though. The next one down the line should give us details of the other side of the truck if the light was strong enough for the camera to pick anything up from that distance."

Cradling the mug, Jonathan leaned forward with interest. Footage came up. The view was from farther away but he watched headlights light up the field as the truck bounced over the dirt. The driver's side came into view. The door remained closed as the truck passed out of the camera's range. Mere seconds later, light flared over the screen as the truck hit the fence off-camera.

"Well, it was worth a try," Julie said. She dragged the baggy sleeves of her hoodie down over her hands.

"Play the infrared from this camera," Jonathan asked.

She nodded and pulled up a new screen. The truck approached in shades of orange and red. They waited until heat blossomed across the screen when the electric fence blew. Jonathan sat back in disappointment. He closed his eyes a moment, resting his head against the back of the chair. All the fancy technology and they couldn't figure out who'd been driving the damned truck.

"Sir, look at this," Julie urged.

His eyes snapped open and he focused on the screen again. A shape moved across the screen, away from the fence and back across the field. Blue and green hues showed it had extremely low body temperature.

The screen split as Julie cued up both the infrared and the video footage and synced them. Nothing was visible on the video. She muttered under her breath, pushed her sleeves up to her elbows, and danced her fingers across the keys. The footage started again, and she zoomed in tightly on the area of the video that should have held whatever was walking across the field. She did something and the contrast changed, once, then again.

Jonathan pointed at the screen. "There."

"I've got him," she said. She focused as tightly as she could and then did something he couldn't follow. A dark shape emerged from the background. A man walked away from the wreckage, hands shoved in his pockets. He wore a dark jacket, a hood drawn up around his face. They couldn't see a single feature.

"He's one cool cat," she commented. "His core temperature is at least twenty degrees colder than a human's."

"Any idea what he is?" a voice asked from behind their chairs.

Julie jumped, but Jonathan had sensed someone was there, recognized the footfall as Mark's. "Not a clue."

"Show me from the beginning," Mark asked. "I came in at the end."

Julie promptly restarted the footage, watching with them as the truck came across the field, as the fence exploded into sparks off screen, and then as the man walked away. When it was over, she swung around and looked at them.

"You did well, Julie. Send us both copies of the footage," Mark said. "In your office, please, Jonathan."

Jonathan reheated the coffee in the microwave. The liquid scalded as he took a drink but he swallowed anyway, needing the punch of caffeine. Outside the window, the night pressed close. It would be dawn soon, but it would be hours before he could get back to bed.

"What's going on, Jonathan?" Mark asked.

"I think we've got a problem," Jonathan said honestly. He checked his email, found the files Julie had sent, and opened them. She'd sent isolated stills of the man, and Jonathan enlarged one to fit his screen. He stared at the mysterious figure for a moment before looking at Mark.

"I think I brought him here," he said. "My last consult down in Carolina didn't end well. Cateera and I couldn't find the killer."

"That's unusual," Mark said.

"Yes, it is," Jonathan said. He wasn't bragging or being arrogant. This was only the second time he and his bondmate had failed to track down the killer. "We just couldn't get a handle on his identity. But I think he knew us. Both of us felt a presence in our heads on more than one occasion."

"He's telepathic?"

"He's something," Jonathan agreed. "It felt like he was laughing at us. And, Mark, I really think he followed us back here."

"Do you just think it, or do you have proof?"

"Nothing concrete," Jonathan admitted. "When Rivera's shields went down a few days ago, I went out there. I felt someone watching us. I can't prove it, but I know there was someone out in the woods. And he was laughing."

Mark nodded. The frown between his eyes said that he believed it, and he didn't like it. "So what's the point of all of this? Why break into the Haven and then walk away?"

"Damned if I know," Jonathan said. He finished the coffee and pushed the mug away. "Maybe he's just taunting us, showing us that he can, that we're not as safe as we'd like to think. Maybe he's planning something and this is a test, or a distraction. Maybe he's mad because I ruined his fun in Carolina.

"Fuck," he said, and pushed out of the chair. "There's something else. Samuelson, the pedophile that Alanna found, he died in jail. What I didn't tell you was what he looked like. I think he died of fear, Mark. He had the same expression I saw over and over on the bodies in Carolina."

Jonathan rubbed his eyes and turned away. The window showed his reflection, a tall, tired man with shadows under his eyes. He closed his eyes and pushed outwards, reaching with the Gift that Cateera had given him. It was harder without contact with the victim but he didn't really need it. Those dead men and women would be with him always. He reached, psychic fingers linked with the deceased, his other hand flung out into the darkness.

And touched something. Icy cold, sharp. The contact was sudden, unexpected, and totally initiated by whoever was on the other end. Cateera was there with him, his anchor, and he used her strength to try to cage the creature he'd reached.

Mocking laughter met his attempts. *It's not as easy as that, Jonathan Burke. I'll let you see me when I'm ready.*

Jonathan staggered back when the contact was broken. His hip hit the chair and he sat. "It's him," he told Mark.

"Human?"

"I don't think so, but I don't know what he is." Jonathan shook his head. The contact felt alien. His skin still crawled. "I think he's playing, though. I think he's having fun. And I think he's angry that we disturbed him in Carolina. Whatever else he is, he's a killer."

Chapter Fourteen

Cashmere gloves and furry earmuffs were the Brownies' way of telling her that it was cold outside. Alanna took the offered gifts with a smile and thanks. The muffs cuddled her ears and the gloves were luxuriously soft and warm. The running suit she wore could handle most weather extremes to keep her core temperature stable.

The cold air outside the mansion was a brisk shock to her lungs, freezing her breath into puffs of twinkling crystal. Clouds had slunk in overnight, obscuring the mountaintops with dark cotton fluff. It looked and felt like snow.

Wait for me, Jekk said. *I'm almost there.*

"I promised I would," Alanna reassured him. She began to stretch slowly, warming her muscles. Her calves protested a little and she worked them a little longer. She didn't want to cramp in the cold. She felt Jekk before she saw him and turned her head to see him lope around the side of the mansion. Long and lean, he flowed with feline grace over the grass. He was putting on weight but he was still far too skinny. Nearly overcome with love for him, Alanna wrapped her arms around his thick shoulders and hugged her face into his fur. He was no longer rejecting her affection, so he must have gotten over his anger at her decision to return home.

Jekk purred, a sound she both heard and felt beneath her hands.

I'll keep you safe, he told her. *The Faelinn didn't find any intruders, but I don't want you to be in danger.*

"I trust you," she said aloud. She began a slow jog down the driveway, letting herself warm up before she increased her pace. He told her about the truck and how he and Cateera had helped the others hunt in the woods for anyone who didn't belong. He was proud that Berren had chosen him to investigate the field beyond the fence. He was also smart enough to understand that it had been a test. Wise enough not to point out to her that he had a place here if he could take it. The pride she felt in him was unmatched.

Reaching the main road, Alanna increased her pace, her running shoes pounding a rhythm on the tarmac. It was so different to run here than it was in the city. She always ran in the mornings before starting work. She knew every trail and footpath around her city. She knew which parts to avoid, and which parts were safe even in the lingering dark of winter mornings. Here in the Haven, she felt safe no matter where she was. Not only did Jekk keep her company, but the knowledge that there were other Faelinn around gave her a lingering sense of safety.

It was a bonus that the terrain here, the ups and downs of the mountain roads, challenged her, strengthening muscles that didn't get as much of a workout on the flat roads of the city.

Running through the small town at the heart of the Haven, she passed a coffee shop that was already open. There was the school, waiting for children to swell it with an equal mixture of boredom and enthusiasm. The sign outside told her that there was a PTA meeting on Thursday night. A ball had been left on the basketball court, just waiting for the right group of children to come along and set it in motion. There was the small bookshop where she'd promised to come back and have a book signing. She waved at the fireman polishing the side of his truck outside the station and received a grin and a smile in return. Lights were on inside the quirky store that seemed to carry everything from groceries to obscure hardware needs. All it lacked were some old men outside playing checkers to complete her mental idea of an old-time mom-and-pop store.

This was a good place, a place where people let their kids play outside without demanding to know where they were each minute of the day. Even with the break-in last night, she felt safe. There was no fear of walking to your car in the dark and being mugged. She didn't feel naked without the pepper spray clipped to her waistband while she ran. It was a place out of time. No new construction to pave over where the Veiler wars had torn down buildings and left scars in the earth.

Just past her halfway point, circling back to head for the Dennisons' mansion, Alanna realized she recognized the houses on her left. The empty house separated Agneta's home from Jonathan's. She slowed to a walk, telling herself that she had the beginning of a charley horse in her calf and needed to work it out. There was no truck in Jonathan's driveway. She imagined he was out dealing with the intrusion.

There was a nice distance between the houses. Residents would be close enough to be neighbors but not so close that they could peek in each other's windows. Jekk took off along the center drive, heading up to the empty house that sat on a small rise. Painted white with crisp navy shutters and trim, it seemed to be waiting for someone to fill it.

"Jekk, we have to get on the road soon, I'm heading back," she said across their private link, unwilling to yell to him and risk waking anyone up.

I want to see inside, he told her.

"I'm sure it's locked," she answered. She'd slowed to a stop, watching him. When he grasped the knob and opened the door, she sighed. She jogged up the path, aware that she was being manipulated. Like Agneta's house next door, it had a wide, covered porch. A set of wrought iron chairs and a matching table graced a corner. Empty hooks between the posts showed where hanging plants would swing in warmer months. She'd put a hummingbird feeder nearby.

Jekk left the door open, and she stepped into a foyer painted pure white. Honey-colored planks polished to a high sheen made up the floor, matching the newel post and banister of the stairs that led upwards and disappeared around a corner. The house had an open floor plan. The rest of the first floor had the same polished floors, but colorful hooked rugs were scattered across them. A sofa and chair pretended to be ghosts beneath white sheets. A large fireplace had been scrubbed clean, a wide mantel begged for photos and trinkets. Most of the room was empty, waiting for someone to fill it with their own furniture. A dining area was raised up a step at the far end of the room. An old crystal chandelier hung in the center of the ceiling but there was no table beneath it. Alanna knew the chandelier would sparkle with a little love and care. A wide butcher's block was a functional barrier between the dining area and the kitchen.

The appliances in the kitchen were state of the art. A long window over the sink had set-in shelves at its base. She could imagine herbs chosen for their scents filling pots. Lemon verbena, rosemary, basil. Alanna shook her head to dispel the vision. She wouldn't know one from the other, and certainly had no use for them in the kitchen. Cooking was not one of her talents.

A stair runner in reds and golds covered the plank stairway. Halfway up the staircase, there was a window seat padded with soft-looking cushions. The second floor held a full bath tiled in a terrible shade of pea green. There was a master suite with a balcony wide enough for chairs and a table. The suite also featured a large bathroom thankfully decorated in more palatable colors. A long, deep tub invited someone to sink into scented water.

There were two other bedrooms on the second floor, one holding a bare twin bed frame and basic furniture. The third room at the back of the house was different. It could quite easily be a bedroom, but she instantly knew what it should be.

Shelves lined one wall. Floor to ceiling, they would hold her collection of research books on every topic under the sun. Her desk would go just there under that gorgeous, wide window. Right there where Jekk had his nose almost pressed to the glass.

I can see Cateera's house and yard, he said. The wistfulness tore at her heart. She crossed the room and laid her hand on his shoulder. Sure enough, when she looked to the right, she could see the edge of Jonathan's house, a wide deck holding a covered barbeque and plenty of seating. A carefully tended yard grown brown in the cold stretched down toward the tree line. There was a large outbuilding, made in the same log cabin style to match the main house. She wondered if that was where he made the stained glass.

The Veil glimmered above the trees. From her desk, she would be able to watch the coruscating colors. At night, they would be stunning. She knew she would be inspired to write here. It would be an ever-changing view. The seasons would play out, changing the landscape. And from up here she would get the occasional glimpse of her sexy neighbor.

It was a good place. It could be her place. Hers and Jekk's. Suddenly, the city held less appeal for her than the trees whispering, the music of the Faelinn calling to each other in the dusk. The people she'd met here and the sense of family that surrounded her. She could make this home.

Closing her eyes, Alanna took a deep breath. The decision was surprisingly easy. Kneeling, she wrapped her arms around Jekk's neck, pressing her forehead to his soft fur. "Yes," she whispered in his ear.

He trembled, a hesitant purr beginning in his throat. *We can stay here, in this house?*

"I'll have to ask Mark, but I don't think he'll mind."

Jekk's purr became loud and he turned his head to swipe his rough tongue across her face. The thought came that it would be an excellent exfoliant as it dragged across her cheek and into her hairline. She laughed at the pure happiness that filled her chest, her own and his. She was still laughing when she looked up to see Jonathan leaning in the doorway.

The exhaustion in his eyes told her he'd gotten little or no rest. He needed a shave and either a gallon of coffee or eight hours of sleep. The lazy way he watched her made her remember their kiss. And made her ache to cross the room and do it again.

"You look like hell," she said, straightening from her crouch next to Jekk. Also adorably scruffy and sexy, but she wasn't going to think about that.

"Gee, thanks," he said dryly. "I like the earmuffs," he said. Amusement tinged his eyes when she snatched them off. "I saw the front door open. What are you doing in here?"

There was no warning. One minute he was leaning against the door frame, and the next he was stumbling forward. Cateera was a blur of white and lavender as she muscled past him, and then she was across the room, winding her sinuous body around her mate's. Her softer purr joined the basso of his and rattled the windows. Jonathan rose from the fighter's crouch he'd automatically fallen into, surprise lightening his eyes.

"I see," he said. "What changed your mind?"

Sidestepping the Faelinn and getting a tail whipped across her hip for her trouble, Alanna smiled at him. "What? Return to New DC and miss out on living next door to you? I don't suppose you do naked tai chi outside every morning?"

"Not normally, but if you let me know when you're watching, I might be persuaded to give it a try."

The images that filled her head reduced her brain to barely operational mush, but she managed to get them under control enough to answer. "I'll be nice and wait until the warmer months. I'm afraid the cold might not show off your best side."

Jonathan snorted back laughter. "I appreciate that."

Thank you.

The soft female tone slid into Alanna's mind. Turning her head, Alanna found Cateera watching her with light-filled turquoise eyes. The depth of happiness and gratitude coming from the two Faelinn awed her. How could she possibly have planned to split them? "Just make him happy," she thought back, reaching to scratch the spot beneath Cateera's ear that Faelinn seemed to like.

Of course, Cateera replied, arching her head into Alanna's touch. *As you will make my bondmate happy. You will be a good mate for him.*

"Oh no," Alanna denied with a quick shake of her head.

"Don't you want to mate with me?" The words were a silky whisper from behind her, Jonathan's breath stirring the soft hair around her ear.

Startled, she spun, wondering when he'd moved. Damn the man for being quiet. Apparently, Cateera had included him on their conversation. Without the heels she normally wore, she had to tip her head back to meet his eyes, an unusual event given her height. So close, she could see the tiny lines radiating from the corners of his eyes. Exhaustion lingered there and in the bruised skin underneath. It would be too easy to reach out and stroke those lines away, to let her fingertips trace the curve of his mouth. Far too easy.

She stepped back. "I'll give it some thought after I see the naked tai chi." Jamming the earmuffs back on her head, she retreated to the door. "I need to finish my run and see a man about a house."

"Alanna, I'm glad you're staying."

The softly spoken words followed her out into the cold morning. And despite wishing it were otherwise, they warmed her.

~

Jonathan tossed his cell phone onto the table. Leaning back in the chair, he let his eyes close. He'd gone home earlier, showered, and changed, but that was all. The muscles of his neck screamed with tension and lifting a hand to rub only seemed to make it worse. It didn't look like there was going to be any sleep in sight, though.

The fence was being fixed. The whole section had to be personally monitored though while the power was down. He'd ordered two-man patrols of the perimeter. The Faelinn could disappear at will, their unique talents camouflaging them. They could prowl without being in danger. His men, though, were targets. Take one down and his Fael would come running. Easiest way to catch a Fael. So, for the duration, there were two on a patrol. It stretched them thin, and he'd called in help from the fire department and volunteers. The Haven could always be depended upon to react as a group.

Sheriff Jacobs had promised to send more patrols out to cover the roads near the Haven. Old man Barnes had been questioned but said he'd been sleeping and hadn't heard a thing. Hadn't seen anything in the past few weeks either.

The truck waited in the garage behind the Playground. It had taken longer than he'd intended to get all the details of the night sorted out. The forensic examination of the truck had been pushed back. Now it was late morning and he needed to head over there and get started on it. Somewhere in that truck there had to be a fingerprint, or a receipt, something that would point them in the direction of who—or what—had launched it through the fence.

There was a knock on the office door. It was a warning more than a request to enter because Mark was already on his way in by the time Jonathan looked up. He grunted a hello and took the large mug of coffee that Mark held out. He drew the deeply caffeinated smell into his lungs, following it up with a long drink.

"Figured you needed that," Mark said, leaning back in the extra chair. He stretched his legs out and crossed them at the ankle. He had a steaming mug of his own.

"I need a vat of it," Jonathan said. He shuffled the paperwork into a more or less functional pile and filled Mark in on everything they'd learned since the man had been there earlier. It was a brief conversation.

"Shit," Jonathan said, and drank the rest of the coffee. "I'm heading over to the garage. I've got the truck in a bay, waiting to be examined. Want to come with me?"

"If you don't mind me watching?" Mark said.

"Nope," Jonathan said and headed out the door.

The day had brightened but still retained the heavy overcast of this morning. The air had the hushed feel that presaged a storm. The world had taken a deep breath and was waiting for the first flakes of snow to fall before it let it out in a rush. Moist cold bit into Jonathan's cheeks when he left the Playground and he shoved his hands into his pockets. Way up high, the pine branches shivered in a wind that didn't quite reach the ground.

Mark kicked at a pile of leaves that had drifted across the sidewalk. They scuttled aside, swirling up before settling into new piles. "So, you're going to have a new neighbor."

Jonathan slid his gaze over to his friend's profile and then away. It wasn't a long walk to the garage, only through a stand of trees and across a parking lot. Just long enough for Mark to annoy the hell out of him. "Looks like. You're letting her use the house, then."

"Of course. I offered her the pick of the unoccupied houses but Jekk wants to be near Cateera."

Jonathan grunted.

"Alanna left hours ago," Mark said. "She's probably close to New DC by now. I have a moving company meeting her tomorrow. She'll be back in no time. Just in case you planned to miss her."

Jonathan stopped. "What the hell does that mean?"

"Rumor gets around quickly. I heard you had a hot date last night." The grin was open now. Mark wasn't even trying to hide it.

The trees ended, giving way to the parking lot in front of the garage. The low brick building and parking lot served a double duty. The Haven's vehicles lined up neatly on the far side of the lot, trucks and vans sharing space with a few sedans and even a limo. The garage itself provided maintenance and storage space. It also offered a place for the mechanically minded residents to service their own vehicles. Five bays stretched away to the right. A single door at the other end led into the office space. There was also another bay, completely separate with its own equipment. Jonathan had insisted on having it stocked with everything a forensic garage would need. Until now, he'd never had to use it.

One of the bay doors was open, a Haven truck jacked up inside. Legs stuck out from beneath the bed, one foot tapping to the faint sounds of a popular country song spilling from a radio. He recognized the boots as belonging to the chief mechanic, Duke.

"It wasn't a hot date," Jonathan denied. Entirely untrue, given the way she'd left him in the driveway. A few more minutes of that kiss and he'd have had her in the front seat of his truck, her legs wrapped around his waist.

Mark's phone rang. Jonathan knew by the happy piece of music that it was Shellie. He headed for the office while Mark answered, wondering if Alanna had his number, angry at himself for even thinking about it.

A frown drew Mark's dark brows together, and he reached out to grab Jonathan's arm, pulling him to a stop. They were almost at the garage door. "Slow down, Shellie. What's wrong?"

The hair lifted on the back of Jonathan's neck. Shellie wasn't one to panic and the look in his friend's eyes told him she was. Something was wrong.

"I'll call you right back," Mark promised. He shoved the cell into his pocket and looked at Jonathan. "She's got a bad feeling," he said. "We need to get out of here."

Chapter Fifteen

S hellie's feelings weren't to be ignored. Jonathan took a step back and then stopped. "Duke's in the bay. Who else is here?"

The ground beneath Jonathan's boots quivered. There was no time to acknowledge it, no time to run. In a breath's time, the quivering gained light and fury. The compression wave lifted him, throwing him across the parking lot. The force of it tossed him against a tree like a loose-limbed doll. Something popped in his side; the rough bark scraped his skin. The ground slammed into him. Heat scorched his face and a great roaring pushed against his eardrums. Molten rain puddled down, igniting the dry pine straw. A blackened cinder block missed his head by inches.

The blast of heat seared across him and he threw up an arm to protect his face from both the heat and the falling debris. He struggled to breathe. Finally, when there didn't seem to be anything else falling from the sky, Jonathan pushed himself up, hissing against the grating pain in his side. Cateera's panicked scream in his head had him reeling and it was pure reflex that let him reassure her he was okay before he was even certain that he was. His leather jacket was smoldering on one arm and he slapped it out. The movement sheared pain through his side, robbing him of what little breath he'd been able to get.

Ignoring it, Jonathan pushed to his knees. The garage was a storm of fire, black clouds of smoke building higher and higher, shot through with angry flame. The roar of it was dull compared to the ringing in his ears. Debris was scattered across the parking lot and around him in the trees. A fire had already started, greedily consuming the dry underbrush. Somewhere, there may have been alarms ringing, but he just wasn't sure.

Mark was sprawled on his back a few feet away. Blood from a gash on his temple gleamed sticky-dark in his hair. Gaining his feet, one arm pressed against broken ribs, Jonathan stumbled to his side. Mark blinked groggily and pushed himself up. His cell phone was ringing.

"The trees are on fire," Jonathan yelled. "Get up!" He used one hand to pull Mark to his feet, bracing him when he swayed. The cut had to be worse than it looked. He led him the few feet to the parking lot where they'd be safe from the smoldering pine straw. Nothing else was falling from the sky.

The garage's roof was gone, blown off in the blast. Fire poured from the office windows, the glass blown out from the pressure. Thick smoke obscured the open bay door, but he didn't see any fire. Duke was inside. Clutching his side where the ribs scraped together, Jonathan ran to the open bay. Smoke blinded his eyes, and he squeezed them nearly shut against the burning and tearing. Drawing a deep breath was out of the question but he did what he could before he stepped into the cavernous repair area. Part of the back wall must have blown out. Cinder blocks lurked to trip him. Supplies were strewn across the oil-stained floor, tools mixed haphazardly with replacement parts. A whole section of roof had collapsed to his left and the heat from the fire sucked moisture from his skin.

There were combustibles stored in supply closets nearby. Pretending they didn't exist, he moved in a half-crouch to the truck. A metal beam from the roof bisected the hood. The ramps jacking up the front end were askew, one completely knocked aside. It set the pickup at a dangerous angle. Duke's jean-clad legs splayed out on the concrete floor, the top of his body still invisible beneath the truck. Jonathan clasped one ankle, giving it a shake. The legs kicked in response. Duke was alive and conscious.

"My arm's stuck," Duke yelled. The sound came out as a croak.

Coughing—what little air there was swiftly being consumed by the fire—Jonathan groped beneath the truck bed. He could feel where the front end pushed against Duke's side, but not where his arm was pinned. Kneeling, Jonathan grasped the wheels of the creeper cart and pulled. His ribs screamed but Duke screamed louder. Jonathan blocked both out. There wasn't any time for mercy. Blackness pressed against his vision and he could feel the world getting dimmer. The creeper resisted a moment, and then came free, sending him back onto his ass. Duke was still pinned beneath the truck. The extra room must have been enough to loosen his arm, though, because he began to dig his heels in and scoot his way out. Jonathan grabbed his calves, and a minute later, the mechanic was free.

The arm was a ruined mass of crushed bone. Wrapping his good arm around Duke, Jonathan half-dragged him out of the garage. Mark was there to take over, and once Jonathan got far enough away from the fire, he collapsed to his knees on the pavement. He couldn't get enough air. His lungs labored to draw it in, but his throat was raw, his ribs screamed, and there just wasn't enough oxygen to be had.

People swarmed around him, helping him to his feet and leading him further from the burning building. He caught a glimpse of a few people with fire extinguishers working on the brush fire. Everyone in the Playground must have heard the blast and come to help. That meant that the fire trucks would be here soon.

A cold bottle of water was pressed into his hand and he took it gratefully. He took a long drink and then had to stop when a wracking cough doubled him over in pain. His cell phone was ringing but he couldn't breathe to answer it. His mouth held a nasty taste of burned chemicals and ash. Cateera was there suddenly, winding around him, shepherding him away from the crowd, away from the many voices that were hammering at him for answers.

Another blast shook the air. From the far side of the building a gas pump shot up, rocketing skyward to disappear into roiling cloud. A second later, gravity pulled it down, tumbling end over end. It cracked the parking lot where it landed.

Grabbing an arm randomly as someone came close enough, Jonathan yelled over the roaring flames. "Get everyone back to the Playground. It's not safe here!"

Anne, the waitress from the night before stared at him with wide eyes. She looked far younger than normal, freckles stark against pale cheeks. Still, she nodded vigorously and turned away to begin yelling instructions.

His phone was still ringing. Looking around for Mark, he grabbed it from his pocket. Mark and Berren were forcing the crowd back toward the road. The fire extinguishers were useless against the burning debris in the trees and the path back through the woods just wasn't safe. A group crouched over Duke where he lay on the tarmac. Now that his eardrums were beginning to recover, Jonathan could hear the screaming of the approaching fire trucks.

Falling back to where the heat wasn't threatening to burn away his skin, Jonathan opened his phone. Pressing one hand against his broken ribs because it seemed to help, he hit redial for the last number. Rivera picked up immediately.

"What the hell is going on?" his second demanded.

"The truck we hauled in exploded," Jonathan rasped. His throat was raw and he had to cough again before he could go on. "The garage is gone."

"I'll call everyone in and send them over," Rivera said.

"No! I want every eye on that fence." Jonathan had to look away from the blaze. It was bright enough to hurt his eyes. Even from his position near the access road, a good distance from the fire, he could feel heat prickling his skin. "If this is a diversion, he'll be trying to use it to get into the Haven. You keep the patrols on that fence, Rivera."

"Yes, sir," Rivera said.

Jonathan slipped the cell back into his pocket. He limped his way to where Mark waited. Every bone in his body felt bruised. His face hurt and he reached up to touch his cheek. His fingertips found blood and the rough edges of a cut in his cheek. The lead fire truck reached the garage. Men began pulling hose almost before it stopped.

"Remind me to buy Shellie a boatload of chocolate," Jonathan rasped. His fingers gripped Cateera's fur. The contact steadied him, kept the pain from dragging him to his knees. Their bond flared to life, and he felt the pressure on his lungs ease a little.

"You'll have to get in line," Mark said. His white shirt was red where the gash on his head had bled, dripping down to coat the shirt collar. His brown jacket was singed in places. His eyes were ringed red and teary from the smoke. "Was it the truck?"

"I think so, yeah," Jonathan said. "Either a remote trigger or a timer. My bet is on a timer."

The fire chief yelled instructions as the men began to direct sprays of water into the conflagration. His grey and red Fael circled his legs. The fierce banding around the Fael's eyes gave him a masked look. Chief Berenger turned toward the trees, his back to the inferno of the garage. He widened his stance, one hand resting on his Fael's shoulders. Fire Sprites flickered and popped, dancing along tree branches and amongst the thick lining of pine straw. The fire extinguishers had slowed the fire, but not put it out.

Even from this distance, his look of concentration could be seen. The red markings on the Fael's sides glowed angrily. Berenger took a step forward. The flames licking at the trees flared brightly and began to shrink. The smell of burning sap was astringent beneath the stench of the garage. Sprites shrieked and cursed, flinging sparks from their perches in the trees. The flames in the straw died first, flicking out to leave charred blackness behind. One by one, the Sprites popped, each tiny explosion sucking flame into nonexistence. When only faint drifts of pale smoke remained and there was no longer a threat that the fire would spread through the woods, Berenger turned his attention to the building.

The clinic ambulance had arrived while they were watching the chief. The mechanic had been strapped to a gurney and even now the attendants were securing him in the back of the ambulance. They were wasting no time getting him to Bethany.

"Duke's going to lose that arm," Jonathan said. He held his ribs tight as a cough ripped through him. Even with bond magic working inside of him, he struggled to breathe.

"Bethany can work wonders," Mark said.

"There wasn't much left but jelly," Jonathan said. Fury as black as the clouds of smoke filled him. He would hunt down the bastard who was responsible for this and make him pay.

"Looks like you could use some help yourself," Mark observed, staring pointedly at the arm held protectively across Jonathan's torso. "They'll send another ambulance."

"I don't need it. It's just a couple of ribs," he said. "Right now, I want to find out what the hell is going on." At his side, Cateera growled her agreement.

The wind picked up, tearing the black clouds of smoke into strands that fingered the tops of the trees. He worried about sparks being picked up and carried to other parts of the Haven, but even as he watched, the fire began to shrink. Hoses shot arching streams of water into the hottest areas. The steam that burped up from the blackened carcass of the garage stank.

The first snowflake drifted down in front of him and Jonathan turned his face up to the sky. His skin felt sunburned. One or two random flakes became three or four and then a dozen. In just a few minutes, they were already settling on his shoulders, in his hair. Shivers rippled through him. His battered leather jacket was not the best choice for standing out in a snowfall.

A car screamed along the access road and came to a sliding stop next to Mark. Shellie launched herself from the driver's seat and into her husband's arms. Her hands moved over him rapidly, testing arms and shoulders for injuries. Delicate fingers pushed back his hair so that she could exclaim over the gash on his temple. Mark put up with her ministrations for a minute and then dragged her tight against him to bury his face in her blond curls.

The sudden stab of loneliness was as painful as his broken ribs. It caught Jonathan off guard.

Your mate should be here, Cateera said. She pushed her head gently against his hand. *She would not let you stand in the snow when you should be inside getting Bethany to heal you.*

"Bethany's busy with Duke," Jonathan reminded her.

Cateera was silent a moment. Her whiskers twitched, scattering snowflakes. *Bethany is waiting at the clinic in town for the ambulance. She will do what she can while they take him to the hospital. Flexa said to send you to the Haven's clinic for help.*

"I'm waiting for Berenger. I want his report."

His Fael tells me that it will be at least tomorrow morning before he can search the ruins. It will still be too hot before then. Raising a white paw bigger than his fist, Cateera poked his ribs. *You see,* she said when he jerked back in pain. *You need help. I cannot help you heal fast enough.*

"You're a nag, Cateera," he told her. The disgusted sound that came from her throat was almost enough to make him laugh. Except that would hurt and he really didn't want that.

Call your mate, she will tell you what to do. Besides, Jekk is worried. He can feel that something is wrong, but he is too far away to speak to me.

He didn't know how the phone got into his hand. But it was there, and he might as well use it to relieve Cateera's worry that Jekk was upset. The number seemed to dial itself and he waited through endless ringing, sure it would go to voicemail. Then Alanna answered and her voice broke like a balm inside of him, even though she sounded curt and frustrated.

"Nice to talk to you, too," he told her.

"Jonathan? What's going on? Jekk is frantic and what the hell is wrong with your voice?"

The smile that tugged his mouth pulled at the cut on his cheek, ripping it open again. He felt the warmth of blood against his cold skin. "Let Jekk talk to Cateera first." He handed the phone to Cateera. The two Faelinn spoke quickly, Cateera soothing Jekk's worry that she was in danger and then explaining what had happened. Linked to her, Jonathan understood Cateera's language, but his human throat wouldn't allow him to make more than the most rudimentary word.

Thank you, she said, rubbing her side against his thigh when she was finished. Her tail wound briefly around his arm, and then she sat, wrapping that tail around her feet. She watched him with calm turquoise eyes as snowflakes settled on her coat.

"Alanna, are you there?" Jonathan asked.

"You idiot! You went into the garage to rescue a man? You could have been killed! What were you thinking? Something could have fallen on you, or there could have been an explosion, or you could have passed out and died from smoke inhalation! You are such a jerk!"

"You're worried about me," he said, satisfaction warming his voice.

"I am not," she answered. "I'm worried about what would happen to Jekk if you and Cateera died, you arrogant jerk."

"No, you're worried about me, I can tell," Jonathan said. The silence on the other end of the phone made his smile widen. It hurt, but he didn't care.

"I'm hanging up now."

"Don't," he whispered. He put his back to the organized chaos of the men fighting the fire and stared instead at the trees, at the snow slowly frosting the pine needles. He didn't want to stare at ugliness while talking to her.

"Fine," Alanna said. "Are you really all right? Cateera said you need a doctor."

"A couple broken ribs and some cuts and bruises," he told her. "I'll be fine in a day or two. Cateera will help. Of course, when you come back, you can nurse me back to health." The thought of her in a nurse's outfit, only barely buttoned, the tops of stockings peeking out from under the short skirt, led to a suddenly very interesting fantasy.

"In your dreams, Burke," she said.

"You have no idea," he told her.

"It would involve an ice water sponge bath and very big needles," she told him archly. But somehow the breathy sound of her voice told him that's not what she was thinking.

"Maybe our bondmates have it right," Jonathan said softly. "Maybe you are my mate."

"Are you sure you didn't hit your head? Or maybe all the smoke went to your brain."

"You want me as much as I want you," he said. "Admit it."

"That doesn't mean we're meant for each other. It just means we're young and horny."

Jonathan's sudden laugh ripped at his throat but he didn't care. "Come home soon, Alanna." He turned when Shellie took his arm, frowning up at him. She dabbed at his bleeding face with a tissue. He shied away, and she took his chin in her hand. "I have to go, Shellie's beginning to mother me."

"Good," Alanna said. There was a pause, and when she spoke again, the words were soft. "Be careful, Jonathan. Please."

Not even the irritating dabbing that Shellie was managing could keep his smile from lingering when he hung up. He slipped the phone back into his jacket with one hand, the other catching Shellie's arm gently. "Stop, I don't need to be fussed over."

"No, but you do need to have that cut cleaned. In case you didn't know, your entire face is black with smoke." She wiped at his cheek again, showing him the bloody black smear. "And those ribs need to be x-rayed."

"You'd better listen to her," Mark said. "It will be a whole lot easier on both of us."

With Cateera adding her own recommendations, Jonathan gave in. Berenger wouldn't have any relevant information for him before tomorrow. Any debris from the bomb wouldn't be found until the fire-blackened wreckage could be safely searched. There wasn't anything he could do here except fret and get in the way. Besides, he could use a couple of aspirin for the pain in his side. He meekly followed Shellie to the car.

The couch caught her as her legs collapsed. Alanna closed her eyes and waited for the unexpected dizziness to pass. The stupid man had gone into a burning building, a building that might have collapsed down on his idiot head at any time, to find someone. She was torn between being furious and being proud. Both emotions confused her.

Cateera says he'll be okay, Jekk reassured her. *She says he's very brave.*

"And very stupid," she answered. She looked into his golden eyes and forced herself to relax. "I don't even like him."

The sound that left Jekk's throat sounded suspiciously like a snicker and she narrowed her eyes at him in warning. In response, he flopped down at her feet and rolled over so that his paws stuck up in the air. The fur on his belly was a soft gold and he looked adorable. Huge, but adorable. She wasn't falling for it, though. Standing up, she stepped over Jekk's prone body and headed for the stairs.

"Come on, we have packing to do if we're going to be ready for the movers that Mark is sending."

We'll go home tomorrow?

"The day after. I have a lot of errands to do tomorrow if we're going to move to the Haven." She shook her head, the thick braid she wore bouncing on her back. "For one, I'm going to have to explain it to my agent. She's just not going to believe it."

Chapter Sixteen

The rasp of Cateera's tongue over his side was finally more than he could take, and Jonathan gently pushed her away. He'd spent a restless night trying to find a position that didn't bother his ribs. The x-rays had shown three cracked ribs. With Cateera's care, he knew they were well on the way to being healed. It was one of the benefits of being a bondmate. The cut on his face had already healed, leaving only a fading red line. With some difficulty, he shrugged into a shirt, ignoring the stabbing pain in his side.

Berenger was waiting for him at the office.

Cateera sniffed in disdain when Jonathan opened the SUV door for her. Frost limned the windows and an inch of snow covered the hood. The storm hadn't amounted to much. Cateera took off at a loping run for the trees. She would join the Faelinn patrolling the fence. Rivera had checked in repeatedly through the night. No further attempts had been made to break into the Haven. Jonathan was torn between relief and anger. He had no way to find the man who was responsible for all of this.

And that frustrated him.

The security center at the Playground was busier than normal. Usually only one man monitored the electronics, watched the cameras, waited for an alarm that almost never came. Today, there were two. Jonathan stopped to speak to them both, looking over the nightly reports. There was absolutely nothing noteworthy.

Stopping by the coffeepot on the way to his private office, Jonathan grimaced as he poured the thick sludge into a mug. He was going to have to hit up the café for a decent cup later. As promised, Berenger was already in the office, feet kicked up on the desk. Ratty black Converse were propped on a pile of unfiled papers. There was a rip in one knee of his faded jeans. With the curls of his dark brown hair and his light gold eyes, he could easily pass for a college student. Jonathan knew for a fact that Jack was older than him.

"Get your feet off my desk," Jonathan said, slapping them as he walked past.

"Wouldn't have had to get comfortable if you'd gotten here earlier," Berenger pointed out. His feet hit the ground and he sat up. "How can you drink that crap?"

"I was a cop; we're immune." Jonathan pulled open the curtains behind his desk, letting in the thin sunlight. The sky was still overcast, but he didn't think there'd be any more snow. He took a long swig of the coffee as he sat. Tasted grounds.

"What have you got for me, Jack?"

Berenger picked up a box next to the chair and pushed it across the desk. "I've been up since dawn," he said pointedly. "Sifting through the wreckage."

Inside the box was a tangle of blackened wire and metal. "What am I looking at?"

"Pretty straightforward timer that was attached to enough explosive to blow the shit out of the garage. Nothing remarkable. No fingerprints, no signature wiring. It's something anyone with half a brain, a computer, and access to the parts could do."

Jonathan shoved his hands through his hair and regretted it when his ribs twinged. "That's it? That's all you found?"

"What did you want, Jonathan? A big shiny arrow pointing to a clue? I can only tell you what I found, man."

"I know; I'm just frustrated. I never had a chance to go over the truck." Jonathan picked up a pen, twirled it between his fingers. "We've never had anything like this happen before. We're lucky there weren't fatalities."

"Maybe the plan was to take out the investigators, or civilians. Just pure luck no one else was there," Jack said. He leaned back and laced his fingers over his lean stomach. "Send in a truck loaded with explosives on a delayed timer. Blow up the garage, taking out whoever happened to be there."

"Why the garage?"

"Why not?" Jack asked. "Maybe it didn't matter. He knew the truck would be taken into the Haven and just figured he'd get lucky wherever it went."

The words had the feeling of truth. It could have been an act dedicated to causing fear in the Haven. The person responsible could be dogshit crazy as well as a cold murdering bastard. "You could be onto something."

Jack lifted one shoulder in a lazy shrug. "It's something to think about. Have you heard anything about Duke?"

Jonathan took another swig of the thick coffee. "Yeah, I talked to Mark earlier. Bethany worked on Duke in the ambulance on the way to the hospital's trauma center. I don't know how she did it, but she managed to get the nerves in a decent state of repair, kept the blood flow going. She gave the bones a decent start at putting themselves back together. He went into surgery where they put in some rods and pins to strengthen the bone. Looks like he'll keep the arm. Bethany will help heal him and he should be fine in no time."

"That's good," Jack said. "Next time, though, don't run into the building. Wait for the professionals. Cateera would have killed me if I'd had to pull you out of there."

Jonathan waved the criticism away. Given the situation, he would do it again. Without a moment's hesitation.

Jack stood, hooking his thumbs in his belt loops. His grey sweatshirt sported the Haven fire department logo. "We'll keep combing what's left of the garage, see if we can find anything else. I really don't think we will, though."

"I appreciate it."

~

Boxes. Boxes stacked two and three high. Boxes with the word "books" scrawled across the side. She had no idea she owned so many books. Alanna opened a box at random, found the cover of a popular chef's latest cookbook staring up at her. Great. Cookbooks belonged in the kitchen, not up here in her study. Not that they really belonged there, if she was completely honest. The cookbooks were her latest attempt to conquer the culinary arts. It had failed. Again. She wasn't even sure why the cookbooks were here. She should have just stuck the box out on the curb in New DC and let someone help themselves.

Pushing the flaps closed, Alanna sat down on a box. Where to start? Shellie was down in the kitchen, arranging the cabinets to her satisfaction. When Alanna complained she wouldn't know where anything was, Shellie calmly pointed out that since it was a new kitchen, she wouldn't know where things were anyway. As long as her favorite coffee mug wasn't hidden, Alanna supposed she could get used to where her plates were.

Putting her hands at the base of her spine, Alanna arched her back, hearing the satisfactory pop. The road from New DC wasn't the worse she'd ever travelled, but by no means was it comfortable. The movers had left yesterday, but she and Jekk had spent another night in the city before driving back to the Haven this morning. Since she'd gotten back, she and Shellie had worked hard to get her new house ready.

The bedroom was livable, clean sheets on the bed, curtains hung. Linens were stacked neatly in the closets meant for them. The most important thing left was her office. Currently it was awash in boxes. One of the overstuffed chairs she liked to relax in when she took a break was almost hidden in the corner.

Jekk padded into the room, a blanket trailing behind him. One corner was held delicately in his teeth. It was the blanket from her bed, the one her mother had knitted for her when she was a child. The one she wrapped around herself on cold rainy days while reading a good book.

This is mine, Jekk told her. He laid down between two stacks of boxes, wrapping the blanket around his paws and resting his chin on it.

"My mother made that for me."

I like it. It smells like you.

Alanna laughed and slid to the floor next to him. He wiggled forward so he could lay his head in her lap, purring when she slowly began to rub the base of his ears. He had a particular fondness for being scratched just below his mangled ear. "I don't suppose I could close my eyes and wish everything put away?"

You didn't even bring everything.

It was true. She'd left most of her living room furniture and the spare bedroom furniture. Things that she would need when she occasionally went back to the city. She didn't want to sell the place. There would be times when she'd want to go back and it would be nice to have a place to stay. She intended to shop for new things. Meanwhile, she'd brought her bed and her entire office. And, apparently, every book she'd ever purchased.

"Need some help?"

Alanna looked up in surprise. She swore her heart went pitter-patter. "Don't you ever knock?" She looked at Jekk who was gazing at her with golden eyes. "And why didn't you warn me?"

He asked me not to. Shellie let him in, her Fael replied. He nuzzled her cheek, tickling with his whiskers. Taking the blanket in his mouth, he walked out of the room. Cateera was waiting in the hallway and followed him down the stairs.

Jonathan smiled. "Nice blanket he has there." He slid a finger under the loose flap of the box with the cookbooks and raised his eyebrows. "Do you cook?"

Small talk. She could do small talk. It gave her an excuse not to grab him and make sure he was okay. There was the faintest scar down his cheek that hadn't been there before. "I can't cook," she confessed. "It's the greatest sadness of my mother's heart that I can ruin any food I touch. I live on frozen food, sandwiches, or restaurants."

Jonathan shook his head. "I'll have to cook for you then."

He cooked? One of her fantasies involved a man who cooked for her. And there was no way in hell she was telling him that. "Take the cookbooks if you want. They're wasted in my house."

Jonathan slid down to sit next to her. Stretching out his legs, he crossed them at the ankle. Everywhere he touched her—thigh, hip, and shoulder—tingled. He seemed to make the room smaller, filling it with heat. "I didn't see a lot of furniture downstairs."

"I didn't bring much," she admitted. She would not stare at the way the tight denim stretched over the heavy muscles of his thighs. She certainly wouldn't give into the desire to touch. "I plan to shop."

"I wondered if it was because you didn't really plan to stay." A smile quirked his mouth as he looked around the room. "Then I saw all the boxes in here."

"I'm addicted to books," she admitted. "Some of them got put up here by mistake, though."

He nudged her foot with his. "Need some help unpacking?"

"Are you offering?"

"Ply me with coffee and I'm all yours." Those sinful blue eyes gave her a cautious look. "You can make coffee, right?"

"I think I can manage not to poison you, if that's what you're asking," Alanna said.

"Then let's get started." He stood and offered her a hand. With a quick tug, she was on her feet and somehow caught in the circle of his arm. Her body didn't mind at all, relaxing into the embrace.

Up close, the faint scar on his cheek stretched from his left temple to his jawline. Alanna traced it with a careful fingertip. His skin was slightly rough with the hint of beard. She wanted to purr. He caught her hand and pressed a light kiss into the center of her palm. It burned there with intoxicating heat.

"I'm all right," he told her.

"I wasn't worried," she said. Her fingers wanted to close around the tingling center of her palm, to save the kiss there. She'd been irrationally frantic but she certainly wasn't going to admit that. "I knew Bethany would take care of you. She took care of your ribs?"

"She was too busy with Duke at first. He nearly lost his arm. She got around to me eventually." He nibbled lightly at the tips of her fingers.

The sensation sent a lovely liquid warmth through her. She locked her knees to keep them from collapsing. His hair was silky and she couldn't keep the fingers of her free hand from stroking through it. It was too long for current fashion, but she loved the bad-boy length and the way it sometimes fell forward to shadow those summer-blue eyes.

"You're staring," he said softly. He bent his head to trace the line of her jaw with teasing lips.

"No, I'm not," she murmured. How could she be staring? Her eyes were closed.

Jonathan's breath was warm as he laughed against her skin. His hands smoothed her ribs, thumbs lingering a moment on the sides of her breasts before sliding down. His fingers tightened on her hips before those wandering hands cupped her butt to bring her tight against him. Every one of her senses focused on him. The urge to wrap one leg around his hips and rub against the hard ridge pressed so intimately to her core was nearly overwhelming. And damn him, he still hadn't kissed her.

"How are you two doing up here?" Shellie's cheerful voice floated down the hall. "I brought you some coffee. Oh!" She stopped in the door-way, two immense mugs in her hands. "I'm sorry."

"Don't take that coffee away," Jonathan said when she started to back out. He dropped a light kiss onto Alanna's mouth and let her go.

Coffee trumped kissing? Really? Alanna glared at his back. She told herself she'd already known he was a jerk, but it didn't change the fact that her body missed the hard warmth of his. Peeved, she yanked open a random box and filled her arms with books. She thrust them without care for organization onto an empty shelf and turned back for another armful.

Jonathan held a steaming mug toward her. His hip was propped on a pile of boxes. Watery sunlight from the bare window spilled onto his hair, brightening the wheat-blond strands. Everything feminine inside of her tightened. She wanted this man. She wanted his body wrapped around her, inside of her. She wanted to lick every plane and hollow of hard muscle, taste every inch of tanned skin. He was arrogant and sarcastic and he made her feel alive.

It must have shown on her face. His eyes darkened to indigo, locked onto hers. The mugs went onto the top of a box. In another heartbeat, he was in front of her, hands tunneling into the tight braid at the back of her neck. She felt the tie loosen. Jonathan's strong fingers separated the strands of her hair. He crushed the waves in his hands, every movement an act of pure possession.

"Mine," he growled. His kiss was hot, wild. She clutched at his T-shirt, fingers balling up the soft cotton to stay on her feet. He nibbled on her bottom lip, swept his tongue over the slight hurt, demanded entrance. The taste of him filled her mouth, dark toffee and spicy male. She was lost in pure pleasure. When his hands curved over her butt again, Alanna gave into her earlier urge and wrapped her legs around his waist. It put the thick length of his erection exactly where she wanted it. The thrust of his body against hers wound that aching pulse of need between her thighs tighter and tighter.

A stack of boxes was hard against her lower back. Digging her fingers into his shoulders, Alanna rocked against him. He growled again, the sound vibrating in her mouth. One hand still held her, his long, talented fingers stroking the denim between her thighs. Alanna whimpered when his mouth left hers, cried out when he sucked lightly at the skin of her throat. She couldn't think at all, didn't really want to. He had her hovering at the edge of release.

"Jonathan," she whispered. Was that really her, that needy plea?

"Tell me what you want, baby," he urged. His tongue flicked at her pulse, teeth grazing the sensitive skin.

Alanna shook her head wildly. She didn't want to admit it, didn't want to give him that much control.

"Tell me," he insisted. His breath tickled the fine hairs by her ear. He nipped her lobe lightly.

Struggling to maintain her sanity, Alanna caught her fingers in his hair, dragging his head up to look into her eyes. "Tell me what *you* want," she whispered. She used her teeth on him now, taking a sharp nip of his chin. His hips flexed, fingers tightened. Indigo with flecks of starlit silver, that was the color of the eyes that held hers. The sexy smile that put a dimple in his cheek told her that she might have made a strategic mistake.

"I want you naked," he said. That growl was still there in his voice, low and sexy, sounding like he'd absorbed some of the Faelinn mannerisms. "I want you under me, your legs locked around my waist. I want to feel you hot and wet around me while I make you scream again and again."

The images he painted made her thighs clench, her core throb with anticipation. He rocked against her, pushing her back against boxes. "I want to taste you, baby, lick every secret place until you know that you're mine and no one else's."

The possessive words should have pissed her off. They didn't because right at that moment, she wanted to belong to this man. Wanted his warmth for her own, wanted his protective streak centered on her. Wanted his body as her own personal playground. His lips were soft as she brushed them with hers.

She spoke against his mouth. "I want—"

The box behind her shifted, sliding back to topple to the floor. It threw them off balance, had her sprawling backwards so that she slammed into the book-filled box underneath. Breath exploded from her lungs; Jonathan's weight pinned her down. Alanna felt the sharp edge of the box dig into the back of her neck, sending a shooting pain down her spine.

"Is everything okay up there?" Shellie's voice held worry.

Alanna nodded, still struggling to catch her breath.

"I dropped a box," Jonathan yelled down to Shellie. "Sorry."

Jonathan knelt, drawing Alanna up gently. His hands soothed the muscles of her back. "Are you all right?"

She nodded, relishing the feel of his fingers kneading the back of her neck. Then she caught the spark of laughter in his eyes and her lips twitched in response. A moment later they were both laughing, sharing a different kind of intimacy. When she finally caught her breath, she leaned her forehead against his.

"You're still mine," he said softly. He pressed a quick kiss on her mouth. "But for now, let's get these boxes unpacked."

Chapter Seventeen

Alanna drove her fingers through her hair, hauling it off her face. This wasn't getting anything done. Damn the man. She saved her work and pushed the laptop closed. The books on the shelves taunted her. The boxes had been emptied, the books tossed in no particular order onto the empty shelves. Now they lurked there. She'd catch a glimpse of one out of the corner of her eye and it would lead to a delicious memory of heat and desire, kisses shared in between emptying the boxes. It seemed Jonathan's taste was meant to linger on her tongue, the scent of his skin to tease her nose when she least expected it.

It kept her awake. She'd expected to end up in his bed tonight. Instead, she'd gotten a chaste kiss at her door and a whispered good night before he'd walked away across the lawn. Just because she'd fallen asleep during the quick drive from Shellie's house where they'd had dinner with their friends didn't mean anything. She liked to think of it as a power nap. When she'd woken up, she'd been more than awake enough to indulge in a little late extracurricular activity.

Instead, she'd buckled down with her story outline and forced herself to try to write. Except that she kept making her hero blond. And he wasn't.

Damn damn damn.

Alanna eased the lace curtain aside enough to peek across the lawn at

Jonathan's house. The back porch light was on, but more importantly, the lights were on in his workshop. In fact, she could see his silhouette against the window. He must have blinds because his upper half was a clearly outlined shadow. Feeling like a Peeping Tom, Alanna watched him move. She had no idea what he was doing, but she was practically drooling when he reached for something, half turning away. The line of his shoulders, the muscles of his upper arms, all magically displayed against the screen.

Enough, her brain screamed. She wasn't going to sleep, she couldn't work, he obviously wasn't sleeping. There was only one thing to do.

The coffeepot was taking its own sweet time. She waited impatiently, switching from foot to foot. Taking him coffee seemed like the perfect excuse to show up at his door in the middle of the night. She was aware she didn't need coffee. That she could show up, drop her robe, and let nature take its course, but she felt much more comfortable with an excuse.

Idiot.

Finally, the coffeepot beeped. Her hands trembled a little, spilled coffee on the counter as she filled her mug. She left the stain there.

It was cold. Her breath puffed out in shock even as the back door closed behind her. She could feel the icy ground beneath the thin soles of the sneakers she'd shoved her feet into. The thin robe was no match for the mountain wind blowing across the yard.

Alanna hustled across the space between her back door and his workshop. Her heart was racing by the time she reached the door. Her nose was frozen and her nipples were tight buds. Holding both mug handles in one hand, she knocked on the door.

A shiver rippled across her shoulders and Alanna almost turned back. This was ridiculous. Waiting in the middle of the night for a man to open a door so she could have a booty call. That wasn't her. Nope. She was half turned away when the door swung open.

"Alanna? What are you doing out here? It's freezing," Jonathan said. His voice, that sexy voice with the lazy Southern undertone, stopped her. Just his voice could raise her temperature by several degrees.

"I couldn't sleep so I brought you coffee," she said, and thrust one of the mugs at him.

Wordlessly, Jonathan accepted the offering and held the door wide so she could come in.

Alanna slid past him into the delicious warmth of the workshop. And stopped. The far wall held a huge stained glass panel. It depicted a battle, Faelinn and humans triumphing over tall, brutish giants. Even with no sunlight coming through, it glowed with color, each panel masterfully chosen and designed. She recognized Setasha, with her flowing ivory fur, and Berren, her fierce mate.

The tools of his trade were neatly organized. Sheets of stained glass waiting to be cut were stacked in special racks on the right. Long worktables ran along the left wall, every surface covered. Another table sat in the center of the floor. It was covered with scattered papers, tools, pieces of glass. There were windows everywhere. She imagined that during the day, with the blinds up, the open space would flood with light.

She drifted forward to the central table. The papers strewn across the surface were mostly sketches. Half-finished renderings of various Faelinn, flowers, even a mermaid. An open sketchbook drew her attention. Her own features stared up at her from the white page. A scatter of arrows led to notes on the side, seeming to indicate colors.

Alanna flipped through the pages. She found sketch after sketch of her. The fall of her hair against her cheek, head tipped back with her eyes closed, one with her and Jekk together. Her hands, her eyes, her mouth.

Jonathan's body brushed hers from behind. She found herself surrounded by his heat, his scent. Her every pore seemed to open up and suck him in.

"You've been drawing me?"

His lips touched her shoulder. "I've been a little obsessed lately." Light fingers brushed her hair away, baring the back of her neck. His lips touched there, too.

Heat rolled down her spine. Alanna leaned back enough to make contact with his chest. "Should I be flattered, or get a restraining order?"

One arm circled her waist, pressing her back against him. His hand rested just below her breast. His mouth was against her ear. He caught her lobe between his teeth, nibbling lightly. "Why are you here, Alanna?"

Pleasure made her knees weak. What he could do with just the barest of contact, the whisper of his voice. Her hands were trembling so she put down the coffee mug before she ruined his drawings. Raising one arm, she stroked her fingers through the crisp silk of his hair. "I couldn't sleep. I couldn't work. I thought you might want some coffee."

The laugh that rumbled through his chest vibrated against her back. He licked the spot where her neck met her shoulder. The sensation shivered over her skin. Desire dampened her panties. Her hips moved restlessly. Need was drugging her, heating her limbs, slowing her thoughts. A teasing thumb stroked the underside of her breast, focusing her attention there. Slow strokes, back and forth, moving slowly higher. Her nipple ached to be touched. When her knees buckled, Jonathan's arms held her up.

He nuzzled that sensitive spot on her neck. "If we were Faelinn, I'd bite you here."

"Why?" she breathed.

His teeth grazed her skin. "To claim you as my mate."

Alanna moaned. Her fingers speared through his hair, urging his mouth to her skin. She arched her back. She could feel his erection pressing hard and thick against her ass and she rubbed herself enticingly against him. His groan was low, animalistic. It vibrated against her skin.

A teasing stroke over her nipple had her trembling on the cusp of orgasm. The silky robe rubbed against her flesh, his fingers plucking her through the thin fabric. With a groan, he tugged her robe open. Bare flesh met his seeking hand. Her name was growled against her neck.

Barely able to breathe, Alanna arched against him, pushing her breast into his palm. She was panting, unable to catch her breath. She tried to turn, but he held her in place. He kicked her thighs apart, pressing into her. One big hand moved deliberately down her belly. Her muscles twitched with pleasure, with anticipation. A shrug of her shoulders had her robe pooling at her feet.

Turning her head, Alanna caught his mouth. His tongue thrust deep, stroking over hers. His taste flooded her. She was surrounded by him. One hand played her nipple with exquisite talent, plucking notes of pure sensation from her body. His other hand finally covered her mound, separated from her by the barest of silk and lace. Heat pressed into her from behind. His jeans were rough against her ass and thighs.

Jonathan's teeth scraped her skin. "Right here," he murmured again.

"Yes," Alanna breathed. She reached back, fumbling behind her for the button of his jeans. When her fingers stroked against him, he sucked in a breath. His teeth bit down. His fingers stroked her clit through the silk.

Alanna blew apart. She screamed his name as pleasure shot through her limbs. She rode his hand while her body spasmed repeatedly. The feel of his teeth pressing into her flesh drove the pleasure deeper, higher, a contradiction that resulted in a fiery explosion rolling through her.

Through gritted teeth, she begged him to be inside her. Jonathan moaned, his fingers bunching in her panties before ripping them off. The tip of his cock nudged her entrance and Alanna pressed back into him, spreading her legs even wider.

"Slow," he said.

"No, fast," she panted. She rolled her hips, feeling him thick and hard. Her body throbbed for him. "Fast now, slow later."

A strangled laugh against her back and then she was crying his name again as he thrust home. He filled her, stretching her tight around him. She could feel his pulse deep inside. It was perfect and it wasn't nearly enough. Not yet. Strong fingers dug into her hips. He withdrew, paused, and thrust again. Sensation slid down her thighs. She tightened on him, making him hiss.

Their bodies rocked. Alanna braced her elbows on the table, her head bowed as she met stroke after stroke. White hot light began to fill her. She reached back for him, her fingers finding his hip.

"I'm here, baby," he whispered. One arm circled her waist, holding her tight. His thrusts were short and sharp now, urgency driving him faster and faster. The light in her head got brighter, the flames inside licked hotter. His teeth found her neck again, locking her in pleasure.

Alanna screamed, her head thrown back. The light tore through her. His arms were her only anchor when the pleasure released, sweeping her up. Her hips lost the rhythm but it didn't matter because Jonathan roared, his hips locked tight to hers while he pulsed again and again deep inside.

Alanna was still panting when he turned her, scooping her up in his arms. Something soft and nubby pressed into her back, Jonathan's body coming down hard and warm on hers. Opening her eyes, Alanna looked up into his. Summer-blue eyes smiled down, promising endless nights spent doing exactly this.

Catching his face in her hands, Alanna drew his mouth down for a long kiss. Her body was still rolling in pleasure, every limb suffused with drugged heat. His skin was smooth and warm beneath her hands. The muscles of his back moved under her palms and she purred at the feeling of all that strength. Bending one knee, she wiggled under him so that his hips were exactly where she wanted them.

Spearing his fingers through her hair, Jonathan changed the angle of the kiss. His teeth and tongue teased her lips before thrusting inside. No one had kissed her like this, finding all the sensitive places, making new ones. She'd started the kiss, but he'd taken control. When he began to harden against her inner thigh, she smiled against his mouth. She scraped her short nails down his back, squeezing the hard muscles of his ass.

Jonathan lifted his head. His mouth was only a breath away. "You're mine," he whispered. She had only a moment to murmur assent before he thrust into her and her body took over.

Jonathan woke to sunshine spilling across his eyes and the insistent blaring of a rock and roll song from his cell phone's little speaker. A warm female body tried to untangle itself from his. A blanket added to the confusion. The cell phone shut off. Blinking sleepily, Jonathan smiled. The warm female body sprawled across his belonged to the woman whose body he'd spent the night adoring. They'd finally fallen asleep when the first hints of dawn began to color the stained glass of the mural along one wall.

Warm lips nuzzled his jaw and he slid one hand down a slender spine, over the soft mound of one perfect butt cheek. She gave a little wiggle, a very interesting wiggle that made his body sit up and take notice.

The cell phone blared to life again. He cursed, feeling around on the floor for his jeans. He wasn't quite sure where he'd dropped them. It was probably the Haven security office again. If it wasn't an emergency, he was going to have someone's head. His hand grabbed cloth and he lifted his jeans. The cell fell out of his pocket and hit him in the shoulder.

Giggling, Alanna slid off him and into the narrow space between his side and the couch. She caught the phone as it threatened to slide to the floor and handed it to him.

He hit the talk button. "What?" he grumbled.

"Now that's a fine way to say hello, me boyo," the voice on the other end said. An Irish brogue rolled through the voice.

Shock had Jonathan sliding his feet to the floor and sitting up on the edge of the couch. "You're no more Irish than I am, Anderson," Jonathan replied. It was a voice he hadn't heard for years. He'd lost touch with his old partner not long after he'd bonded with Cateera. Once he'd quit the force and moved to the Haven, he'd let those attachments go. It was his fault. Now, this call from the past spiked his curiosity.

"Sure I am, only two generations removed on my mother's side," the voice replied, this time without the brogue.

"My great-grandparents on my mother's side were from Germany," Jonathan replied. "That doesn't make me German."

"You've just lost your roots, man," Anderson replied. "Go find yourself some schnitzel."

Jonathan laughed. His old partner still amused him. "You didn't call me at nine a.m. out of the blue to discuss food. What's up?"

"We've got a situation." Anderson's voice grew serious, no hint of laughter now, only pure cop. "They want to bring you in."

Jonathan grabbed a sketchpad and a pencil from a side table to take notes. Alanna sat up behind him and circled his waist with her arms. She pressed a light kiss to his shoulder. He squeezed her fingers quickly. "Talk to me."

"Over the past eighteen months, we've had six adolescent boys disappear off the streets. There may be more, but they come from the streets and that population is fluid. Not every missing kid is noticed. We've found five bodies, the last one two weeks ago. He'd only been dead about a week, but the remains showed signs of long-term abuse and we believe he may have been kept prisoner. Yesterday, another boy was snatched, only this time, he wasn't homeless. Neighbors saw him waiting for the school bus first thing in the morning. One of them reported seeing him get into a blue sedan. He never arrived at school. The car matches the general description of a vehicle seen near two of the other abductions."

"You want to find him before he's killed," Jonathan said, pencil still on the paper.

"Damned straight I do," Anderson said. "I've spent over a year on this case, and I'm getting nowhere. I've heard you can find killers, Burke. I can't let another boy die."

"You've got access to a body?" Jonathan asked. Cateera's awareness stirred in his mind. She was listening. He felt the wildness inside of her rise, knew her hunter was stirring.

"Bodies are in cold storage," Anderson said. "But we have some clothing. Can you work from that?"

"I don't know, maybe," Jonathan answered.

"Will you? I don't know what your consulting fee is, Burke, but they've approved some discretionary funds."

Thrusting his fingers into his hair, he pushed it back from his forehead. Too much was going on here. The intrusion into the Haven and the ensuing explosion needed to be solved. There were still angles to work. The killer that had followed him from Carolina was a thorn he needed to pluck.

And there was Alanna. He needed to make sure she understood that she was his. He'd known it from the moment he'd seen her kick Samuelson, her bare feet bruised and bloodied. It had taken his brain a little longer to catch up with his gut, but it had. He wanted to spend the next few weeks imprinting himself on her skin so that she would always know he was hers. It wasn't an entirely human reaction, but it felt natural all the same. Even now she was a warm presence pressed to his back, reading his notes over his shoulder.

She is your mate, she will understand, Cateera told him. *So will Jekk.*

"Won't make it any easier to leave her," Jonathan replied along their link. He felt her understanding roll through him.

We will go, Cateera decided. *Children should not be killed.*

It was only because he knew her, was so deeply attached to her, that he caught the thread of buried grief. Her kits had been taken, used, and sacrificed. Nothing would ever erase those memories from her mind. Saving children now was part of what she was. They rarely turned down cases where children were involved, even if it was only to bring their killers to justice.

"Don't worry about any fees, Anderson. I know how tight the department's budget can be. Cateera and I will be there by this afternoon."

There was a sigh of what could only be relief. "Thanks, boyo. I'll make reservations for you at the hotel around the corner."

"All right, see you in a few hours."

Going back, he thought. He'd never planned to go back. With the old gunshot wound sending phantom pains through his shoulder, Jonathan put down the phone.

"Tell me," Alanna said softly.

He turned and tumbled her back against the couch cushions first. After a long good morning kiss that didn't come close to satisfying the need that had him hard and throbbing against her thigh, he propped himself up one arm. Her hair was tangled darkness on the pillow, her lips swollen. It was her eyes though that caught him. The dark grey of the sky just before the storm broke loose, they stared up at him with a warmth that almost had him calling Anderson back and telling him to solve his own murder. Instead, he stroked a gentle finger across her lips and told her about the call.

"How long will you be gone?" she asked when he was finished.

"A few days at most. I'm sorry," he said. He closed his eyes when she trailed her fingers through his hair. When her hand cupped his cheek, he turned his head to press his lips to her palm.

"When do you have to leave?" Alanna asked.

Jonathan smiled. He caught her hand and nipped the ends of her fingers. "Soon, but I still have plenty of time."

Alanna arched one dark brow. One foot ran slowly down the back of his calf. "Time for what?" she asked archly.

He lifted his hips from hers enough to slip one hand between their bodies. His palm covered her mound, feeling her heat. His fingers found her wet and ready. He teased her with his fingertips, drawing a low moan from her throat before sliding those same fingers deep inside of her. "Time enough to make you scream my name again," he whispered, and covered her mouth with his.

Chapter Eighteen

Just over two hours after the phone call, Jonathan was out the door. Part of that time had been spent talking to Mark and calling the security office to let them know where he'd be. He'd instructed Rivera to call him immediately if anything else happened. Cateera met him on the porch, her ears quivering with the need to go, to find, to save the child. It was rare they were called in before the victim was dead. In this case, with multiple victims and the remains of one, he was given the opportunity to save a living soul. Usually, his talent was needed only when it was too late, where there was nothing to find but the killer.

Tossing the go bag he kept packed with everything he'd need for a few days away into the SUV, Jonathan turned to look toward Alanna's house. She was dressed in sleek, warm running clothes, ready for her morning jog. But her eyes were on him, her fingers buried in Jekk's rough fur. Cateera bounded across the lawn to her mate. He met her at the bottom of the steps, rubbing his body along hers to imbue her fur with his scent. Jonathan wanted to do the same to Alanna.

"You're going now?" Alanna asked when Jonathan climbed the steps to stand in front of her.

"Yes," he said. A soft strand of dark hair had escaped the woolen hat she'd pulled on, and he gently smoothed it back. He let his fingers linger on her cheek before curling his palm around the back of her neck and bringing her closer.

"Will you miss me?" he asked, his mouth a breath away from hers.

"Your ego is limitless," she told him. Her eyes told a different story, and her fingers curled into the T-shirt he wore beneath his jacket.

Alanna's bottom lip was soft between the gentle nip of his teeth. "I'll miss you," he confessed softly. Even after their night together, the surprise in those stormy eyes made him smile. He licked her lip lightly and watched her eyes close, felt her sway closer. And gave into the need to taste her completely. When her tongue slid along his, welcoming him, he drew her up tight. He loved the way her fingers feathered through his hair, loved the soft sounds that escaped her. He needed her, needed this

"How long will you be gone?" she asked when he finally let her speak.

"A couple of days," Jonathan told her. "It depends on how things go." He missed it when her fingers dropped from his neck, smoothing over his shoulders before gently pushing him away.

"You'd better go then." Her breath was a puff of ice crystals.

Alanna looked so adorable in the purple knitted hat and the earmuffs, a far cry from the elegant, buttoned-up-tight woman he'd first met. The one who had smelled like heaven and made every nerve in his body spring to life in irritated awareness. And Jonathan knew if he lingered any longer, he wouldn't be going anywhere.

He allowed himself one last kiss before stepping back. "I'll call tonight."

Jonathan saw her nod, saw her catch her bottom lip between her teeth, and made himself walk away. She was still watching as he pulled the SUV out of the driveway and headed for the Haven's gate. Cateera let out a long sigh, already missing her new mate, and laid her head on her paws.

We should bring them with us, she said.

"No," Jonathan said firmly. "A murder investigation is no place for her."

Her Gift would be good here. She could find the child.

"If we find the killer, then there's no reason for either of them to see anymore ugliness."

The Fael agreed with him, her understanding and an odd protectiveness toward Alanna washing through him. His bondmate had already incorporated Alanna into their family. She would protect her as fiercely as she protected him. He was smiling as he left the Haven and turned the truck toward the roads that would take him to Hampton.

∼

The old city, one of the oldest in the original United States, had once been part of a larger metro area. Perched on the point of a peninsula, it had been the home to a number of military bases prior to the Veil Wars. Coupled with the oystermen and other fisherman in the area, it had been a vital, powerful community. Now the river was gone, emptied in the Cataclysm brought on by the advent of the Veil. Over the past three quarters of a century, the riverbed had dried and the city had spread. It was still a pivotal port for the Eastern States with its marine terminal and naval bases, although both of those had moved their docks to account for the new coastline. The oystermen had moved on with the loss of the river, following the migrations of the marine life post-Veil.

Jonathan still found it nearly unbelievable that the city hadn't been destroyed in the upheavals, both the geological and the social that had followed the Cataclysm. He remembered the first time that his grandparents had taken him out to what had been the center of a river he'd never seen and told him how things had been. He hadn't believed them until they'd taken him into the city museum and given him the tour of the relics and photos that remained. His fifth-grade science project had been a scale model of the area before the Cataclysm, complete with a pump that cycled water down the river and into the bay. He still had the first-place ribbon.

The central police building looked the same except for a new paint job. It was strange to pull into the public lot rather than the reserved spaces for the department. The sky was grey, spitting down rain. The wind that blew his hair back brought with it the scent of the sea. Beneath it curled the scents of the fish-processing plant perched on a narrow inlet a few blocks away. Cateera sniffed, making a low sound of interest. He caught her wondering if there would be time to track down the delicious smells.

The inside of the precinct hadn't changed either. It still smelled of stale air and bad coffee. The same posters promoting the anti-drug programs and Officer Smart still hung on the wall next to the front desk, surrounded by the latest batch of wanted posters. He glanced at them and saw more than one familiar face. Seemed like most things didn't change.

"May I help you?" The voice floated from the general vicinity of the large monitor behind the counter. The woman didn't look around, still focused on whatever was on the screen. Cateera sat in front of the tall counter, her eyes and tufted ears visible above the scarred top. Jonathan knew the moment the receptionist saw her. The woman's shoulders jerked, her head whipped around. The squeak of fear preceded the sudden backwards propulsion of the chair by mere seconds.

Before Jonathan could intervene, though, the receptionist was on her feet and cautiously peering over the counter. Gently teased silver hair caught the dull light of the fluorescents and glowed. The smile that spread over the carefully lipsticked mouth was childlike in pleasure and had Jonathan smiling in response.

The quick clack of heels on tile brought her from around the desk. "Well aren't you the most beautiful thing I've ever seen!"

The slow nod was regal as Cateera accepted the words as her due.

She may scratch my ears if she wishes, Cateera told him.

Jonathan felt his lips twitch and worked hard to hide his amusement. When he passed on her words, the woman acknowledged him for the first time, even as her coral-tipped fingers moved to do as Cateera had instructed.

"You must be Detective Burke." The soft accent was pure south.

"I'm not a detective anymore," he said.

"You are around here," she informed him tartly. "Detective Anderson is waiting for you." Distracted by Cateera's rumbling purr, she smiled at the Fael. "I'll buzz him and let him know you're here."

"I remember the way," Jonathan said. "If that's all right?"

Homicide had its office on the third floor. Clusters of desks grouped in twos ranged around a room too small for them. A visitor might think that the ones below the bank of windows on the far wall were the best spots, but Jonathan knew from experience that it wasn't true. During the winter, those desks became draft central with icy air slipping in around the uninsulated windows. The summer brought its own problems with the afternoon sun baking those same windows and concentrating that heat right onto the heads of the detectives sitting at the desks.

The place was noisy, but almost deserted. Phones rang at empty desks before clicking over to voicemail. Jonathan's old desk belonged to a brunette detective now who was hunched over a laptop, her eyes fierce behind her glasses. A row of pictures lined the front of the desk, although the anemic spider plant drooping over the filing cabinet behind her looked to be the same plant he'd ignored when the desk had been his. The lieutenant's door was open, the blinds lifted so he could keep an eye on the squad. It was always that way. Now, though, the office was empty. The air in the squad room was a mix of stale heat, staler coffee, and greasy fast food. Cateera's nostrils quivered and then she sneezed violently.

It smells of mouse, Cateera informed him.

That was one thing he couldn't smell. Jonathan was smiling when the detective at the desk closest to the door looked their way. Thomas's dark eyes widened with recognition. He pushed the chair back from his desk, giving him room to thump his feet up onto the desktop as he lounged back. Dislodged sandwich crumbs tumbled from his tie.

"Well, if it isn't the prodigal detective. Come to save us incompetents, have you?"

It wasn't just the physical surroundings that never changed. "How's the wife, Thomas?"

That destroyed the mocking light in the man's eyes. "Ex-wife. The bitch is still trying to get half of everything."

"Half of everything still a lot of nothing for you?" Jonathan asked.

The quick pop of middle fingers aimed his way told Jonathan he'd found a sore spot. Cateera rested a clawed paw on the edge of the desk and slowly peeled back her lips to show two-inch long incisors.

"You know animals aren't allowed in the building," Thomas snapped. He moved to push her paw off the desk. It was only quick instincts that allowed him to retain the top knuckles of his fingers.

"Careful, she doesn't like you," Jonathan warned. He rested his hand on Cateera's shoulders, feeling the tension. "She doesn't take kindly to being called an animal."

"What the fuck is she, then?" he asked.

Jonathan would lay money on Thomas being a member of the Human Rights Alliance. Bastards believed any non-human was an animal and therefore devoid of rights. It was all about outward appearances and genetics, not at all about sentience. Which was probably a good thing for them, Jonathan thought, considering most of the Righters didn't seem to have much intelligence of their own.

He is a moron, Cateera announced, looking up at her bondmate. *He is very lucky I am a forgiving sort of animal, or I might leave him a souvenir of my visit. He should have a rat or two in his drawer when he opens it.*

Jonathan didn't want to tell her to do it, but the thought of Thomas opening his desk to find a couple of headless rats on top of his files provided a great deal of satisfaction.

"Burke, you made it."

Anderson strode across the room, all long legs and bunched muscles. The man was built like a top-heavy beanpole, thick on top and long and spindly on the bottom. The result of a human/troll pairing, Anderson looked like the two halves of his heritage just didn't agree.

"Yeah, traffic wasn't too bad." He grabbed his old partner's outstretched hand and felt himself pulled in for the male form of a hug. Anderson's hard thump on his back nearly knocked the air from his lungs.

Keen brown eyes studied him. "That is not a regulation cut, boyo," Anderson informed him, his fingers tugging hard on the blond hair curled over Jonathan's collar.

Jonathan eyed his friend's shaved head. "I like the cue ball look."

"So do the ladies," Anderson said, winking as he rubbed a broad palm over his scalp.

"Like you'd ever get a real woman to pay attention to you," Thomas commented.

"Ignore him," Anderson advised. "We keep him around because we're an equal opportunity employer and even assholes need jobs."

"Fuck off," Thomas snapped. He took his cell phone out of his pocket and swiveled his chair, giving them his back.

Grinning, Anderson led him out of the squad room and down the corridor. "We're set up in a conference room."

The room was the same as Jonathan remembered with its concrete block walls and institutional green paint the color of old mint toothpaste. Dry erase boards lined the walls, pictures of the victims tacked to the slick surfaces. Notes were scribbled around the pictures, some more legible than others. The long table in the center of the room was covered in files, stained pizza boxes, and empty water bottles. The smell of burned coffee saturated the air.

"Welcome to my home away from home," Anderson said with a broad wave of his hand. "And now, are you going to introduce me to your beautiful partner?"

The lavender-striped, white Fael purred at the compliment. She gave a quick shake from nose to tail to make sure every inch of fur lay just so.

Jonathan stroked a hand over her head. "This is Cateera, my bondmate. Cateera, this is Leo Anderson, my ex-partner."

Anderson offered a hand, and Cateera placed her broad paw in it, her fingers gripping his. They shook as equals.

"Place looks like a ghost town," Jonathan commented. "Where is everyone?"

"The LT's wife is in labor and it's not worth his life for him to be anywhere but at her side. That woman scares me. Got a couple of guys out looking into gang-related fatalities, and my partner's at the dentist."

"The LT would never have allowed that when I was here. Has he mellowed?"

"Nope, but Beatrice lost a filling overnight and her dentist fit her in. She's a good cop, been busting her ass with me over this case."

Jonathan shrugged off his jacket and tossed it over the back of a chair. He rotated his shoulders to get the last of the stiffness from driving out of them and walked over to the first board. "So, fill us in."

The photo on the board showed the remains of a youth, the level of decomposition making it impossible to determine race at first glance. Jonathan studied it while listening to Anderson's recitation. No ID on the body, but the statistics scribbled next to the picture listed him as a Black male between fourteen and eighteen. Height five-seven, weight at autopsy one hundred ten pounds. Eyes and hair, brown and brown. Even with the level of decomposition, Jonathan could see a series of small burns across the chest, the notes agreeing with his thoughts that cigarettes caused them. There were places on the back, thighs, and upper arms where it looked as if flesh had been peeled away in patches. He pointed them out to Anderson.

"These postmortem?"

"No," the detective replied tightly. His mouth was pressed into a thin line, eyes flat with fury. "Medical examiner lists them as antemortem. The boy suffered."

Cateera whipped her tail in agitation, ears laid flat against her narrow head. The sound that rumbled from her chest gave voice to the depth of anger she was feeling. She paced the room, returning to look as he moved from picture to picture. All of them bore similar injuries. All of them showed signs of sexual abuse. What he found interesting was that although the ages seemed to be clustered in middle adolescence, the ethnicity ranged across the board. He was aware that predators tended to remain within their own ethnic group. Whoever this monster was, he didn't seem to care what color the boys' skin was.

Great, a non-racially biased predator. What a step forward for humankind.

The concrete block wall, painted that lovely shade of institutional green, was cold against Jonathan's arm as he leaned against it. The narrow, barred window didn't provide much of a view, but it was still better than the torn, abused bodies in the pictures.

We will find him, Cateera said. She smacked him with her paw until he looked down and into her turquoise eyes. *We will find him, and the detective will put him in jail. And then we will go home to our mates.*

That made him smile, he couldn't help it. The thought of Alanna swept a clean wind through his mind, settling the horror and allowing him to move beyond it. "All right, my precious one, let's get this done."

"Okay, Anderson, let's see what you've got."

Anderson swiped a hand over his shaved head. "What do you need? I'm not sure how this works."

"I need to touch something of the victim's," Jonathan told him. "Sometimes, I need to touch a body, but I'd rather try the sanitary way first."

Anderson grunted. "Can't say I blame you." He went to a pile of boxes in a corner and hefted one, depositing it on top of a pile of papers on the table. It wobbled a little, slid, and then steadied. The case number was printed neatly across the side. Pulling a pair of latex gloves from his pocket, Anderson shoved them onto his hands before opening the box. Inside were several sealed plastic bags, evidence codes inked across the surface. Anderson's electronic badge doubled as a scanner, and he ran it over the evidence code and input a series of passwords. The lock on the sealed bag clicked and glowed green.

The hoodie was grey with black stripes and sized to fit a young male. There was a streak of dirt on the sleeve, but otherwise it looked to be in good shape. Jonathan pulled out a chair and sat, anchoring himself. Cateera leaned up against him. They didn't need physical contact for their powers to work, but it was a matter of comfort for them both.

"I can't use gloves," he told his ex-partner.

Another input of codes, and then Anderson passed the device to Jonathan. Jonathan pressed his thumb to the touch pad, waiting as it registered his identity, and then passed it back.

"That takes care of the bureaucracy," Anderson said. He took a chair as well, hooking his feet around the legs. "Besides, your prints are on file as exemplars. How does this work?"

Jonathan stared at the hoodie. Light from the overhead fluorescents glinted on the silvery zipper. There was a stain that looked a lot like a mustard drip on one side. Cateera leaned in, taking a long slow sniff.

Mustard, she confirmed. *Sweat. Detergent. The smell of a dog. It must be a pet because the scent is pervasive. A truly offensive cologne.*

"In other words, a teenage boy," Jonathan said.

The Fael at his side chuffed in amused agreement.

Wrapping an arm around Cateera's shoulders, Jonathan ignored the hoodie for a moment. "I don't really know how it works," he admitted to Anderson. "When I touch a body, or something from the victim, I can somehow tune into the killer. I'll need a map program to locate him for you, though. And coffee."

"Shit, I should have offered," Anderson said. He went to the communication panel next to the door and keyed in a number. When the voice answered, he instructed them to bring coffee to the conference room.

"Anything for you, Cateera?"

He has manners, she told Jonathan. *I will have cream.*

"They don't have cream. You'll be lucky if you get milk."

They should have prepared for me, she said with a sniff.

Jonathan passed along her request, enjoying the sight of his trollish friend frowning. Anderson repeated Cateera's preferences before joining him back at the table. "While we're waiting, tell me what you've been up to," Jonathan said.

"Working my ass off," Anderson said. He loosened his tie, released the top button of his shirt. "A lot of politics right now. The Alliance has opened up shop because this is such a huge spot for the Oceanborn. We've had some assaults on both sides. There've been two murders in the last year, one a selkie, one a Merman. Diplomatically, it's a nightmare. Both murders are still unsolved, but I know—I *know*, Burke—the Alliance is behind them."

Jonathan propped his elbows on the table, leaning forward. He carefully avoided contact with the hoodie. "We've had problems with them in the past trying to capture one of the Faelinn, but nothing recently. We haven't been problem-free, though. We've had issues with portions of the security system going off-line unexpectedly. Other minor annoyances. But a couple of days ago, we had a truck crash through the fence. The driver walked away. Moved the truck to the garage and it exploded. Injured the head mechanic, destroyed the garage."

"You don't think the Alliance is behind it?"

Jonathan shook his head. "No. I had a case in Carolina just before the problems started. Couldn't track the killer. I think he tracked me instead. Scary bastard. We don't think he's human and we haven't been able to catch him yet."

"But he's come to play in your backyard. Better hope the Alliance doesn't hear about him. They'll use it as another argument to shut the borders and cease all contact with the Veilers."

"Yeah," Jonathan agreed. "And that worries the shit out of me." He pushed a hand back through his hair. "We're all on high alert, but we can't stay that way forever. I've got my people running down every lead, but there just aren't that many."

"I'm surprised you agreed to come out here," Anderson said.

"If it had been anyone else, I wouldn't have," Jonathan admitted.

The knock, followed by the door opening, drew their focus away. A young officer carried in a tray with two steaming mugs of coffee and an old bowl. His eyes widened when he saw Cateera. A stumble had the coffee sloshing over the mugs' rims. Anderson deftly rescued the tray. Cateera sat primly, her tail curved protectively over her front paws.

"I couldn't find cream," the officer said hesitantly. "I brought half and half instead. Is that okay?" He looked like he was afraid he'd be eaten if it wasn't acceptable.

The lavender-swirled Fael began to purr, pitching it loudly enough to be heard. The officer's shoulders visibly relaxed.

"Anything else, sir?" he asked, daring to glance away from Cateera.

"No, that's fine," Anderson said. "Dismissed." He made shooing motions with his hands and then rolled his eyes when the door closed again. "Shit, he makes me feel old."

Grunting agreement, Jonathan took a slurp of coffee. It tasted like runoff sludge, just like he remembered. The caffeine kick would help, though. Using his Gift would eat up his energy reserves. Ignoring the scalding temperature, he took another long gulp and then set it down.

Straightening the slide of files across the tabletop into a semi-neat pile, Anderson uncovered the flat black screen in the center of the table. He pulled out a hidden keyboard and activated the hologram system. Sleeker than it used to be, the magickal components replaced the stream of highly dense air with an energy field that maintained a much clearer image. An area map projected up into the center of the field, showing the entire metropolitan area.

"That's good," Jonathan said. "I'll have you narrow it down as I key into the killer's energy."

Cateera returned to his side, still licking off the droplets of half and half from the tiny hairs around her muzzle. She'd used the bowl with grace; few knew about the fingers hidden in Faelinn fur. The dark purple tufts at the ends of her ears quivered as she rested her front paws on the table. Drawing in a slow breath and then releasing it, Jonathan reached for the link between them, expanding it so that it went beyond mere communication and awareness. Power swelled, doubling and redoubling, as they both focused on their bondmate connection.

So connected to her now that he felt the subtle shift of her fur beneath his skin, their senses linked so tightly that he could catch the vinegary tang of dried mustard on the hoodie, he reached for the garment. The fabric was soft, well worn. It would feel good against the skin. He ran his fingers along the sleeves, feeling a subtle stiffness at the elbow where dirt was ground in. The cuffs were stretched out, and the faintest glimmer of a pair of tanned forearms flashed onto the interior screen of his mind.

Focus on the forearms. Bring them into view. The image shivered, and then was gone. Jonathan felt Cateera reach for the image, bringing it back. It steadied for a moment and then snapped out again. He stroked his hands over the soft cottony material, slid them into the front pouch. Warmth. There'd been a cookie there once, though the forensic team had painstakingly removed all the crumbs.

Cateera drew the scent of the garment into her lungs. He could smell and identify each of the scents through her. It really was awful aftershave. A flash of a razor, one of his mom's, stolen from the pack under the sink. Carefully shaving the sparse growth of hair on the tip of his chin. Jonathan could see him in the mirror. Short dark hair, almost military in the closeness of the cut. Light eyes, blue or grey, hard to tell.

They fixed on that image. Pushed into it. Anderson had said the victims were street kids. He needed a more recent fix from the hoodie. School hallway, the clang of lockers slamming shut. Bumped from behind, elbow to elbow with the press of kids, rushing to algebra. Lunchtime. Flicking a spoonful of mashed potatoes across the table when the monitors weren't looking.

"Further, precious one," he urged through their link.

The expansion of their Gift, two unique talents, their bond the catalyst. Walking in the cool afternoon, backpack heavy over one shoulder, hood pulled up against a light salty-smelling drizzle. Not wanting to push his own expectations of a street kid's environment into the mix, Jonathan accepted the images as the most recent he would get. For whatever reason, the runaway aspects of the youth's past were hidden.

A step further now, Cateera right there with him. Feeling for the killer. Negative energy packed between the warp and weft of the fabric. The faint acid taint of fear. Breathing it in and following its length, tracking back to the cause. Pushing harder, sliding down that microscopic thread. To nothing.

Jonathan took a shuddering breath. He thrust his arms into the sleeves. The hoodie was too small to put on, but the feel of it stretched around his forearms tightened his focus. Cateera whined low in her chest, and he wrapped one arm around her shoulders, feeling the muscles ripple as she leaned into him. Wrapped in the boy's scent, feeling the warm body of the Fael under his arm, Jonathan closed his eyes again. Following that fear scent, he slid down it, mental aerobics that stretched the psychic muscles activated by Cateera's bonding.

Killers had a smell to them, as if they'd been marked by their actions. A blight on their mental signature. The acrid bite of fear came from the victim. He was hunting for the putrid odor of the murderer.

And there was nothing.

Chapter Nineteen

Keeping a tight wrap on the boy's identity, Jonathan opened his eyes. Sweat dripped from the ends of his hair, dampened the back of his shirt. "How long has he been dead?"

"Ah, well, as to that," Anderson began. He rubbed a finger along the side of his nose. "This is from the last victim. We don't know if he's dead yet. The sweatshirt was found at the bus stop."

Cateera growled low in her throat. Her fury echoed his, only Jonathan didn't let his lips peel back over his teeth. The appearance of her thick ivory canines caused Anderson to scoot his chair back.

"I told you that's not how it works," Jonathan said. He pulled his arms free of the warm material, carefully folding the hoodie and placing it on the table. As long as his hands were occupied, he could keep them from tightening around his ex-partner's throat. "Why are you wasting our time?"

"I'm sorry, boyo, I had to try," Anderson said. He kept a wary eye on Cateera who was still growling, her long tail lashing the floor. "If there's any chance at all we can find him before he's killed, I'm willing to take it. I don't want to find this boy's corpse."

Shit. Jonathan understood. He really did. He'd probably have done the same thing if the situation were reversed. "You should have told me," he said. "We would have tried for you, but I should've known ahead of time."

"Now that you know, can you try again?"

"It would be a waste of time. Our Gift just doesn't work that way."

We know someone whose does, Cateera said.

"I don't want her seeing this," he answered. "We can find this killer. We'll be home in less than two days."

Too long. We could be home in the morning.

"We'll try," Jonathan said to Cateera. He took a long drink of the now-cold coffee, grimacing as the acid hit his stomach. To Anderson, he said, "Do you have something from one of the other victims?"

The back of his neck was tight and Jonathan rubbed a hand over it, trying to loosen the muscles. Using his Gift was a mental exercise that took a hell of a toll on his body. He burned calories like no one's business, his muscles always feeling as if he'd run a marathon. When he was done here, he'd want a huge pizza and a hot shower. And a couple of aspirin for the headache he knew he was going to get.

Anderson retrieved another box and within minutes, a filthy sneaker slouched on the table, the high-top sides drooped over. Brown smeared the toe and it wasn't clear at first glance whether it was dirt or blood. The smell of decomposition lingered, and Jonathan knew without asking that a corpse had worn this.

"First victim, but not the first found," Anderson said. "No ID, adolescent Black male."

The pictures on the white board showed the shoe still attached to a decayed foot. Fixing the image in his mind, Jonathan reached for the sneaker and closed his eyes. He ran his fingertips over it slowly. Holes were worn into the rough canvas on the outside edge. The laces were missing. The empty grommets were cold to the touch. He ran the tongue between his fingers, feeling loose stitching on one side. The tread on the sole was nearly gone, worn away by extended use. The seams where the canvas met the rubber were coming loose. The shoes had seen hard use and probably hadn't fitted properly for a while. Finally, Jonathan brushed his fingertips over the brown staining the toe. Blood. It echoed through him, reverberating hollowly like a broken bell. Cateera's agreement made him clutch the toe more tightly, and images came.

A broken house, porch sagging enough to nearly reach the ground. Orange condemned notices taped to the door instead of the windows because the panes were gone. It smelled like old urine, sickness, and rot. The smell burned his nose. Cateera hissed but didn't fight as he took her deeper.

Inside, nothing as comfortable as even a moldy mattress. Cardboard boxes flattened, stained, bug-infested. It was his bed, the house, the place he'd squatted in for weeks. He had nothing; anything worth taking was long gone. He was lucky to have shoes. An ache bit at his stomach, a hated companion. It was a wanting inside of him that never went away, not even on the days when he collected enough loose change to buy a burger. And it was still better than what he'd run from.

Pushing deeper, Jonathan's fingers trembled. He knew what it was to sell himself for a meal only to have the money stolen away. He knew the sickness that came from a bad fix, and the cravings for the next one. Loneliness so sharp and deep it cramped his heart. Holding tight to the person he sensed through the shoe, Jonathan went further.

Blood warmed beneath his fingers, dripped with life and its fading essence onto the dirty rubber. It coated his fingers and he clutched it with mental muscles, traveling through the viscous stew of memory and pain to squeeze at the source. A sliced vein, the merest slash of open wound. No quick death, just an endless drip of pain as his body was torn over and over from within.

Cateera keened, her distress so intense Jonathan shook with it. Sweat ran down his face but he couldn't spare a hand to wipe it away. His muscles cramped tightly with effort.

His will a sharply focused force, he bullied his way beyond the smell of death. Another scent tickled the base of his skull, low and pervasive. Purposely drawing in the stink of it, he let it flow through, catching its essence, and filtering it to Cateera. She yowled as she accepted it, but concentrated, scenting it in ways he couldn't.

"Map," he choked out. The pinprick of knife's point in his vein, tearing him open. The hand that held the knife was slender, long-fingered. A dusting of dark hair across the back. Grasping that hand, he fought to hold it. It slithered from his grip. Breathing deeper, the decayed stench of killer driving the memory of every pleasurable scent from his mind, Jonathan reached for the hand again.

Not far, Cateera said. *Within three miles.*

"He's close," Jonathan said to Anderson. "Tighten to a three-mile radius."

"Shit," Anderson said. "He's under our nose." He two-fingered the keyboard and the holographic map zoomed in until the police station was at the center of a relatively small circle. He tightened it further, bringing up the names of the streets.

Jonathan coughed as the acid-poison smell choked him. The sweat running down his back was cold with the ice of a grave. He filtered the essence of it through the bondmate link. Cateera didn't need to feel the physical horror of it. It was bad enough that she suffered its core.

"East of here," he said as she fed him the direction.

The shoe was mangled in the vice of his fingers. Jonathan stood, leaning over to peer at the map. He felt like two people. His own personality was pushed aside by the murderer's desire, the lingering spirit that infected the blood on the shoe. His eyes traveled the streets, recognizing names, his own mental map overlaying the holograph. He'd known the neighborhood intimately at one time, a collection of old houses built at the turn of the last century, sturdy enough to survive seasons of hurricanes and the apocalypse of the Veil. Newer houses mixed in but still managed to maintain the illusion of old stateliness. Gables and gingerbread, widow's walks that looked out over streets instead of waterways. Old growth trees, oaks, and crepe myrtles big enough to shade even the third-floor windows.

It didn't seem the type of place to hide a murderer. Jonathan knew, though, that the outside walls of a house rarely gave an indication of the ugliness that might dwell within. A lovely suburban rancher with carefully manicured gardens might shelter a well of domestic violence. He'd seen it too many times.

Cateera guided him through the narrow streets. Jonathan noted the street names as they passed by on his mental screen: Rosewell, Jasper, Applewood. The headache had started at the base of his skull, a dull drumbeat that was slowly climbing. He pushed through it. They were so close, the poisoned smell filled his lungs.

Cateera growled, a whine of sudden frustration. The street names began to roll backwards in his head as she circled, the mental ghost of her struggling to follow the scent she could take from his mind. The shoe was twisted out of shape from his grip; Jonathan's fingers cramped so tightly around it he wasn't sure he'd be able to straighten them. He pulled images from it, the dripping blood, the slowing heartbeat. The knife. He willed himself to *see*, to grasp the man who'd stolen the boy's life and track him down.

The moment of failure shot a pain through his head that had him reeling back from the table. Jonathan's cry echoed Cateera's as his back hit the wall. The shoe hit the floor at his feet, his cramped fingers clutching his temples. Whoever had been at the end of that murderous scent had felt him coming and cut him off short. There was nothing left. Not even a mental waft of scent to guide him.

"Shit, boyo, are you all right?" Anderson asked as Jonathan slid bonelessly to the floor.

Cateera growled at the detective, warning him away from her bondmate. Jonathan wrapped an arm around her shoulders, grounding himself in the silky feel of her fur, the warm cinnamon scent of her skin. He could feel her heavy pulse beating beneath his fingers as he managed to straighten them. The rebound of his power snapping back, cut off so suddenly, made his stomach threaten to revisit the vile coffee he'd had earlier.

"Give me a minute," he managed at Anderson's repeated question. Cateera's pain pulsed at him and with an effort, he drew it into himself, giving her relief. She protested, but he ignored her. He would not let his bondmate suffer when he could so easily aid her through their link. He'd deal with the pain himself. He took a deep breath. His knees weren't quite ready to support him yet, but when he looked up at Anderson, the man's face was in focus.

"The murderer felt me coming," Jonathan said. "He just cut me off."

Anderson blinked in confusion. He offered a hand and hauled Jonathan to his feet with an easy flexing of his troll-like shoulders. "I'm assuming that's bad."

"Yeah." Jonathan staggered to a chair and almost fell into it. He groped for the nearest cup of coffee, not caring whether it was his, and sucked down a big gulp.

Anderson picked up the discarded shoe. He stared at it, turning it in his big hands. "Is that normal?"

A short, rough laugh escaped Jonathan's throat. "No, it's not normal." His hand automatically reached to stroke Cateera's neck as she laid down on the floor next to him. She leaned her head against his leg.

"So, what does it mean, then? You can't find him?"

"Not only can't I find him, but the bastard knows we're coming," Jonathan said. He stared into the empty mug and pushed it viciously away from him. It teetered on its base until Anderson stopped it. "No human can do what he just did."

Anderson's eyebrows drew down in a scowl. "So, he's a Veiler?"

"I'd say so, yes," Jonathan agreed. He scrubbed at his eyes with his hands. The images of blood and horror lingered, and no amount of rubbing would make them go away. "And he's got some definite magic skills." A worm of suspicion began tunneling through the pain in his head.

We can try with another child, Cateera said. *We must try, Jonathan. We cannot let these deaths continue.*

He looked down into her startling turquoise eyes. The intelligence there, the determination, always rocked him. "I don't know that it would help, but if you're willing to try, we will."

Then we will, she said. *Do we have access to a body?*

"We're willing to try again, if you can get us access to a body," Jonathan said.

Open relief eased the lines on Anderson's face. "That's not a problem, Burke. Do you think it would help?"

"I don't know," he replied honestly. "But Cateera wants to try, so we will."

"Thanks, Cateera. You have no idea how badly I want to get this bastard."

Tell him I do, she said. *I really do.*

≈

The smell. How could he have forgotten the smell? He'd been to a lot of murder scenes when he'd been on the force, even more since bonding with Cateera. He'd tracked a lot of murderers. There was something about the combination of decomposition, recycled air, and industrial-strength cleaner that his brain had erased. No doubt as a defense mechanism. Cateera sneezed, shaking her head, and Jonathan smiled when Anderson absently blessed her. Water from his rain-wet hair dripped down his neck. At least down here in the basement, they couldn't hear the thunder.

The diener checked the file against the freezer door before pulling open the drawer. Cold dead air puffed out. The body was covered with a white sheet. A rounded bump for the head, two smaller bumps at the other end for the feet. The two ends were not that far apart. It hurt Jonathan's heart to know that an adolescent lay beneath that mourning drape.

"You know the routine," the diener said around the wad of gum in his cheek. It popped, the sound unnaturally loud in the room. "Don't forget to shut him back in when you're done. Had a guy last week forget to do that."

"Thomas?" Anderson asked.

"Yeah, how'd you know?"

"Lucky guess," Anderson said.

Jonathan's headache had retreated to a workable level of pain. A sub loaded with everything and three bottles of water had done wonders to reenergize him. Cateera had eaten all the meat out of a sub and lamented that he hadn't brought any of Gina's meat rolls with him. He wished they'd had time to stop. He had a fondness for her cheesecake.

"You ready?" Anderson asked.

"Go ahead," he said.

Lifting the sheet revealed the pale, mottled body of a boy in his early teens. Heavy black stitches marred the chest and marched down the distended stomach. The body showed signs of advanced decomposition. He listened as Anderson read the information he'd gathered on the boy. The medical examiner estimated the body had been dead for three weeks before it was found. White, male, between fourteen and sixteen years of age. No ID, no trace on the DNA. The state of the teeth led the coroner to believe the boy had never seen a dentist. It indicated a low-income background, or a home with sheer neglect.

The body showed cigarette burns consistent with the photos Jonathan had seen back at the precinct. He pulled the sheet aside to examine the arms and found the cut he'd expected. It was in the same place he'd felt the mental knife enter the other victim's arm. All the blood had been washed away, of course, but the slice gaped enough for him to see the striated muscle inside.

"Poor kid," Jonathan murmured. He smoothed back the dark hair from the boy's brow, saying a quick prayer that he'd be able to find some justice for him and the others.

"Laptop is up," Anderson said. He'd pulled a sliding tray up to the side of the freezer and initiated a map program. "It's not as good as the holomap, but it will have to do."

Cateera's long white whiskers trembled a little as she looked at the boy. She nudged his shoulder with her nose and then briefly lay her head alongside his. The sorrow that flowed through their link made Jonathan close his eyes against the sudden urge to cry. No way in hell was he going to do that in front of his ex-partner.

"Ready?" he asked his bondmate.

Yes, she answered and laid her paw over the back of the hand that rested on the boy's forehead. It was more for comfort than anything else, but they both needed it.

Chapter Twenty

Jonathan closed his eyes, centering himself, and pushed his awareness through his palm and into the shell that had once been a boy. Everyone left a smudge of themselves behind. Even a napkin at a restaurant held a faint imprint of the person who'd used it. The spirit was long gone from the body, but that imprint remained, like a fingerprint on glass. Sliding into it, Jonathan pulled it around himself like a coat.

Street corner hangout. Music pounding into his head from a stolen player. His hips moved to the rhythm with no conscious thought. He could smell bad fish. Too far in the past. Jonathan pushed forward, impressions streaming past. A car slid up to the curb. Dark blue, four-door sedan. No logo visible, but Jonathan made it for a Toyota Camry, older model. The driver-side window rolled down, but the man's face remained in shadow.

Skipping forward. The car smelled of stale sausage biscuits. There was a gripping hand on the back of his neck, forcing him down. A sharp sting. Jonathan tried to escape it, but his limbs were already beyond his control.

It was so dark and the smell made him want to vomit. There was a nightmare in the corner, and he thought maybe he was home in bed, and the closet monster was with him again. A flaring orange glow touched down on his chest. Jonathan screamed. He could smell the barbeque scent of his skin burning.

I'm here, Cateera said. *We are safe.*

He struggled to hold on to his own personality, to push the pain far enough away that he could deal with it. He struggled to keep his eyes open, but all he could see was that dancing orange pain so they kept squeezing shut. Pain and fire so deep inside that it was stealing who he was, changing him into a hollow receptacle that was slowly filling with terror. Claws and teeth latched into his head, into his brain, feasting on the agony and horror, sucking it up with dark glee. Jonathan couldn't stop screaming.

Drifting away, all that he was and might have been feeding an insane appetite. Catching onto that hunger, Jonathan forced himself toward it, following it to its source. He hit a wall, rebounding so hard he felt the mental bruises. Eyes turned to look at him. Pale eyes, a soft baby blue so innocent and unassuming that they couldn't possibly belong to a killer, regarded him through the darkness.

"I see you, Burke." The voice didn't match the eyes. Rough gravel carved the words into his flesh, and Jonathan recoiled in surprise. It was enough to sever the connection.

Pain beat in his temples and he struggled with nausea. Cateera supported his weight. Despite the frigid temperature in the room, Jonathan's shirt was plastered to his back with sweat. He could still see those eyes, and he had the nastiest feeling they could still see him.

A bottle of water found its way into his hand. Jonathan raised it to his lips and didn't stop drinking until it was empty. Even then he could still taste the fear.

"That didn't go well, did it?" Anderson asked.

"What makes you think that?"

"Could be that you were screaming loud enough to bring an audience that I had to throw out," he answered.

"Ah shit." Jonathan looked down at the far too young boy whose life had ended so horribly. "I'm sorry. I can't help."

"Maybe another body?" Anderson asked hopefully. He flipped the sheet back over the boy's face and slid the drawer back into the wall. Jonathan stopped him when he reached for another handle.

"The killer saw me and cut me off." He didn't mention the words or the feeling of threat that had imbued them. "There are two of them,

Anderson. I'm nearly positive. One who does the torturing, and one who watches. That one isn't human, and he's the one who cut me off."

Jonathan didn't say that he thought the Veiler reveled in the horror the victim was feeling, eating it like it was the finest delicacy.

"Did you see him?"

"Only his eyes," Jonathan answered. "Pale blue. A white male with pale blue eyes. And a car. Toyota Camry, dark-blue, four-door sedan."

No location, Cateera said. *I could not reach any closer than before.* She rubbed her cheek against his. *He frightens me.*

"You're safe, precious one," Jonathan told her. "You'll always be safe with me."

I know, but this creature is following us. What if he catches us?

"I won't let that happen." He slid a reassuring hand through her fur. "We'll guard against him."

Anderson slapped the laptop closed. "So, except for a vague location, and a car, we're no closer than we were before. The lieutenant is going to have my balls for breakfast. I pushed hard to get you here."

Jonathan didn't like failure. He especially didn't like that the Veiler who'd been behind the gruesome deaths in Carolina and who'd followed him back to the Haven also seemed to be behind the deaths here. Why? Was he trying to be caught? Jonathan didn't think so. Anderson had said that these deaths had been going on for over eighteen months. Far longer than his case in Carolina. Maybe Jonathan was just unlucky enough to have run into a multi-territorial killer. If such a thing existed

He also had more than a sneaking suspicion the Veiler was enjoying himself. That he thought of Jonathan and Cateera as adversaries and this was all a game to him. Perhaps it wasn't coincidence that Jonathan had been drawn back to his hometown.

"I'm sorry, Anderson," he said.

The apology was waved away. "Not your problem, boyo. We'll just have to track him the old-fashioned way. At least now we have a general location. We can start canvassing the neighborhood, knock on some doors. We'll catch him."

The combination of the chill of the room and his sweaty shirt made Jonathan shiver. The pain beating in the back of his head was making him nauseous. Overall, it had shaped up to be a shitty afternoon. Jonathan knelt in front of Cateera, framed her face in his hands, and ruthlessly pulled at her pain. She tried to shake him off, push him out, but in this he was always stronger. Still, he had to close his eyes and struggle to breathe for a minute as the pincer-like tightness where his skull met his spine threatened to suck him down.

Outside it was still raining. The sky was a peculiar grey-green, the rain icy cold. Once the sky would have made people worry about tornadoes, but Jonathan knew it was nothing more than the Veil miles out to sea reflecting off the dense flat clouds. He stood in the parking lot, face tipped back, letting the rain sluice away the ugliness. The failure.

A low whine alerted him to the fact that Cateera was not nearly as happy with the weather as he was. Her fur, dense and thick now with winter, was enough to repel the water. Not like his jacket, which was soaking up moisture like a sponge.

"I'm wetter than you," he told her.

But that is your choice. I am forced to stand here in this rain while you deliberately try to absorb enough of it to prevent a flood. I do not like my ears getting wet. To show just how much she didn't like it, she hissed at him. A muddy paw, claws retracted, smacked at his thigh.

"Doesn't like the rain?" Anderson guessed, coming up behind them. Water ran down his bald head, beaded in the thick line of eyebrow, and dripped.

Jonathan unlocked the door to the SUV and quickly got out of the way when Cateera hurried to jump inside. "What female does?"

Anderson snorted. He shifted the laptop case under his other arm and held out a hand. "I'm sorry I made you come all this way for nothing."

Jonathan shook his friend's hand. "I'm sorry we couldn't help. Be careful of this guy, Anderson. Whatever he is, he's a nasty son of a bitch, and now he knows you're closing in on him."

"Maybe that'll make him screw up. All we need is one little mistake and we'll have him. Maybe we'll get that last kid back alive." He rubbed a hand over his wet head. "You heading back or staying in town overnight?"

Going home, Cateera said. Her turquoise gaze pierced him through the window.

"We'll stay overnight. I need a good night's sleep before I can drive."

"Let me take you out for drinks later. You can meet my partner. She'll want a couple beers after the dentist. And if the Novocain hasn't worn off, we can make fun of her dribbling them down her shirt."

Jonathan weighed the need to sleep off the headache against the pleasure of hanging out with an old friend. "Meet you at eight out at Old Beach?"

"You got it," Anderson said with a wide grin.

The bar was located on what had once been the boardwalk of Buckroe Beach. Now, the beach was down a long hill. The Cataclysm had changed the area that much, not only drying up the James River, but lifting parts of the small city above sea level. The Eastern Shore, the long peninsula that sheltered what had been the Chesapeake Bay, was long gone. The bay was gone. Now the ocean pounded hard against the shore with nothing to soothe its fury. The bar sat on the cliff above, and on stormy days, the view was wild. On calm days, with the tide out, the beach would stretch for half a mile before hitting water. On hot, humid days, the smell of brine and fish permeated the air. Rainy days did the same thing. Luckily, the interior of the bar reeked of overused cooking oil and the warm yeasty smell of beer. He breathed it in and was instantly filled with nostalgia.

It smells bad, Cateera said. *Very, very bad.* She was invisible beside him, using her camouflage magic in this place where she wasn't sure of her welcome.

Jonathan laughed, lifting a hand in greeting to the barkeeper. Joe had added to the tattoos he wore as his life story, a family swirl around his left eye now proclaiming his wedded state. "It doesn't smell bad."

Your poor human nose only smells a tiny fraction of what I smell. It is a very noxious odor. She crowded up against his legs as the door opened behind her, sending in a gust of damp air. Jonathan stepped to the side to compensate for her shove. It was either that or end up on the floor. The newcomer gave him an odd look when he found his way blocked by something he couldn't see. He sidled around, eyes locked warily on Jonathan.

Is there something to hunt here?

"It's raining; you don't like the rain."

I like this smell less.

"There are geese, deer if you can find them. You can fish at the beach if you want to brave the water."

She nipped his wrist, holding it gently between her jaws. He returned the gesture of affection with a good scratch beneath her chin. "Make your way to the hotel when you're done. I won't be too late."

He couldn't see her when he opened the door to let her out. What he could see though were the patterns of her footprints making circles in the rain puddles. "Be safe," he sent after her.

Always.

Jonathan wove his way through the packed tables, stopping to say hello to people he'd known when he lived and worked in the area. This was a cop hangout, a place for them to relax without having to keep one eye on the door. Only the stupidest of troublemakers would try to come in. Anderson had scored a table in the back, a six top that currently had about ten chairs pulled up to it. He waved Jonathan over, tapping the back of the one empty chair at the table.

"Glad you could make it, saved you a spot," he said. His voice was raised to be heard over the chatter of drinkers and the howls of sports fans watching a game on the big-screen TV in the corner.

Jonathan slid into a seat covered in duct-taped red vinyl, and a beer magically appeared in front of him. There were four pitchers scattered on the table, all of them nearly empty. He took a long pull before acknowledging the enthusiastic greetings shouted his way. Most of the people at the table he knew from his squad days. A couple of them were detectives now. There were a few unknown faces, and he memorized names as they were introduced.

A woman leaned around Anderson, extending a long, narrow hand. "Hi, I'm Beatrice, the asshole's partner."

Grinning, Jonathan shook her hand. He approved of her name for Anderson. She had dark hair pulled back into a tight ponytail, a thick spray of freckles over her nose and cheeks, and a smile that broadcast energy. "How's the tooth?"

"An hour and a half waiting, and thirty minutes in the chair. I should have arrested the damned dentist for wasting my time. But at least I can chew again." She demonstrated by sticking half a potato skin dredged in sour cream into her mouth.

Jonathan snagged one of the skins off the plate in front of Anderson and bit into it. He'd eaten, but he was still hungry. The expenditure of energy when he used his Gift was astronomical. He'd probably lost close to four pounds, and his muscles screamed for sustenance.

"I heard you have a Faelinn," Doughtry said. He sat across the table, narrow shoulders hunched over his beer. He worked in the computer squad now, though Jonathan remembered him from the academy. He'd always been a computer geek, spoke code better than English.

"Yeah, I'm bonded to a Fael," he said, gently correcting the man. A lot of people confused the plural Faelinn for the singular Fael.

"Cool, where is it?"

"She's a she, dumbass," Anderson said, tossing a pretzel across the table. Doughtry caught it neatly in his mouth like a seal catching a fish.

"Well, where is she, then?"

"Hunting," Jonathan answered.

Despite the noise in the bar, he suddenly had the attention of everyone at the table.

"Hunting what?" Doughtry asked. A mug of beer was poised halfway to his mouth.

"The slowest human she can catch," Jonathan said with a straight face. "She picks the slow or elderly out of the crowd and stalks them for a while for fun before taking them down. One bite to the throat, and they're dinner."

The Adam's apple in Doughtry's throat bobbed up and down. "Are you serious?"

Jonathan leaned in close. "How fast can you run?"

Doughtry went pale. The mug in his hand jittered just a little.

Anderson dissolved into full-bellied laughter. "Ah shit, boyo, he got you."

"Yeah, yeah, laugh it up," Doughtry said. He looked Jonathan in the eye, the corner of his lips twitching as he tried hard not to join in the laughter. "Just for that, you can buy the next round." He drained the mug and slammed it down onto the table.

A squealing, warm weight wiggled itself onto Jonathan's lap, wedging curvy jean-covered hips between his waist and the table. Arms slipped around his neck and a skillful mouth suddenly entertained his. He tasted bubblegum before breaking the seal between their mouths. He looked into bright brown eyes, knowing who she was just from the taste of her.

"Jonathan! You're back," Louise said. She leaned in, her lips brushing his ear. "I've missed you."

Not quite sure what to do with his hands, Jonathan let them rest on her waist. It seemed safest. He was very aware of Anderson's keen interest and was very careful not to look over at his ex-partner. "Hey, Louise, how have you been?"

"Lonely," she told him. Her lush bottom lip pouted prettily. "These morons don't know how to treat a girl."

"That's not true," Anderson protested. "All you have to do is agree to be the mother of my children and I'll worship the ground you walk on."

She turned her head to look at him, her soft brunette hair tickling Jonathan's cheek. "See there, that's your problem, Leo. The worshipping needs to come first."

"She has a point," Jonathan said.

"Not where I come from," Anderson said. "I learned it at my papa's knee. Babies first, then the queen treatment."

"Sugar, your papa was a troll," Louise told him.

Since that was true, Anderson couldn't argue. "Whenever you change your mind, sweetheart, you let me know. We'll make beautiful babies together."

"I'll keep that in mind," she said with a wink at Jonathan. She wiggled a little on his lap to get comfortable. "How long have you been back in town?"

"Since this afternoon. I'll be heading home in the morning."

"So, the night is ours, then?" Her voice was low and husky.

Jonathan shook his head. He brushed his lips across her smooth cheek. He was gentle for old times' sake because he'd once enjoyed her company very much. "Sorry, Louise, I'm involved with someone."

"Oh," she said, drawing back. There was a smile in her eyes though that told him she wasn't overly disappointed. "I should have asked." His lap was suddenly empty, but he got a glimpse of very nice cleavage when she bent down to whisper in his ear. "I hope you're not listening to Leo. His romancing skills are awful."

"I think she likes me," Anderson said, his gaze glued to her ass as she walked away with a promise to bring back more beer and food.

Jonathan shook his head and finished his beer. "You're serious about the babies, aren't you?"

"Oh yeah," Anderson said. "She's perfect."

"In that case, I suggest you really rethink your strategy. Human women have a whole other set of priorities."

"It worked for my mother," Anderson said bullishly. "And my folks have been married for nearly forty years."

Having heard stories about how Anderson's parents had gotten together, Jonathan just shook his head. "I don't think that's going to work for Louise. In this case, I really recommend the worshipping first."

Anderson's big fingers tightened around the mug's handle and threatened to snap it right off. He mumbled something unintelligible under his breath and glared in the direction of the bar. "Maybe if I bring her the head of the bastard who's killing those boys, she'll have my babies."

"I don't think that's a good idea," Jonathan warned.

"You didn't win your woman over with a blood token?"

About to answer in the negative, Jonathan thought about how he'd killed Oktar to free Jekk. He'd done it for the Fael, not for Alanna, but he wondered if she'd be impressed if he told her about the fight. "We're all a bunch of Neanderthals," he told Anderson.

"Finally, a man who's self-aware," Beatrice said, peering around Anderson's side. "There might be hope for the species yet."

Pitchers of beer appeared on the table. Louise was a study in professionalism as she cleared away empty appetizer platters. She wiped up a spill of beer, tossed down a stack of clean napkin, and disappeared back into the kitchen.

Chapter Twenty-One

"I wish I could have been there today," Beatrice said, raising her voice to be heard over the sudden frenzied screams of cheering sports fans in the corner. "I wanted to see how you work."

"Don't believe her," Anderson said. "She just wanted to see your Fael. She's furious I didn't take pictures."

"I'm sorry," Jonathan said. "If I'd known I'd have introduced you before she left." He followed the bond link to tell Cateera she was missing an adoring audience.

The ocean is wet, she snapped at him. *It is worse than the rain.*

"Have you caught anything?"

Of course. Fish are stupid. Now let me eat.

"It's a shame your talent is only with dead people," Anderson said. He downed half his beer in one gulp, considered what was left, and drank that too. "At least we know that the last boy taken is still alive. That's something at least."

Jonathan pinched the bridge of his nose, trying to push back the lingering headache. He hated the thought of an innocent child being tortured because he hadn't been able to find a killer. The guilt had taken up residence in the tight knots of his shoulders, and in the ache of his heart. He could call Alanna. He knew she would come. But then she would have to step into his world, see the violence and ugliness he worked with, and he didn't want that for her. Let her find lost keys and puppies and maintain her innocence.

Her innocence was shattered when she found Amber Leigh, Cateera said. *If she finds out that you made this decision for her, she will not be happy with you. She should be allowed to make up her own mind about how she and Jekk will use their Gift.*

"I know," he said. And that was the kicker. He did know. But that didn't mean he had to like it. He sat back, letting the familiar odors and rhythms of the bar soothe him. Nothing much had changed here. The floor tile was still the same scuffed black and white. Half of the chairs were mismatched. Even the people were the same. There were a few new faces to break up the monotony, but if pushed, he was pretty sure he'd be able to call up names to match most of the faces. The only real difference was that he felt like an outsider looking in.

A burger appeared in front of him, loaded with bacon and cheese. Louise winked at him, pointedly ignored Anderson, and sashayed away. He had the sudden feeling that he'd been used. The very obvious way she was ignoring Anderson told him that she wasn't ignoring the other cop at all. And he found that very interesting.

"You should ask Louise out for dinner," Jonathan told Anderson around a mouthful of beef.

"Why? To build up her energy for baby making?"

When Anderson had finished whacking him on the back, he felt bruised but was no longer choking on burger. "No, to get her to spend some time with you, idiot. Feed her, listen to her, and don't mention babies."

"But babies are—"

Beatrice slapped Anderson's shoulder from the other side. "Listen to him, asshole. It's not like you're getting anywhere doing it your way."

"Better give her a blindfold though," Doughtry said from across the table. "So she doesn't have to look at your ugly mug while she's eating." He leaned back to dodge Anderson's long reach. It looked like he'd had some practice at it.

Louise wove her way through the tables, a tray balanced dexterously on her arm, two pitchers of beer in her other hand. She deposited them at a nearby table, chatted for a moment, and then moved off with a smile. She came to lean against the table at Jonathan's side.

"How's the burger?"

"It's good," he said, and kicked Anderson under the table.

The man coughed, shot Jonathan an angry look. When he looked at Louise, though, there was nothing but adoration in his eyes. "I'm taking you to dinner Thursday night."

She blinked in surprise. "I see. What if I say no?"

"You're not going to," Anderson said. His hands were clenched into fists on the table. "Thursday is your night off. I'll pick you up at your apartment at seven."

"How do you know where I live?"

"I'm a cop," he pointed out.

"So you are. Make it six-thirty. Don't you dare be late." She was gone before Anderson had a chance to reply.

A wide smile took control of his mouth and he slapped Jonathan's back again, nearly knocking him forward into his food. "She's going to have my babies."

Beatrice's laughter was contagious and after a moment, even the half-troll cop joined in. When they'd all managed to catch a breath, Doughtry shook his head. "The world is ending; Leo has a date."

"And if we catch that damned killer before then, I'll give her his head as a present," Anderson announced. He looked at his partner. "Feel like pulling a few more hours tonight, since you spent the day lounging around with your mouth open?"

"Bite me, asshole," she said, but reached for the jacket slung over the back of her chair.

"Listen," Jonathan said. "I might be able to help."

"You going to try again?" Anderson asked. The hope in his voice was tangible. Beatrice stopped with one arm in a sleeve to look over.

"No," he answered. "But I know someone who might be able to find the living boy." He didn't add that the boy might not be living at all. None of them wanted to consider that. "Her Gift is for finding missing things."

"That include people?" Beatrice asked.

"You talking about that writer?" Doughtry asked. "I read about her in the eNews. Didn't she find a kidnapped kid just recently?"

So Jones had written about her for his paper. It shouldn't have surprised him, but it did a little. The man had reported on a tragedy his own family had suffered. Jonathan wasn't sure how he felt about that. He'd have to look up the story. See the slant of it. See whether Jones had painted the Faelinn in a good light.

"You know her?" Anderson demanded. "Why didn't you mention her before? How quick can she get here?"

He was never going to forgive himself. Alanna was going to have to touch that boy's hoodie, and if her Gift worked at all like his, she would see him wherever he was, whatever was being done to him. It wasn't a call he wanted to make, but Jonathan knew his conscience wouldn't allow him to ignore the chance that they could find the boy alive.

"Yeah, I know her," he told them. "I'll call her and let you know what she says."

"Convince her," Anderson said. The lovelorn male was gone; the cold cop was back. "I'll clear her fees with the lieutenant."

Jonathan shook his head. "I doubt she'll want money. Neither of us will. We'll find this kid and the bastard who took him, I swear it."

Somehow, his SUV headed away from the direction of the hotel. Instead, he found himself driving down to the ocean. Cateera was still there, waiting for him. Despite her complaints about the wetness of the water, she had lingered at the shoreline. He understood. He found the sea breeze and the never-ending sound of the waves soothing. Maybe it would clear the feel of failure from his soul.

The rain had slowed to a misting drizzle by the time he parked in the dark lot. The streetlights had been shot out and no one had replaced them. Digging in the glove compartment, Jonathan found the old Hampton PD parking pass he'd squirreled away and stuck it on the dash.

Cateera ghosted out of the dark, making a deliberate show of rubbing her wet fur against his hip. He smiled and gave her chin a good scratch. "Catch enough to fill you up?"

I had help, she said smugly and showed him the memory of a playful Merchild flinging fish at her from the waves. The waves sparkled with phosphorescence, the rain a shower of glittering jewels. Her night vision was so much keener than his. She saw the world in a whole other way, saw things he would never glimpse except through her eyes. Just past where the swells began to crest, the Merchild rode the waves, hair like strands of red seaweed plastered to his narrow face. His nose slits were open to accommodate the air, and the pointed teeth in his lipless mouth shone like mother of pearl. With each leap from the wave, he slung a plump fish at the beach, laughing when it splashed into the shallows and Cateera retrieved it to feast on the moist flesh. The pungent taste of fish filled Jonathan's mouth, and he found himself wishing for a bottle of water.

Your taste buds have atrophied, she informed him. She fell into step beside him as he ran down the steps to the sand. He headed for the waterline, and once he reached it began a slow jog down the beach, just above the reach of the water. The tide was still coming in, although he judged it to be almost time to turn.

Lights from the houses up above didn't quite reach the water, so Jonathan found himself running nearly blind. The rain was almost gone, but the clouds remained, no stars peeking through to throw even the tiniest light on the sand. If it wasn't for the odd glow of the Veil reflected from the clouds, he wouldn't even see his feet on the sand.

Cateera loped along beside him, on the opposite side from the freezing waves that tried to lap at his feet. Jonathan hurdled a small tongue of water that had worn a ditch into the sand, increasing his speed. Lights from a boat bobbed on the horizon. The rhythm of the waves, the even beating of his feet on the sand lulled him. His mind slowly emptied, the tension of the day, the memories of pain and terror all falling away. All that mattered was the scent of salt, the dark, and Cateera's silent companionship.

A blazing light shot over the waves. Jonathan stopped, bracing himself for what was coming next. He warned Cateera barely a second before a loud boom burst against his eardrums. She cried out in pain, her paws covering her ears while she balanced on her haunches.

What was that? she demanded. She shook her head, rubbing at her sore ears.

"That was an Oozlefinch," he told her. "You just had the privilege of seeing it in flight. It flies backwards at near light speeds. It used to be a local legend until the Veil proved it really existed."

Cateera grumbled, peering after the lingering light far in the distance. *If I see it again, I will eat it.*

Jonathan laughed and began to run again. He left behind the lights from the houses on the cliff. Scrub trees grew above the dunes. Nature was taking over. Out of the corner of his eye Jonathan caught a flash of light in the waves. Without turning his head, he watched carefully. After a few minutes, he became aware that the Merchild Cateera had been playing with was pacing them. The light was a faint reflection off of iridescent scales. Gradually slowing his pace, he finally stopped when they reached a piece of beached wood large enough to sit on. It was old, smoothed by water and time, and just above the high tide line. Taking off his shoes, Jonathan dug his toes into the cold sand and waited to see what the child would do.

Cateera approached the waves, careful to stay just out of reach. She backpedaled once, nearly landing on her rump when an overly ambitious wavelet splashed too close to her paws. Out in the water, the child stopped and watched them carefully. Only his eyes were visible above the waves. A tiny crab ran over Jonathan's foot, disappearing into a hole when he moved. Slowly the Merchild approached, drifting closer with each approaching wave.

He should be more careful, Cateera said. *He does not know what kind of human you are.*

"Didn't you tell him I'm a nice guy?"

I did, but he does not know if I am lying or not. He is foolish.

A fish came sailing out of the dark, landing neatly next to Cateera. She took it gently in her paw and tossed it back. The next wave deposited the child on the beach. He pushed up on his elbows and stared at them out of slanted dark eyes. His tail with its stiff dorsal fin was covered in fine scales that picked up the ambient light and tossed it back as a shimmering rainbow in the dark.

Jonathan stayed very still. He couldn't judge the male's age. He had little experience with the life cycles of any of the Oceanborn races. He knew enough to recognize that the boy was still prepubescent, with the soft cheeks of childhood. The thick red layers of his hair curled at the edges where they weren't plastered wetly to his face.

"No more fish?" he asked Cateera. His accent was hard to understand, the vowels carrying the odd intonations of the moving tide.

The Fael shook her head. When he reached out a hand, she dared the water to allow him to run his webbed fingers through her fur. He clicked in contentment and then laughed when she rubbed her face against his.

He is adorable, she said.

Jonathan couldn't help it, he laughed. The child froze, eyes wide and alert.

"She said you are adorable," Jonathan told him softly. "And she thanks you for all the fish."

"I am not a guppy," the child replied. His dorsal fin twitched in aggravation. "I am a strong warrior."

There was a sudden sharp cry from the waves and the strong warrior disappeared, slipping back into the water so quickly Jonathan wondered if he'd even been there.

We have another visitor, Cateera warned.

Very slowly, Jonathan stood up. An adult male strode from the waves, a phosphorescent shimmer of water on fading scales revealed the thick muscular thighs of a man. He stood in the foam at the edge of the water, blatantly aggressive. Jonathan studied him quietly, waiting for him to make the first move. Except for the fact that he was wet and nude and had just appeared from the sea, there was no indication that he belonged to the Mer race. His features had taken on a distinctly human cast, the thick seaweedy strands of his hair softening to silken waves that poured down his back. A thick torque of woven shells and teeth decorated his throat, matching armlets around his biceps. A long, thin dart gun rested against his shoulder, ready to be brought to his lips and used. Jonathan knew that the poison tipping the dart would kill him inside of a minute.

Cateera was crouched to attack, her ears stiff, her tail twice its size. Lips were drawn back from razor-sharp incisors. The Merman would be able to take either Jonathan or his bondmate, but he would be dead before he could shoot the second.

"We meant no harm," Jonathan said quietly.

"The Fael was within killing distance of my ward." His accent was far lighter than the boy's, exotic but completely understandable.

"He helped her fish," Jonathan replied. "She doesn't like to be wet."

"My ward is foolish. He knows that he cannot trust humans and yet he allowed himself to get within harm's reach."

"Kids don't always listen, do they?"

A sharp shake of his head and the briefest twitch of the Merman's mouth told him he agreed. "No, they don't."

"You've had some trouble recently, I've heard."

"I wouldn't call the slaughter of my people trouble," the Merman said.

"I meant no offense."

A long silence as the Merman studied him. After a minute, he let out a call, the clicking, musical song similar to a dolphin's. There was a splash out beyond Jonathan's sight and he realized that the Merman wasn't alone. He should have known. Only a fool would trust solitary travel so close to shore after the recent murders.

"My name is Kikirik."

"Jonathan Burke. I used to be on the police force here. I know the murders are being investigated, but if you need someone to contact, I can give you a name."

"That would be welcome," Kikirik said. "The human liaison we're forced to deal with seems more inclined to downplay the slaughter and cover it up with platitudes. I'm not even sure he swims."

The last was said with such disdain that Jonathan laughed. He found himself liking the Mer warrior, despite the blow gun that remained close at hand. "Homicide Division, Leo Anderson. He's aware of the murders. Whatever you do, refuse to speak to Thomas. He's a Human Righter."

"Thank you. I will send Anderson word and ask to meet with him." Kikirik lowered the blow gun from his shoulder, resting one end in the sand. His skin reflected a faint sheen of scales below his knees. The rain had started again, slow drops that threatened to turn harder.

"Anderson's investigating the disappearance and killing of human boys here in town. Have you heard anything about that?"

Dark wet hair slithered over bare shoulders as Kikirik tipped his head to the side. "No, I'm sorry. We don't pay much attention to human news."

Privately, Jonathan thought that they should. Keeping up with human politics alone would make them safer. Perhaps they left that to their own liaison. Cultural isolationism was not smart in these tense times.

The Human Righters were getting bolder, their political power stronger. Eventually, something was going to blow.

The slow fat drops of rain suddenly became a drenching sheet. Kikirik tipped his head back and laughed as it sluiced over him. Jonathan cursed. The rain found its way down the back of his jacket. The Merman took a step backward and dived into an oncoming wave. He disappeared and then his head popped up yards from the shore. "May the waves keep you safe, human," he called out and then he was gone.

He should keep his ward under better control, Cateera said. *Too many things could happen.*

Jonathan leaned over and hugged her wordlessly close. "Let's go and get dry and then call Alanna."

Despite the rain, a low purr rumbled through the air. *I knew you would see it my way.*

Chapter Twenty-Two

Alanna stretched her back, trying to loosen the muscles that had tightened up during the long ride. She wasn't used to driving the big SUV. Mark had insisted she take the larger vehicle for the long drive to the coast. The vehicle's frame was reinforced to handle the weight of a fully grown male Fael and provide him with enough room to be comfortable. The trip to New DC and back had made it obvious that her sedan wasn't constructed to carry that kind of load.

The trip across the state had been arduous. Snow slowed her in the mountains. Once she hit the lowlands, it melted into rain, heavy sheets of it that fought the windshield wipers. The roads were narrow, winding through miles of forest, skirting the areas destroyed by the Cataclysm. When she'd reached the coast, Alanna had engaged the GPS, setting it to the address Jonathan had given her. His call the night before had interrupted her writing, but she hadn't cared. His voice through the phone wrapped around her like warm velvet. Just listening to him made her melt. He'd sounded angry but after a few minutes she'd realized that it was the situation that caused the tension in his voice. The case he'd outlined caused a cold lump to form in her chest. His request for her to come had filled her with dread, but there wasn't any question of saying no.

The perky GPS voice announced that she'd reached the city limits of Hampton. Jekk turned restlessly in the back, pacing from one window to another. The long main road was a concrete line separating shopping areas, auto mechanics and restaurants. She stopped at a light and craned her neck around to stare at her bondmate.

"You're making me nervous," she said, grumpy. "Would you settle down?"

They're waiting for us, he said. *Cateera said they've missed us.*

Maybe that was true of the Fael for her mate, but it didn't necessarily mean that Jonathan had missed her. He'd said he would when he kissed her goodbye, but that didn't make it true. She'd missed him, though, unreasonably so as far as she was concerned. Just because he looked good and tasted better didn't mean a thing. Missing him implied there were emotions involved. One night of wild sex didn't mean there was emotion. She didn't want to have missed him.

Obeying the GPS directions, Alanna turned, following a twisting road. A sign proclaimed that she had entered Historic Downtown Hampton. A brief flash of wording and she was informed that the city had been founded in 1610, the earliest continually occupied English city in the new world. Downtown held a quirky mix of government buildings, shops, and apartments. It had more style than what she'd seen before, a mix of cobbled streets lined with trees, and paved roads. The official buildings were the stark, spare construction that had been thrown up hurriedly after the Cataclysm had changed so much of the landscape. The GPS signaled their arrival by issuing a command to turn left into the parking lot of a big grey square building. The parking lot glistened with puddles. Weak sunlight was trying to battle its way through the clouds. She wasn't sure it would win. The clouds looked like they had more to give.

Jekk stuck his massive head over the passenger seat's headrest. He'd been doing it for most of the trip. More than once she told him to haul his furry butt up to the front seat, but he'd refused every time. Being too close to the front window apparently made him feel sick. Her bondmate didn't like cars. His ears were sharply alert, his entire focus on where they were going.

She's there, he said, nudging Alanna's head with his.

Alanna had already seen them. There was no missing Jonathan's long, lanky frame, the tousled blond hair. No ignoring the way her stomach fluttered when he straightened away from his own SUV. The space next to him was empty and Alanna pulled into it, trying to calm the beating of her heart. The second the SUV was in park, Jekk pushed the door open. His happiness spilled into her as he greeted his mate.

Alanna was smiling when she exited the SUV. Water splashed up from the pavement and she was glad she'd worn boots, even with the fashionable heels that gave her an extra three inches. Leaning back in for her purse, she felt warm hands settle on her hips. Forgetting everything else, she straightened, turning, those broad palms sliding with her movement.

No chance to catch her breath before Jonathan's mouth took hers. There was passion there, enough to heat her blood and turn her knees to jelly. But there was something else, too, and it made her loop her arms around his waist, her hands inching under the black leather jacket. The muscles were tight, and she soothed them with slow circles of her palms. With a shudder, Jonathan buried his face against her neck.

"I don't want you here," he said, his voice ragged. His breath was warm, his lips tickling her skin. "I don't want you exposed to this."

Alanna sifted her fingers through his hair. It was silky and damp. The muscles at the back of his neck were tight and she began to massage them gently. Damn it, she *had* missed him. "I can handle it."

"You shouldn't have to," he told her.

Leaning back to look into his eyes, Alanna frowned. "I'm not a wilting lily. I spent a month riding with the New DC police as research for my fourth book. I've attended a full autopsy. I've seen death."

"Not like this," he insisted. "And it's not the dead bodies I'm worried about. It's what you'll see when you connect with the missing boy."

The harsh rasp of his words made her stiffen. Images of what she'd seen from Amber Leigh flashed through her mind. From what Jonathan had told her over the phone, what this boy might be going through was exponentially worse. Until now, she hadn't realized what that would mean for her.

"You can still change your mind," he said.

A line had formed between his brows, his eyes fiercely intent. He wanted her to change her mind. She could see it and it made her feel unreasonably obstinate. She hadn't come all this way, through crappy weather, only to turn back without attempting to find the missing boy.

With a light fingertip, she traced the line, continuing down over his nose to linger on the curve of his mouth.

"No, I really can't, Jonathan." She replaced her fingertip with her lips for a long moment before drawing back to smile up at him. "Tell me they have decent coffee here."

"I could," he said. That stray dimple creased his cheek as he echoed her smile. "But it would be a total lie."

The building was warm, she'd give it that much. Despite the long gentle ramp and the decorative fountain at each side, the charm ended with the doors. Institutional, that was the word that came to mind. No doubt back when the city was being rebuilt, funds had been in short supply for amenities like nice carpet, central air, open spaces. She'd bet the proceeds from her last book that the fountains outside had been added within the last decade.

The possessive palm at the small of her back guided her through the hallways, into an elevator. Cateera had taken Jekk to the stairwell. There just wasn't enough room in the small elevator for the four of them. And Alanna wouldn't have wanted to test the machine's weight limits like that anyway. When the doors opened and spilled them into another hallway, she caught the scent of burned coffee. She really wished she'd taken the time to stop for lunch and a large takeout cup of well-brewed caffeine.

The Faelinn had beaten them to Homicide. Both of them stood facing a desk where a man wearing a sleek grey suit and a stained tie stood frozen. Jekk had angled his body so that he shielded Cateera. Every eye in the place was on them, and there were plenty. Beside her, Alanna could feel the sudden tension in Jonathan's body. Jekk's thoughts were wild, full of fury. The hair along his spine had risen, his tail puffed twice its normal size. He stood inches taller than his mate, his chest broader, his teeth longer.

"Jekk?" she asked cautiously. She started to go to him, but the noose of Jonathan's fingers around her wrist stopped her.

"Back down, Cateera," Jonathan snapped. The Fael pointedly ignored him. A low rumbling growl shivered up from her throat.

"Get your animals away from me, or I swear I'll put a bullet between their eyes," the detective said. His voice was cold but touched with a tremor of fear. It was then that Alanna saw the gun in his hand, the barrel steady and aimed at Jekk.

"Put the gun away, Thomas, or I'll have your badge," Jonathan said.

"The hell I will," he said. "Your animals are threatening me. They're obviously feral and should be kept in cages at the zoo."

A fine tremor ran the length of Jekk's body. Alanna caught a glimpse of memory from her bondmate, a cage too small, pain and fear and abuse. She realized only the tiniest sliver of control kept him from launching himself over the desk. He'd snap the detective's throat before the blast from the gun had died away. And the bullet would no doubt kill him.

Shaking off Jonathan's hand, Alanna stepped forward. Jekk ordered her back, trying to push his body between her and the desk. The finger on the trigger tightened just a little more. "If you shoot him," she said softly, "several things are going to happen. The first is that his mate will have your throat in her jaws before you can take your next breath. If you survive that, which is doubtful, you will have to deal with me. Since I will be protecting my bondmate, I won't hold back when the pointed toe of my boot connects with your genitals. Your testicles will burst from the pressure as the force of my kick drives them upwards into your lower abdomen. Your penis will be crushed. Your initial reaction will be to double over from the pain, probably falling to your knees. My kneecap will impact with your chin, snapping your mouth closed and forcing you to bite off a chunk of your tongue. That may or may not become lodged in your throat as you suck in a breath to scream again. If you're lucky, you'll choke and pass out. If you're not, you'll still be conscious when your colleagues disarm you. You can only hope that one of them takes pity on you and calls an ambulance immediately. Judging from the looks on their faces, I think you may lie there awhile."

The detective stared at her in stunned silence. The gun trembled just a little.

"Thomas, save yourself the humiliation and put the gun down." The whip of voice came from the man standing in the doorway of an office across the room. "Now."

"They threatened me," he insisted. The color had fled his face and his eyes darted between the growling Faelinn and Alanna.

"They walked past his desk and Thomas pushed it with his foot and rammed it into the white one's side, sir," a petite, dark-haired woman said. Her arms were crossed over her chest, the shoulder holster black against the white of her button-down shirt.

"I said put the gun down, Thomas," the lieutenant said. "I won't ask again."

The hand holding the gun wobbled and then the detective slowly lowered the weapon to the desk. The sound of it hitting the wood was shockingly loud in the room. Immediately, the female detective moved forward to pick it up. With a practiced move, she removed the clip and pocketed it.

Jekk slowly turned his head, nuzzling his mate's cheek. He never moved from his protective spot between her and Thomas. Jonathan knelt at his bondmate's side, running careful hands through the lilac-swirled fur over her ribs. A low whine slipped from her throat as he found a sore spot. Both sets of male eyes, human and Fael, fastened on Thomas with a fury so fierce it burned.

"My office, now, detective," the Lieutenant ordered.

Thomas didn't argue this time. Never taking his eyes from the Faelinn, he walked backwards, hitting a desk with his hip. He reeled around, anger painting his skin in shades of red, and scooted past the lieutenant into the office.

Alanna was shaking when she dropped to her knees beside Jekk. The adrenaline drained away to leave her feeling sick. The massive golden Fael beside her nuzzled his mate one last time and then turned to wrap one muscular leg around Alanna's shoulders. She returned the hug with both arms around his neck, her face so hot against his cool fur.

Don't ever put yourself at risk like that again, he snapped in her mind.

Startled, Alanna pulled back to see him staring at her intently, the pupils dominating the amber of his eyes.

I can protect myself. By doing what you did, you asked me to choose between protecting you and Cateera. I do not want to have to make that choice. I can't live without either of you.

"If he'd shot you, you might have died. And that's something I can't live with," she told him. "I'm not about to let some twisted asshole put your life at risk. You're just going to have to deal with the fact that you're not alone anymore. We're family."

The black faded abruptly from his eyes. His rough tongue delicately touched her cheek. *We are a family. You were very fierce.* There was pride in his thoughts.

"Then we make a good team." She hugged him hard again, feeling the bunch and release of his muscles as he returned it. Her knees weren't quite so shaky when she stood up. She felt even better when the warmth of Jonathan's hand stroked the length of her back.

The room was no longer silent. They were still the objects of attention, but it was assessing now, the detectives discussing what had happened. More than one of them glanced repeatedly at the office where Thomas paced. A hand thrust towards her, and Alanna took it without thinking. She found her fingers squeezed in a tight grip, brown eyes looking steadily into her.

"I'm Lieutenant Duncan. I'm very sorry for Thomas's behavior. This wasn't how I would choose to meet a consultant."

"You're not responsible for his actions," she assured him.

"He's a part of my unit; I'm responsible for everything he does while he's here," Duncan said.

"I'll be pressing charges," Jonathan said. "He assaulted Cateera."

The two men clasped hands briefly. "Good to see you again, Burke. When you're through with the consult, come see me. I'll handle the details of the charges personally."

Alanna wondered what the charges would be. The Veilers had gained rights over the years, but there was still a very fuzzy line about certain things. If they tried to press charges of animal abuse, Jonathan wouldn't be satisfied. In fact, she'd hazard a guess that he'd be furious, and she wasn't sure what he'd do then.

"Hey, you beat me here," a loud voice announced from the door.

Alanna glanced over her shoulder to see a bald man holding a cardboard cup carrier packed with tall coffees and a white bag. The dark suit he wore had to be custom made to fit the breadth of his shoulders and the narrowness of his hips. The smile he wore faded slowly as his brows drew together, the light brown eyes narrowing as he keyed into the room's tension.

"What's going on?" he asked.

"Thomas finally went too far," the woman who'd disarmed the detective said. "I hope like hell one of those coffees is for me."

He handed her the carrier. "Dark roast, extra cream," he said absently. "What did he do?"

"The last thing he's going to do in this department," Duncan said. "If you'll all excuse me, I have some things to take care of." The lieutenant nodded at Alanna before scanning the room. "Is no one working? Are all your cases closed?" The quick movement of detectives back to their desks was impressive.

"What happened?" Anderson asked.

Beatrice, his partner, filled him in quickly. By the time she was finished, Anderson's face was the furious mirror of Jonathan's. He knelt in front of Cateera and very gently smoothed the fur along the side of her head. "I'm very sorry, Cateera. I know it won't help, but I bought you an entire carton of cream."

The Fael extended her tongue and very lightly touched it to his cheek.

Anderson turned to Jekk and extended a hand. "We haven't met, but I'm Leo Anderson. If you like cream, I have one for you, too."

The golden Fael placed his paw in the detective's hand and shook. Anderson's huge hand was only slightly smaller than the Fael's. "His name is Jekk," Alanna said. "And he thanks you for the cream."

Anderson straightened from his crouch, his eyes scanning her from bottom to top as he did. Alanna waited for him to meet her eyes, and when he did, arched one dark brow at him. He had the grace to look embarrassed. Some women might have found that slow scrutiny acceptable, but she didn't. When he offered a hand, she took it reluctantly.

"Detective Leo Anderson," he told her. "I'm a troll."

Alanna blinked, taken aback. She let her eyes run over him, aware that she was giving him the same scrutiny that he'd given her. It would explain the width of his shoulders, the slight overhang of his brows. But his teeth appeared normal, his skin smooth, so she wasn't sure if he was trying to excuse his behavior, or give her his parentage.

"Only half," Jonathan put in. "That half just can't help himself." His hand had settled warmly in the small of her back, his fingers stroking lightly. It was terribly distracting.

Anderson's partner shuffled the cup carrier from one hand to the other. The cups wobbled dangerously. She introduced herself, holding the cups steady. "We appreciate you coming," she said. "I assume one of these is for you. If you need it as badly as I do, then follow me. We have a room set up."

Alanna took an immediate liking to the petite woman. Since Anderson had supplied the coffee, she supposed she should be more charitable to him, too. Her heels made a staccato clicking on the worn linoleum of the hallway. Jekk was a warm shadow at her side. Beatrice commented on her boots and Alanna felt herself relax just a little.

The pictures on the board dominated the small room when Beatrice ushered her in. Breath caught in her throat, Alanna walked over to examine them. Jekk whined a little, crowding her while he looked, too. She reached for him blindly, tears gathered behind her lashes. They were all so young. Just boys. And the terror on their faces, those that retained a discernable face, showed that they'd suffered horribly.

"You don't have to look at those," Jonathan said. His breath was warm at her ear, stirring tendrils of the hair that had escaped her bun. She leaned back just a little until her shoulders met his chest.

"Yes, I do," she said. Her fingertips grazed the smooth finish of a photo. The pale body, even with decomposition well started, showed long, straight wounds. She was pretty sure a sharp blade had caused them. "I need to see what this monster has done."

Starting at the far left, she examined each photo, read each bio, all the details of the deaths and body dumps. She committed each one to memory while inside her heart filled with pain. Every one of these boys had been snuffed out without hope and the knowledge of it nearly broke her. Seeing them, the garish photos documenting each wound and degradation, made her want to shut down. She wanted to go back to her nice little world where she could make up stories with happy endings where no one ever hurt the way these boys had.

Jekk reared up to place his big paws on either side of the photo at the end. His nose nearly touched the glossy paper. Standing on his rear legs like that, he towered over her. The deeper stripes in his golden fur were dull with the wash of his own emotions. She felt them as keenly as her own. There was a killing edge to his thoughts that satisfied her own desire for revenge against the monster who'd hurt the boys.

His nose touched the last photo. *We can save this one. He's still alive.*

Alanna gave her bondmate a quick hug and then turned to see the others watching them silently. "I have no idea how to do this, but let's get started."

A space was clear at the table, and Jonathan pulled out the chair for her. She smiled a little at his chivalry, trying to appear calmer than she felt. His hand passed over her hair, lingering warmly on the back of her neck for a moment. It was a comfort.

"Will it bother you if we watch?" Beatrice asked. "I've never seen anyone do this before."

"I have no idea," Alanna said. "We'll find out." She took a long drink of the coffee, finding it strong and sweet, with a lingering hint of chocolate. Perfect.

There were some details with the recording of her information. Her thumbprint was scanned. When both detectives were satisfied, Anderson opened an evidence box revealing a striped sweatshirt. As he lifted the shirt, she saw a hood flop loosely. She kept her hands in her lap, hit by a sudden reluctance to touch it. Jekk leaned over the table, his whiskers trembling as he took a long, slow smell.

"Jonathan said you might need to touch something that belonged to the missing boy," the detective said. He nudged it a little closer to her.

A glance at Jonathan showed her he was watching closely. A reassuring smile touched his mouth. The lines of strain around his eyes told her how important this was. She wished he would kiss her, just once for courage. It was crazy; she was a grown woman who didn't need a man for support, but she needed it from him. Surprise flickered in his eyes and he glanced at Cateera. His hand cupped Alanna's cheek, fingers stroked the strands of dark hair that wisped around her face. The lips that covered hers were warm and lingered long enough for pleasure to loosen the muscles of her shoulders.

"I'm right here," he told her softly.

A long breath shuddered out of her. "Thanks," she said, and reached for the hoodie.

It was soft. The fabric was worn and she got the sense it wasn't because he didn't have others, but because this was his favorite. She fingered a thick seam at the top edge of the front pouch. It had been mended at one end. The stitches were neatly done. And that was all.

"What do I do, Jekk?"

Amber gold eyes narrowed. His tail beat a ruthless rhythm on the leg of her chair. She could feel the vibration along her spine. His mind expanded within hers and Alanna felt herself fall into him. Her senses sharpened. She closed her eyes against the sudden glare from the overhead fluorescent bulbs. She could scent Cateera, the musky warm smell of her pelt. And Jonathan, all spicy male heat. She breathed them in and then allowed them to fade into the background.

It was funny, but even with her eyes closed, she could still see the hoodie. Senses other than sight were working now. She could see every fiber, every machine-knitted stitch. There was a grommet missing on one side of the hood where the drawstrings came out. Dirt ground into one sleeve. A mustard stain.

We'll track the boy, Jekk said. The voice that spoke to her was richer and deeper than usual. It occurred to her that the normal link between them was used at only a minimum of its potential. *It will be like tracking an enemy. Only I won't kill him.*

Jekk's mind flexed, and hers stretched with it. The last two times had been spontaneous. This time the movement was purposeful. The ghost of a sweatshirt settled around her shoulders. It was warm, comfortable. Alanna shuddered. It was like walking alone at night. There was a destination, but the trip itself was frightening. A chill settled around her. It was really cold in here, why hadn't she noticed it before? Goosebumps ran down her arms, her legs. She tried to curl into a ball, to cuddle what little warmth there was inside of her. Her limbs were frozen in place and no amount of struggle could get them to move.

He's cold, Jekk said softly. He was at her side, walking that dark street with her.

A jerky movement of her head passed for a nod. She tugged at her hands again, but straps dug into her skin. The only warmth was the wet leak of blood around her left wrist. Panic boiled in her stomach. Her eyes opened, but she was sightless. Cold and dark and so very scared.

"I don't want to do this," she cried. Only on the privacy of their link could she admit such a thing. His love surrounded her and she knew that he would never leave her. It gave her courage to look further, to delve deeper into the weave of the hoodie she wore as a phantom mantle.

Cold. Dark. Strapped down, face pressed into rough wood. She took a breath, and leaped the last chasm. Instantly, pain battered her. Ramming, tearing agony splitting her from behind. She was being torn into pieces. The acid burn of vomit coated the back of her throat, and Alanna struggled to swallow it back. If she didn't, she would choke with the gag in her mouth.

There was sound, too. The slapping of bare flesh. Grunts of pleasure and muttered obscenities. A low, gravelly voice that murmured instructions, suggestions for increasing the pain. Her soul shied away from that voice.

Black, cloying fear snaked tendrils into her mind. It insinuated itself into all the soft places, the safe places. Memories were sent fleeing, every shadow of hope driven away. It swelled until there was only the terror and the pain. And then it sent visions. Lost, so small in a forest of legs. Looking and looking for safety only to find that there wasn't any. No one to rescue her. No one to care. Fingernails, claws, clattering under the bed. The sly tug of the sheet as those hands teased for her feet. She tried to curl into a ball, but she was tied down and those hands were touching, pulling, feasting.

And she was screaming around the gag.

Hands caught at her, wrapping her tight. Fighting to get free, she lashed out. Somehow, someway, despite the restraints, her fist found solid flesh.

I'm here! I'm here! I'm here! echoed in her head. Love and reassurance warred with the fear, and she clung to the lifeline. It pulled her up, though black globs of nightmare clung to her flesh.

"Come back, baby," the words urged. "Look at me."

See us, Jekk commanded. His soft fur relieved her abraded flesh. The lightest of licks wiped away the gelid darkness from her arms.

"Open your eyes," Jonathan urged. Gentle hands framed her face. "Look at me."

Light replaced the dark. Summer-blue eyes stared into hers, the flecks of silver catching the light. There was a red mark high on Jonathan's cheekbone, and she lifted a hand to touch it lightly. Her hand hurt when she flexed it and she realized she must have hit him.

"You went too far," Jonathan said.

Alanna didn't want to look away from him. He knelt so close, his hands anchoring her to reality. She was afraid that if she stopped seeing him, the world would dissolve again into a nightmare. She threw one arm around Jekk, clutching him close, and curled the fingers of her other hand into the soft material of Jonathan's shirt.

Words tried to come, but her throat was shut and only a croak emerged. A bottle of water shoved into her line of sight and Alanna stared at it a moment, realizing she was going to have to let someone go to take the bottle. Jekk nudged her arm away, making her take the water. It was cold and tasted better than anything ever had. It had been days since she'd been allowed to drink freely.

You're still attached to him, Jekk said. *We can track him.*

"How?"

Just feel where he is, feel that tie between you. We can find him.

"Is she okay?"

Anderson sat on her left, past Jekk. His hands were fisted on the scarred table. Beyond him, Beatrice was pale, looking as if she'd suffered along with Alanna. That made Alanna wonder just what they'd seen, what they'd heard. She'd been screaming, hadn't she?

"I'm all right," she murmured. The words weren't very strong, didn't sound very convincing.

"You went so far," Jonathan said. "You can't do that again, Alanna. I won't let you."

Spine stiffening, she glared at him. "That's not a decision you get to make."

The smile that tugged at his mouth told her he'd meant for her to react, meant for the words to snap her out of it. She leaned forward and pressed a hard kiss to his mouth. That more than anything anchored her.

"He's still alive," she told them. Tears burned her eyes and she covered it by taking another long drink of water. "He's being hurt."

"Do you know where?" Jonathan asked.

Without thought, Alanna pointed south.

Beatrice tapped something into a keyboard and a holographic map beamed out of the center of the table. It was only then that Alanna noticed the extensive hardware grouped in a recessed hole. She stared at the map, not making any sense of the glowing lines that marked streets.

"Pull up the area we were looking at yesterday," Jonathan said. Immediately, the map tightened, streets coming into sharper focus. "We both agree on the general direction, but I couldn't get enough of a grip on the killer to pinpoint him. If you can follow the boy, we can find him."

Jekk's claws dug short grooves into the scarred tabletop as he leaned forward to put his nose closer to the hologram. The map wavered sharply, falling out of focus as his nose disturbed the projection. He sneezed violently, shaking his head.

It smells bad, he informed her.

"We have a saying about cats and curiosity," Alanna told him. "Perhaps it applies to Faelinn, too." She realized that they were all waiting for her, so she gave the map her full attention. It looked like any other city map; nothing stood out. But she could still feel that pull to the south. "I'm sorry, the map means nothing. All I know is that he's in that direction." Again, she pointed.

Jonathan and Anderson shared a glance. As one, they pushed their chairs back and stood. "I'm driving," Anderson said.

"We'll never get the Faelinn in your car," Jonathan said. "You can follow me. I'll drive while Alanna tracks."

Chapter Twenty-Three

Whimsical houses lined the streets of the neighborhood. Square Cape Cod styles nestled in the shadows of gingerbread Victorians. A single-level sporting stone walls and wooden beams echoed the Tudor fashion of centuries ago. It seemed as if the people who rebuilt the neighborhood after the Cataclysm chose whatever style appealed to them. It was a charming mix, but Alanna saw little of it. Instead, her eyes were closed as she concentrated on the fragile link that remained between her and the kidnapped boy. Jekk was with Cateera in the back seat, but he was the anchor in her mind.

"How are things going up there?" Anderson's voice came through the cell phone in its rest on the dashboard.

"We're getting there," Jonathan said.

There was a mental tug to the left, and Alanna pointed. She felt the truck drive a little farther, and then turn. The connection sharpened. Terror twisted through the link. She couldn't bite back a low moan. Warm fingers curled over hers, squeezing gently for a moment. Jonathan placed her hand on his thigh, providing a physical anchor for her. She clenched her fingers into the hard muscle.

There was a scream. She jumped in her seat, staring around wildly before realizing that it was in her head. "Turn here!" she yelled. The scream morphed into an animal howling. Pain and fear had stripped all sense of humanity from the boy. It threatened to overwhelm her but Jekk's mind wrapped her in safety, allowing only a narrow link to worm its way through his protection. Now she stared at the houses, strained against the seat belt. So close!

Abruptly, the link shuddered. Agony peaked and sliced right through Jekk's protection. Spikes drove into her midsection, splitting her. There was a knife slicing into her arm, deep enough to shred muscle, scrape across bone. Acid burned along her nerves. She writhed against the restraints but they wouldn't yield. There was no way to escape the pain battering her. No way to clutch her arm where the blood flowed away. No way to force back the fear that squeezed her mind in pincers of darkness. Scenes of horror and betrayal twisted in her mind. Inside her head was blackness, and it laughed as it ate. She was crying and the tears burned. The blackness ate that too. And then she shattered.

"No!" Denial screamed from her throat. Blackness sucked her down, the link dragging her down the path of death. She struggled to hold onto the boy, unwilling to let him go. Jekk pushed hard, his razor-sharp teeth biting at the link, tearing it. She fell free.

"What the hell is going on?" Beatrice demanded through the phone.

"He's dead," Alanna said. The path still beckoned at the edges of her soul. Entropy reached for her, a seductive siren of nothingness. Bile boiled up. She shoved the door open, uncaring that they were still moving, and vomited onto the street. Wave after wave of nausea spasmed her stomach. Her body kept her earthbound while her mind tried to yank her away.

The SUV came to a sudden stop. Jekk was there immediately, nimble Faelinn fingers releasing her seatbelt. He was deep in her mind, pushing away the desire to float away. Love filled her, coupled with desperate fear. She turned her face into his furry neck, breathing in the sunlight scent of him. The feeling of nothingness fell away. Shivers of reaction threatened to pull her apart. Strong arms eased her from Jekk's care. She came to rest on Jonathan's lap where he now sat on the curb. She curled into him. He made her feel safe. He always made her feel safe.

Jekk nuzzled her, his whiskers tickling her cheek. Safe, she was safe. The spicy scent of Jonathan's skin filled her nose. Jekk's fur and the roughness of his tongue soothed. She was safe.

At the end of the street, tucked under a massive crepe myrtle, was a pale yellow Victorian. The shutters and curlicues were white. It was crisp, clean, and held a darkness that encouraged at her fear. "He's dead," she managed to choke out. The finger she pointed at the house was trembling.

"Ah, shit," Anderson cursed. He'd joined them at the side of the street. "Are you sure?"

Alanna nodded. Her cheeks were wet with tears and she rubbed them dry. It didn't seem to make a difference.

Taillights flicked on ahead of them. A navy sedan pulled out of the driveway. The driver was an indistinct shape through the rear window. Jonathan stiffened. Anderson cursed, running back to his vehicle. The car slowed at a stop sign ahead and turned left. Anderson gunned the engine and tore after it. Scrambling out of Jonathan's embrace, Alanna headed toward the house. She stumbled, ankle twisting a little as her heel teetered under her. Let the others chase the killer. She needed to see the boy, needed to mourn the light that had been ripped from her mind.

Jekk outpaced her, racing ahead to veer into the Victorian's yard. Jonathan's urgent voice didn't slow her down. Cateera ghosted past, her white fur glowing as it picked up the last rays of the setting sun.

"Alanna, stop!" Jonathan reached for her, his hand grazing her arm. She twisted free, flying up the front steps. Her heels tapped a sharp beat on the old wood.

"Damn it, Alanna, you can't go in there!"

The doorknob refused to yield to her frantic twist. Jekk threw himself against the wood. It shuddered but held. A low growl vibrated from his chest. Two windows flanked the door and Alanna ran from one to the other, trying to see inside. They were painted black. Frustrated, she turned to Jonathan.

"I have to get in," she begged. "I have to see!"

"Anderson is following the car. We have to wait for backup. We can't compromise the scene, Alanna."

The growl that came from her throat wasn't terribly different from Jekk's. She fisted Jonathan's shirt, yanking him down. "I need to get in there." She saw the moment in his eyes when he gave in to her desperation.

"Do you hear screams?" he asked her. "I hear screams." Using his elbow, he punched out the pane of glass beside the door. He reached in and a moment later, the door swung open. Alanna tried to dart through, but he grabbed her arm and held her back. "I don't think so. Not again. You follow me and do what I say."

The words "or else" went unspoken, but Alanna heard them loud and clear. She stepped aside to let him go first. The black gun in his hand had appeared as if by magic. Before she could step across the threshold, the two Faelinn muscled past her.

We won't allow you to be in danger, Jekk said. *You can't keep running into dangerous houses.*

Muttering curses, she followed them inside. The foyer was dark, the only light filtering in through the open door. The walls were painted a muted red. What appeared to be a paint-by-number still life lurked in a cheap frame on one wall. Doors led off on either side and a narrow dark hallway ran the length of the house. Piles of yellowed papers lined the walls. Discarded bags, fast food wrappers, and garbage littered the floor, dark planks barely visible under the filth. A stairway disappeared around a landing halfway up. The risers were an obstacle course of garbage, stomped flat in the center where someone had worn a path.

Jonathan waited, the gun held at his side. His head was cocked as he listened to the silence.

"Stay here, do not move," he told her again. "I'm going to make sure there aren't any surprises upstairs." He glanced down at Jekk, whose ears lay flat against his head. "Watch your bondmate."

Jekk growled at him, insulted. *Of course, I will watch you. Your mate should know that.*

Alanna wrapped her arms around herself as Jonathan moved slowly up the stairs, Cateera close on his heels. Her heart skittered when he disappeared around the bend.

Something rustled under a pile of trash bags, or maybe it was even inside of one. Alanna froze and then slowly eased away. Tickling fingers teased her calf, and she whirled to find a filthy sweater sleeve dangling from between piles of bags.

Smells like rat, Jekk said. *This man lives like the worst of the Kellian.*

Alanna wanted to back out the door but she'd made a fuss to get inside and wasn't about to leave now. She just wished Jonathan would hurry. The golden Fael at her side moved forward a step. His ears twitched.

The long tail began to whip from side to side. He took a deep breath and promptly sneezed.

This place is foul, he complained. But he took another breath, and another.

"What is it?"

There's something here, he told her. He took another cautious step toward the hallway.

"The boy is dead," Alanna reminded him. The sorrow pierced her heart again and she swallowed hard.

I know. This is something else. Jekk opened his senses to her. Immediately the stench of the place overwhelmed her and Alanna gagged. She covered her mouth, fighting not to vomit again, not wanting to compromise any possible evidence. Gaining control, Alanna sensed what Jekk did, an insistent tickle in the back of her mind.

"What is that?" she asked him.

The Fael hesitated. *Stay here.* He began to stalk slowly down the hallway.

Oh hell no, not another bossy male. Alanna followed him down the dark hall, ignoring his displeasure. Her heel sank into something soft and she hopped to one side. Her shoulder knocked a box. It teetered dangerously and she shoved it back with one hand, quickly stepping over a minor avalanche of trash. Jekk's growl deepened as they passed a series of closed doors.

The hall ended with a wall of papers bricked together and tied with string. There was a narrow opening to the right. Jekk squeezed through, blocking the opening so Alanna couldn't advance. She shoved against his haunches and he reluctantly moved forward. She stepped up onto a pile of garbage and followed him.

The kitchen was a copy of the foyer, only with more food. Filthy dishes piled on the counters, filled the sink. Garbage overflowed everywhere. Alanna saw a roach nearly the size of her hand scuttle across a plate and disappear behind a bowl. The smell was beyond description. A large table was barely visible, its surface an extension of the cluttered counters. Dark curtains were shut along one wall. The windows of the back door boarded over with cardboard. If the overhead light wasn't on, she would be standing in darkness. The clearest space in the room was around the table and even that held a litter of empty cans and papers.

Jekk whined. One furry paw scraped at a series of plastic bags, spilling coffee grounds and something rancid and green onto the floor. He turned from side to side. His entire body quivered. Alanna caught his anxiety. The hairs at her nape prickled to attention. There was something here. She felt it through Jekk, but even without him, she still would have sensed something wrong, something out of place.

A thump and a rustle came from behind her. Remembering the size of the cockroach, Alanna shuddered, afraid to look. Then Jekk howled, leaped past her in a blur of golden fur. Something slammed into her back and knocked her forward and she fell hard against the table. Her hands skidded on the pile of filthy dishes. Split vision showed both the plate next to her cheek and a man's face torn with a terrified expression. Disoriented, Alanna closed her eyes. She still saw the man's face, realized it was through Jekk's eyes.

Swiveling, Alanna saw her Fael standing on the chest of a man sprawled out amongst the discarded food and garbage. The weight of Jekk's paws on his ribcage didn't leave much room for air. High-pitched wheezes escaped from his throat.

"What the hell are you doing in here?" Jonathan demanded. He pushed through the narrow doorway a bare second in front of Cateera. His eyes were blue fury. Cateera leaned over the man on the floor, putting her face within a breath of his. Her lips peeled back in a dangerous growl. She looked about an inch away from ripping out his throat. The wheezing grew more terrified.

"Don't harm him," Jonathan instructed. He looked down at the man. "I'll get to you in a minute. If you move, I'll let them play with you." The man squeaked.

Jonathan's gun disappeared back under his jacket. The fingers that wrapped around her upper arm were hard. "I told you to stay put. What part of that didn't you understand?"

Alanna's first instinct was to tell him he wasn't the boss of her. But she looked up into his eyes and decided that wasn't the best plan. Instead, she let her fingers trail down his cheek. "I'm all right. Jekk and I sensed something and we had to look."

Those blue eyes closed for a second, and when he looked at her again, the anger had faded into a sort of resignation. "You're never going to listen, are you?"

"Maybe you shouldn't give me so many orders," she suggested. "We found the bad guy."

"So I see," he said.

Before she could respond, there was a commotion from the front of the house.

"Back here," Jonathan called. A moment later, Anderson appeared in the doorway. He eyed the narrow opening and then bulled his way through. It was a miracle that nothing toppled. His partner, Beatrice, didn't have that problem.

"What the hell are you doing in here?"

Alanna refused to look at Jonathan. "We heard noises," she told the detective.

Anderson's eyes narrowed.

"There were screams," Jonathan said mildly. "We were hoping there was a chance to save the boy."

"If you've screwed up my crime scene, I will kick your ass," Anderson promised.

"Understood. Victim's in the attic. You'll need the medical examiner," Jonathan said.

Grief boiled in the back of Alanna's throat. She swallowed it down, but it was hard.

"What happened with the car?" Jonathan asked.

"Bastard just disappeared on us. He went around a corner, and when we got there, he was gone." Anderson kneeled to get a good look at the man who'd finally fallen silent. "But it seems like you found another one."

They all stared at the narrow-shouldered man wheezing under Jekk's paws. He was balding, wore small wire-rimmed glasses, and had eyes that spun wildly in their sockets.

"Should we let them eat him?" Beatrice asked.

"He'd probably give them food poisoning," Jonathan said. "I hear sirens. I think your backup is here."

Alanna spent the next hour sitting in Jonathan's SUV. The house was cordoned off. Police cars had blocked the street, keeping back the inevitable news crews. At the edges, curious neighbors pushed up against the tape barrier and craned their heads to get the best view. Alanna watched the forensics squad arrive, was there when the curses began. She overheard the supervisor complain that it was going to be weeks before they could properly go through the house. She didn't envy them the job.

When the medical examiner released the body, the EMTs quietly wheeled out the body bag. She watched in numb silence as it was placed in the back of the ambulance and driven off. Jonathan wrapped her hand in his but she barely felt it. Jekk pushed against her mind, offering comfort despite his own grief and disappointment that they had failed.

She must have slept because when she heard the tapping sound on the window, she opened her eyes to find that her head was pillowed on Jonathan's shoulder. Straightening, she bit back a yawn. The sun was down but the night was lit police lights. She doubted any of the neighbors were going to get any sleep that night.

"I'll need you both at the station in the morning," Anderson said. He looked tired. The circles beneath his eyes were beginning to take over his face. "I'll be here or at the station most of the night so you might as well get some sleep. Unless you want to listen in when we interview Elliott?" He raised his eyebrows at Jonathan.

Jonathan's fingers tightened on hers, and shook his head.

"Didn't think so," Anderson said. "We'll get your statements tomorrow."

"Okay," Jonathan said. "We'll be there first thing."

The half-troll detective nodded, patted the truck's roof, and stalked back to the house.

The Faelinn came out of the shadows where they'd been patrolling. Jekk opened the back door, waiting for his mate to leap in before he followed. The whole vehicle settled noticeably as they made themselves comfortable. Jekk pushed his head over the seats, purring when Alanna reached to scratch his chin. She was ready to go home, and was happy to find that home meant the Haven and not her place in New DC.

The hotel sat on the banks of an inlet. The smell of salt water teased her nose and Alanna stopped as she left the SUV to breathe it in. It seemed to blow some of the cobwebs out of her brain. There was a marina next door, and she could see tall masts bobbing on the dark water. The faint slap of waves on a wooden dock came to her on the breeze. If the night wasn't so cloudy, she thought it might be beautiful. As it was, she shivered a little and fell into step beside Jonathan. The arm he put around her shoulders tucked her close.

"I've booked a second room for the Faelinn," he told her.

The Faelinn shivered into invisibility in front of her. Apparently, they didn't feel like starting a fuss in the lobby. She glanced at the man who was holding the heavy door for her. "Do either of the rooms come with pizza? I'm starving."

Chapter Twenty-Four

The king-size bed looked too inviting to resist. Alanna sat down, feeling the ache of tension in her very soul. She thought about just lying back and letting sleep take her but there was no way she wanted to wake up and smell the stench of that house still lingering on her hair and skin. Jonathan put her suitcase on the floor. She should get up and find fresh clothes but it seemed like so much work.

Denim-covered thighs replaced her view of the suitcase. The shiver that went down her spine had everything to do with the man standing in front of her. He'd run his fingers through his hair too many times and the blond strands were disheveled, falling over his forehead. She wanted to wind her fingers through them and pull his head down to claim that sexy, smiling mouth. Restless heat flared between her thighs.

Something of that must have shown in her eyes. He dropped to his knees in front of her. Strong fingers curved around her nape and tugged her close. She got her wish, the cool silky strands of his hair tickling her fingers. There was no teasing in his kiss, just pure intoxication. He nudged her knees apart and moved between them, molding her body against his while he devoured her mouth.

Alanna thought he'd give her gentle seduction, tenderness to drive the visions of death from her mind. Instead, he gave her heat, fiery pleasure that swept through her from toes to fingertips. She didn't know he'd pushed her backwards until she felt the mattress hit her shoulder blades. That was okay. The hardness of his body in front, the mattress behind, made her feel protected.

The line of his jaw was salty when she nipped it. The murmured groan that rumbled from his throat, the flexing of his fingers on her hips, told her he liked it. So she did it again. In response, he fisted her hair, pulled her head back to flick his tongue against her pulse. The sensation shot through her, made more intense when he dragged his teeth over the sensitive spot.

Skin. She needed skin. Alanna dragged his shirt from his pants, flattening her palms over his smooth back. She felt the muscles flex under her hands as he pulled her own shirt from her waistband. Then her brain stopped functioning because his broad palms stroked up her rib cage, taking the shirt with him. She raised her arms obediently as he pulled it off.

"More," she demanded. He nipped her collarbone before tracing his tongue down the strap of her bra, across the swell of her breast. Tingles of pleasure zipped down to throb between her thighs. When he tugged the cup of her bra down, licking her nipple, Alanna cried out. Her hips flexed, rubbing restlessly against him. She wiggled her fingers between them, found his zipper, fumbled with the button of his pants. The hard flesh beneath her fingers tempted too much and she teased her fingernails down his length.

Jonathan's turn to tug at her zipper. One hand slipped inside, deft fingers stroking slick folds. The sensation of his finger sliding over her clit was enough to propel her right to the edge. She moaned a plea, her knees trembling. One arm curved around her ass, drawing her up against him. She needed him, needed him now inside of her, and she wiggled her hips, helping him pull her pants down and off. And then he was lifting her.

The first thrust was enough to make her scream.

Snuggling down, Alanna wriggled a little closer. Jonathan's arm tightened around her, his lips lightly brushing her shoulder. It was beyond nice. Every muscle was limp, steeped in pleasure. She felt safe, sheltered. It was funny how he made her feel that way. Everything he'd done since they'd met had protected her in some way. If she'd thought about it, she wouldn't have pegged herself as a woman who needed protection. She'd always made her own way, done for herself. The knowledge that he was there, though, strong, sure, and ready to stand with her, was good. This was good.

"Are you okay?" he asked softly.

Alanna thought about it. The death of that boy would always be with her. She'd held him inside of her mind, experienced every horror, felt it when he gave up and flung himself into death. She might never get past that. But for now, the grief was at bay.

"I am now," she said. She turned her head and pressed a kiss to his warm skin. "But I'm starving."

"I'll order something."

"I'll take a shower," Alanna said. She leaned over him. "You could wash my back."

He grinned. The dimple in his cheek teased her, and she kissed it lightly. "We'll never get food if I get in that shower with you. You need to eat."

"There you go trying to take care of me again."

Long fingers stroked the hair back from her face. She leaned into the caress. "Get used to it," he murmured. "You're mine."

That shouldn't sound as good as it did. In fact, it should have pissed her off, and a few weeks ago, it would have. But if she was being honest with herself, it was true. She was his on a very basic level. Looking down into his blue eyes, his body warming hers, she realized she was in love with him. She could even pinpoint the moment when it had happened. The night of her Awakening, when he'd followed her through the woods, willing to do whatever it took to make sure she was safe while she'd tried to find something she didn't understand.

A little overwhelmed, Alanna rolled out of bed. "If what you're ordering is pizza, Jekk wants one with all meat. And I eat anything but anchovies."

He was laughing while as she walked to the shower.

～

Sleep slipped up on her. Drifting in a twilight drowse, Alanna spun out a fantasy. The arms around her whirled her in a waltz, her feet dancing across the floor. When had Jonathan's face become that of her current hero? The man in her book was dark to Jonathan's light. But the scene she was imagining between her characters featured the man who held her now. Throwing back her head to smile into his eyes, she met a visage of wood. Splinters poised above her eyes. Her dancing partner was gone. The arms that wrapped her close became cold, rough wood. The faint melody drifting in the air became footsteps, voices rattling off technical details. She wanted their attention, but the ball in her mouth prevented speech. The tightness in her throat, the dryness, kept her from even moaning. She instructed her legs to lift with the hope that the voices would hear the thump against the wood, but her muscles refused to work, too weak. The hands chained behind her back had long since lost feeling.

Despair, the sure knowledge that she would die in this place, this fucking box, made her cry. Except there were no tears, no moisture left in her body to shed. She gathered herself, marshalling her strength for what would probably be her only chance to make someone hear her. Waiting for a silence in the thumping of feet above, Alanna forced a scream past her throat. It was barely a whimper.

Alanna screamed, the full force of desperation propelling her up and out of Jonathan's arms. Disorientation held her a moment. Hands caught her arms and when she tried to struggle, the low male voice that soothed her brought her back.

"We have to go back," she panted. A shaft of light from the streetlamp outside fell through the crack in the curtain, highlighting Jonathan's hair.

A strong hand smoothed her skin. "It was just a dream, baby," Jonathan whispered.

Alanna scrambled out of bed, looking around the dark room for her clothes. "No, we need to go back. We missed something." She blinked in the sudden lamplight but spotted her underwear across the room.

Jekk scratched at the door, demanding to be let in. She turned the knob with one hand, holding the lacy strip of cloth with the other while stepping into it. He pushed against her, nearly knocking her over.

Be faster, he urged. He growled at Jonathan, found the man's jeans and with a toss, flung them at his feet.

"Jekk hears it too," she said. She hopped her way into her pants, yanked a T-shirt over her head. "We have to go. We missed someone."

"There was no one else there," Jonathan said, even while he pulled the jeans over his lean hips. He stopped a moment when Cateera purposely stepped on his foot. They locked eyes, and then with a sigh he grabbed a shirt from his overnight bag. "All right, fine, I've been overruled. I'll drive."

By the time they reached the hotel garage, Jonathan had called Anderson. The detective promised to meet them at the house. "He was still at the station, questioning Elliott. He doesn't play nice when he's tired, so watch out."

Alanna nodded. She kept trying to recapture the dream, the sense of the person who was trying so desperately to be heard. There was nothing now, not even a niggling at the back of her mind. Hopefully, when they got to the house, something would tell her where to look.

"This had better be good," Anderson said. His face was fixed in a scowl, brown eyes sharp with irritation. His shoulders were hunched down in his jacket. The old-growth trees puddled shadows on the sidewalk. There was virtually no light coming from the house. The windows were all covered to keep the secrets inside.

"Alanna thinks we missed someone," Jonathan said. He wasn't so sure of that but kept it to himself. Jekk seemed very sure, too, and Cateera had spoken for her mate. He glanced at the woman at his side, but her eyes were fixed on the house.

"The only people inside are the forensic team. You dragged me away from the interview for that?"

"He's still in there," Alanna said. Her voice was hollow to Jonathan's ears. She started across the wet grass, her bondmate pressed to her side.

Anderson caught her arm. Jekk's teeth missed his hand by inches. Quickly, Anderson let her go, hopping back out of range. "You can't go in there," he snarled.

"I've already been in there," she reminded him.

"Can you really be sure the rest of the place is empty?" Jonathan asked. He caught Alanna's icy fingers in his. "With the mess in there, are you really sure?"

Scrubbing blunt fingers over his face, Anderson gave in. "You have fifteen minutes to find this person. Any longer, and you're out."

"Thank you," Alanna said, and began walking again.

Jonathan allowed her to lead the way this time. He stopped her outside the front door, holding her back when Anderson went inside. "Wait for him to clear it with the forensic lead." He tugged her to him, running warming hands up and down her back, but he could tell she wasn't aware. She'd gone somewhere else in her head. He understood. When he was searching, he was the same way.

"You've got to be kidding me." The voice drifted out of the door. Irritated and very southern, the stomp of heavy feet followed it. The door banged open and Jonathan met the gaze of the man dressed in a white coverall and green plastic booties. Not bothering to introduce himself, the forensic supervisor leveled them with an angry gaze. The ID tag clipped to his protective suit read Buchanan. "You want to come in here and make a mess of my scene?"

"It's already a mess," Alanna snapped back. Her shoulders had straightened, her chin tipping up in that stubborn way she had. "The boy in there is dying. The longer you give me crap about it, the closer he gets."

The man's nostrils flared, but it was Anderson who received his wrath. "Just one," he said, waving his finger in the detective's face, "just one screw up, and it's on your head."

"Understood," Anderson replied. Then stepped back to let them into the house.

Stepping away from Alanna, Jonathan watched as she knelt next to Jekk. Her narrow frame was dwarfed by the Fael's shoulders and chest. Even though the Fael was still underweight from being kept in a cage and forced to fight, he'd filled out a lot in the past few weeks. He would easily outsize the other males at the Haven. Even Berren, the Alpha.

Slender fingers disappeared into Jekk's ruff as Alanna rested her forehead against his. Jonathan let them work, wondering what it was that made her so sure there was still someone hidden here. His need to pick her up and cart her away, to take her somewhere safe and love her until she promised never to leave his side, was so strong he found himself clenching his fists.

The pair abruptly headed down the hall to the kitchen. He remembered her saying earlier that they'd sensed something there. At the time, he'd thought it was the killer, but what if it had been something else? Someone else?

Slipping through the narrow doorway between the leaning towers of paper, Jonathan moved back against one of the piles of garbage and filthy dishes stacked against the wall. Anderson joined him, a question in his eyes. Jonathan shrugged. Whatever Alanna was sensing, it wasn't anything he had the power to feel.

Hands on her hips, feet planted on a filth-covered pile of cardboard, Alanna turned in a slow circle, studying every crevasse, every nook no matter how narrow between the hoarded mess. Part of the detritus along one wall had been moved. A door was there, leading to a room Jonathan hadn't seen. It may have been where Elliott had been hiding. Beyond the stacks of boxes, he could see more of the forensic team.

"I know you're here somewhere," Alanna said. "I can feel you, but I can't find you. Please do something, anything, to let me know."

They were all silent, waiting for an answer. Waiting for anything.

"Please," Alanna begged again. "I promise you that you're safe. We'll keep you safe, no matter what. Just scrape your heels, move your head, anything."

Silence. A voice in the next room, complaining about the crap everywhere. Nothing here in the kitchen.

Alanna's eyes met his. The grief that poured from those grey eyes tore him up.

"Please," she said again. "You reached out to me, you know who I am. I've come to get you out. Jekk and I are here, just help us find you."

Anderson was shaking his head. Jonathan knew his ex-partner was about to call an end to all of this, and he completely understood why. There was no one here. Echoes of victims, ghosts of horror, but nothing alive. No one left to rescue.

"Damn it! I'm talking to you," Alanna yelled. "You make a sound or I swear I'm going to walk out of here and you'll die in that prison!"

The outburst of temper startled them all. If it hadn't been for the tears streaking her pale cheeks, Jonathan would have thought she really meant it. He moved forward, reaching out to her. And there was a scrape. A subtle rub of sound. Cateera growled, and Jekk turned and snapped his teeth at her. She fell silent.

"I hear you," Alanna said. She dropped to her knees, scraping through the garbage with bare hands. Jekk began to dig beside her, moving cans and empty containers with his broad paws.

"This piece of floor was bare before, do you remember?" Alanna said when Jonathan knelt next to her. "When I fell against the table, I knocked things onto the ground. Jonathan, there were scrape marks on the floor."

"Stop!" The forensic supervisor stopped her from moving anything else. "I heard it too. Let me get some men in here to do this properly. We need to preserve the scene as much as we can."

Alanna hesitated. Jekk's hiss of breath sounded like a question. She glanced at him, and then stood up, moving backwards. "Please hurry," she whispered. He nodded even as he was calling to the crew in the next room.

"We're going to need an ambulance," she told Anderson. Jonathan wrapped his arms around her, drawing her trembling body back against his chest. She leaned into him, her arms covering his, fingers threading through his own. He pressed his lips into her hair. She smelled of jasmine. It was his favorite scent.

Barely fifteen minutes passed before the floor around the table was clear. The scrape marks were pale against the stained wood. The table legs had worn them deep, and the paleness signified that the table was moved often. Too often to let the dirt discolor them. Buchanan was down on his hands and knees examining the floor.

"There's an opening here," he said. "About the length of a body." He scuttled back and stood, dusting his gloved hands off on his legs. Waving his people forward, he looked back at Alanna. "Don't know how you knew it, but you were right. There's something here."

The table was dragged out as far they could manage. When Buchanan knelt again, Alanna shouldered her way to his side. When Buchanan opened his mouth to protest, Anderson shook his head. Jonathan figured he'd join the party too, and knelt at Alanna's side. She gave him a grateful look.

Carefully, Anderson slipped his fingers into the grooves in the plank floor and lifted.

The smell that hit them had them all rearing back. Rot and feces ripened the air, and Jonathan threw his forearm over his nose in an effort to hold down his dinner. He forgot about the stench when he saw the boy who'd been hidden under the floor.

$$Chapter\ Twenty\text{-}Five$$

The space was narrow and short. An adolescent male was squashed inside. Filthy dark hair and bloodied feet pressed end-to-end. The box had been constructed to fit tightly against narrow shoulders. His arms were behind him, and there was no way he could have moved them. Duct tape bound his ankles together. It was so much easier to see the parts instead of the whole.

Alanna reached out to touch the boy's cheek. He startled away from her. The ball gag that stretched his mouth so wide was obscene. The wounds that marred his skin were worse. The boy was naked, covered in a mix of his own filth and blood. Ribs and joints were knobbed beneath his skin. Long cuts had been carved into flesh stretched tightly over his bones. Some of the slashes were crusted over but a few oozed pus. Tears streamed down cheeks speckled with tufts of dark beard. Jonathan ratcheted his age up by a few years.

"We've found you," Alanna murmured. "You led me to you and you're safe now."

Fierce green eyes blinked up at her. Unaccustomed to the light, tears streamed down his gaunt cheeks. He closed his eyes, turning his head away. Jekk leaned his huge head into the space and very delicately licked the boy's cheek.

Jonathan took Alanna's hand and tugged her to her feet. "Let's get out of the way. Let them help him."

When she looked like she was ready to protest, he leaned close, his lips brushing her ear. "He's embarrassed, baby. He doesn't want you to see him like this."

Understanding brought tears to her eyes and she let him draw her back against the wall. Jekk and Cateera stayed with the boy, supervising as Anderson helped him sit up. The ball gag was removed, provoking a bout of coughing. Someone found an unopened bottle of water and held it to the boy's lips. Most of it went down his chest.

When the ambulance arrived, Anderson beckoned them to follow him out of the house. When the night air wrapped around him, Jonathan took a deep breath. It smelled achingly sweet.

Anderson pressed his palms hard against his eyes and then ran them back over his bald skull. "I have never seen anything like that. That son of a bitch at the station better hope I don't get him alone."

"If you do, I get a turn with him," Alanna said fiercely. She glanced back at the house. "That place should be burned to the ground."

Jonathan agreed but kept it to himself. He was afraid to guess what other horrors the place might hold.

"I owe you an apology, Alanna," Anderson said. "I don't know how you found him, but thank you."

She graced him with a smile, even though it didn't chase the shadows from her eyes. "I find lost things."

And it truly was as simple as that.

"Between Jonathan finding killers and you finding the lost, you're a hell of a team."

"That's why I'm keeping her," Jonathan said. He waited for her to argue and when she didn't, he felt like he'd won a prize.

"There's nothing else you can do for him here," Anderson said. "You may as well get some sleep. Just come by the station in the morning."

"No," Alanna said fiercely. "I'm going to the hospital with him. I promised him he'd be safe."

"He'll be safe," Jonathan said. "The police won't leave him."

"And neither will I," she informed him. Jonathan knew that stubborn tilt to her chin, that look in her eyes, and resigned himself to being awake for the rest of the night.

~

The perpetual day of the hospital waiting room was as nerve-wracking as the wait. Exhausted to the point of insanity, Alanna wished for just a few minutes of darkness. The fluorescent light in the far corner had a ballast problem and flickered incessantly. Even with her eyes closed, it was annoying. Gentle fingers smoothed her hair, stroked her neck and shoulders. It should have been relaxing, but the slideshow of horror that played ceaselessly in her head kept her tense.

"You should get some sleep," Jonathan whispered.

Giving up, Alanna lifted her head from his lap. "I can't," she said. "I keep seeing him in that horrible box. How could anyone do that to a person?"

"Some people are just born wrong," Anderson said. He'd entered the room, juggling three paper cups of coffee. "The boy's still in surgery. That bastard did a number on him."

Alanna took a cup of coffee. It smelled burnt but at this point anything would help. She sipped. It tasted worse than it smelled. She'd slipped off her shoes earlier and now buried her toes in Jekk's side, the thick fur feeling wonderful against her skin. He grunted in his sleep but didn't move. At least he had the sense to sleep when he could.

It had been a chore to get the Faelinn into the hospital. The two refused to camouflage themselves. They said they'd earned the right to be present and wouldn't sneak in just to make things easier. Security had been called, hospital rules about animals quoted. It was only Anderson's authority, the badge hooked to his belt, and the blazing anger in his dark eyes that had swayed the staff to reluctantly allow them entrance. Quoting the Statutes, which theoretically prevented discrimination against non-humans, and the threat of a few phone calls to different rights groups, Anderson had convinced them that an argument about this was not in their best interests. Now, periodically, a curious face peeked into the waiting room to see one of the elusive Faelinn.

"Any idea who he is?" Jonathan asked.

Anderson swallowed his coffee, not seeming to mind the taste. "Not a clue. He wasn't saying much, and his prints aren't on file, which means he's not listed in the Missing Children's database."

"Why was he kept alive?" Alanna asked. "The others were all killed and dumped, but he was left alive. What is it about him that's different?" Unable to bear the taste of the coffee, she set the cup on a small table next to a pile of old magazines.

"That's a very good question. It'll be one of the first I ask when he's out of surgery and able to talk." The detective drank the last of his coffee and made a respectable toss to send the cup into a garbage can across the room. "How did you know he was there? I thought you had to touch something to connect with a lost person."

Alanna opened her mouth to answer, and then reconsidered. It was a good question. So far, everything she'd found had been through a connection with an object. As far as she knew, she'd touched nothing belonging to the teen. "When I was at the house earlier I sensed something. When Elliott jumped out, I thought it was him. All I know is that I was half asleep and I heard him call me."

"You heard him call you?" Jonathan asked. "Not the other way around?"

"I didn't know he was there, so yes, he called me. Why?"

"I'm not sure," Jonathan said. He lifted her hand to his lips, kissed her knuckles.

"Detective Anderson?" A white-coated doctor stood in the doorway, eyes glancing around the room.

Anderson stood.

The doctor joined their group. His stethoscope was hooked around his neck, the chest piece tucked into a breast pocket. The ID clipped to the same pocket gave the name Hallenbeck, Stephen. His gaze lingered on the two Faelinn sprawled across the floor, the sun-gold Fael still sleeping, the lavender-swirled female watching carefully. He glanced at Alanna and Jonathan. "Are you relatives?"

"No," Jonathan answered.

"They're consultants with the Police Department," Anderson said. "Ms. McLean found the boy."

"It's a good thing you did," Dr. Hallenbeck said. "The patient is drastically malnourished and dehydrated. There are numerous burns and cuts on his body, many of them infected. He has several broken ribs. He's been repeatedly brutalized and has suffered internal damage. Did you catch the man who did this to him?"

"We did, yes," Anderson said.

"Good. I'll be happy to testify when he goes to trial."

"Will he be okay?" Alanna asked.

"He's stable," the doctor said. "If we can get his strength built up and get a handle on the infections, he should come through it. He made it through surgery so I'd say his prognosis is pretty good."

The relief that swept through Alanna made her light-headed. "Can we see him?"

"He's not awake," Hallenbeck said. "You need to wait until he's recovered more before you start questioning him."

"I don't want to question him," Alanna said. "I just want to see him. I promised him he'd be safe."

"He won't know you're there," he said. "I don't need you disturbing my patient. And before you go flashing your badge at me, detective, the boy is my patient. I have authority over him."

Alanna reached out, putting her hand on the doctor's arm. "Please, just for a few minutes."

Dark eyes studied her for a long moment. "Five minutes. I'll have an orderly take you to his room."

The orderly took them up to the surgical ward. Jekk paced at her side, still sleepy. Alanna had to shut herself off from him because otherwise she'd be falling asleep while she walked. She could feel her own exhaustion pressing against her mind, urging her to rest. The drain of power today had been too much. She needed to sleep.

Seeing them, the nurse on duty at the station hurried around the counter. Anderson flashed his badge, heading her off before she could speak. "Official investigation. Hallenbeck already approved it." Not quite true, but the nurse looked at him, at his badge, and gracefully gave in. She gave them the room number and went back to work.

Jonathan held the door open for Alanna. Jekk slipped through ahead of her, followed by Cateera. Only after they judged the room safe did the two Faelinn move aside to let her in. The steady beeping of the heart monitor, the antiseptic smell, the tubes and wires, all of it combined to overwhelm the narrow shape in the bed.

Alanna moved quietly to the boy's side. The pale face she remembered from the house was relaxed in sleep. He'd been cleaned up, some of the grime scrubbed from his skin. The dark hair she remembered was still greasy. She guessed his age was around sixteen or seventeen, though it was hard to tell. She had a feeling he'd be a handsome kid once he recovered. Bandages covered his arms, hiding some of the knife wounds. The IV taped to his arm dripped nutrients and antibiotics into him. Judging by how he looked, he was going to need a lot of both.

Jekk put his paws on the bed, leaning over to give the teen a good sniff. *He smells odd.*

"It's the hospital," Alanna answered.

From the other side of the bed, Cateera leaned over the boy to nuzzle his cheek. She began to lick him gently, purring softly. He stirred a little. He turned his head on the pillow, not to get away, but to get closer. Jekk pushed against his hand, and the fingers curled tightly into Jekk's fur. A long sigh escaped the boy's throat.

"I think he likes them," Jonathan remarked.

The boy's eyes blinked open. There was a moment of disorientation before his entire body stiffened. Cateera crooned to him, her lavender-tipped whiskers tickling his skin. He raised a cautious hand to touch the soft fur at the side of her head. Her purring grew louder. The boy switched his attention to Jekk, stroking fingers through the Fael's thick fur.

The moment he registered the presence of people, his whole body went taut. The green eyes sluggish with sleep and drugs grew wide with fear. The touch of color in his cheeks fled, leaving him as white as the sheets. He tried to scramble away, but the tubes in his arms held him captive.

"It's okay," Alanna said. She moved forward, but stopped when he cringed. "I'm sorry, I won't come any closer. My name is Alanna. We found you in that house, do you remember?"

A pause while those green eyes flicked from one of them to another. Cautiously, he nodded. Cateera licked his cheek.

"This is Jonathan, and the bald guy by the door is Detective Anderson. The white Fael is Cateera and the golden one is my bondmate, Jekk." Both of them nodded hello, but the boy's eyes didn't shift away from hers. His fingers were white-knuckled as they gripped the Fael's fur. "You're in the hospital. You've had surgery and the doctor told us you're going to recover from your injuries. How well is up to you."

Alanna waited while he processed that. She saw the understanding grow in his eyes, knew when he realized she wasn't just talking about his physical wounds. "You're safe here, and I'll make sure you're safe when you get out."

His eyes were the most expressive she'd ever seen. The suspicion that narrowed them was obvious.

Alanna smiled. "You don't have to believe me."

Someone tried to push the door open. Anderson held it closed. His half-troll strength meant that it didn't budge again. Instead, hard knocking and an angry voice disturbed them. It was the nurse, telling them their time was up. She threatened to call security. Anderson opened the door a crack, snarled something at her, and pushed it closed again. Silence followed.

"They're worried we'll disturb you," Alanna said. "I just needed to know that you were safe. Before we go, will you tell me your name?"

The suspicion darkened. He licked dry lips. His gaze flicked to the pitcher of water and then away.

"You can only have a sip if you trust me to get it for you. You probably shouldn't have any at all because you just came out of surgery, so we'll start slow."

The indecision was obvious. Alanna moved slowly to the table, poured an inch of water into a glass, and offered it to him with a straw. His eyes never left hers as he took a careful sip. His head dropped back onto the pillow with exhaustion.

"Did you get them?" he asked. His voice was hoarse. "The two guys. The one who owns the house and the scary one. Did you get them?"

Anderson appeared at her side. Jekk blocked his path to the bed, keeping himself between the detective and the boy. Anderson gently petted Jekk's head. "We have Justin Elliott, the owner of the house in custody," Anderson said gently.

The teen's eyes flicked around the room. "You didn't get him. He'll find me. I need to get out of here." He coughed and pain drew harsh lines on his face. Alanna wordlessly held the straw to his mouth.

"You didn't get Kerwyn," the teen said. His eyes dilated with fear and he let the Faelinn go to begin pulling at the bandages on his arms, trying to remove the IV. "I have to go. He'll find me."

"Stop," Jonathan interrupted. "Leave the IV alone, or I'll call the doctor. The Faelinn will keep you safe. We won't let you hurt yourself."

The boy in the bed froze. Whatever he sensed in Jonathan's voice, it caused him to slowly drop his hands to the bed. "You don't understand. He can get in my head."

"I've met him," Jonathan said. "Brutal guy, sends you nightmares you can't escape from."

"That's the guy," the teen said. His voice was a bare shiver of sound.

"For more reasons than I'm going to share now, he's going to die," Jonathan said. His voice was glacial frost. "I swear it."

Green eyes grew wide with the promise before he gave a jerky little nod. Jonathan nodded back.

We'll stay with Eric, Jekk said. *We won't leave him alone.*

"Your name is Eric?" Alanna asked. Just when she thought he was he was relaxing, he stiffened again. "Jekk told me. The Faelinn won't leave you while you're here. They won't let anyone hurt you."

"They can't stop him," he said. His eyes closed. His voice was bleak. "He'll kill me."

"Then help us find him," Anderson said. "Give us a full name. Is Kerwyn his first or last name?"

"It's just Kerwyn," Eric said. He turned his head, blocking them out. No amount of coaxing made him respond. Alanna shared a helpless look with Jonathan. He lifted a shoulder in a quick shrug. Alanna looked back at the young man in the bed. He looked so pale, ashen against the white sheets. The way he was curled in on himself, it was hard to tell how tall he might be. She released his hand only to smooth the hair flopped into his eyes. He flinched. Alanna almost drew back. Instead, she stroked again, continued to stroke until she felt some of the tension melt away.

"Jekk and Cateera will stay here with you. They won't let anything happen, I promise. We're going to go, but we'll be back."

Anderson stepped forward. "I'm going to post an officer outside your door. No one will come in who isn't authorized."

Eric didn't respond, but his fingers found Jekk's fur again.

We'll keep him safe, Jekk assured her.

"I know, dear heart," she told him. She gave Jekk a quick hug, inhaling the warm scent of his fur before following the men out of the room.

"I have some arrangements to make," Anderson told them. His cell was already in his hand. "I'll see you back at the station. You still need to give your statements."

"We'll see you there," Jonathan assured him.

"Yeah, you will, boyo, and I'm going to pretend I didn't hear you swear you're going to kill someone." A sharp poke in the chest accompanied the words.

Jonathan said nothing.

The sun had come out of the clouds and burned Alanna's eyes when they left the hospital. Midday was already slipping away. The wait during Eric's surgery had eaten away at the day. Back at the SUV, Alanna closed her eyes. "That poor boy," she said.

Strong fingers wound through hers, and Alanna turned her head to look at Jonathan. "I'm going to call Mark," he told her. "I want him here. This is a lot more complicated than it seemed at first. I want Eric protected."

"Tell him to bring Riordan," she said.

The initial surprise in his blue eyes slowly changed to contemplation. "You're right, I think they'd be a good fit." He hit speed dial.

Alanna stared out the window, only partially looking at the parking lot. She didn't see the cars circling the lot looking for a space. Instead, she saw that withered, broken body in the bed. Fury made her hands clench, her nails digging into her softer palms. What had been done to Eric was beyond her world experience. She couldn't even imagine, didn't want to imagine, the things that had been done to him. She almost wished that Anderson hadn't shown up last night. It would have been so satisfying to kick the shit out of the bastards who had imprisoned Eric. Maybe forensics would find something that would identify the second man. Maybe she'd still have a chance to enact a little justice.

"He'll be here tomorrow," Jonathan said, interrupting her thoughts.

"Meanwhile, he's going to contact an advocate for Eric." He started up the SUV, threw it into gear, and backed out. "You look like you're ready to drop."

"Oh Jonathan, you say the nicest things," she said.

The flash of his grin warmed her. The desire in his eyes made her hot. "After we give our statements, I'll take you back to the hotel and we can get some sleep."

"Sleep? I thought you had more imagination that that."

The low rough laugh that filled the SUV made her stomach flip flop. "We'll work on my imagination when you're not likely to fall asleep."

The smile that curved her lips was still there when she drifted off halfway to the police station.

Chapter Twenty-Six

The statements had been written, printed, signed, and filed. Alanna wasn't sure how coherent hers had been. Her head throbbed, the tension in her skull tightening her shoulders into one giant knot. She couldn't remember the last time she'd been this tired. Jonathan looked marginally better. He hadn't used his Gift twice in the last twelve hours. She thought about putting her head down for a nap and decided against it. She wasn't sure the battered table had been scrubbed in recent memory. She did know that if she drank anymore of the stationhouse coffee her stomach was going to become an acid volcano.

"We're dismissed," Jonathan said, poking his head into her interview room

"Oh goodie," she replied, and pretended not to sway on her feet when she stood. Instantly, Jonathan was at her side to steady her. She leaned into him with a sigh. "My hero."

"I thought I was an arrogant, rude jerk," he said.

"Absolutely," she answered with a smile. "But I'm tired, so right now you're my hero."

Jonathan laughed. They were halfway out of the homicide division when Anderson's voice cut through the din, yelling Jonathan's name.

"Don't answer him," Alanna whispered. "Let's just make a getaway."

But Jonathan did answer, and that was how Alanna ended up in the jail, staring through the bars at a dead body.

A pen protruded from Elliott's eye socket. Not much of the pen, because most of it had been shoved deep into his brain. His face was a rictus of pain and horror. Alanna leaned against the wall. The concrete blocks were icy against her back. Bands of cold sunlight fell through narrow windows and striped the floor. Eyes stared at her from the other holding cells. She wasn't supposed to be here, but she'd grabbed hold of Jonathan's arm when they'd learned that Elliott was dead, and she hadn't let go. She knew that had been a bad idea.

Jonathan stood at the cell bars, his hands bunched into fists. She could just see Elliott's body past him. "Where did he get the pen and paper?"

"I can tell you that after I review the tapes," the sheriff's deputy said. The Sheriff's Department controlled the city jail and the holding cells in the police station. They were responsible for the prisoners' safety. If they'd allowed someone to smuggle Elliott a pen, they would be in hot water.

"No matter what the video shows, it was Elliott's accomplice who did this," Jonathan answered her.

"Couldn't be," the deputy said. "No unauthorized personnel allowed past the gate."

"He would have looked like one of you," Jonathan said.

"You think it's the bastard who's been following you?" Anderson said.

Jonathan nodded. "Yes."

Alanna frowned. Someone was following Jonathan? This was the first she'd heard of it. "Who's following you?"

Jonathan turned, positioning himself so that she could no longer see into the cell. When he tried to take her hand, she slapped his fingers away. "I'll explain everything when we're at the hotel."

"Everything? Why didn't you explain everything before we got this far?" She didn't care that they were suddenly the most interesting thing on the block.

"I didn't want you to worry," he answered.

She leaned close. "You're not my hero anymore."

"Back to arrogant, rude jerk?"

"Do not try to make me smile," she said. She poked him hard in the chest. "The minute we get somewhere private, you are going to tell me everything."

~

The engine fell silent. Alanna hadn't spoken for the last five minutes of the drive from the jail. Jonathan sat waiting for her to explode. He'd filled her in on what was happening, starting with his failed consultation in Carolina, his suspicions about the explosion at the Haven, and finally the death of the serial pedophile they'd caught. She'd remained quiet when he told her about how Samuelson's face had worn the same expression as the victims in Carolina. The pedophile who'd kidnapped Amber Leigh had died wearing an expression of extreme terror.

Now he waited. She looked exhausted. He wanted to wipe away the dark circles under her eyes and hold her while she slept. He was turning into a lovestruck idiot. That should have bothered him more than it did.

Alanna turned to face him, tucking one leg beneath her. "I think I know what we're looking for."

That was the last thing he expected her to say.

A car drove past them around the looping track of the parking garage. "Let's go up to the room. We'll order room service and you can tell me what you think. I'll make some calls and make sure that Cateera and Jekk get dinner, too."

Alanna bit back a yawn and nodded. "Thanks, Jekk says he's hungry."

It was nearly an hour later when they sat down to the feast on the small table in their room. The smell of the steaks was almost as distracting as Alanna's bare shoulder. The robe she wore kept slipping down. Jonathan wanted to tug it down even further. Maybe all the way off. If he did that, though, they'd never eat, and he wouldn't hear her theories about who was behind the killings. Why did she have to be so distracting?

"When I was doing some research for my third book, I came across an obscure reference to a Fae that ate fear."

Jonathan put down his fork. "Fear?"

Alanna nodded. She speared a slice of steak, moaned at the taste. "The Fae instills fear in its victims and feeds off the energy. A lot, like incubi and succubi, feed off sexual energy. The Fae gets inside its victim's head and takes over the fear response. In this case, the more horror the victim feels, the more the Fae feeds. I ended up not using the research but it's always stuck with me. I can't think of a worse way to be violated."

Jonathan dragged part of a roll through the steak juices and leaned forward. "You are amazing."

"That's a given," Alanna said with a smile. "But why?"

"Because this thing has been in my head. He's taunted me, laughed at me, and if I wasn't bonded to Cateera, I think he would have eaten my brain from the inside out. With just a few words, you've cleared up the mystery of what it is I'm dealing with."

"We're dealing with," she said.

"I want you far away from him," Jonathan said. He fed her a forkful of baked potato. "I don't want him coming after you."

"It might be too late for that," she said. "I was in the boy's head when he was being tortured there at the end. The Fae may have felt me there. If he's following you at all, he'll know that we're involved."

Shit. Jonathan hadn't thought of that. His only focus had been to make sure she was protected. It had never occurred to him that by involving her in the case, she might be targeted. He hadn't wanted her here because of the heinous crimes against the boys. He hadn't wanted her to see any of it. Maybe what he should have been worried about was the danger he was putting her in.

"Don't," she told him.

"Don't what?"

"You've got that he-man look on your face. The one that says 'me big man, protect little woman.' I don't need you to protect me. I'm quite good at that all by myself."

He couldn't help grinning. She looked adorable and sexy as hell in that fluffy robe. Her shoulder was peeking out again. He reached out and ran one finger under the fabric, easing it down a little further. The midnight strands of her hair shivered over his hand. Alanna's stormy grey eyes glared at him.

"You can't distract me with sex," she told him.

"I can't?" He teased the fabric a little lower. The curve of her breast enticed him to stroke there too. He was pleased when she sucked in a sharp breath.

"No, you can't," she said. "Aren't we supposed to meet Mark at the hospital in a few hours?"

"Yes," Jonathan agreed. He slipped his hand underneath the robe and discovered that she was naked. Her nipple was hard and his stroking fingers drew a moan from her. It was enough to drive him to his feet and toss her over his shoulder.

Alanna laughed breathlessly. She slapped his ass. "What are you doing, Burke?"

"Acting on my he-man urges," he answered, and tossed her into the center of the bed. The robe loosened further, giving him a long strip of creamy skin to admire. She pushed herself up on her elbows, her breasts thrusting up.

"What does that make me, then?"

"Mine," he said simply. Dropping to his knees, he pressed a kiss to the arch of her foot. Even there she smelled like jasmine. She was begging by the time he reached her thighs. Screaming his name a few minutes later.

The remains of a meal were smeared across the plate. Jonathan examined it with a keen eye, noting that the doctor had given Eric a very bland diet. Toxic green Jell-O cubes were still wobbling in a little bowl. Soggy crackers floated in a bowl of chicken broth. The round scoop of mashed potatoes hadn't been eaten, just rearranged. Only the carton of milk had been opened. The boy hadn't eaten much. That worried him. He'd obviously been starved. Of course, the faint smell wafting up from the soup was enough to turn anyone off their food.

"Did you get any rest?" Jonathan asked. He hooked his foot around a visitor's chair and pulled it to the side of the bed. It was as uncomfortable as it was ugly.

"They gave me stuff to put me to sleep," Eric complained. "I don't want it."

"You had surgery yesterday," Jonathan pointed out. "What they gave you is probably for the pain."

"I'd rather have the pain. I can concentrate on it and it keeps him out of my head."

Jonathan glanced over at Cateera. The day was cloudless and she sprawled in a puddle of sunshine on the linoleum. It sparkled on her coat. "I really think Alanna has this thing nailed," he told her.

I think you're right. Your mate is very smart.

Jonathan remembered the connection he'd made while trying to track the killer. He remembered the awful glee that had invaded his mind for a few moments before Cateera had wrenched him away. It seemed that having a Fael bondmate afforded him some protection from the Fae.

"Maybe your doctor can find something that dulls the pain but doesn't knock you out," Jonathan suggested.

"Yeah, whatever." Eric aimed the remote at the TV hooked up on the far wall and began to scroll from channel to channel. They went by in a blur of sound and color.

Jonathan leaned back in the chair, kicked out his legs, and stretched. Alanna hadn't arrived yet. She'd headed across the street when they'd parked, promising him that she'd meet him in Eric's room. He had no idea what she was up to. Anderson had been by earlier, according to the guard at the door. Jonathan hadn't talked to him since Elliott's death.

The boy in the bed was ignoring him with an intensity that made a smile tug at Jonathan's mouth. He wore fear like a mantle, disguising it with the sullen intensity that only a teenage boy could manage. He refused to give them any indication of how long he'd been held captive. Judging by the healed-over wounds beneath the fresher ones, it had been weeks, maybe longer. Jonathan couldn't begin to comprehend how he'd survived.

"I have a friend coming by," Jonathan told him. "His name is Mark. He's going to make sure that you get whatever help you need. He'll find your family and bring them here, if you want."

"No!" Eric denied, struggling to sit up. Cateera crooned to him, raising her head from her paws. "I'll run before he comes. I won't go back to them." His thin face became even more pinched. Green eyes wide with fear and panic locked onto Jonathan's.

Jonathan had seen that face before on victims of abuse. As a policeman, he'd been first on scene for too many domestic calls to ever forget that haunted look in a victim's eyes. "How old are you, Eric?"

"Why?" the boy demanded.

"Because I'm asking politely."

Green eyes in that battered face narrowed suspiciously. "Sixteen."

Jonathan welcomed Cateera when she joined him, pushing her head against his. He obediently looped his arm over her shoulders. Her head was on a level with his, only twice as big. Her whiskers tickled his cheek. "At sixteen, you can sue for emancipation. Mark will help you with that, if it's what you want. He's a good guy."

"Yeah, sure. And what's in it for him?" Eric asked bitterly.

Jonathan leaned forward, elbows on his knees while his hands dangled between his legs. "You'll have to ask him when he gets here."

The teen turned his face away. He withdrew into himself, his narrow shoulders hunched forward. He began to rapidly change TV channels again.

"Tell me about the guy who got away, Eric," Jonathan said.

Eric responded by turning onto his side, shutting him out. Studying the knobbed spine revealed by the loosely tied hospital gown, Jonathan was torn between pity for the boy, and anger against the people who'd hurt him. "I used to be a detective," he said softly. "Here in Hampton, in fact. Then Cateera found me, and my life changed. When a Fael bonds with a human, changes occur. We get Gifts. There are theories at the Haven that the Gift is based on our natural talents, but no one really knows for sure.

"I find killers. It's both similar to what I used to do, and completely different. Now I just have to touch something that belonged to the victim, and I can mentally track the killer. I tried that with the man who held you. He found me instead and invaded my mind before Cateera pulled me free. And then he blocked me out. I couldn't track him anymore. In the few years I've been bonded, that's never happened before. I've never failed before.

"So tell me about him, Eric, because I want to get the bastard before he starts taking more boys."

Alanna is coming, Cateera told him.

"Have Jekk ask her to wait before she comes in," he said. "Say please."

I will speak to Alanna, and I am always polite, she protested. *Especially to your mate.*

He tucked away the little nugget that Cateera was speaking directly to Alanna. He'd have to be careful to remember that. In the meantime, he waited for Eric to answer. The teen had rolled back over and was staring at him.

"Kerwyn got into your head and you were able to get away?"

"Cateera got me away," Jonathan corrected.

"I couldn't get away," Eric said softly. "He got in my head and I couldn't kick him out. Can she keep him out of my head, too?"

"No, I'm sorry. Only bondmates can do that."

The tangled dark hair fell into his eyes again when he gave a short nod. "Figures."

Jonathan had a lot of questions, but he knew he needed to start on safer ground if he was going to get anywhere. "What about the other guy? The one we got last night."

Fury made those green eyes dark. "That bastard! All Justin wanted to do was fuck me, cut me, and burn me. He has a thing for cigarettes." Unconsciously, he touched his chest and the wounds that were hidden beneath the gown. "The things he did were no big deal. I've had worse."

Anger swelled, the bitterness of it burning the back of Jonathan's throat.

"He's a slime, but he's weak, you know? I mean, I got the feeling that he'd never have done any of it on his own."

"So, he was the follower, Kerwyn was the leader."

A short, hard nod of Eric's head. "He pulled Justin's strings. I think he drove him half crazy. Probably put pictures in Justin's head, too. And the bastard deserved every one of them." He fell silent. The channels resumed racing across the screen.

Jonathan waited, sensing there was more. He could see the struggle on Eric's face. The boy was tough, had obviously been through hell, but he wasn't as hardened as he pretended to be. Not with that expressive face wearing every fear.

"It was Kerwyn," Eric finally said. "He's one who put the pictures in my head, who made me see things that weren't there. He's the one you need to find. He's the monster."

"What did he look like?"

"I don't know," Eric said. His fingers picked nervously at the blanket. "He stayed in the dark. I never saw his face. He'll find me again. I can still feel his hooks in my brain. No matter where I go, he'll track me down."

"We won't let that happen," Jonathan said. He'd intended to tell Eric about Elliott's death, but kept it to himself. He didn't want to reinforce the boy's fears that Kerwyn would find him no matter where he was.

The bitter laugh was more suited to an old man than the sixteen-year-old boy in the hospital bed. "You won't be able to stop it."

"Then we'll just have to track him down," Jonathan said.

"Good luck with that," Eric said.

There was still another question that pulled at Jonathan's mind. "What did he want with you, Eric? They kept you alive. What did the monster get out of it?"

The eyes that met his were older than time. "What does any monster want, you moron? He wanted all of me."

The door opened, admitting the nurse's aide. In the hallway, Jonathan caught a glimpse of the police officer assigned to watch the room talking with Alanna. Jekk took the opportunity to slip through the open door to greet his mate.

"You didn't eat much," the aide fussed, looking at the tray on the bed table.

"That's because it's not food," Eric replied sullenly. "I want a burger."

The nurse picked up the tray with a quick smile. Her purple scrubs were covered with cheerful smiley faces. "I've tasted the hospital burgers. They're not food either. Besides, the doctor has you on a restricted diet."

Jonathan caught the curse Eric muttered in the nurse's direction. From her expression, she did too, but she ignored it. She'd probably heard worse.

"I'll see what I can do about dinner," she promised. Balancing the tray on one hand, she opened the door with the other. Alanna grabbed the door, held it open, and entered the room behind her.

"Hey Eric, how are you feeling?"

"How am I supposed to be feeling?" he asked her. "Do you think I'm ready to stroll through the fucking daffodils?"

Jekk made a short, harsh sound in the back of his throat. Eric's eyebrows winged upwards, his mouth dropping open. His pale skin reddened and then he looked at Alanna from underneath his lashes.

"Sorry, ma'am," he told her.

"It's okay," she told him. "And don't ma'am me. No matter what my furry protector says." She handed him the bag swinging from her arm. "I got you something. I imagine you'll get pretty bored in here before they let you go."

Eric took the white shopping bag suspiciously. He opened it and his eyes widened.

"I wasn't sure what kind of music or anything you'd like," Alanna said as he pulled out the box holding the tablet from the bag. "So, I stuck some gift cards in there. You can get what you want, music, books, apps, whatever."

"You got this for me?" Suspicion and cautious excitement threaded the young voice.

"Yes."

"Why? You don't even know me."

Alanna was silent for a long moment before she spoke. "Jekk likes you. I trust my bondmate. I thought it might make the hours here easier to bear."

"Yeah, okay," Eric said. His fingers were tight around the box. "Thanks."

Jonathan slipped his arm around Alanna's waist and drew her against his side. She leaned into him, turning to smile. His brain turned off. Just like that. All he could think about was that soft mouth, and what it had done to him just a few hours ago. Oh man, this woman was going to make him lose his mind.

His cell rang. He fished in his pocket for it. Seeing the number, he reluctantly released Alanna and went out into the hall. "Burke," he answered.

"Hey, partner, we've got a problem."

Jonathan ignored the partner reference. It was too easy to fall back into that pattern. "What's up?"

"We've reviewed the security tapes. Several times. I've had the video guy go over them frame by frame. You gave Elliott the pen."

The words didn't compute for a moment. "What?"

"The footage shows you walking back to the holding cells and passing a pen and paper through the bars"

"You're shitting me," Jonathan said.

"I wish I was. Of course, you were writing out your statement at the time, and we have video of you doing just that. So who the hell was passing notes with Elliott?"

Jonathan ran his hand through his hair. He filled Anderson in as quickly as he could on Alanna's theory and on what Eric had said about his other captor's mental abilities.

"Forensics is still at that damned house," Anderson said. "They'll probably still be there a year from now, but maybe they'll find something."

"I doubt it," Jonathan said. "We're not dealing with a human."

"Doesn't sound like it," Anderson said. "This whole thing is a fucking mess."

Jonathan couldn't do anything but agree.

Chapter Twenty-Seven

The hospital took a collective breath when Mark Dennison walked through the doors. The administrator, Doug Dalton, scurried from his nest at the top of the building and squawked around the foyer uselessly. Alanna had to hide a smile because Berren was purposely switching from one side of Mark to the other just to make the administrator nervous. Riordan thought it was a game and scampered back and forth, tumbling over himself to race Berren.

Mark stalked through the lobby, tall and stern in a custom-made pinstriped suit. His dark hair waved back perfectly. The briefcase he carried was top of the line, probably costing more than any of the nurses made in a year. He had the power to draw all eyes to him, not because of the Fael at his side, although that was an issue, but because he wore power like a mantle.

That and the fact that he could buy the hospital outright without batting an eye.

Jekk padded across the mauve-swirled carpet to meet Berren halfway. Jekk lowered his head and Berren licked the spot between his ears, accepting his greeting and submission. Alanna greeted Mark with a kiss on his cheek, and smiled at Berren. She leaned down to pick up Riordan when he mewled and stretched up the length of her thigh. He settled in her arms contentedly, completely uncaring that he weighed enough to make her lean to one side. His purr rumbled through his body and into hers.

"Thanks for coming," she told Mark.

"The situation sounds serious."

"We're giving the young man the best of care," Dalton said, nearly walking backward to keep Mark's attention.

"I'm sure you are, Mr. Dalton," Mark said smoothly. "I understand that you and your staff have gone out of your way to accommodate our Faelinn." There was an underlying edge to his voice that made Dalton blink in confusion.

"Well, you're certainly welcome. Here at Hampton General we go out of our way to treat all races."

Alanna glanced around the foyer. Not a single person lingering in the padded chairs looked like a Veiler. Of course, it wasn't always obvious when a person wasn't human, but she'd bet her next royalty check there weren't more than one or two Veilers in the room. Maybe in the entire hospital.

The elevators were momentarily an issue. There was no way two full-grown Faelinn, a juvenile, and three adults were going to fit the weight limits of the car. When Jekk headed for the stairs and the rest of them followed, Dalton hesitated.

The portly man stopped at the stairwell door. "Well, I'll leave you here. I think you know your way to the ward, Ms. McLean. If there's anything I can do for you, Mr. Dennison, please don't hesitate to have someone call me."

Riordan wiggled in her arms, and Alanna pressed a kiss between his ears before gently putting him down. He raced up the stairs after the two adult Faelinn. The lavender tip of Cateera's tail remained just out of reach as he chased it.

Mark laughed and followed the Faelinn up the stairs.

At the top of the stairs, Riordan begged to be picked up again. Alanna obliged, nuzzling the soft fur of his ruff with her cheek.

He can walk, you know, Jekk said. *You're coddling him.*

"I know," Alanna said. "But you're too big to carry. Does it bother you?"

Jekk snorted and butted his head against her shoulder. *No, but he's a male and he can walk.*

"Males need love, too," she told him. "Sweetie pie."

He bared his teeth at her. The nurse walking towards them stopped, her eyes wide. The tatter-eared Fael swiped her fingers with his tongue as he walked past and she squeaked.

Reaching Eric's room, Jekk pushed against the door, his weight opening it. Alanna fell back. "I think Riordan and I will hang out in the waiting room until you're ready for him."

Mark smiled. "I think that might be wise." He chucked the kit under the chin, long fingers scratching for just a minute. "Wait just a little longer, Riordan, and then you can see if he belongs to you."

The look on the midnight-blue kit's face could only be described as pouting. His royal blue ears flattened a little and he mewled at Mark. "You'll last a little longer, Riordan," he told him. He squeezed Alanna's upper arm gently in thanks and slipped into the room behind Berren.

"Well, kiddo, it's just you and me for a bit," Alanna told the small Fael. "Want to go and meet the nurses?"

The faintest touch in her mind of agreement. Smiling, she set him on the floor and followed him to where the nurses were watching him with wide eyes. Nothing like a baby of any species to get a female's attention.

"Who the hell are you?"

Mark flicked a glance at Jonathan, who was lounging in a chair in the corner. No help there. The blond man just kicked out his feet, crossing them at the ankle and waited for the amusement to begin.

Berren stepped forward. Cateera met him at the side of the bed, her head lowered so that her alpha could lick the silky fur between her ears. Mark noticed that the boy's attention went immediately to the two Faelinn. He even leaned forward to see them better, though the movement obviously caused him some pain. It gave Mark time to study him.

The boy was propped up in the bed, surrounded by wires. An IV ran into one scrawny arm; electrodes monitored his heart rate, respiration, and oxygen levels. Bandages covered one arm and peeked out the top of the hospital gown. He looked too small and pale for his age. The scruff of dark hairs on his upper lip showed his truer age.

"He yours?" Eric demanded, indicating Berren with a jerk of his head.

"Yes," Mark answered.

"I guess that makes you special."

"It makes me lucky," Mark answered. He grabbed the second chair in the room and pulled it next to the bed. Berren sat beside him, the Fael's eyes never wavering from Eric's face.

"Why's he staring at me like that?" Eric shifted a little.

"He's trying to figure out if you're worth our time," Mark said. Berren's lips spread back, showing long, pointed canines. If it was his version of a smile, it certainly wasn't reassuring.

"Fuck off, I don't need to impress you," Eric snapped. He turned his head away, but not before Mark caught a glimpse of shame in the boy's eyes. He immediately felt remorse, but had a feeling this kid wouldn't respond to coddling.

"My name is Mark Dennison. I'm head of the Haven. Do you know what that is?"

"Some kind of creepy secret society where you dress like assholes and run around in the woods chanting?"

Out of the corner of his eye, Mark could see Jonathan struggling not to laugh. It didn't help. Even Berren and Cateera chuffed their amusement. "We only do that once a month. And never during the winter. I don't know about you, but I don't like my balls sucked up into my abdomen."

The crudity of the words did what politeness hadn't. Eric laughed.

"Seriously, man, who are you and what are you doing here?"

"I'm Jonathan's friend. He called me and asked me to come because you need some help."

"I don't need nothing from nobody."

Wincing at the grammar, Mark wished for a giant cup of coffee. He had a feeling this kid was going to give him one hell of a headache before he was done. "When you get out of the hospital, where are you going to go? I understand you won't give anyone information about where you come from."

"It's none of your business where I'm going."

"Maybe not, but if you think you'll just be walking out of this hospital free and clear, you're wrong. The police won't let you, for one thing. Social Services will put you into the foster system."

"I won't stay."

Mark shrugged. "That's up to you. Jonathan and Alanna thought I might offer you an alternative."

Green eyes darted to Jonathan and then back to Mark. There was a cautious look in them. "I ain't gonna be your bitch."

"I'm sure my wife will be happy to hear that," Mark said drily. "There might—might—be a place for you at the Haven. With the Faelinn."

"With one of them?" There was no missing the cautious interest in Eric's voice.

"There would be rules."

"Yeah, whatever," Eric said. He snuck a glance over at Berren. "Can I have him?"

Berren snorted hard enough to ruffle the black hair crowding Eric's eyes. The teen reared back, a look of shock on his face. "Do they all talk in my head?" he asked.

"The Faelinn are a telepathic race," Mark said. "It's rare for them to talk to anyone other than their bondmate. He must like you."

"He said I can't be his," Eric said.

"No, he's my bondmate. But if one chooses you, then you're theirs for life."

"How do I make one choose me, then?"

"You can't make a Fael choose," Mark said. "No one really knows how it works."

Eric sighed. "So, what do I have to do? Sign over my soul to you?"

"Only if you want to dress like an asshole and run around in the woods with us," Mark said with a straight face.

Eric blinked, his eyebrows drawn together. It took him a moment, but he finally realized he was being teased, and a smile tried to lift his lips. Mark thought it was a good sign. "You'd come to the Haven as my ward. You would live with us. Your education would be a priority, and you would go to school. You would obey house rules."

"Sounds like prison," Eric complained.

"You'd be safe," Mark said. "No one would hurt you or take advantage of you."

"Why would you do this for me? There's gotta be a catch."

"I'm asking myself that same question," Mark said. "You seem like a whole lot of work to me."

"Shellie will love him," Jonathan said, speaking up for the first time.

"Yeah, God help him," Mark said. "She's my wife. She's a nurturer. It won't be easy for you, Eric. We could do a trial run, at least until the police catch the bastard who hurt you."

Thin fingers plucked the blanket. "Maybe. But I could leave whenever I want, right?"

"Not exactly," Mark said. "You could leave, but you'd be in the hands of Child Protective Services."

The door opened and a speeding ball of black and midnight-blue fur streaked into the room. Losing traction on the waxed floor, Riordan lost his footing, slid under the bed, and came out onto the other side. Berren chuffed sharply. Riordan's ears flattened, his tail lowered, and his belly hit the floor.

"Sorry," Alanna said from the door. "It was either let him in or have every nurse in the hospital clustered outside the door."

"Wow," Eric breathed. He was leaning so far off the bed that in another inch he'd be on the floor. At the sound of Eric's voice, Riordan raised his head, angling it so he could look up at the teen. Eric sucked in a breath and forgot to let it out.

Mark realized he was holding his own breath. He watched as Berren gently licked the kit and then nudged him. Riordan's tongue flicked lightly at the older Fael's nose, and then he jumped lightly onto the bed.

Carefully, oh so carefully, Riordan snuggled up to the boy whose arms were already hugging him. The purr coming from his throat was deep and loud. He tucked his head under Eric's chin and closed his eyes.

"His name is Riordan," Eric said. His arms clutched the Fael possessively. "He says when I'm stronger, he'll be my bondmate."

Mark smiled. "Looks like you were right," he said to Jonathan.

"It was Alanna's idea," Jonathan answered. He tugged her down onto his lap. "I just passed along the message."

"Good call," Mark said. He eyed the two for a moment, pleased at the progression of their relationship. It was nice to see his friend looking content.

"To become his bondmate, Riordan will bite you. There's more, and I'll explain everything a little later. There are benefits to both of you."

"So, like a vampire?" Eric asked. His fingers hadn't stopped stroking the dark fur. Riordan's eyes were closed.

Alanna laughed. "Not quite," she said. "He'll only bite you once. Which is good because Jekk still eats everything in sight." The golden Fael reached over and smacked her in the thigh with his paw, making her laugh.

"Eric, it wouldn't be a bad idea if you bonded soon. It will help you heal," Mark said. The eyes of two youngsters fixed on him. Human and green, framed with thick lashes. Fael, slanted, and a deep aqua in color. He thought how opposite they were. The human was damaged, tough, and full of fear. The Fael was sweet, innocent, and full of joy. Flip sides of the coin, and he knew they would be perfect for each other. "If you're going to be a bondmate, you'll have to come back to the Haven with me. You'll be my ward and you will stay with us until you're at least eighteen. Those are my conditions and they aren't open for negotiation."

Eric and Riordan looked at each other. The teenager's fingers were buried in the young Fael's fur. As one, they looked at Mark and nodded.

Chapter Twenty-Eight

"Dinner is ready," Jonathan said, leaning in the doorway. Alanna's fingers flew across the laptop. Her silky dark hair was drawn up in a high ponytail. Her lips moved a little while she wrote, a habit that never failed to make him smile. It was like she was dictating the story while simultaneously writing it. She looked good sitting at his desk with the sun slanting over her shoulder. He hadn't told her yet that he was remodeling a spare room on the second floor for her to use as a study. Eventually, he was going to convince her to move in with him. In the three weeks since they'd come back from Hampton, she'd spent as much time in his house as they had in hers.

Alanna didn't even look around when he walked up behind her. She jumped a little when he laid his hands on her shoulders, groaned when he dug his fingers into the tight muscles and began to knead. "That is so good," she said, leaning her head back against his hard stomach.

Leaning down, he grazed the sensitive side of her neck with his lips, tasted the warm skin with his tongue. "Turn off the laptop and I'll show you what else feels good."

"I thought you said dinner was done," she teased, swinging the desk chair around to face him.

"It will reheat," he said. He tugged the tie from her hair, letting the dark strands spill over his fingers. Wrapping them in his fist, he took her mouth in a long kiss. He loved the low moan she made, the way she softened and melted into him. Dropping to his knees, he pulled her legs around his waist, tugging her forward until he nestled between her thighs. The need to plunge inside of her, to claim her again, was almost overwhelming.

The sound didn't register at first. The tortured howl outside the house began low and wound higher and higher. It penetrated his awareness at the same time Cateera's panicked voice exploded inside his head. He jerked away from Alanna, who was already pushing him back. Her eyes were wide, scared.

"Riordan," he said, picking out the one word that Cateera kept screaming in his head.

Alanna struggled to her feet. "He's gone," she confirmed.

The cell phone was in his hand before he reached the stairs. Mark didn't answer. Cursing as he took the stairs two at a time, Alanna right on his heels, Jonathan speed dialed Security. He could barely hear over the cacophony from both inside his head and out. He shrugged into the jacket Alanna thrust at him, shoved his feet into boots, and then was out the door, breaking into a run across the yard.

"I'll follow you," Alanna said, hopping on one leg to tug on a second boot. The snow crunched under their feet. Breath frosted the air around them as they ran.

"Riordan disappeared into the Veil," Jonathan told her as they reached the SUV. The headlights swept over the house as he backed out of the driveway. The Faelinn of the Haven were converging on the spot now. Through Cateera, he knew that Mark would meet them there.

"He would never go in on his own," Alanna said.

"No," Jonathan agreed. "But Eric is with Mark, so they didn't go in together." Through the trees, he caught a glimpse of a sleek body racing at the side of his vehicle. Cateera blended so well with the snow, her lavender swirls darkened to grey for camouflage. Fury and fear had tempered her initial panic. Still, the emotions overwhelmed him, made it hard to think.

The road didn't go as far as they needed. Pulling over, Jonathan parked the SUV on the grass. Cateera met them, whining deep in her throat before disappearing into the trees. Alanna squeezed his hand and they took off after the Fael.

The silence of the woods was unnerving. Clouds obscured the night so the path beneath the trees was pitch black. Only the crunch of their feet and the regular panting of their breath disturbed the air. It seemed as if even the birds were afraid to disturb the night. The snow was thinner beneath the trees, only a few inches deep. His boots ate up the ground. He stopped long enough to hold a snow-covered limb aside for Alanna before continuing. The woods changed slowly, normal earth trees becoming interspersed with Veiler varieties. The Veil wasn't static, and when it moved it sometimes left things behind.

The trees ended when the ground tumbled down to a frozen creek. Water gurgled beneath the ice, tumbling down from the spring higher on the mountain. A few feet past the opposite bank the Veil shimmered and danced.

Faelinn lined the banks. Dozens of eyes turned their way when they burst into the clearing. Their colors were dimmed, camouflaging them among the trees, snow, and rock. Hunting colors, Jonathan thought. They were clustered in groups but each one was alert. He felt the weight of their regard for a long moment before they turned back to the Veil. Mark wasn't here yet, but Berren approached him, ears erect and eyes direct on his.

Riordan and the twins were roaming, the Fael's gruff voice spoke in his head. As alpha of the Faelinn, Berren made it a habit to speak to all the bondmates on a regular basis. *The twins are still terrified but their mam pieced together part of what happened. Something came up to them and put nightmares into their heads. They ran, but Riordan didn't follow. He disappeared and his trail leads straight into the Veil.*

"Nightmares?" Jonathan questioned.

That's how they describe it, Berren confirmed.

Mark came out of the tree line. There were others with him, and at a quick glance Jonathan identified Jack, the fire chief, and Rivera. The one who caught his attention, though, was Eric. The youth had changed in the three weeks since he'd joined the Haven. Bethany had worked to heal the physical ailments, allowing him to recover quickly from the surgery and the months he'd spent as a prisoner. Eric's black hair was shaved close to his head. It made the stark bones stand out under his pale skin. Even so, his face had softened considerably over the past weeks. Between the

Brownies' cooking and the healing powers of the bond with Riordan, he was recovering well.

Alanna went to him, sliding her arms around his narrow shoulders. She was one of the very few people the boy allowed to touch him. He shuddered, his forehead resting on her shoulder. He was a few inches taller than her, nearly Jonathan's own height. Even from here, Jonathan could see him trembling.

Cateera slipped her head under his hand, an unspoken plea for reassurance. Jonathan scratched the dense fur between her ears and under her chin. The weight of her against his thigh was considerable but she only leaned there a moment before leaving his side. She rubbed her body against Eric's legs until he slipped away from Alanna and dropped to his knees to embrace the white Fael, burying his face in her neck.

"Did your Fae take Riordan?" Mark asked. The man's face was grim. There was a dusting of snow on his collar, in his dark hair.

"The video's being analyzed now," Jonathan said, referring to the security cameras placed the length of the Veil. There wasn't an inch that was free of surveillance. "At first glance, it shows the kits bouncing from rock to rock in a race along the stream. Then the twins are screaming and racing for the trees. Riordan looks like he's being picked up and then he disappears into the Veil. Beatrice is analyzing the footage now, but you and I both know that's who it is. How's Eric?"

Mark looked over at his ward, still kneeling in the snow with Faelinn clustered around him. "He heard Riordan screaming for him, and then nothing."

"I think he's in shock," Alanna said, joining them. Her hand slipped into Jonathan's and he squeezed her fingers gently.

"We have to get Riordan back," Mark said. His grey eyes scanned along the bank, a line of concentration between them.

"The monster took him."

Jonathan turned to find Eric behind him. The teen's mouth was set in a hard line. Those green eyes of his were sunken in bruised sockets but they glittered with anger.

"The monster took him," Eric repeated. "Kerwyn tracked me here, and he took Riordan to get to me."

"You don't know that," Mark said.

"I do know that," Eric said firmly. He looked far older than his years. Older than he had any right to look. "I felt him through Riordan. He'll keep Riordan and he'll hurt him unless I follow."

"Why would he take Riordan instead of you?" Alanna asked. "If he could get into the Haven, he could just as easily have waited for an opportunity to snatch you."

"But that wouldn't have been as much fun," Eric said. His green eyes were bleak. "This way he can terrify me with what he might be doing to Riordan. Sweeten me up a little so he can drink me down later."

"Shit," Jonathan said, scraping his hands back through his hair. The kid was probably right.

"Well, he's going to be disappointed because you won't be following him," Mark said. "I'm not letting you through the Veil. If it is Kerwyn, he's not going to get another chance at you. We'll wait him out. If he wants you, he'll come back here."

"I'll die first, and so will Riordan. He's still a kit. He needs me."

Jonathan shared a glance with Mark, acknowledging the truth. As new bondmates, the bond between the two was precarious. It wouldn't take much to sever it and kill them both. The fact that Eric hadn't Awakened yet made it worse. "I'll go after him," he said. "I'll hunt him down and bring Riordan back to you."

"You won't be able to find him," Eric said. "Kerwyn will hide, and then he'll destroy you. It's what he does."

"I can find Riordan," Alanna said softly. "He's lost and finding lost things is what I do. I'll just need something of his."

"You can have me," Eric said. "I'm his. We'll find him together."

"No!" Jonathan and Mark were nearly in unison.

"There's no way in hell I'm letting you cross the Veil," Jonathan swore. Alanna's eyes were the color of storm clouds. Her chin had the stubborn tilt to it that he recognized.

"You're crushing my fingers," she told him gently. Jonathan loosened his grip, rubbing his thumb over the back of her hand as an apology. "You're not going to let me do anything," she continued. "You're my lover, not my keeper."

Blue eyes narrowed, a dangerous glint shining in their depths. "Alanna—"

She cut him off before he got any further. "I can find Riordan, Jonathan. I'm Eric's best chance of getting him back before it's too late. If you think I need protecting, then you're welcome to come along."

"I can track Kerwyn now that I know what he is," Jonathan said. "I've touched his victims; I should be able to trace him."

"And if he hides himself from you? He's done that before," she reminded him. "If I'm hunting Riordan at the same time, we double our chances of getting him back."

Jonathan felt the truth in her words, but he didn't have to like it. He didn't want her in danger. The thought of her across the Veil, in hostile country chasing a madman through Kellian territory, scared the shit out of him. There were too many ways for her to be hurt. Losing her was not an option. "We're not done talking about this," he said tightly.

The cold fingers of her other hand curved over his cheek. "Whatever you say, Jonathan." Her smile was deceptively sweet.

We will all go, Cateera said. He picked up the image of "all" from her thoughts. Alanna and Eric bundled up in cold weather gear at his side, Jekk and Cateera sleek predators ready to hunt and kill.

Despite the gravity of the situation, Mark looked amused. "Wait until you've been together fifty or sixty years," he told Jonathan. "You'll learn the females always win."

Chapter Twenty-Nine

The Veil crackled in front of them. The sound was so faint that unless you were standing only a foot or two away, you wouldn't hear it. But Alanna was standing close, and she did hear it. It spat like an angry cat. A tendril reached out, a long narrow finger that inched across the distance between them. She jumped back, colliding with Jonathan, who put a steadying arm around her shoulders. The questing tendril snapped back.

More than an hour had passed since Riordan's abduction, the time filled with frenzied activity. Now they were back at the site where he'd disappeared. A pack weighed down her shoulders. A long knife was strapped to her belt, another in her boot. She had no idea what she'd do if she had to use them but felt safer knowing that they were there. A coat as light as a kiss and as warm as a summer afternoon was buttoned to her neck. A hat was pulled down low enough to cover her ears. The gloves she wore were sleek and warm. Goggles hung around her neck to protect against snow blindness. Short of an out-and-out blizzard, she was ready for whatever would come.

"How long do you want me to wait before I send a recovery party after you?" Mark asked.

"Three days," Jonathan replied. "If we're not back by then, things have gone really wrong."

Alanna saw the look that passed between them. She knew they were worried about Eric. Both he and Riordan were young, and Eric was still fragile emotionally. Physically he wasn't as strong as he could be. Too much separation between the bondmates and they would both start to suffer. Eric hadn't Awakened yet, and that was a concern. If he and Riordan weren't reunited soon, neither would survive.

"Are you ready?" Jonathan asked her. A grey cap covered his bright hair, making the blue of his eyes even sharper.

Wordlessly, Alanna nodded. Her stomach roiled in fear. She was woman enough to admit she was afraid of the Veil. Too many spooky stories as a child about what could come out of the Veil, or what could take you in. She refused to acknowledge that this was much like one of those stories. Something had taken Riordan in.

Calm, and a fierce determination soothed her as Jekk pushed comfort into her thoughts. He wouldn't let anything happen to her. She was his bondmate and he would protect her. She smiled down at him, marveling again at how this magnificent creature had chosen her. His ragged ear flopped a little and she smoothed it with her gloved hand. He'd changed his colors, settling on the mottled grey and brown of a wind-blasted winter landscape. Their chameleon abilities never failed to fascinate her.

"Hold onto my arm and don't let go," Jonathan was telling Eric. "I don't want us to get separated in the Veil. It can be disorienting. Alanna, Jekk will guide you."

"What if we can't get through?" Eric asked. His nose was red with cold. He rubbed at it with a gloved hand.

"Then I'll go alone and bring Riordan back to you," Jonathan replied. He wore his sword strapped to his back, the hilt rising above his shoulders. He looked like a warrior, tall and strong and ready to save the world. She felt a curl of heat low in her belly. Crazy woman, she told herself sternly, but she couldn't help but take a long look at his ass when he turned away.

She was still smiling when Jekk drew her into the Veil.

It surrounded Alanna like cold taffy shot through with static. It tingled against her exposed skin, lightly at first but quickly becoming painful. As she sucked in a sharp breath, it filled her mouth and nose. Another breath and she couldn't breathe. Jekk dragged her forward and when her grip on his ruff loosened, he grabbed her wrist with his strong teeth.

Breathe, Alanna. It's an illusion, he told her.

Her chest was burning. She made herself draw in a breath and then release it, but it felt like she was filling her lungs with thick syrup. The bright swirling colors started to darken and blur. She stumbled and Jekk supported her. Ahead of them, Jonathan's back disappeared into the Veil's colors. Panic trapped her, beating black wings inside her skull.

I'm here, Jekk yelled. *I won't leave you. We're almost through.*

The disorientation was too much, her lungs struggled too hard for air, and her brain was screaming. There was nothing to focus on; there was no up or down, only fading colors and electrified syrup filling her up. Arms wrapped around her and her feet left ground that she couldn't even see. A mouth pressed to hers, breathing air into her desperate lungs.

And then there was cold. A biting wind blowing across her cheeks. The pressure on her skin was gone. She began to cough, the thick goo of the Veil replaced with thin mountain air. Slowly she became aware that she was cradled in Jonathan's arms, her cheek pressed to his jacket. She curled her fingers into his collar, breathing in the warm scent of him.

"Please don't ever make me do that again," she said.

Opening her eyes, Alanna found herself the focus of four concerned gazes. Jekk pushed his head into her face, nuzzling her nose with his cold one. She wrapped her free arm around his neck and hugged him tight. Eric knelt by her knees. His face was carefully blank, but he scowled when he saw her looking his way.

And there was Jonathan. His face was pale beneath the grey hat that covered his hair. His eyes were fiercely blue, full of slowly fading panic. "Can you breathe now?" he asked.

Alanna nodded and then let out a little squeak when his mouth took hers in a fierce kiss. His hand covered her throat, holding her while his kiss expressed all the desperate fear he'd experienced when she'd nearly suffocated. Alanna felt warmth slither through her veins, pushing out all the winter cold and the last of the shock from the Veil. She forgot that they were the center of attention. She forgot everything except his taste and the way he made her feel.

It was a shock when he broke away to lay his forehead against hers.

"Damned woman, don't scare me like that."

There was only one way to answer and that was with another kiss. It was brief this time, though she gave his bottom lip a quick nip when he drew back.

I told you to breathe, Jekk chastised. The voice rumbling in her head was gruffer than normal.

Eric stood up, shoving his hands into his jacket pockets. "Just like a girl to get excited over a little sparkly stuff."

She gaped at him, and then began to giggle. The terror of nearly suffocating was fading. She indulged in one last taste of Jonathan's mouth and then struggled to her feet. The Veil shimmered behind her. "So what are we all standing around for? Let's get going."

Cateera yapped agreement.

Jonathan shook his head though and handed her a bottle of water. "Take a minute, Alanna. Some people can't make it through at all."

The water was icy and felt good on her stressed throat. She stowed the rest of the bottle in her pack. It was only then that she felt well enough to look around.

It was sunny. It had been nighttime at home, but here it looked like late morning. The light provided a panoramic view of treeless mountain slopes dropping down from where they stood. The Veil had led them out onto an outcropping of rock two thirds of the way up a rock-strewn slope. They were above the tree line and she could see the green smudge of pine further down. The sky was a sharp blue, unlike the cloudy day they'd left behind. It sparked off the windswept snow, shadows lying like deep pockets of night beside the rocks poking up from the granite slabs beneath. The wind was icy, the air was thin, and Alanna thought it was as different from where they'd come from as the earth from the moon.

"Why's it so different?" Eric asked.

"The world here isn't quite the same geographically as ours," Jonathan said. His eyes scanned the slopes. "There's a theory that the Cataclysm wasn't just about our worlds colliding, but about our side of the Veil aligning itself more physically with this one. So the sides are very similar, but not exact. Have either of you noticed that there aren't any tracks?"

Alanna hadn't, but now that he'd pointed it out, it seemed obvious. "Are we sure this is where Kerwyn came through with Riordan?"

We're sure, Jekk said. *We can't smell him on this side, but we know.*

Eric scowled. "He can screw up your mind. He can make you see what he wants you to see."

"Illusion," Alanna said.

"Can you talk to Riordan from here?" Jonathan asked.

Eric shook his head. The skin of his face was drawn tight. His eyes were haunted wastelands. "No."

He was breaking Alanna's heart. She peeled off one glove. "Then let's see if I can feel him," she said.

The bones of Eric's hand pressed too firmly under his skin. She linked her fingers through his, pleased at the strength of his grip. The trust in his eyes warmed her even as it made a brief spurt of worry burn into her stomach. What if she couldn't find Riordan? She pushed that thought from her mind, gave him a quick smile, and closed her eyes.

Jekk pushed his head under her other hand, his body shielding her from the wind. She leaned against him. Worries skittered around her mind. The Veil crackled behind her. She was going to have to go through it again to get home. The landscape was inhospitable. What if one of them got hurt? What if she couldn't track Riordan? Icy wind touched her cheeks, chapped her lips. Her fingers were cold and so were Eric's. Trying to push all those thoughts away, Alanna concentrated on the connection between herself and the teen. Gradually, she became aware that her hand was growing warmer. With that warmth came images.

Darkness. Pain. Terror. Dreams of fire and loss. A grief so deep it was a pain. A feeling of suffocation. Heat all around. Flames dancing so close to his eyes that even when he screwed them shut the flames threatened to burn his sight away. Alanna struggled to find her way through it all before it engulfed her, too. She screamed Eric's name into the darkness and felt his sudden shocked awareness. The images peeled back, the taste of terror cut now with shame. Inside the darkness where there was only the two of them, woman and teenager on the cusp of manhood, she made him a promise that she would never speak of his memories.

Riordan. The name of his bondmate. He gifted her with it, with the pure sweet joy the kit had shown him. Fur softer than anything he'd ever felt, eyes full of profound trust and deeper love. The soft rumble of a purr.

Taking all those things, Alanna cast the essence of them out into the world and waited to see what would come back. A tickle in her mind grew into surety. Riordan. He was hungry and afraid. He was terrified to make a sound because the last time it was met with the smack of a heavy fist. He'd tried to bite but a bruising punch on his muzzle had left him dazed and sick. She tried to tease her way into his mind, but shadows blocked the path. They roiled like smoke and from their mass came the occasional glimpse of fang and claw. Nightmares encased his young mind and she couldn't get through.

Alien intelligence stroked against hers. Curiosity full of barbs designed to hook prey grasped her. With a startled cry, Alanna pulled away. Her fingers clutched a piece of smoke, thick like dirty cotton, and pulled it with her. For a moment, Riordan's mind shone through the gap. As hard as she could, she pushed reassurance and promises at him, and then she was flying backwards through the empty darkness.

Hands locked together so tightly they were bloodless. Her own and Eric's. Taking a shuddering breath, Alanna realized her eyes were open. She and Eric were on their knees in the snow. Jekk's breath warmed her cheek. She was sheltered between his paws. She could sense Jonathan's warmth at her side though he was careful not to touch her. Jekk and Cateera flanked Eric.

"He's alive," Eric said softly.

Alanna nodded. She didn't want to release his hand. So much pain there. She'd sworn an oath to keep his secrets, though. Peeling her fingers open, the pain of returning circulation curled her hand against her chest.

"He's alive," Alanna repeated. She felt a pull now, a tug to the left and down, and she knew if they followed it they would eventually reach the kit. Her fingers trembled when she pointed the way.

Eric scrambled to his feet, immediately heading in the direction she'd pointed. Cateera raced ahead. Her broad paws left tracks in the snow, making it easier for Eric to walk. Jekk nuzzled Alanna's cheek a last time before he ran to join his mate.

"Are you okay?" Jonathan asked as he helped her to her feet.

Alanna pulled her glove back on and then dusted snow off her knees. "We need to find him quickly, Jonathan. He's so scared."

"Then let's go," he said. Catching her gloved fingers in his, he started down the slope after Eric.

Chapter Thirty

Alanna adjusted the goggles. They pinched her temples. She'd taken them off earlier, and within five minutes, she had trouble seeing anything other than the glare of the sun off the snow. Her throat burned from the cold, her thigh muscles ached, and the hawks she was seeing might as well have been buzzards circling above, waiting for her to die. She had reached the conclusion that she was not a mountaineer.

All her internal complaints vanished when she looked at Eric. His eyes were hidden behind the black lenses of his own goggles, but the strain was visible in the set of his mouth. His skin was buffed red from the cold. A fine tremor made his steps sloppy in the snow. It was hard enough navigating the uneven ground and the deep snow without your body betraying you. She was worried that they wouldn't find Riordan in time.

It became obvious that they were following a trail. There were no tracks in the snow, but it wound unerringly down, finding the easiest places to descend. They were forced to stop only once, when Alanna's sense of Riordan's location led them to a dangerous drop-off. The two Faelinn split up and scouted to each side, searching for a safer path. Jekk found it, a tumble of snow-tipped boulders that provided an adequate if slippery place to descend. Once past that point, Alanna pointed again and they resumed their pace.

It was easier once they reached the tree line. The snow wasn't as deep under the sweep of fir branches. Tracks showed them the secret ways of rabbit and deer. Once they crossed the distinct paw prints of a Fael. Jekk paused, sniffing along the tracks before leaving his own scent puddle at the base of a tree.

It's the trail of a native Fael, Jekk said. *He's not close enough to bespeak or I'd ask for his help.*

"Are we getting closer?" Eric asked. He'd dropped back to match his pace to hers. He pushed his goggles up onto his hat. His eyes burned with fatigue. It reminded her that less than a month ago, he'd been a prisoner trapped in the floor of a madman.

Alanna concentrated on the pull in her chest. It was stronger. With a little effort, she brushed up against the roiling mass of blackness that encapsulated the kit. Only for a moment, though, because when she did, that frightening glee turned her way and reached for her.

"Yes, we're closer," she said. Fear twisted her gut. Even that small contact left her trembling.

"We should stop and rest," Jonathan said. They'd been moving at a steady pace for several hours. The cold had worked its way into their bones.

"I don't need to stop," Eric said. He'd dropped his goggles down again and his eyes were invisible behind the lenses. "Let's keep going."

Jonathan shrugged out of his pack and sat on a fallen log. He stretched his long legs out in front of him. The hilt of the sword rose behind his shoulders. "You go ahead then," he said to Eric. "We'll catch up eventually."

Alanna froze, staring between the two males. She noted that Cateera had flopped down next to Jonathan's legs though Jekk continued scanning the trees. She shrugged out of her pack and sat next to Jonathan. The log was cold, but it felt good to sit. She snuggled up against his side. His arm encircled her shoulders, claiming her.

"I need to get to Riordan," Eric said. His hands were screwed into fists. "He needs me."

"He needs you strong," Jonathan said. He opened his pack and reached inside. "Rest for a few minutes. Drink some coffee, have some food. You'll be stronger."

"Coffee?" Alanna asked. She leaned over to peer with interest into Jonathan's pack.

"It's probably cold," Eric mumbled.

"Nope," Jonathan said, pulling out a fat thermos. "The Brownies spelled it to keep it hot." He twisted off the top and steam escaped. "There's a thermos in yours, too."

Despite his scowl, Eric shrugged off his pack. He found the thermos. When he unscrewed the top, the smell of tomato soup wafted through the air. "Cool," he said, and poured it into the cup. Apparently, food was enough of an enticement to keep him in one place.

They made a quick meal of coffee, soup, and sandwiches. The Faelinn shared the contents of the thermos in Alanna's pack, thick meaty chunks in warm broth. Soft chocolate chip cookies quickly disappeared. While she ate, Alanna looked at the two men with her, the two Faelinn pressed close, and thought how very much like family they were. There was Jonathan, who was apparently her mate. She was head over heels in love with him. Even though he hadn't said the words, she knew he felt the same way, knew it in the way he smiled at her, the brush of his hand across her hair, the way he kissed. He was hers. Jekk, her bondmate, her friend. They would be together forever, and it was a comfort to know that he understood every nuance of who she was and accepted her anyway. Even Cateera, his own mate, with her precise way of speaking and her heart so generous and full. She was slowly allowing Alanna to come to know her. Finally, there was Eric. With his night-dark hair, they could have been siblings. She missed her family, though she'd moved away from them years ago. She found that he easily fit into the role of little brother. There, on the side of an alien mountain, hunting for a madman who wanted to hurt them all, she was happier than she had any right to be.

Wind rustled the branches above the group, knocked down the occasional clump of snow. Bushes quivered with hidden life although nothing was brave enough to peek out with the Faelinn so close. A hawk's cry pierced the quiet as it rode the currents overhead.

Wiping up the last of her share of soup with a piece of bread, Alanna sighed. "Better."

"Now can we go?" Eric demanded. His muscles were so tight he was shaking.

"Pack up and then we're on our way," Jonathan said. "Alanna, you still have the direction?"

She nodded, sliding a thermos and their trash into her pack. "Just out of curiosity, are we heading toward the Kellian?"

"No," Jonathan said. He pointed down slope in another direction. "At least Kerwyn'sS leading us away from their settlement."

"Why didn't he just wait on the other side of the Veil for us?" Eric asked. "Why make us march all over this damn mountain to get to him if he wants me so bad?"

"To wear you out, most likely," Jonathan said. "He probably has a site picked out for an ambush and is just waiting now."

Alanna confirmed that. The pull was steady. Even with their break, it hadn't lost its intensity. Wherever he was, he was waiting for them. Resting up. "I can still feel him, Eric."

After several more hours, the slope of the mountain began to even out. The trees were thinning. They were in a natural bowl, surrounded by snow-covered peaks. Behind them, near the crest of the mountain, the Veil glittered with the light of the setting sun. Before long, the valley would be too dark to travel.

Jonathan took the lead. He set a hard pace. Alanna felt the burn in her thighs and calves. The two Faelinn left them to scout ahead, invisible as they moved through the trees. Only the tracks of their passing marked where they'd been.

The steady pull in Alanna's chest grew stronger. It was so much different than the first time she'd tracked through the woods. Then, on the night of her Awakening, visions kept her blind to her surroundings. The power of it pulled her forward with no thought to safety. There were only vague memories of Jonathan pacing her, guarding her from whatever danger waited. At his heart, he was a protector.

"I can feel him," Eric exclaimed. He surged forward, would have abandoned them if Jonathan hadn't reached out and snagged his arm, hauling him to a stop. He struggled. Jonathan hauled him close, giving him a little shake.

"Calm down," Jonathan hissed. "If you can feel Riordan suddenly, then it's Kerwyn's doing."

Eric pulled off his goggles and threw them into the snow. Her eyes looked fevered, too bright and glassy to be healthy. His gaze darted from tree to tree. The tremor Alanna had noticed earlier had become a full-bodied shaking. She thought he looked ill.

We see him, Jekk informed her. *We don't see Kerwyn, but we see Riordan.*

Alanna shared a glance with Jonathan and knew that Cateera had passed along the same information.

"He's very close," Jonathan said, his voice low enough that only the two of them heard. "You're Awakening, Eric. I don't know what that means for you and Riordan, but I do know that if you rush into this, you'll get both of you killed. Can you control yourself, Eric? If I let you go, can you wait here?"

Eric trembled, but gave a quick nod. Watching him, Jonathan let go and then silently eased his pack to the ground. He motioned for them to do the same. Alanna left her pack beside his. One hand reached nervously for the knife at her side, touching it to reassure herself it was still there. A second touch found the other knife safe in her boot. Her stomach was queasy. It was one thing to track Riordan, but to think about facing the monster that had tried to worm into her thoughts was an entirely different thing.

He can't reach you through me, Jekk said. He nuzzled her cheek, his whiskers tickling. *You found him. Let us do the rest.*

"I'm not going to sit on a log like a helpless princess waiting for the men to save the day," she snapped back. Fear made her words sharper than she'd intended. "Besides, you said you can't see him."

We couldn't see his tracks either, but they're there. Eric can see them now. I need you to be safe.

"I love you too, Jekk. But I don't need you to babysit me."

"Is Riordan okay?" Eric asked. Overly bright green eyes demanded an answer.

Jekk allowed her deeper into his mind, and suddenly she was seeing through his eyes. There was a small clearing, the snow pristine. Nothing had walked there since the last snowfall, including the young Fael. He quivered in the center of the clearing as if he'd been dropped. He was curled into a ball of pure misery. His eyes were closed, his dark blue tail covered his nose. Even so, there wasn't a mark on him. All the damage had been done inside his mind.

"He looks okay, just scared," Alanna said. She gave Eric's shoulders a quick hug, and was startled at the heat pouring from his skin.

Hard lines carved Jonathan's face. He was focused. The eyes that had looked at her earlier with such warmth were now iced over. Something inside of him had switched. She found herself thinking that he'd never looked sexier. If they'd been alone and not about to face down a monster capable of mind rape, he'd have a hard time keeping her from ripping his clothes off. She gave herself a mental shake and concentrated on what he was saying.

"I'm going to circle around to the other side of the clearing. I want the two of you to continue and join up with Jekk. No one, especially you, Eric, enters that clearing until I give the word. Is that understood?"

Alanna nodded. Beside her, Eric gave a reluctant nod. He was practically vibrating with barely controlled energy.

"Kerwyn's here," Eric said. "I can feel him, even if the Faelinn can't see him. He's going to try to get into my head."

"Fight to keep him out," Jonathan said. "It might keep him occupied long enough for us to find him. If he does get in, try to keep him there. Again, it might distract him. Your Gift is Awakening, Eric. You need to stay in control as long as you can."

Eric nodded. "Mark told me about it. But Riordan comes first."

"Understood. Alanna, I want you to help Eric break through to Riordan, if you can. Eric will stand a greater chance against Kerwyn if the two can connect." Reaching up, he loosened the sword in its scabbard.

Alanna caught his hand. "Be careful."

A hard kiss on her mouth. It swept her under and she caught his arms to hold herself up. It was over far too fast. His forehead rested against hers for a moment before he stepped away. He tugged his goggles back into place. Eric's hand shot out and Jonathan gripped it for a moment before he slipped away into the trees.

Eric looked at her. There was something seriously wrong with his eyes. The green had been swallowed by the black of his pupils.

"Are you all right?"

He ignored the question. Gloved hands settled the goggles over his eyes. Turning his back on her, he jogged into the trees. She trotted after Eric. The teen moved quickly through the trees, intent on reaching Riordan. She caught up to him, touching his shoulder to let him know that she was there. He flinched but didn't slow down.

Jekk blocked his path. He blended with the snow and trees, all white, grey, and brown except for his golden eyes. Eric tried to move around him, but the big Fael blocked his way. He stared Eric down and it was only when the youth stopped trying to dodge him that Jekk turned and led the way.

The back of Alanna's neck prickled. She knew she was being watched. The sensation was visceral. A quick scan showed nothing. Wherever Kerwyn was, he was completely hidden. It scared her.

Jonathan is in place, Jekk told her. Jonathan must have been moving a lot more quickly than they were. Just as she thought that, Jekk stopped. Eric let out a low moan. Jekk grabbed the teen's wrist and held him back. Eric struggled until Jekk tightened his grip to the point of pain.

The trees had thinned enough to see the small clearing. Shrubs pressed against their legs, and thin bare branches poked up from the snow. The snow was eerily unmarked. Not one paw print marred the surface. Not even the distinctive mark of a rabbit bounding through the snow disturbed the whiteness. Riordan lay in the center. He didn't move or acknowledge Eric's presence in anyway.

Alanna circled the teen's waist. "You won't do him any good by rushing out there."

"Kerwyn already knows we're here," Eric moaned. He twisted free, yanked his arm from her grasp, and raced into the clearing. Droplets of blood stained the snow behind him. His wrist bled where Jekk's teeth had scraped the skin. Gathering up the ball of fur that was Riordan's terrified body, Eric held him tightly.

And they disappeared.

Shocked, Alanna's instinct was to rush into the clearing. Jekk body-checked her, forcing her back into the trees. Her hands curled into fists but she stayed where she was. Instead, Alanna searched for Riordan's mind. Something was wrong. They couldn't have gone far without being seen and she hadn't taken her eyes off them for even a second. Reaching for him was different now. She'd found him so he was no longer lost, and their connection was tenuous. He felt nearby. The blackness surrounding the Fael's mind pushed eager tendrils toward her. Mentally she dodged them, trying to weave herself between, looking for cracks.

The Fael's mind blossomed, bursting free of the darkness. His nightmares fell away. Alanna had a moment where the kit's mind connected to hers, then, quick as a heartbeat, she was pushed out. She felt the connection between the two bondmates snap into place. Her gift of finding the lost was no longer needed, and she was unceremoniously booted.

Taking a deep breath, she opened her eyes. She hadn't even noticed that they'd been closed. Eric's footprints disturbed the pristine snow of the clearing, but otherwise caught the light of the late afternoon sun. It glittered with frozen rainbow points. In the center huddled the teen and his kit. She smiled, satisfied that her talent had a happy ending this time.

We're a good team, Jekk said. *This is a good use of the Gift. No more violence for a while.*

She heartily agreed.

Something hard closed around her throat, pulling her backwards. Off balance, Alanna staggered back and collided with a hard body. Jekk howled, his teeth bared as he lunged forward. A hot slice of pain across her throat made her freeze. Jekk pulled himself up short. His golden eyes were fierce with fury.

I didn't see him, Jekk said. *He came out of nowhere.* His nostrils quivered. *He has no scent.*

"If you or your beast moves, I'll slice your throat." The voice slithered into her ear, hot breath scalding her skin. Something wet trickled down her neck.

"Jekk?"

I won't let you be hurt, Jekk swore. And then howled as their minds were torn open, blackness boiling in to invade even the tiniest crevice of thought.

Alanna screamed. Fire blistered her skin, the smell of her own roasting flesh clogging her nose. As quickly as it came, the fire blinked out and now she was struggled for breath as fathoms of water compressed her from all sides. She felt her skull begin to tighten, her eyes shrinking in their sockets. Her chest burned for lack of oxygen and when she gasped for breath, dirt poured into her open mouth. The weight of it crushed her chest, her ribs creaking as they struggled to protect her heart and lungs. Something wiggled against her cheek and then a sharp pain stabbed the spot. Another and another, bits of her flesh being torn away as sharp rodent teeth chewed.

Jekk tried to reach her, tried to draw her out of the darkness. Instead, it engulfed him too. The pressure of bars against their skin, a cage too small for their size. The gnawing hunger from days without food and only a minimum of water. The smell and taste of blood and being so hungry that you were willing to cannibalize your own. Large teeth now tearing at them, going for all the tender spots, and they were unable to move to fight them off.

And then the worst of all. Loss, the aching loneliness of it. Calling and calling but receiving no answer. Alanna felt her heart clench in her chest, an emotional anguish so deep it robbed her of thought. Instinctively reaching for Jekk, she found that he'd been walled off from her and she was completely alone in the dark. Jonathan was torn from her heart with bitter words and the laughter of purposeful rejection.

Alone in the dark now, and things lurked just past the reach of her fingers. She snatched them back, tucking them under her armpits. She could feel unseen things reaching for her. The terror overwhelmed her and she screamed. Her screams echoed off damp stone walls, rebounding to fill her ears with her own horror. Over it all rode the despair of the knowledge that no one would ever come for her. She was alone, would be alone forever. No one would miss her or mourn her passing. There was nothing but the darkness and what lurked within it.

Until the laughter came. And then it was so much worse. It rolled through her, touching places that were never meant to be reached. It stripped her bare, shone light into the places no one ever wanted to see. Every ugly thought and deed she'd ever had was flayed open and picked through. And the laughter rolled on.

There were no further depths she could sink into, nothing more she could have stripped away. Until the laughter in the darkness began to feed. The long acidic tongue slurped at her. She writhed, trying to escape, but there was nowhere to go. The darkness held her taut while the delicacy of her fear was lapped up. The sounds of delight curdled her blood. Her sobs only added flavor to her fear. He was going to eat her away until there was nothing left. She would die there in the dark, alone.

~

The underbrush provided good cover. Jonathan crouched behind a bush denuded of leaves. He waited silently for Cateera to tell him that Alanna and Eric were in place. His bondmate was invisible a few yards to his left. He watched Riordan. The little kit cowered in the snow, shudders wracking his small frame. Jonathan knew it was a mix of cold and terror. Even as thick-furred as the Faelinn were, they weren't equipped to lie in the snow like that for extended periods of time, especially not the young ones.

Eric burst from the trees. He floundered through the snow, dropping to his knees next to Riordan. Cateera snarled. Jonathan cursed loudly in his head. The kid was a damned fool. Would it kill him to follow instructions? His eyes scanned the surrounding trees. He could feel Kerwyn nearby. The prickling feel of a killer itched at his skin. Cateera swore over and over that she couldn't see or smell him.

The scream froze him. Ice shifted through his veins, stopping his heart. Alanna's terror brought him to his feet, his whole body vibrating with the need to respond. Cateera whined frantically. She couldn't reach Jekk, could only feel the horror of whatever had invaded his mind. Her panic ate away at his control. He stepped forward, away from cover.

"Ah, there you are," Kerwyn said.

The man appeared behind Riordan. With an easy grace, he grabbed the kit from Eric's arms. A long knife in his other hand pressed into the kit's fur. The tip forced the Fael's narrow head up. Wild-eyed, Riordan mewed in terror.

Eric scrambled back, crab-like, on his hands and feet. His face was slack with fear.

"Put the kit down and I'll let you live," Jonathan said. He could hear Alanna crying, her sobs so desperately heartbreaking it was killing him not to rush to her side.

Kerwyn laughed. "You don't get to let me do anything. I've tasted your frustration, suckled on your anger. You touched me that first time and I felt the depths of you. It took so little to lure you to me again. And you came prancing like a little lap dog. You've come closer to catching me than anyone has in all my years." He smiled, lips drawing back over polished white teeth. Humor danced in his soft blue eyes, the kind of humor you'd see in a clown's eyes right before his flower squirted acid into your face.

"I'm going to enjoy sucking you dry," Kerwyn said.

"You know the problem bad guys always have?" Jonathan asked. "I saw it over and over when I was on the force. I've seen it in movies and read it in books. Single biggest problem is that you gloat."

Cateera hit Kerwyn from the side. Her teeth clamped onto his wrist, tearing his arm away from Riordan's throat. The knife dropped into the snow.

Laughter rolled through the clearing. Kerwyn popped out of existence, and then stepped out of the forest to Jonathan's right. Cateera spun, snarling with rage. Her fur spiked, her ears laid back against her skull. The lips that peeled back revealed long ivory teeth capable of snapping a man's neck in one bite. She stalked over the snow, her broad paws distributing her weight so that she didn't sink far into the drifts. Kerwyn watched her come.

The sword felt good in Jonathan's hand. He wasn't entirely sure when he'd drawn it, but its heft reassured him. He allowed his bondmate to stalk their prey, waiting for the chance to finish Kerwyn off.

The monster stood his ground, mocking Cateera with a smile. "Here kitty, kitty, kitty." That hideous smile split his face. "I know your secrets, kitty. I know how they tore the kits from your side. I know how they cried for you, for their mother. Do you know what happened to them? Shall I show you?"

Cateera howled, her leap carrying her the last few yards to where Kerwyn stood. He was gone by the time she landed. Her body convulsed while a shriek of horror and mourning ripped from her throat. She fell into the snow, her sides heaving while she panted. Her eyes were wide open but saw nothing more than the images he'd pushed into her head.

The grief was almost enough to bring Jonathan to his knees. The three kits were stolen from her and he felt the loss as if it was his own. The darkness washed inwards, threatening to take his vision from him. He saw one kit thrown into the circle with a hungry Fael, saw its fight as it was ripped apart and consumed.

Cateera! It's not real. You know it's not. Jonathan shouted the words into her head, trying to push the images out by sheer force. Wild with grief and fury, his bondmate turned mental teeth on him, snapping and biting until he was forced to withdraw.

Laughter behind him had Jonathan spinning around. Nothing there. Not even any footprints in the snow. He felt impotent, needing to protect the ones he loved but unable to find a target. "Are you afraid to face me, you bastard?" he shouted.

Kerwyn stepped from the trees to Jonathan's left. Another from his right. A multitude of Kerwyns appeared around the clearing. Each one looked as real as the next. Long shadows on the snow grew from their feet. All of them were smiling that wide, insane smile. "I'm not afraid of you, Jonathan Burke. I brought you here. I followed the threads in your mind to find all those places and people you call home. I'm going to make you suffer the deaths of each one of your companions before I feed from your hatred and despair. And then when I'm done with you, I'm going to take my prize, my sweet boy who got away. He will last me such a long, delicious time."

The snarl ripped from Jonathan's throat. He whirled to the left, the long naked blade in his hand slicing through the Kerwyn that stood the closest. The sharp sword sliced easily through flesh, the spine resisting only a moment. The two halves gushed blood into the air, the sword flinging droplets into the trees. The torso and legs hit the ground separately and popped out of existence.

Jonathan moved to the next and the next. Each body collapsed without a fight, disappearing when he chopped into them. The blood remained, mocking him as the heat of it melted the snow. The certainty that he could spend an eternity killing Kerwyn again and again grew in his heart. The knowledge tasted of failure. He would lose Cateera to the nightmare of her kits' fates. His bondmate had shut him out and the loss of her was an aching hole in his soul.

A slice and a head went spinning away from his blade. A spray of hot blood coated his cheeks before the body disappeared. He could hear Alanna's sobs, the unending torment as sharp as a knife in his side. He would lose her, had already lost her, and his life stretched out over empty years. He would be alone. The moan built up in his chest before ripping from his throat. He couldn't protect them; couldn't protect his family. He would lose them all because he couldn't even kill one single man. Failure dragged him to his knees. Kerwyn's laughter hit him. He no longer had the desire to fight it. There was no one left to fight for. The blade fell from his fingers.

Boots approached, crunching the snow. They stopped inches from his hands. Hard fingers knocked his hat aside and curled into his hair. His head was yanked back painfully. It didn't matter. He deserved it for failing to save them all. A mouth swimming with shark's teeth grinned down at him.

"Tasty," Kerwyn announced. "All that macho heroism stirred up with the lovely tang of defeat." He leaned down and kissed Jonathan. Sharp teeth ripped into Jonathan's lips, a burning tongue licking at the blood. "Delicious. Now let's see how much tastier we can make you. Who's going to be first?"

Kerwyn pretended to think, one finger poked into the flesh beside his mouth. The stringy curls tumbled around his cheeks bobbed a little. "Oh, I know, let's start with the little woman."

Another Kerwyn, this one carrying Alanna's unconscious body, stepped into the clearing. One of her arms hung loose, nearly trailing the ground. Her skin was as pale as the snow. Tears trailed from her eyes, sobs tormented in the still air of the clearing.

"Isn't she lovely?" Kerwyn asked. His fingers tightened in Jonathan's hair. "I said, isn't she lovely?"

He'd lost her. Jonathan stared at the woman he'd wanted to spend his life with, seeing her broken because of him, because he'd failed to protect her. He tried to close his eyes, to stop seeing her, but Kerwyn wouldn't let him. If only he'd been strong enough to find Kerwyn before now. He'd failed at that too. Jonathan moaned. If he'd found him, he could have killed him, but it was too late.

Taking the moan as agreement, Kerwyn danced a little in the snow. He giggled and it sounded like the bubbling of acid-eaten flesh. "Shall I make her scream? I can, you know. I think we should, it sounded so lovely before."

Jekk stalked out of the trees. His muscled chest rippled beneath his fur with every step he took. Hope tried to flicker to life in Jonathan's chest. Jekk was her bondmate, he would save her. The Fael stalked over to the pseudo-Kerwyn and stopped. The gold of Jekk's eyes had been swallowed by the black. Saliva dripped from his teeth, pink and frothy with blood from biting his tongue. The doppelganger disappeared and Alanna dropped into the snow. Jekk shrieked and one massive paw swiped across Alanna's chest. Claws rended the coat she wore, flaying it open. Another swipe would draw blood.

"He was trained for this," Kerwyn whispered into Jonathan's ear. "Starved until he was insane with the desire to feed before being tossed into the circle. The winner had the pleasure of eating the loser. A wonderful game. So ripe with ugliness." He smacked his lips.

Jekk's flanks quivered. His paw lifted, claws extending. His whole body shook. Kerwyn smiled and danced, each movement ripping at Jonathan's scalp. The pain he felt was sucked up with ferocious glee. His mind provided the inevitable conclusion of this little play: Alanna screaming while Jekk's blood-stained muzzle rooted around in her stomach cavity.

"No, no, no." Jonathan heard someone chanting it raggedly. Thought maybe it was him, but his throat was locked tight.

From the center of the clearing, Eric and Riordan staggered towards Kerwyn. The teen's eyes were black, his cheeks flaming with fever. His body seemed to have grown within the winter coat. He wavered in the thin, cold air. In the swiftly falling dark, Jonathan saw an aura of light hover around him. Riordan stalked at his side. There was no laughter in the Fael's eyes, no kittenish humor and exuberance for life. Instead he shared the same grim look etched on Eric's face.

Kerwyn let go of Jonathan's hair to turn to face the two. He began to laugh, sheer merriment twisted with arrogance. "What an unexpected development! This is fun! You think you can slip my leash, boy? I've known every twist and turn of your mind. You're mine and will be until I tire of you. Now go back to your fiery hell and wait for me." He shook his fingers at the pair in a shooing motion.

Eric took another step forward. "No."

Kerwyn shivered with ecstasy, his head thrown back. "Defiance. So delicious," he murmured. "I was right to keep you alive for so long."

"No," Eric said again. He lifted a hand, knotted his fingers into a fist, and jerked his arm toward his chest.

Kerwyn dropped to his knees, his squawk of surprise spiraling upwards into a squeak of fear.

"You won't hurt my friends," Eric said.

"Stop it," Kerwyn said. He struggled to get to his feet, but his legs kept collapsing beneath him.

"You like to make people afraid of you," Eric said. His eyes glowed with green fire. Images danced there, and one by one they sprang up out of the snow. Sharp-edged things with teeth and claws. Creatures that chattered at Kerwyn as they launched their fist-sized bodies at his legs and scampered upwards. A beast made of smoke that edged closer and closer, taunting Kerwyn with the flash of an eye, the snap of a smoky tendril. These and more came from Eric.

Squealing in fear, Kerwyn battered at the multi-legged creatures that swarmed his body. He screamed as a tentacle made of mist caressed his cheek. It left sucker marks on the skin. Something tore a chunk of hair from his scalp and flung it into the snow.

"I can make more," Eric promised. "Everything you fear, every nightmare you've ever had, I can make you see them. I can make them real. You're mine now, and I'm going to keep you for a very long time."

The grip on Jonathan's mind eased and then fell away. Suddenly free, the import of what Eric was doing blossomed in his mind. He crawled forward to reach his sword, his fingers tightening around the haft. Gripping it, Jonathan used it as a crutch to gain his feet. None of the creatures paid any attention to him, circling the now-writhing Kerwyn and mocking him with their hoots and cries. He would have to fight his way through them to reach the monster.

"No, Eric!" Alanna screamed the teen's name. She'd woken from nightmares to see Jekk standing over her, his paw raised to fight off her attackers. All the terror that had smothered her had disappeared. She wasn't alone. Her bondmate would always be with her. Ignoring the wash of dizziness, she sat up and threw her arms around his neck. Jekk gave a long groan, and the mix of emotions that flooded their link nearly overwhelmed her. His rough tongue tried to scrape off a layer of skin on her cheek.

Eric's voice was very loud in the clearing. It had grown dark, the trees a black circle around them. Only the moonlight provided light to see by; the moon and the light that surrounded Eric. She saw a mass of crawling darkness, knew that Kerwyn was somewhere inside of it. Eric and Riordan stood so still, energy pouring off them bright enough to show her the tableau. She understood immediately that he was Awakening and whatever his Gift was, it had brought Kerwyn to his knees.

Eric took a slow step forward. One raised hand moved and fisted and Kerwyn's screams grew louder. Eric was torturing him the same way Kerwyn had tortured them all. The desire for revenge was natural; the need for it almost irrational. What Eric was doing now would change him in ways he would have to live with for a very long time. She didn't want that for him. She didn't want a death to blacken his soul. She cried out his name and ran for him.

The light surrounding the two bondmates held no heat. It didn't hurt when Alanna flung her arms around Eric's narrow shoulders. His body was rigid, every muscle quivering with strain. "Don't, Eric. Don't kill him."

The youth tried to shake her off but Jekk was there too, standing over Riordan protectively. Cateera joined them, rubbing against Eric's legs. Her sleek head pushed at his hands. The hand that was fisted so tightly loosened to grip her fur.

"He should die," Eric said. "He has to die."

"But you don't have to kill him," Alanna said fiercely. Her hand smoothed over the velvety stubble of his hair. "You don't have to become what he is."

"I'm not him!" Eric shouted. Those lantern-green eyes flared at her and then washed over with tears. "I'm not him," he said again, and now his voice was little more than a whisper.

"I know, sweetheart," Alanna said. She tugged him to her and was glad when one of his arms circled her waist. "I know you're not. You're a good man and whatever your Gift is, I know that you won't use it like this, to kill someone. You're better than that."

"Am I?"

Those soft lost words made her cry. "Yes, you are. If I ever have a son, I want him to be as good and brave as you are."

Those narrow shoulders shook now and Eric collapsed into the snow, reaching for his bondmate and holding the kit close. Tugged down with him, Alanna continued to hold him, hold them both now, her hand rubbing soothing patterns onto his back. Jekk's front legs cradled her, his warm cinnamon smell surrounding her.

A sound made her look up. The creatures that Eric had summoned popped away one by one like the illusions they were. They left a bleeding Kerwyn in the snow. They may have been illusions, but since Kerwyn had believed them to be real, the wounds they inflicted were real. Jonathan stood behind the huddled figure, the killer of so many innocent children cowering at his feet. She met Jonathan's eyes once, understanding his intent. She gave a short nod.

The sword flashed in the moonlight on its downswing. Kerwyn's head bounced once and came to rest face down in the snow. She was glad; she didn't want to have to see his face again. Jonathan wiped the blade clean on Kerwyn's back and then sheathed it. He looked across the snow at her, and Alanna understood what it had cost him to take the life. She also knew he'd done it gladly to spare Eric the responsibility. Lifting her arm, she made space for him at her side and when he joined them, she held him tight.

Someone had wound colored lights through the Tree's branches. Either that, or they had spontaneously grown there. Alanna wasn't sure. They twinkled in between the branches, casting multicolored sparkles on the leaves and the grass below. She smiled. It seemed like everyone in the Haven had shown up for the party. The ones who weren't sprawled on the grass had either found places in the branches or were crowded into the restaurant. It was wonderful and loud and she couldn't think of a better place to be.

Warm arms slipped around her from behind and Alanna leaned back into Jonathan's embrace. "Having a good time?" he asked. "The party is partially for you and Jekk, you know. It's not often there are two new bondmate pairings so close together."

"I know." She turned her head to smile at him. "Eric is recovering, I think."

Down below, the young man was sprawled bonelessly on the grass. Riordan was flopped at his side. Paws far too big for his small body poked in the air. The kit seemed to be sleeping off the huge meal he'd just eaten. His bondmate was idly rubbing his tummy. There were other teenagers with them. Every so often, Eric would laugh at something one of them said.

"He's a good kid," Jonathan said. "Mark will be a good influence."

"It didn't take long for Mark to get the paperwork done to make Eric his ward."

"There's not much Mark can't do when he wants something," Jonathan said. He grinned when Jekk leaped down beside them. "I haven't seen Cateera," he told the Fael.

I'm hiding from her, Jekk said. *She's It.*

Tag was his favorite game.

"He's recovering too," Alanna said when her bondmate ran along a nearby branch and down a hidden set of stairs.

"He's lucky he found you." Jonathan nuzzled her neck and then turned her in his arms. Her bones liquefied when his hand made a slow journey up her side and back down. Clever fingers slipped beneath the bottom of her sweater and began to stroke pleasure into her skin.

The kiss left her breathless and aroused.

"You found me, you know," he whispered.

"I did?" Her hand stroked his cheek, feeling the roughness of a day's growth of beard and smiling. "I didn't know you were lost."

He turned his mouth into her palm for a moment. "I didn't know either, but you found me all the same. You're going to have to keep me, now."

She already knew she had no intention of letting him go. She only pretended to think about it.

"Well, then I guess I'll keep you," she agreed. She stroked his hair and tugged his mouth back to hers. When he whispered words of love against her lips, she smiled. She was home.

About the Author

Sarah Husch is an avid fan of books, coffee, and tequila. She lives in southeastern Virginia with her husband and a clowder of psychotic felines. When she's not writing (which is often because she's a professional procrastinator), she's walking, painting, or stitching.

9 781946 462213